Acknowledgements

Forever grateful to so many …

With deep appreciation, I thank everyone who wrote reviews for The Black Rose, especially Bob Cooney, Bob Grotz, Mike Jensen, Mike Kern, Rob King, Jack McCaffery, Kevin Noonan, Dave Pauley and **Celeste Whittaker.**

Special thanks to my brother Rich for bravely giving The Black Rose its first read and my sister Liz for giving the novel the second and final read as well as all her encouragement and insights in between.

Also, this thank you page wouldn't be possible without my friend, Barry Joseph, enduring the reads of three drafts and countless discussions. And thanks to Barry's wife, Joan, for her insights during our discussions.

Thank you to my brother John for shooting the cover photo and my brother Paul for his home and hospitality while I embedded in Strathmere and Sea Isle.

Thanks to my father, Jack Callahan, for his love, support and understanding over the process of writing.

D0107317

I appreciate the guidance, suggestions and expertise of editor Dennis Mathis and publisher Joseph Martino. I highly recommend both!

An extra special thanks to my wonderful children, Mary and Jackson, truly Gifts from God, who added inspiration through their hard work while in college and my brave little wife, Donna, who supplied more inspiration as she works to completion of her MBA.

And with the deepest gratitude and love for my mother, Barbara Hayes Callahan, who when I first started this trilogy process, read the first draft of what now is sequel to The Black Rose, writing a note to tell me everything that was right with the story and the writing before appropriately concluding, "Kevin, this was a very nice try."

So, with the help of so many, this is my nicest try...

THE BLACK ROSE

by
Kevin Callahan

Dedicated to *me* dear mother.

Publishing with J.A.M.

makes your words stick...

Callahan Services, LLC

Printed in the United States of America
Published May 2017

Cover Design: Kevin Callahan & Joseph A. Martino
Interior Layout Design: Joseph A. Martino
Cover Photo: John Callahan

For more information on this title please visit:
www.PUBLISHwithJAM.com and
www.CallahanServices.us

Book Reviews

If you've ever stepped onto any of the thousands of basketball courts in the Philly area for pick-up games and all that they entail on and off the court, this is the book for you. If you haven't, this is still a book you will find thoroughly thought-provoking and enjoyable. The main characters are all dealing with their different internal struggles, but somehow find a way through with the help of each other and their Christianity. Kevin Callahan does a terrific job of showing how people of different ages intertwine the lessons learned on the basketball court to their challenges in everyday life. The Black Rose will extract all sorts of emotions and thoughts from the reader. A wonderful read.

Bob Cooney, Sportswriter
Philadelphia Daily News

A culturally challenging piece set at the Jersey Shore that's got game... and a dirty secret buried in the dunes. Existence precedes essence in this 'fookin' crazy ride over the Townsend's Inlet Bridge to Avalon with Kevin Callahan.

Bob Grotz, Sportswriter
Delaware County Daily Times

Something extraordinary has been produced by one of this generation's finest Philadelphia sportswriters, Kevin Callahan. He doesn't merely capture a time and a place. He throws his arms around a life, tackling big issues, providing an original narrator, not even considering easy answers. He also writes about basketball like Naismith couldn't have imagined, and about a particular section of the Jersey shore with the same expertise he writes about disappointment and heartbreak. He tackles race with his heart and his brain. He tells a tale that keeps you reading, with characters you know or wish you did. These Bounce-passers come alive in his hands, with their need to stay in the middle where the action is, even if life kept on pulling them to the side.

Mike Jensen, Sportswriter
Philadelphia Inquirer

I have been a friend and colleague of Kevin's for most of my adult life. We played basketball together at the Palestra (he was taller, and much better). We enjoyed a sunset or two together over cold drafts looking out from the Deauville Inn in Strathmere, NJ. I only wish we did it more often. In this work, he has captured many of the places and scenes from the South Jersey shore that have defined my annual summer vacations. The way he brought them to life hit home for me. I am a native of Philadelphia (Northeast), and a devoted Strathmere/Ocean City visitor. But aside from the descriptions of things so familiar to me, it was the way he dealt with people and relationships that really set his story apart. I know some of those people. And the subject matter of why maybe we can't all get along better in this world of ours is often kept in the background for whatever reasons. Perhaps it's a fear of coming to terms with our own feelings on such matters. So, a little enlightenment is never a bad thing for one's perspective. Kevin has made us at least think, about stuff that is important. And here all these years we thought what actually mattered was winning that pickup game so we could keep playing. And it is. But it's just a part of it. The reality is there's so much more out there. I thank Kevin for reminding me. It's easy to lose track. Can't wait until the next time he's buying me a mug or two at our favorite spot. Until then, he's given me memories of great times gone by. Hope this brings back some for you too.

Mike Kern, Sportswriter
Philadelphia Daily News

Kevin, I love your book. Love it! It's heartfelt, authentic and full of hope.

Rob King, Senior Vice President
ESPN SportsCenter and News

Excellent work! My nephews will get a kick out of their father's name being included in a novel.

For a legendary story-teller whose grasp of the Philadelphia-South Jersey basketball culture is unmatched, I'll take Kevin Callahan for my team and you can have the next three picks.

Jack McCaffery, Sports Reporter
Delaware County Daily Times

The Black Rose is a fascinating, no-frills look at a specific culture - playground basketball - and the diverse people who play it and live it. Kevin Callahan knows that culture as well as anybody and he captures it perfectly. He makes the characters and settings come alive, and after reading The Black Rose you'll be ready to lace up your Air Jordans (or Chuck Taylors) and head to the playground.

Kevin Noonan, former award-winning Sports Columnist for the Wilmington News Journal

A perfect swish – timeless story of beach and ball.

Dave Pauley, Head Basketball Coach University of the Sciences, Philadelphia

The Black Rose is an impressive first novel. It takes you back to playground basketball days where friendships were formed in between the lines on the court. Where you would stay all day and into the night playing games, often times with people you never knew but got to know intimately after the daylong games. The story runs deep and has so many paths. A black young man from Newark is friended over social media by a white young lady, but athletics is something they have in common, basketball in particular. The deep knowledge of the Jersey Shore comes through in the book and the experiences and landmarks are so detailed. The descriptiveness makes you feel as though you are taking that ride in that car with them as they head into Avalon. You can literally feel the bumps in the road and see the drawbridge in the distance. It's an impressive book that leaves you wanting more. The issue of race is a thread of the book, from the black police officer that is beaten, to the Byrd character, who grew up in Newark, but has lived a pretty privileged life to this point and had never seemingly experienced too much racism. To be among mostly white people in a shore town where he is unfamiliar takes him out of his element. Yet, his confidence, polish and ability to fit in, in different circumstances, plus his skill on the court, seemingly allows him to flow right in, in an unfamiliar surrounding among a very interesting cast of characters. That is something that sports will often do. The book makes you want to pick up a ball and head down to the shore and call "next." Many friendships have been forged on the courts over the years and the book lets you know that it's a common experience, no matter where you grew up. I look forward to the next installment to see what happens next on the courts.

Celeste Whittaker, Metro Reporter
Courier-Post

Introduction

The Black Rose examines the lives of three seemingly different people – a white father and his daughter and a black male – during summer basketball games and their drinking together afterwards.

These seemingly meaningless pick-up games and their bellying-up to the bar while still dripping in sweat are filled with racial tension, personal discovery and inter-generational friction that spark spiritual growth.

The idiosyncratic main characters – Byrd, Pete and Andie – share a sad combination of disappointment in their current circumstances and resignation of a future that falls short of their dreams and aspirations. They are what America has become.

In between the dribbling and the drinking, the novel explores race, religion and sexuality in America over the last five decades. The story is set in real-life places around Sea Isle City and Avalon, New Jersey under the backdrop of 50-year-old childhood friends still playing pick-up basketball games "at the courts" and how they are now joined by their 18-year-old sons – and the main character's daughter – who are turning out like them.

The fictional characters are mostly from the Philadelphia suburbs and who attended Ursinus College, where some of their kids are going. Real life former players at Aronimink swim club like Eddie Hastings and Tom Ingelsby, along with their great Villanova team are used as reference characters.

Hopefully, *The Black Rose* offers how to better understand race differences in America by simple one-on-one interaction and crossing over into each other's lives. By portraying seemingly different characters – just like black and white people in America – coming together playing basketball, the novel shows how a black young man, Nate, and a white old man, Pete, can not only coexist, but also grow to love each other and how better days are ahead through hope and a Christian connection to the cross.

Mostly, though, the novel is about acceptance and ephphatha...

Table of Contents

THE BLACK ROSE

Chapter 1

The black-and-white striped traffic gate at the rusting drawbridge is broken in half. The bottom piece is stuck pointing straight up as if daring me to cross over the choppy inlet to the unknown other side at my own risk. For sure, the missing top half was used to whack the black cop over the head last summer. There is a reward for discovering which one of these white guys down here knocked him into a coma. The snitch money will pay back my parents for me whiffing on landing a college basketball scholarship that we all treated as my birthright.

We wait at the foot of the Townsends Inlet Bridge, next to a yellow sign that says SUNSHINE AND MEMORIES, blocked by a white-and-green jitney shuttle unloading the last of the Friday night drinkers from downtown Sea Isle City. The drunks stumble around in the roadway. Some reverse their tracks in the middle, bobbing and weaving back to the other side. Meanwhile, Andie is sitting here red-faced and pissed.

She revs the sputtering engine of her pop's extended-cab pickup, and I jam both feet to the floorboard. Out her driver's-side window, the top fringe of the sun pokes out over the Atlantic Ocean.

Andie lays on the horn. She pauses, and pushes again and again. The rapid beeps stutter offbeat from the laboring truck motor. Birds, the size of my fist, scatter from the bushes flanking the bridge on both sides. Suddenly she floors the pedal. Without even sticking her head out the window to see if drunken traffic is coming the other way, she swerves around the shuttle van.

She speeds up the bridge that connects the bottom of Sea Isle, her summer home, with the narrow strip of land ahead that I think is about as far south as you can go in New Jersey. "Paradise," Andie says, taking both hands off the wheel to double point where we are racing to play basketball at dawn.

On the other side of the bridge unrelenting rows of white-capped waves crash against the jetty protecting our destination: Avalon. Suddenly a rogue wave rolls completely over the rocks, splashing violently onto the causeway. In the split seconds of stillness between Andie's beeps I hear scores of sleepy birds coming to life. They are chirping in the trees bunched above the bushes scattered on the sandy white dunes shaped by the overnight winds and divided by the aging bridge.

The traffic light coming up to the tollbooth is green. The sign reads: CARS $1.50 NO E-Z PASS.

The pavement widens around the narrow tan tollbooth. Beyond the wind-washed structure, there's a block concrete building on the bayside with a padlocked white door. A yellow newspaper covers a cracked window, but the wind flaps the broadsheet open enough for a quick view of the four corroded levers that must operate the drawbridge.

The toll collector sticks his feet into the chilled air, the only part of him we can see.

"Boo," Andie yells at the sleepy worker. "We gots *fookin* winners."

Without moving his untied sneakers, the

man slides a hand out of the booth.

"Morning, Andie."

"You gots a dollah fiftee?" she asks me.

While she slaps the toll collector's hand and grumbles at him something about how a person ought to pay to *come* to Sea Isle, not to leave it, I read the plaque next to the blockhouse: FEDERAL EMERGENCY ADMINISTRATION OF PUBLIC WORKS. *Emergency*? I think, transfixed looking at the bolted joints in the guardrail above the sign, which drip with rust.

The metal grid of the bridge rumbles beneath the pickup's tires as we cross. Three startled seagulls launch themselves off the ancient railing and arc above us, flapping toward the bay side.

I look down to where the rail disappears into mist and rocks. A glint of fresh sunlight points to a shiny-new yellow equipment shed at the foot of the bridge on my side. On the ocean side of the inlet, waves spray over the rock wall that guards the causeway.

"I *wants* to live in the draw bridge house up here," Andie says, thumbing back at the little concrete bunker building.

"There's a cozier dig down there in the shed," I tell her.

When I glance back, Sea Isle is just a vague curve of sand. The dunes rise higher than the streets, which are lined by duplexes. The houses all seem to have wrap-around decks. Up ahead, the dunes on the Avalon side are strung with wooden snow fences and rows of planted grass.

Smack. A low flying bird hits the truck's

front fender on my side and disappears. The tires seem to tremble. I feel a chill and realize how much more ocean-like the air is suddenly.

A round sign on the passenger side of the road has a picture of a flying seagull. It reads: DUNE DRIVE. That's the same road I was on when I took a bus to Sea Isle yesterday. I came from Atlantic City, where my dad had dropped me off. We'd come that far on a yacht owned by one of my pop's clients, a judge. We sailed down from his marina near the Statue of Liberty.

My pop and the judge are playing golf this weekend in the shadow of the Trump Taj Mahal Casino at the famous Atlantic City Country Club. That's where the term "birdie" was actually coined. My pop always wanted to play there. Our last name happens to be Byrd.

The summer homes in Avalon are dark. There are no cars in the driveways. This isn't surprising since school isn't out until next month. Some houses have construction vehicles backed into their multi-color paved driveways.

A couple blocks into the island, Andie points with both hands to the public park that must be her paradise: stretches of manicured grass and some picnic tables, a baseball diamond and empty tennis courts. She jabs her index fingers at the fenced-in hoops courts where shadowy figures are already scuffling around in the half-light, showing their age as no one jumps for a rebound, instead boxing out.

"Gots winners," she pierces through the truck window with an intense Irish-like accent. Her awkward, throaty voice is almost as deep as a dude's, which creeps me out.

One of the shadows on the court charges at us like a bull on Red Bull as Andie slows our drive-by. He's a red-faced man with thick hair, not balding like probably the others, wearing a raggedy green No. 24 jersey over a black long-sleeve shirt. She once again floors it, passing him.

Looking back, I see a half-empty water bottle sailing toward us. The plastic container crashes into the truck bed, rattling around with a bunch of empty aluminum beer cans.

"He did it," I say.

Slamming on the brakes, she rips, "How can, y-y-you say that?"

"It's obvious."

"So, you're like that," she says, "You... stereo... typing..."

"Like what? The crazy dude ran at us... a water bottle flies... splats in the truck... the old dude did it... he threw the bottle."

"Oh, that," she gruffs.

Stepping on the gas, Andie barks "we gots fookin *winners*" again. This time emphasizing "winners" as if the old ballers can't hear her declaration. Probably, these old guys have as many liver spots as Andie has freckles. She wants to be damn sure her team will play next against the winners of this pick-up game already rolling before the locals here started to sip their Saturday morning coffee.

Looking back again I see the empty playground swing next to the basketball courts swaying back and forth. Moving, perhaps, from the slight early morning breeze, or maybe from the tug and push of the rising sun and the fading moon. Or, just possibly, the echoing shrillness of Andie's shouting stirs the swing into action.

There is something about her words. Not just the way she says them... but her words seem worn and faded... perhaps, like my dreams... my hopes... of playing major college basketball.

Andie rolls through the stop sign on 8th Street at Dune Drive. For some reason, in the middle of a boulevard divided by a wide groomed strip of grass, Andie pounds on the brakes. Then she looks both ways before poking ahead. She rolls the stop signs at First Avenue and Avalon Avenue, whizzes along past a stretch of super-sized homes on the right side and even larger houses on the left, which are backed up to the inlet.

At last the pavement widens into a turn-around, where a guardrail signals the end of land and the beginning of the Atlantic Ocean. On a sandy black-asphalted parking lot Andie skids to a stop. Empty beer bottles spill out from under the seat and roll around our feet. Yellowed newspapers fly off the dashboard. An old red baseball scorebook, which was stuffed under the middle armrest, slides out over the cup holders. A frayed piece of the cardboard cover breaks off as it comes to a rest on top of our lemon-lime Gatorades.

Andie leaps out, leaving the engine running. Ignoring the wooden ramp leading over the rocks, she instead jumps the four-foot seawall. Her bony legs are churning as she races halfway up a sand dune, digging in like an Ethiopian marathoner on her bare, blistered feet.

While I sit on some rocks, worrying what the blasting sand will do to my new shiny black Nike Air Jordan "Son of Mars" $139.99 sneakers, she's up on a long rock jetty prancing around like a mutant combination of Mick Jagger and Michael Jackson. I watch her outlined against the shining wave-washed gray rocks looking like a drunk dancing puppet of white and pink skin. Now she's hopping up to her ankles into the crashing surf and whipping fistfuls of sand into the ocean. Much of the sand blows back into her red face as she stares wide-eyed and defiantly at the sun which is, by now, floating on the horizon.

Andie then sprints up the beach to the real dry stuff, scoops up two more fistfuls of sandy white powder, and sprints back to windmill more sand into the ocean. She zigzags, chasing the shadow of a seagull, and comes racing past me with specks of sand on her cheeks, shouting, "Hustle up Byrd! Start throwing elbows," spitting out sand.

I heard her raspy, scary voice for the first-time last night. I've known about her since the end of our high school basketball seasons a couple months ago, when we Twittered-up. Andie doesn't do Facebook like the rest of us. She had heard we were going to the same college. She said we needed to play ball, and this is what she commanded, pounding the courts starting at 7 am.

I Google-Earthed the satellite view of Avalon the night before I came down here, so I could picture where I am now, as if I were one of those seagulls. We're stranded on a spit of land, a barrier island. You can start at the bay, walk a few blocks, and stare at the Atlantic Ocean. The opposing sides of the isle may be just short stroll from the bay to the ocean, but the truck ride across is a very long journey.

My sister also did some recon for me. Sea Isle came up in some Twitter hashtags she searched. One included a book club woman who posted she was...

Putting together book basket for family of Sea Isle cop, P.T. Mann, beaten on beach at end of last summer, in coma. Want to join in? If so, please PM me.

My sister showed me some nastier hashtags about how, if #OfficerMann were a white cop instead of an off-duty black cop, SOMEONE, probably an innocent black dude, would be in jail by now.

She sent me another tweet saying how the cop was cracked over the head with a wooden plank, perhaps from one of the promenade benches, when leaving a bar in Sea Isle.

Someone replied: Everyone knows the score down there. If you're a black dude, F'SHURE you don't want to be around Sea Isle after dark.

I'm a black dude.

Andie is standing with her arms stretched out, crucified in the wind, bathing in the rising sun. Eventually she struts back to the parking lot, wincing like Lucifer when she steps on a broken shell. But her face suddenly converts, and she is now glowing like an American Girl doll as she walks up to me.

"So, what was the sand dance about?"

"Stirring the spirits within," she tells me. She lifts her chin up to the sky and inhales deeply through her peculiarly wide nostrils.

"*Boo-yah*," I tell her as if I'm ESPN's Stuart Scott, bobbing my head. I lift my arms up and tilt my face to the clouds. I close my eyes.

"You don't get it, do you? This isn't some meaningless pickup game boyo. Not for these fooks. You *gots* to bring the wood ... always bring the *wood.*

"And besides, you *gots* to gauge the wind down here to adjust your shot. You *gots* to dial in the universe, if we're going to beat these old fooks."

We gun back toward the basketball courts with the empties rattling on the floor. Again, we roll through two stop signs and then she slams the brakes in the midpoint of the boulevard, looks both ways, and says with a satanic smile, "We're coming for you, you old fooks, we're sending you to ass-sisted living," as sweet as you can possibly make trash talk sound.

We're still two blocks away from the court but we can already hear grunting and squeaking sneakers. A gruff voice orders to "get *back* on defense or play on the *fookin* swing set."

A block later, she starts screaming out the window, "We gots fookin winners. We gots fookin winners."

We're both looking straight ahead at an elderly gentleman tugging on the leash of a little dog in the striped crosswalk directly in front of us, but Andie seems indifferent. She keeps screaming.

The dog is a terrier.

My heartbeat revs erratically like the truck's engine until Andie eventually slams on the brakes and plows up inches short of the crosswalk.

The gentle dude and his furry companion are wearing matching Penn State sweaters.

"Hey poochie," Andie yells through the open window while rolling the stop sign. "Hey Koonce. Did your old lady leave you and you got a pooch to poke? Doggie looks a bit old to romp."

The air, swirling in the cab with the beer empties, is suddenly summer-warm. The smell of burnt rubber catches up with us.

"Well, hello, Andrea," the elderly gent calls to her in a cheery voice. He dutifully tips his cap.

His lil-ole dog isn't donning a matching lid.

We're 20 yards or so away from the closest basket, near enough for me to match-up the contorted faces with the grunts and insults we've been hearing for the last two blocks. Now slaps from hand checking rattle like a rapper and the play is down the *other* end of the court. Suddenly the action rushes back up-court toward us as we're rolling to the curb.

From out of the snarling pack swirling around under the nearest basket, a taped-up hand, reaches up for the ball… but another hand scores.

Andie yells out the window, "Winners! We gots fookin winners!"

The pack looks up.

I'm framed in the window of a pickup truck from which some kind of tribal taunt keeps being hurled. A still life portrait of a young black man someplace he shouldn't be. But no one engaged in this break-of-dawn, full-court freakin pickup basketball game even gives me a second look before they sprint – yeah *sprint,* trailing the ball handler – back down to the far hoop.

One of the smaller old guys, maybe around six-foot in his old-school high tops – I recognize him as the red-faced guy with thick hair who threw the water bottle into the truck - slams the ball after the basket is scored off a rebound.

"Box the fook *out,*" he barks, kicking the ball out the gate opening of the fence. He wipes his taped-up left hand on the floppy sleeves of the black shirt he's wearing under the green jersey, number 24. His sweat drips on his black high-top sneakers, the same Converse Chuck Taylor All-Star canvas kicks the hipsters at my corner Starbucks wear. He wipes the blood seeping from under the taped hand on his ass, leaving fingerprints on the gray mesh shorts snugged up to the middle of his thighs.

The ball rolls to a stop in front of Andie.

"Nice fookin mouth," she yells at Mr. 24, snatching the ball up with one hand as she slams the door of the truck with the other. "You kiss your boyfriends here with that mouth?"

With the ball tucked under her right armpit, she uses her left hand to sweep up her red hair and knot it into a ponytail. Then she lets the ball drop, it bounces, and she hurls it left-handed over the eight-foot fence behind the basket.

"Nice left," a tall, slender guy with glasses calls out to her. "Good to see you're working on the weaker side."

"Thanks, Uncle Matty."

Another tall guy, but with a beer belly the size of the ball, the unfortunate dude who failed to "*box the fook out*," catches her lob pass with both hands like it's game-point possession.

"Nice gut, Pops Meags!" she yells to him. "Good to see you been working on those abs all winter."

"Hey Mr. Mitch," Andie says, picking out a guy wearing two knee braces, "I got me boys coming hard at you old fooks this summer. You gonna need a walker not braces."

An argument breaks out over who knocked the ball out of bounds. No. 24 barks, "You can't-remember-squat fooks just scored."

I tug on Andie's ponytail, saying softly, "He did it."

"Don't say it. How can you say that?"

"He kicked it."

"Oh ... but the other team just scored."

"What did you think I meant?"

"We gots winners."

"Don't we choose sides?" I ask her. "Where I'm from, we pick teams. You know? Freedom of choice?"

"We gots *fookin* winners," Andie huffs, snarling and smiling out of the same side of her mouth while chewing on a mixture of M&M's.

I studied Latin the past four years at St. Anthony's in North Jersey, just a 3-point shot across the Hudson from Lower Manhattan. I think for a moment that she's speaking some similar dead language. She's admitted she did some "powerful" drinking yesterday afternoon before I arrived, so I guess she could be just messing up her phonetics.

Andie's fake Irish patter is wearing on me, and I really want to go ghetto slang on her. But I don't want her or her b's down here to think I'm from the hood. I'm not. Still, I want to tell *her* to play her own damn self and not be a busta.

My mom used to scold me, growing up, whenever I slipped into "poor" English. "No one will respect you if you talk like an indentured servant." She never used the word *slave*. I rolled with her terminology and always spoke with dignity when she was around. On summer nights, we played scrabble and diagrammed sentences she'd underlined in her mystery novels. She always corrected my verb tenses, even around my high school friends.

Today, I tell myself, I will speak properly like Tony Kornheiser and his partner Mike Wilbon on the ESPN show *Pardon the Interruption*. Not like Stephen A. Smith, trying to use big words that don't fit just to impress.

I have always been good at fitting in. Today is going to be my fitting-in Final Four.

Yeah, I've met a few Irish-wannabee types before, like the Leprechauns floating over to New York on St. Patrick's Day. They magically appeared on New Jersey Transit, which I took to high school in Jersey City when Exit 15 on the Turnpike was backed up, and it was scary as a flash mob being closed up with Paddy Paraders.

But honestly, none ever sounded quite as determined to be a fake Irishman as Andie, all five-foot-freckled-nine of her, charged up to play basketball here in spotless Avalon, tucked between Sea Isle and Stone Harbor like that ball under her arm, where a Penn State or a Villanova University banner hangs from the decking rail of every other house.

My dad told me that back in his day, in the early '80's, the courts in Avalon attracted loads of big-time Philly college players.

I knew of the Philly players, but they were blacks. Ballers like Wilt the Stilt Chamberlain and Earl the Pearl Monroe and Hank the Tank Gathers. Well, I didn't really *know* them from having seen them. I picked up on them from my Play Station Legends game video.

I wonder why Andie wants me to play here in the first place, but I dare not ask her. I already see her as a clock that doesn't tell time.

Popping M&Ms one at a time now, she doesn't seem quite real. I downed a few beers last night, too, knowing I would probably be the only black guy playing.

Unable to lift his arms much higher than his beer belly, Pops Meags pushes a low line-drive shot from the foul line. The ball slams the bottom of the front rim, crashing straight down on the head of the angry guy, Mr. 24. He dives to the asphalt for the ball. Mr. Mitch jumps in and rolls on top of him. They wrestle flat on the ground.

They flop over each other a few times before Mr. 24 pushes himself up with the bloody hand on old Mitch's chest and the ball squashed under the floppy sleeve of his other arm.

"Bros, *you are on the same team*," the slender man with glasses stresses.

"Matty you know he's still going for his 1,000[th] career rebound off the ground," Pops Meags says, helping Mr. Mitch to his feet.

Mr. 24 takes a few steps with the ball before dribbling. No one calls walking or travelling, or whatever they call going for a stroll without bothering to dribbling down here.

"You gots fookin winners?" he yells at Andie, though he's looking right at me, as he runs backwards up mid-court after making a breakaway layup. "There're no winners here, lass," shaking his moppy head, "just players and spectators."

Matty and Pops Meags jog back to play defense. Adjusting his knee braces, Mr. Mitch just *walks* really quick back on D.

"He might still have all his hair, but he's lost his mind," Matty chirps.

Walking to the court, Andie snaps, "Who took me fookin tape?"

I pass her the roll of white athletic tape she dropped in the thick grass. The old trees and lush sod make this place look like an asphalt oasis. Even the courts I come from aren't this shiny nice, and I live in an uppity neighborhood now. Older players say you used to be able to see the Twin Towers standing on the bleachers at half court.

She kicks the tape toward the bleachers, already gleaming in the early sun, and bounces along carrying her basketball sneakers, white leather Converse High Top Trainers she holds high and tight, as if they're too good to touch the ground, though they probably cost only $60.00. She walks barefoot, stopping to wipe the sand off the soles of her feet in the grass still wet from the sprinklers. She nods and then waves to Mr. Koonce, the Penn State guy with the look-alike dog she almost ran over.

"Why did you freak when I said the red-faced guy did it? When he threw the bottle? When he kicked the ball?"

"You know. I know you have to know the black cop was beaten last year down here. Everyone thinks he did it. There is even a British film company that wants to do a documentary show on what they called a *chilled* case... the producer called me and asked to talk to him."

Andie points up to three guys our age hanging around the bleachers. "These fooks are our fookin teammates in the next game," she tells me. "We're the five fookin winners. Me and you, Mitch, Mac, and Meags." Her voice booms like the morning announcements over the intercom at St. Anthony's.

Even with her red hair and freckles, Andie doesn't look as Irish as the three young dudes, my new teammates, Mitch, Mac and Meags, maybe because she's got some color left over from last summer and isn't as worn-pale as these boys. They definitely are around our age. High school, almost college kids. They sit on the sparkling metal bleachers looking like they sort of want to play, but not nearly as amped-up as Andie. They look very sleepy. She's yelling, poking, prodding at everyone to game-up, though she still hasn't put on her sneakers.

"Meags, my man," she says to the biggest of the guys on the bench. "How the fook are you?"

"Better than Pops," he tells her. "He can't even hit the top of the rim. His gut is bigger than all your pop's stories."

"This here's Byrd," she says, nodding over at me.

Meags stares me down to my shiny high-tops and then back up to my head, shifting his eyes rapidly between my ears.

My black buddies, my b's, call me Grant Hill or "Dookie" just like Jalen Rose, now a talking head with ESPN, called the former Duke star an Uncle Tom in the Fab Five documentary on the 20th anniversary this year of Michigan's Final Four team in 1992. ESPN ran the show all during March Madness.

Now I am down here the weekend before Memorial Day for what Andie says is the Camaraderie Classic tomorrow, a tournament organized by one of the old guys. The Fab Five documentary must be still on everyone's mind … like the cop in the coma.

On the way here, at the Wawa convenience store in the center of Sea Isle, the clueless counter guy was a pale older dude who looked normal enough. But he also looked like he never played ball with teenagers. He was amused when Andie bought a bag of peanut M&M's and regular M&M's, opened them both up at the counter and mixed them together in a plastic bag used for the soft pretzels.

Andie munches the M&M mixture, one at a time, while we squeeze in real "teammate tight," as she says on the bleachers, actually way too tight for me. Meags, practically on top of me, is already sweating as much as his dad out on the court.

"Yeah, we got winners, Andie," Meags says, rubbing her red head with a towel as she hands him some M&M's.

"Take some pep pills," she commands with a mom's plea, "we need to win to stay on, boyo."

He spills a few of the mixed candy, and a dog burrows from under the bleachers to gobble all the colorful pieces.

"What the fook? Hold onto me goods," she scolds the sheepish Meags. "You, boyo, better not drop the fookin ball."

The all-black neighborhood of Newark where I grew up was near the Prudential Center, 'The Rock," home of the New Jersey Devils of the NHL where my dad holds season tickets. We didn't have any fences around the courts. When my dad started rising on Wall Street, we climbed the social stairway to our white neighborhood where we live now, where only the tennis courts are fenced in to keep the balls from bouncing out and lodging under the street cleaner trucks.

It makes me think there's a reason why these guys, racing up and down the court like it's the Final Four, need to be fenced in. They're animals. The gate shouldn't even be open; these guys shouldn't be allowed to get loose as a matter of public safety. Who *dives* for loose balls in pickup games? Is the asphalt softer down here in this gilded seaside town?

While nibbling on M&M's, Andie focuses on each dribble like her only goal in life is to get out there in the next game and start winning. She spits when a pass is deflected in front of her. A deflection means the wait is a split second longer.

The ball skids out of bounds. Except from when it was booted out of the enclosure by the angry guy, this is the first time I've seen the ball off the court. These guys all make safe bounces passes like every possession is game point.

The loose ball hits the fence at Andie's feet. The clang reverberates metal-on-metal, like the beer cans slamming in the back of the truck when she pounded the brakes in front of Koonce. The fence is solid as their hand-checking defense, tight as the tension in the salt air.

Man, it is only a few minutes after seven *a.m.* and the game is already boiling. Andie wants in, she wants to play *now.*

I hand her the tape I picked up earlier from the grass. She flips the white roll back to me and says, "Cover up the earrings, boyo. Your baby dreads aren't long enough to shield your diamonds." She mumbles something about the man giving me "the fookin fits and shits."

She wipes her feet dry with Meags' towel and snatches back the roll of tape. She starts taping her scabby ankles, both ankles, while I peel off a length and tape over my earrings. Both ears.

Although this is just a meaningless run, the first of a hundred games we'll play this summer, we are *taping up.*

"I need to play a lot," I tell her, not knowing what else to say.

"I know what you're thinking. You think you need to work on your game so you can transfer to a Division I college," she says. "I know, everyone thinks D-3 is for losers."

"Well, my dad tells me playing with lower level guys a year or two will make me want to work harder," I say.

"I know, your b's back home probably - no *definitely* - think *you're* the fookin loser."

Andie leans over the bench edge, stretches the white athletic tape around her skinny ankles like she is suiting up for gladiatorial combat.

There are welts around her ankles where tape has cut her before, sores on top of scabs on top of scars. I gape at her wounds like a stunned motorist passing an 18-wheeler wreck on the Jersey turnpike. There's a girl thing somehow about this wrapping, like a ballerina lacing up slippers. She's using the tape for support, but she'd be better off buying Jordans than Chucks.

She yanks off a slice of wrinkled tape, and a scab opens. Now there's blood.

"Let's put it on these fookers," she says. "No fouls down here, Byrd. Make *them* make the call. You don't call fouls."

I've played pickup ball before. I'm not just this high-level AAU bred kid who's always played ball with officials. I know there are no refs in pickup. The ten guys playing make their own calls.

I don't know any of these guys from LeBron, but it looks like Pops Meags or any of these relics, especially angry Mr. 24, would call a foul on me in a Hoboken heartbeat.

A tall guy with a Villanova baseball hat on backwards catches a bounce pass on the wing and drives baseline. A guy in a long-sleeve sweatshirt that says Braca's reaches out and whacks him across both arms.

Nobody calls it.

"Call a fookin *foul,* Pinck," Andie yells.

"Fookin Old Mac wears long sleeves to hide his welts from hacking so much," she says to me sideways. "The game is dragging like Pinck's saggy ass at Braca's after one brew."

I check the tape over my earrings. If I get into a wrestling match over a loose ball, I could lose an ear but the tape won't come off. But that won't happen, I'm not grappling these cave men with more hair on their necks than their heads.

These guys aren't fitness freaks. They don't dress the part. They could be taking a break from a demolition job. Half of them have paint on their sneakers. They're wearing ripped t-shirts advertising pubs that probably aren't in business any more.

"Hey, Andie," Old Mac says, rolling up his sleeves while sprinting down the court, "who brought L'il Wayne?" Before she can open her mouth to respond, he's back in the scramble for a rebound.

Smiling like L'il himself, I undo my laces and pull them tighter, tighter than I ever tied them before. I feel my teeth grind as I set the knot. My toes tingle.

"There have been black guys down here," Andie says to me. "I don't remember any coming back for more than two weekends in a row. Play strong and maybe you'll survive to tie the record.

"The black coma cop used to ball with us here. He'd play a game early in the summer and wouldn't come back to after Labor Day. Every summer it was that way, always giving it another chance."

Old Mac whacks Pinck so hard on a follow-up his Villanova hat sails into the pole holding up the basket.

"Good fookin defense," Mr. 24 calls the mugging.

"I'll settle for survival," I confess to Andie. "I'm not looking for *any* kind of record."

"That's what the black cop said about playing against him," she says, tucking her ponytail into the back of her shirt while nodding to old No. 24 anguishing over a late outlet pass.

"One thing you gotta realize is," she continues, "is that these are *old white guys* so they're always on defense. Everybody's a guard. They're guarding how the game should be played. They move without the ball and don't hug the 3-point arc, not so the game doesn't pass them by, but that's how they win. Box out and move without the ball… mostly boxing out.

"They've got you pegged as a dude trying to slide your way through Division 3 college ball."

"That's not it at all," I say, turning on the smile so she catches my irony. "I want to learn to play basketball *God's* way, the way Jesus wanted the game played, like a D-3er."

Andie pulls the ponytail out of her shirt and playfully whips my tensed forearm.

"I've been coming down here all me life, playing ball with these car wrecks, though they weren't so rusted back then," she says. "I came down as a wee kid, shooting on the side court, waiting to grow up. I listened to *all* their stories. Not once did I hear one of them lament how they wished they played Division 1. Not one of them."

"Now that's a pile off my mind," I tell her. "Divisional resentment tugs at the quilt of society, frays the fabric of hoops unification."

"I didn't know you were black at first," Andie says. "Your Twitter photo was the St. Anthony team picture, and somehow I thought you were the one white guy."

"Is that why you invited me down here? To be comfortable among my own kind?"

"Sort of." Andy looks over my shoulder at the three lugs down the bench, propping up their chins on their fists and yawning. "Take a good look. They're your new teammates at Ursinus."

I flash the thumbs up to them, but they don't seem to notice.

"I'm pumped I tweeted you, bro," Andie tells me. "I'm amped you're actually here."

"Fookin A!" Pinck screams after missing a tap-in. He picks up his Nova hat next to the pole and puts it on, backwards.

"Need my fookin hat," he says. "Keeps the sun out of my eyes."

"Fook the hat," Andie yells at him. "Ed

Pinckney didn't miss with Patrick Ewing hanging all over him in the championship game "

"You weren't even born yet for the '85 game between Nova and Georgetown," Pinck spews, jogging down the court, already trailing behind the play. "How the fook would you know?"

An old guy, wearing blue Penn basketball shorts blotched with gray paint, yells over to Andie as he sprints up the court, "Hey look. It's little *Andy* from *Toy Story*. She's all grown up."

The ball sails out of bounds and through the open gate. The game stops. Everyone laughs.

"Hey, my man, Action Jackson," she says, smiling at him.

A drop of sweat hangs off the tip of Action Jackson's cocked nose as he runs to retrieve the ball. He comes over and hugs Andie really tight. He's wearing a shamrock-green Phillies shirt, which takes me a Hackensack heartbeat to recognize because the Phillies wear red uniforms.

They don't do the black hug, shaking hands and a simultaneous chest bump, but they really hug. Like Andie might be with this guy off the court, I think, squeezing each other like it matters.

A guy with bad teeth and the bluest eyes I've ever seen looks over to me and smiles, which creeps me out until he says to Andie, "Hey, you brought Woody. You bringing Woody to college with you?"

"Haha, I got it the first time," she tells hm.

The guy struts over and gives me a knuckle punch. Drills my hand really hard.

"That's White Magic," Andie tells me when he turns away. "He likes to think they call him that because of his point guard prowess back in the day, like Magic was to the Lakers.

"He fookin wishes," Andie goes on. "He can't even assist an old lady walking across the street. He got the nickname because he brags about all the supermodels he's boned."

"I can see it," I tell her. "He's got a champion's smile."

The game plods on with the knuckle-draggers on the court swearing like freshmen trying to impress seniors.

Then a guy soaking in this torn the ROCKING CHAIR BAR AVALON N.J. t-shirt turns an ankle. Writhing under the basket near the street, he conjugates the f-word like a linguist on meth.

"That's Black Jesus," Andie says. "Now, *he* could play, back in the day. He had a spin dribble like Earl Monroe, who they called Black Jesus on the Tunstin Playground courts in West Philly."

"Am I missing something? Earl The Pearl *was* black. They oughta call this dude *White* Black Jesus."

This guy with the legendary spin dribble hobbles to his feet, but plops down again holding his ankle and sprays another fire hose of f-bombs, this time louder. A nice-looking blonde lady who stopped starts push-running her kid in a stroller across the street.

"Fook, a longer wait." Andie says spitting. "Easy on the fookin language, Black Jesus, will ya! You scared crazy Catrina and her baby away."

"In my house, I never heard my mother or father curse," I tell Andie, tying the string on my shorts.

"That's fooked up."

Andie lasers in on the red Boston University mesh basketball shorts I'm tightening.

"What, you think your gonna fit in down here wearing Terriers' gear? You should pull 'em up higher, bro."

"I got the right, go easy. My dad played for Rick Pitino at BU in the early 80's."

She ignores me. "Scrape him up! Start the game!" she yells at the court.

"Pitino, of course," I continue, trying to show off my knowledge of the game, "just took Louisville to the Sweet 16 two months ago, after going to the Final Four last year."

"Drag him the fook off the court if he can't run," Andie barks as White Black Jesus refuses help getting to his feet. Eventually he hops up on his own and tries to walk it off. He limps down the far end of the court near the swing sets.

"My dad loves Pitino," she tells me. "He says Pitino created this statistic called deflections. He calls it a hustle plays anytime you get your hand on the ball, so he counts them too, just like rebounds, steals, assists and points."

"Deflections, my dad says, disrupts the game, too," I agree. "He says it's the most important stat."

"That's why they throw bounce passes," she says, "so their passes won't be deflected."

Another guy drops on the court, clutching his ankle under his high white socks, stretched up to his knee braces.

"Come on Old Man Mitch, you are *disrupting* the game getting hurt," Andie barks at him. "You need a tissue?"

Andie tells me, "Down here, any time you can just get your hand on the ball, just *do* it. We *need* to disrupt the hell out of these old fooks. They play so tight together. Just deflect the ball."

"Right. My dad said the same before big games against our North Jersey rivals St. Patrick's and St. Benedicts."

"That's baby ball," she bites.

Old Man Mitch fights for a rebound and somehow outlets the ball to half court. He hobbles to trail the fast break. When there's no quick basket, the ball kicks back out to Old Mitch, who drains a three-pointer on one leg.

"You should turn your fookin ankle every game," a guy barks from our side of the fence. He's wearing a yellow Master's golf polo shirt. "You shoot better on one wheel Big Mitch the Bitch."

"Kiss my white ass Daddy Wheels," Mr. Mitch screams to the heckler. "When you'd get down Wheels? How are the kids?"

Andie unties her right sneaker. She reties it tighter, using both middle fingers to snag the laces taut.

The stragglers arriving now bop around with their sneakers untied, insulting and high-fiving each other while keeping an eye on the play inside the cage.

These arriving late-twenties or thirty-something guys, now maybe a dozen waiting to play, not counting us five winners, don't really talk or converse. They *interrogate* each other.

"You know, this could be like some sociology study," I say to Andie. "I'm thinking of majoring in sociology."

Andie unties her left sneaker. She reties it, yanking the laces like she pulling-up roots. Her sneakers are so tight she must be squeezed taller. I peek over and think we're almost eye-to-eye, and I'm 6-foot-2 in socks.

"Back in the day, the native Americans played lacrosse with hundreds of Indians on a side," I teach her. "One match rolled on for days. Players *gots* killed. I saw a documentary on Discovery Channel."

"Sounds like an Irish wake." Andie says staring at her sneakers, as if considering whether to retie them. "You know the difference between an Irish wedding and an Irish wake?"

"One less drunk," I say, having heard the joke every year from the Leprechauns on the train.

"I mean, look at these guys," I tell her. "They're like dogs sniffing each other's butts. What neighborhood? What school? What parish? What town? When did you get to *that* school? Did I play Little League ball with your brother? I know he wasn't good enough to play basketball for the varsity squad as a sixth grader because he couldn't make a left-hand layup yet. Did I drink with you last night?

"So, do they come here for the game, or is the game an excuse to come here?"

A layup clanks. A scream of anguish follows. Mr. 24, who missed the gimme, pushes the rebounder with two hands and storms down-court to play defense yelling, "I suck."

"You sook so bad old man!" Andie yells at him in her fake Irish tongue.

"We're still up, 14-fooking-13," he shouts at her, his moppy-hair rigid with sweat. He stiff-arms the guy wearing the green Phillies jersey. He *leans* on Action Jackson while running with him, covering him from half court to the baseline before sliding in the lane to play help defense.

"You do know the game is 15, no win by two, when teams are waiting," Andie says to me as she sprays on sun block.

"I thought the game was to 11?"

"Fook, yeah, it's to 11. But you have to win by two, it can't be 11-10," she says staring at me like I'm really L'il Wayne. "If you don't get up two points, you just play to 15 straight… you only need to win by one fookin point."

"I'll ponder the algebra," I tell her. We might actually play soon.

"Genius, how you going to major in sociology if you don't know the basic social-structure protocols?"

Andie struts toward the court like she's disgusted talking to me. I'm alone. I squeeze the tape over my earrings.

I hear her ask this guy standing by the fence, if he was "a fookin altar boy" at some parish.

"Say hey to Amazin," she yells over to me.

He carries the morning newspaper, the *Philadelphia Inquirer*, in his right hand and reaching out his left hand to shake, sideways. "Tim

Grace," he says. He makes the sign of the cross over my head with the morning *Inky*.

"Amazin Fookin Grace," Andie booms.

Then she asks another guy, "Aren't your fookin parents from…" some town that sounds like Havertown.

"Yeah, I'm from H-town, right on the other side of Llanerch Country Club off Route 3," I hear him tell her. "But I got Township Line blood running through me, I grew up in The Hill."

Andie asks this skinny, good-looking guy she calls Weed, who must be six inches taller than her, even pumped up from the tight sneakers, if his fookin cousin played at Bonner. Weed is standing next to a guy around my age who looks like him.

"Say hello to Sprout," she says, punching the young guy playfully on the chest, where his t-shirt reads MING'S DINER. "Son of Weed."

The guy with the bad teeth, White Magic, tugs up his droopy shorts and positions himself in front of another guy in ratty gray sweatpants. "Hey, I know you," White Magic says to him. "I used to *bless* your fookin wife when I was an altar boy, right there in the confession box."

They laugh like reunited brothers. Sitting on the bench, our three teammates are yawning.

"Nice fookin kicks Meags," Andie says turning to the bench, looking at the tall guy wearing old Air Jordan sneakers with colored paint on them. "Way to decorate."

"These puppies? My dad's," he alibis with a shrug. "Forgot to bring mine down."

Looking at the guy sitting in the middle,

Andie digs, "Cool fookin shorts Mac."

He's wearing old-school snug Bob Clarke Gym shorts with holes in them and a peeling Flyers logo.

"My pops. Forgot mine," he offers.

"Hey Little Mac, hey Little Meags," I say for no reason besides trying hard to fit in, at least show some respect, that I remembered their names. "Hey Little Mitch."

"What's your name bro?" Meags asks me.

"His last name is Byrd," Mac reminds him.

"So, what's your *real* name?" Meags asks.

"Seriously?"

Meags stares at me.

"My full name is Nathaniel Bartholomew Byrd," I tell him with my best British accent, trying to sound self-deprecating.

"What. The. Fook!" Mitch says, astonished. "So, what, your folks were the Pilgrims' help? They come over on the *Mayflower*?"

"You sound like the little journalist guy from The Guardian, who called Andie from England yesterday afternoon when we were drinking, saying he wants to write a story on the cop beating last summer," Mac says. "He said the Brits love to read about *chilled* cases, and solve them before the Americans can."

"Yeah," says Meags. "You could be a professor at Penn State or Nova with a name like that." He wipes sleep from his eyes. I wonder how he came up with those particular colleges. Then I see another house right across the street flying Penn State and Villanova banners downstairs and a Notre

Dame flag on the upstairs porch.

"It's good to see Penn State and Notre Dame fans getting along," I say. "Living under the same roof."

"The people upstairs are different from the guys downstairs," Andie says, cutting me short. "Brilliant bros. They inherited a one-story wreck from their parents, hired a contractor to slap on a second level. They rent out the lower floor and sit up on their ass watching Notre Dame."

"FOOK!" I hear this primal scream from the court. Angry Mr. 24 heaves the ball through the opening of the fence. It bounces twice and hits Andie in the knee.

"Fookin about fookin time!" Andie yells as she lobs the ball back at him.

The first game is over.

"My hamstrings are tight. I think I will stretch for a while before playing," I tell Andie.

"Tape 'em," she says.

Mr. 24 slouches in the lane down one end of the court. "I can't believe we lost to a bunch of fookin old fooks," he yells.

Mr. Mitch slams the ball off the backboard with a long baseball pass. Limping over to the winners and unstrapping his knee braces, he shakes hands with the rest of the losers moping over to the bleachers where we're waiting to play.

Andie paces.

"Introduce me to your friend," says the angry guy, wiping his forehead with his jersey.

"This here's Byrd. He's going to school with us," Andie says, bending over to pull her laces tight.

"You know that ... Dad."

The angry old man is *her* angry Old Man?

"Any relation to the Larry Bird?" he asks before I can reach out to shake hands.

"Sorry. We spell it B-y-r-d."

"Okay with me, as long as you're not a *d-i-c-k*," he shrugs, grabbing his crotch with his taped hand.

Even younger black guys know about the Bird vs. Magic duels in college and in the NBA. There was a Broadway play called "Magic vs. Bird." Last year some guys on our high school team played in an all-star game - North Jersey vs. New York City - and I went to Madison Square Garden to watch and saw the title on the marquee.

"So... Larry Legend," I say. "The Celtic himself. Even at, what, fifty?" I wish I hadn't said that.

"He's 56. Born December 7, Pearl Harbor Day. The day before the Feast of the Immaculate Conception."

"Bird was my favorite player in Play Station growing up," I tell him. "My dad thought he was God when he played college ball in Boston."

He stretches his back like it's killing him, and looks me up and down. He sticks out his untaped hand.

"Pete," he says. Then he walks away.

"Now you're in," Andie says when he's out of range. "Bird is the Supreme Leader to these guys. If this were Iran, they'd be marching up Larry Bird Boulevard chanting 'Larrytollah.'"

As I begin to stretch while walking on the

court, bending over to touch my toes, acting like my hamstrings are really tight, another old guy comes over and looks me over like I'm livestock.

"Hey, this here is Byrd," Andie announces to the big muscle guy wearing an XXL tank top stretched over his bulging chest.

"Where did you find him, Andrea?" the guy asks, rubbing his pineapple head he must shave daily. "Where'd she find him, Pete?" he yells.

"What the fook? Fookin Leyne!" Pete screams. "You're late! We had to use fookin Meags. We fookin lost because he's hung over and you can't drink and bounce back in the morning."

Leyne shrugs his giant shoulders and rubs the top of Pete's messy hair.

"Looks like he's a player," Leyne says, glancing me over again.

"I'm not so sure. He looks like he has a little whitey in him," Pete says.

"Yeah, he looks like Stephen Curry."

"Fook," Pete says. "We'll take him on *our* team if he can shoot like Stephen fookin Curry."

"Shee-it, we'll take him if he can shoot like Curry's *old man*, Dell, who lit it the fook up at Virginia Tech, back when shorts were short" Leyne says, tugging on his long black shorts. "So, you think he plays any D?"

"Come on Andie, fook, you got winners, let's get the fook going," Pete snaps at his daughter like she's his booze buddy. "You Lads are cutting into *me* drinking time."

Thankfully, at least for Crazy Catrina, the mommy who ran-pushed the stroller across the street, and her kid now playing on the nearby swings, the cars coming into town from the bridge onto Ocean Avenue, a block or so from the bay, are increasing and muffle Pete's hoarse cursing.

I must have walked on the court because Mac, Mitch, Meags and I are hanging around Andie under the basket. I stand close to her.

She turns around. "Back off," she tells me. "I'm not the Pope who will forgive your sins."

"I'm hoping you keep me safe," I say, massaging my right hamstring.

"Stop rubbing your onions. Put out your hand," Andie orders.

I'm thinking she is going to do some bonding-ritual handshake before our first game, like we're b's or bros or something.

"Stick out your fookin *hand*."

I do. She turns my hand up and pours in the mixture of M&M's she grabbed from her below-the-knee shorts' pocket.

"Relax, bro. Chew."

On my first warm-up attempt from inside the foul line, I square-up text book ... but don't jump very high. I want to make the shot. I know they are watching.

I shoot an air ball.

"Birdie, Birdie, Birdie. My man. You should be able to shoot here." Pete says with a sort of menacing reassurance. "Fook, this is the Boston Garden of summer basketball. *Every* player can shoot here. You don't come here if you can't shoot. This ain't the new Fleet Center where you just slash to the basket. It's the Boston fookin Garden."

"Actually, the Celtics play in *TD Bank* Garden," I say under my breath so only Andie can hear me.

She steps on my feet. Andie juts her chin sticky with sun block against my chin.

"You don't need to look like them," she says. "You don't need to talk or drink like them. You just need to play ball, and play smart, like them. Make fookin open shots."

And then she smiles. Her teeth are perfect - except a missing bicuspid.

I will listen without hearing here, which is why I am here, to learn, pretending to learn the art of bounce passing from a bunch of white guys playing a meaningless pickup game like it's life or death when all I really want is the reward money… and not to end up like the poor coma cop who tried to coexist with these mad men.

The pretty mother, Crazy Catrina, and her kid in the stroller leave the playground as Andie reties both sneakers and her dad tears off the tape from his hand, throwing the bloody-white ball behind the unsuspecting mom. The empty swing next to the courts swings, slightly swaying back and fro, as if keeping time where time has stopped.

Chapter 2

I rebound for my new teammates, passing up taking any more pregame shots. I stand under the basket and two-hand the ball out to them, snapping my wrists on each pass as if I'm a kid at camp trying to impress the counselor. My head burns like the fever I got as a kid.

When I got the fever, the balls wouldn't stop bouncing, pounding my aching head, scorching my seven-year-old soul.

Why I had one particular dream, I never knew. I only knew the same dream returned every time I got the fever. It was like the heat ignited my deepest thoughts and fears and then melted them right out of me.

As a kid, I seemed to get a fever twice a year. Each time, even while half asleep, I waited for the dream, always hoping for a different ending.

The dream was short. It always started with me having the ball a few dribbles from half court. I always wondered how I got the ball. Was it a rebound? Was it a steal? Not a pass?

I always took a few dribbles, crossed half court and then launched a desperation shot to the basket. This meaningless dream came to mean more than extra lunch money to me. The dream meant so much I even practiced the shot, aiming the launch from half court for my last shot during every backyard solo session. Even for my last shot after every practice session in high school.

In my dream, on the ball's flight to the hoop, I saw the scoreboard. We were down two points, always 64-62, and my 3-pointer, if good, would be the game winner. The gym was packed. Everyone was standing. A roar engulfed the court when I rose from the last dribble and transitioned into the shot.

A sudden haunting hush always followed my release.

In my burning sleep, I was smiling. The ball was going in the basket. I could tell. I knew.

Suddenly, though, from the bleachers arced thousands of other balls. Everyone else threw a basketball toward my basket. All of the other balls hit the basket in the same instant as mine did. No one was able to tell that my shot swished through.

I screamed trying to tell everyone it was my shot that went in, but suddenly I was covered with basketballs. No one could even see me.

At the bottom of the pile and always right in my face was my ball. I knew it was my ball because there was always a black rose inscribed on it. My mom had drawn the budding black rose on it with a Sharpie.

Perhaps, she knew I liked Jalen Rose. Back then I thought I was going to be a 6-8 point-guard, too. Even though my dad was just over 6-foot and my mom was well under that's what I thought. Also, both sets of my grandparents were shorter than my mom, Barbara, or Barb as her book club friends call her. Still, I thought I was going to be 6-awesome-8 like Rose.

And in my bed, after the dream, fully awake, I would lay - or lie... I've been schooled at home, Montessori pre-school, and my private grade and high school for the for the last 15 years to speak proper English, so I am not going to stop just because I'm around these Neanderthal old guys "down da shore." I don't want to sound like the black ESPN and TNT announcers wearing horned-rimmed glasses and buttoned-collared Oxford shirts and who still always mix up their verb tenses, making us look dumb - while staring at the far wall of my bedroom with just a crucifix and simply wondering why did God make me?

Always, for about six seconds while in this trance, I would edge so close to the answer. And just as I was about to find out, really know why, all these black roses on all these basketballs would completely overwhelm my thoughts.

I was not so asleep and much more awake than I always thought, but when the answer of why I was here, was knocked out of my head by those black roses, I wanted to start the dream over again. But as hard as I tried I couldn't.

I thought about the dream over and over, I would hope that the black roses would never appear. But they always appeared in those ensuing fever dreams... just as the basketballs always appeared to come out of the stands.

I haven't languished in that dream for probably 10 years. And I don't think about God either like I used to anymore. I mean really think about God ... and about why I am here. I stopped thinking of all life's whys. The only "y" I thought of was the "y" in my name – Byrd. I was thinking just of myself - until last night.

But this time, the dream followed drinking with Andie, who snuck brews to the center of town where the bus had dropped me off. This time the dream was not during a fever. Perhaps my virgin shot of warm Irish whiskey, some fire water called Middleton, stoked the dream. At first the whiskey burned going down. It made my windpipe sting. And then my brain stirred in its warmth with familiar old thoughts.

Even in this whiskey-drenched dream, after I shot and all the basketballs covered me, under the pile, the ball I saw right in front of me was inscribed with a white rose! A white rose bud.

And there was one other difference. The game was played outdoors in this dream. In my sleep, I had sweated over a meaningless summer league game.

I was burning hot under the basket. I must be still dreaming after having to tape over my earrings while getting ready to play my first game on the hyped Avalon courts – "the Paradise of Playgrounds," as Andie called it at Wawa. I don't expect a good ending either here, just as in my fever dream.

"Byrd, huh?" another of these 50-something-old guys with a concrete block for a head asks on the sideline.

"Yeah, Wog," Andie says. "Byrd is from up North Jersey, he played for Saint Bob Hurley at St. Anthony."

Wog shakes his rock jaw, which is as square as a backboard, up and down first and then around in a curious circle.

"You guys killed us in the Tournament of Champions three years ago. My son played against you defensive animals. He was a sophomore," Wog says. "You beat us, bad, bro."

"You must be from Camden Catholic," I say with true admiration and not from fear that Wog would rip my head off and feed my brains to the seagulls and then let the cowering dog lick my skull dry.

"You guys smacked Catholic's ass around like Gerry Sandusky gone Wild in the state showers," Pete yells from the far end of the bleachers.

"Because of Coach Hurley, we're a national power," I shrug. "Maybe not Bobby Knight," I add trying to appease them, "but he's a great coach."

"Indeed," Pete says, "grand, indeed."

Tragically, at least for my dad, I only started my senior year and not as a sophomore or junior. But in my defense, some eventual blue chip college recruits wait their turn to play for St. A's, even though it is a little Catholic School.

"Each year, it seems the diocese threatens to close you down," Wog says about the Jersey City school without a gym.

"Yeah, but our famous basketball alumni keep kicking in more money," I answer, hoping the guys down here appreciate my honesty.

"Yeah is right," Pete says, dribbling a ball toward me, "alum like Coach Hurley's son, Bobby Jr., who played with Grant Hill at Duke, and is helping his brother, Danny, coach at Rhode Island, keeps mighty St. A's floating."

"I got so desperate I even had hoped the Hurley's would like me enough as a player to offer a scholarship," I slip, knowing with the words barely out of my mouth I shouldn't have said them.

"Balls," Pete barks, pushing the ball in my chest, "Although the Rhode Island Rams are down, it's still Division 1."

"Oh, I know, I would've gone to Mystic Island if it was D-1, just so my dad could say his kid got a ride," I say. Angry Pete nods.

Truthfully, playing at Rhode Island would've been painful, though. We vacationed in nearby Cape Cod as a family each year where I dreamt of playing for Duke, when I just knew I would win a national championship with the Blue Devils.

"Bro," Andie says, "you boyos could ball out at St. A's."

Andie is going to Ursinus to play for the women's basketball team. We're both stuck playing Division 3 somewhere in lil Collegeville, Pa., which I didn't even visit until after my high school season, still hoping for any D-1 offer.

Looking at her in the sun, her really red hair on top of her really red-orange face must piss off her dad. Not that his daughter has red hair and he is a boring brown head, but that his girl doesn't have white sheriff cowboy-hat skin like him.

They don't really look alike as much as the other guys do with their dads.

She seems really close friends with the other three dudes, I am going to be playing ball with down here. They are also all going to Ursinus. I think their dads and Andie's dad all played together at Ursinus when they were our age.

They couldn't have played with any athletic guys way back then in the early 1980's, when there wasn't even a 3-point line. All they did was backdoor layups. My dad said whites and blacks balled differently. It was like each race was justifying their lifestyle, with whites making precision, purposeful bounce passes for layups or short bank shots and blacks slashing, flying to the hoop for twisting reverses or dunks.

I am different, an anomaly for any era. I'm black, but not a typical slasher. I am a shooting guard, but only 6-foot-2. Jump shooters like me swarm every suburb in America. Except down here in Avalon, where kids probably grow up holding their skateboards while hanging by the shops on the grassy boulevard as their 30-something techie dads play Madden Football on their smart phones and work iPads.

In the real basketball world, where college coaches recruit high school standouts, two or three 6-2 players camp out behind the 3-point line in every game. Sadly, especially for my dad, I am the only one of the starting five from our New Jersey Tournament of Champions title team who didn't get a scholarship to Division I.

Even our St. Anthony's sixth man hooked a full boat - a 6-8'er who is unfairly still growing into his body - got a ride to James Madison to play for coach Matt Brady. I was the smallest of the starters at St. Anthony's. Our point guard was 6-3.

These crazy, crippled Irish guys here aren't the tallest or cleanest, but they all pack big shoulders. They must swing from the overhead lights in the bars all night.

While bending over and wiping my hands on the back of my low-cut socks, I check out my three new teammates with confused curiosity.

Our real big guy, Meags, is 6-7 of all bones. He's tall, skinny and really white, like stale milk.

"Tommy Meagher was the man at mighty Monsignor Bonner High School," Andie boasts.

"Down here?" I ask innocently.

"In Pennsylvania, in the fab fieldstone-house suburb of Drexel Hill," she responds like an annoyed high school teacher. "The Hill is Sea Isle North... or Sea Isle is The Hill South. Either way, it's an Irish mass migration into South Jersey. The Hill is filled with Irish families living a half hour outside Philly and Sea Isle is filled with Irish guys, half out of what remains of their mind."

The other big guy is Mac. He's all muscled up. Even at 6-5 or so, he looks stocky like a beer keg. Although he seems like a hard-ass while warming up now, taking a few 3-point shots, I am relieved he is on my team. I mean, Andie's team.

During warm-ups, Andie pep talks each of us. She points down the other end of the court, directs us who to cover like planning a gang fight.

Both Meags and Mac look like the two old guys in the first game. The father-son duos could pass as brothers... just separated by 30 years and more than a few beers.

"Byrd Man," the younger Mac says, examining me, thinking. He points down the other end of the court, closest to the pretty moms pushing their kids in the swings, as a ball thrown by Andie hits him in his sequoia tree trunk of an arm. "You got the fat fookin guy."

"I already told him who to fookin cover," Andie bites into him.

No one looks fat. They just have beer guts. One guy appears thicker, has hammers for hands.

"Hey fat fook, my man Byrd gots you," Andie taunts, laughing and pointing down to the thickest guy in the long white gym shorts, which look like long pants since his legs are just as white.

"Watch your ball, Righty," Andie screams down to our foes, "we'll knock the other one out."

"Easy Andie," young Mac pleads a lil bit.

"Righty?" I ask, but wishing I didn't.

"Yeah, he lost his left nut to testicular cancer as a kid… so the old guys all call him Righty," Mac says with a burst of forced laughter.

"It was his right onion he lost," Andie says, "which is why they call him *Righty.*"

Man, this Mac, I will have to kiss his ass. I know the law of the courts better than the eight ESPN channels on my bedroom remote.

"Thanks Mac," I say after he passes a ball back to me. "Good rotation."

My shot – stiff like at the end of a St. A's practice - rattles every side of the rim. I finally make a warm-up jumper after eight or nine shots.

"Nice shot, good rotation," Andie's dad yells, "Balls, hey now, Byrd's good."

I know all about Irish guys. Coach Hurley is one. His players at St. A's aren't Paddys. They are all real athletic, some coming from across the river in New York City, but mostly from all over North Jersey like me. I commuted from Rumson. My adopted small, leafy rich town, multiplying its wealth in the shadow of the Statue of Liberty torch, is about an hour drive from St. Anthony's.

My dad pads his pension and 401k as a commodities broker in New York. He hops the Staten Island ferry across to the city each day just like many of the dads from my neighborhood, except they are all rich and white. My dad fits in, though. He easily jokes with them. He makes them feel like they know basketball even though they don't have kids good enough to play at St. A's.

My mom shuns what she calls the "brokering-of-bodies" to play. She is Scotch-Irish – a Hayes. She has six brothers who are as white as Andie's dad. Five of them still live in Rumson. One brother moved out to Colorado. He owns an Irish Bar called "O'Shayes Saloonery" in Longmont, not far from Denver, deep in Mormon country. My mom would rather sell players to high schools than go drinking, but she likes the alliteration of the bar's name.

I was recruited, really just contacted, my junior year by BYU, so my parents and I stopped on the drive out to Utah to see her brother. I was actually thinking of going to Brigham Young until they kicked the only black guy off the team this year for having sex. I can't believe the other BYU guys do all their balling on the basketball court.

Still, I hoped to get an offer, but after no more recruiting bites from BYU, or any other D-1 schools, I chose Ursinus, about an hour drive west of Philly and a distant dream from the Big Five.

Even North Jersey guys like me coveted the Big Five. But neither Villanova, La Salle, Saint Joseph's, Temple or Penn offered me a scholarship. Dr. John Giannini at La Salle and Phil Martelli at St. Joe's showed up at a few games. . . really great guys, but like I said, there are 6-2 guards who can play and flash grades, too, all over the prestigious Philly Catholic League, where the Big Five is worshipped like Matthew, Mark, Luke and John... and Lord Jesus Himself.

I sure wasn't at the level of Villanova and Temple and I wasn't smart enough to get in Penn.

On the ride over this morning, Andie told me little Big Mac is Jimbo McManus. Oddly, he lives in Camden, the poorest city in the country with the highest crime rate, right across the river from Philadelphia. He must live in a single-parent home. Maybe that is why he is so strong looking, to protect his mom.

Mitch is Jimmy Mitchell. He is about an inch taller than me. But he looks slower than me going backwards. I bet he can shoot his ass off. A guy who isn't athletic and plays basketball just has to be a sniper. And he topped 1,000 points last season at St. Joseph's Prep, a prestigious high school stuck next to decaying row homes in the center of Philly – we played there my sophomore year, didn't leave our coats in the lockerroom. He must have his act together. He lives in Moorestown, which was voted a few years back by Forbes Magazine as the best place to live in America, somehow better than idyllic Rumson.

Moorestown is only a 20-minute ride east of Camden – the worst place and the best place in all of America separated only by a few strip malls.

Both towns are only about an hour or so drive down the Atlantic City Expressway, which stretches east from Philadelphia to the home of the Miss America Pageant, and then into the Garden State Parkway, which runs parallel to the ocean from the bottom of the state to the top near me.

I need to know my escape routes.

The hot moms pushing their kids on the swings distract me from planning to run north and lamenting how I played with and against D-1 players the last four years at St. A's, but now here I am with a tight A-hole and I am stuck with three D-3 Irish guys - Meags, Big Mac, and Mitch - and a freakish and freaky-looking girl who says *gots*.

With each bricked shot, I move closer. I shoot inside the foul line with only my right hand as if I am practicing my form at summer camp.

I might as well be doing backdoor layups.

"Boyo, make some warm-up shots," Andie says, shoving the ball at me. "Drink more Gatorade, bro."

"We're going to bash these old guys," she brags to a gang of college-age guys, who are moping down to the courts.

I wave to a collective stare from the cluster.

Andie hits me with another ball.

"This is basketball, not life," she injects. "We choose how to play the game, ya know bro."

"This is all real inspirational stuff, thanks sis," I say, fearing without any conviction.

Somehow, for Andie, the words of her story seem already told. She is like a lady professional golfer, who grew up on a putting green at the country club since her dad was the pro at the course. All her putts are already read for her. She just has to close her eyes, make the stroke and listen for the ball to drop in the cup... plunk.

Confusing to me, too, as if her Wiki page is already written for her. I can't think too long about where her life is going, though, not while seeing the guys who lost the first game, who didn't shut up, now slumped on the bleachers, heads in hands. They don't talk to each other... as if this was their first loss ever... as if they don't have jobs... as if their wives don't even like them... as if their kids don't have scholarships to college.

One of the cell phones on the bleachers rings, a bare-chested Pete stops wringing out his sweaty black long-sleeve undershirt, reaches over two guys and grabs the phone, flips it into the metal trash can by the fence with the anointed duty of flipping a coin into the church collection basket.

"Fookin kids these days," he grumbles, "can't even go to the courts without their phones."

"Whew, I thought the ring was your defibrillator going off," Leyne says, smacking Pete's sweaty ass. "Either that or the Sea Isle cops finally calling to arrest you."

"Yeah fook the phones, all this technology cost me my job," old Mitch says, slapping Pete's saggy chest. "Now I can't even find a bartending gig because all my friends give the jobs to hot girls with big boobs..."

"Your man-boobs are looking good, bro," Leyne says. "Here, Dolly, strap my shirt as a bra."

"And I can't even get a job with my landscaping buddies," Mitch continues, squeezing Pete. "My boys hire Mexicans all-year round."

"Hey, at least you can still hit a jump shot in the wind down here," the shirtless Pete smirks.

"Yeah, but we fookin lost."

"Fookin-A, right, now a bunch of kids are playing in our places," Pete says, throwing his long-sleeve shirt in the trashcan on top of the ringing cell. He tugs on the cutoff green No. 24 shirt, taps the numbers on his peacocked chest and orders, "Boys, let's bring the wood."

I don't remember getting to game point in the first game, like I was playing mired in the muddled trance as a kid wondering about God and why I am here. I don't even know how we scored.

I do know I haven't made a stinkin' shot. I must have taken seven or eight already in this game only to 11 points - by ones - and I have not made a bleeping basket.

And I am the kid who played at the great St. Anthony's, the gifted one without the sunburn and freckles. I am the athlete. I am the bro, the boyo, who thinks he invented the game.

At least the young guys, my new teammates, can use the excuse their sunburned past hinders them. I have no excuses... except that my mom is white.

White Magic is puking. He leans up against an old tree by the benches, where this motley looking pit bull is cowering. The dude hugs a basketball while losing his breakfast. Really, he doesn't care the playground moms see him heaving. The tree is bigger than the rest of the trees, but not so big the coffee drinkers on their decks across the street can't see him puke, too.

None of the old guys seem to care, or notice, like this is White Magic's pregame routine.

"Thank God for the Puke Tree," old Pete Duffy yells, throwing a bottle of yellow Gatorade at the dude. The top pops off, splashing half the drink on the feet of his Whiteness.

"Holds you up during tough times," Andie says about what I don't know, pushing me to run back harder on defense. "Keeps you from shaking."

The tree? Basketball? Booze?

I can't shake how I shot three air balls. I'm consumed by White Magic puking. I've stopped shooting, but now I can't stop watching the guy heave - and the game is on the line.

On each of my misses, our big guys, Meags and Mac, just crashed the boards hard, as hard as a Coach Hurley practice, as if there was definitely going to be a rebound. Then, Andie and Mitch just picked up their men full court to keep them from fast breaking… as I mope about my miss.

In this first game with these young guys, I learned before game point now how nothing bothers them. Well, no bad play, at least. They just go on to the next play.

"Pick 'em up," Andie yells after diving and deflecting the ball out of bounds.

Looking around instead of focusing on the game, there is already another team of five mulling behind the old guys waiting to get on the court.

"We gots fooking winners," Pete yells again from the sideline as he walks over to his puking buddy, nudging him to drink the Gatorade.

It isn't even 7:30 in the morning, it isn't even summer yet, but there are three teams of five waiting in packs to play the winners.

"C'mon it's fookin point," Andie demands while zig zagging backwards on defense, covering her man bringing up the ball. "We can't get assed-out. We'll have to fookin sit... with the losers."

"Turn his ass four times before half court," Pete barks at his daughter. "Turn him, baby, turn."

I am tighter than Andie's rock-solid butt.

"Don't let them score," Andie says, determined to win as her dad is to rattle me. "Your man doesn't score... doesn't score... doesn't..."

Andie, I know, won't let her guy score. No way. Andie is only 135 pounds, tops, but she is a rock. She is all shoulders and triceps. She is square like she does fingertip pushups before bedtime prayers and in the morning. But she isn't bulky, just strong looking. Fit like a P.E. teacher.

She spits out of the side of her snarling mouth and grinds in her man's face, or "up in his grill" as she constantly reminds us how to play our men. Her guy is left-handed, a point guard type. He is the team's best player and leader.

He played at some small school, I heard Mitch say after the guy scored on a spin dibble, short jumper in the lane with Andie all over him, for the game's first point as her dad yelled, "nice fookin D."

Actually, Andie had whacked his elbow as he came out of his spin and squared up, Andie mumbled "fookin ball," calling her foul. But the guy followed through nicely on his shot, touching all net. The point counted.

Some guys foul all the time, but they never call "ball," like the left-handed guy covering Andie.

He kept fouling her after the first basket. But Andie didn't show she cared. Or maybe she doesn't, like what doesn't cripple her makes her better. She just kept going hard to the basket, pounding this stutter-step dribble, lowering her shouldering, willing her way into the lane, figuring out how to score, using her left or right hand, going straight-in or under the basket, or pulling up for a short jumper and then saying, "nice D Lefty."

I knew she has "onions" - as ESPN announcer Bill Rafferty and Andie now calls stones - after the first basket. She blew by the left-handed guy, scored on a straight right-handed layup, and got whacked across the forehead. Andie didn't blink. She just yelled, "Pick 'em up!"

"Call your own fouls," Lefty says after whacking Andie again.

"I'm not a p-p-pussy," she stammers with anger, without calling for the ball.

Now, on game point, she commands, "Pick up your man, boyo" again.

I scored about 11-points a game this year for St. A's, but now realize I just had open shots in high school. I wasn't covered by Andie.

We were really good, actually great because we had four other guys on the court with me at all times who could score. I was never doubled teamed. My man always helped-out or was digging down low so I had open shots.

I made about 5 or 6 of 11 or 12 shots a game. Add one free throw or so and there was my 10-12 points a game. I rarely toed the foul line. I didn't have to drive to the basket for good looks.

Even with my man, Black Jesus, draped all over me, I haven't been fouled in this game either. He grinds in my grill even with his lame ankle.

"Just move without the ball, we'll get you a good shot," Andie orders again to me, like she has on each possession of this war when I've run by her bringing up the ball with my head down, my mini-dreads bouncing above my eyes. "No softies, let's make a layup, boys. Move."

She pounds her dribble, crossing over at mid-court, going behind-the-back to change direction again, working her butt off to get me a good shot on game point. Mac picks down for me at the box as Andie passes the ball with added top spin because she bounces it all the way across to the weak side and an open Mitch.

Mac sets a screen with his elbows down and low for me to come to the elbow of the foul line.

A 15-foot open shot to win… to justify…

Mitch whips the ball to me angling off the pick. I catch and square up, but Black Jesus closes. Andie steps in front of him. She picks Black Jesus solid. He fights over her, but Andie holds ground, her body arcing backwards under the pressure.

This is the best screen I've ever seen… without moving.

I should be thinking of making this shot, but I can't help admiring Andie's pick.

She kind of dips her shoulder and spreads out her right elbow as wide as possible so Black Jesus can't get right on me. And this is after Andie planted him like a pulling guard with her body.

But Andie won't cheat and move. B-Jesus slides over the pick a little, stretches his hand up.

I jump as high as I can on the shot. I don't have to, but I want to show the old white guys that I can jump … at least.

Air ball.

"If they win, let Byrdie shoot," old man Duffy yells. "Just box out when Byrd man shoots."

"Layups, boyo. Roll off the pick to the hole," Andie lashes in my face. "Pick 'em up, or will be assed-out. Your man doesn't score."

Andie is right. You can't shoot in this wind coming off the ocean. Maybe she can since she tests out the wind with the sand at the ocean, and the old guys who must sleep here over night.

I want - no need - to show these old guys, especially her old man, and my future teammates what I am packing, that I got oversized onions.

Damn, I played for the great St. Anthony's. None of these old guys or their kids did.

Lefty doesn't want to bring the ball up. I wonder if he lost an onion, too. Or Andie took it.

Right one? Left one?

Sliding, Andie forces Lefty to turn toward the middle of the court and yells, "Mitch, double."

Mitch is already there. Lefty picks up his dribble. They double his ass.

At St. Anthony's, we doubled everything. Last year, I doubled Michael Gilchrist, the 6-6 McDonald's All-American from our rival St. Patrick's in North Jersey. He is now Kidd-Gilchrist since he uses his late uncle's name as well as his late dad's name, and plays for John Calipari at Kentucky, who played against Pitino and Louisville in the Final Four in March.

Interesting how life is connected through basketball. Wonder if these old white guys have the same basketball connections as me?

With a surge of confidence, I rotate to Mitch's man, Pinck. I am pumped, I am going to snatch a steal and waltz in for the winning layup.

Lefty sees me rotating and in an instant, two-hands the ball over his head to my man, who has the whole left side free to coast in for a layup. He catches the ball around the foul line and busts toward the basket with his head up... and a smile.

Out of nowhere Meags rotates and blocks the shot, smacking the ball up against the fence, I look away to where White Magic sits next to his puke, knowing my man almost beat us.

The ball bounces back and hits the whining dog hiding under the bench. The mangy mutt squeals as loud as the pack of honking seagulls circling above, spectators soaking in the game.

Pete sprints over like someone whacked his baby. He cuddles the dog. He kicks the ball.

The airborne ball bounces sideways off a baby stroller and backwards near the old tree, right into the puddle of crusty puke.

After Andie smacks Meags on the ass,

rejoicing "Big block, baby bro," she shuffles over to the ball and pats White Magic on the head. She scoops up the ball, studies the puke, and pokes the slumped over zombie, "I remember me first Jameson. Or was it Middleton?"

Andie wipes the ball on the grass, appearing to clean off most of the puke. She rubs the ball using both hands and forearms and yells, "Point, no one fookin scores." She offers the ball to Lefty to inbound.

"There's vomit all over the ball," Lefty snaps, not grabbing the ball, letting it drop to the ground and then kicking it back toward the dog.

"It's puke, not vomit," Andie says, strutting over to the ball. Everyone, I mean all the 20 or so dudes around the court, the ladies in the playground, the kids in the swings, the old guy, Koonce walking his dog with the matching Penn State shirt, the seagulls swirling above, they are all watching her. No one is looking at me.

The guys waiting to play creep a step closer to the court and lean their stunned faces against the fence. I'm frozen at mid-court.

She picks the ball up, wipes each side of the ball across her face.

"It's all fookin off."

Andie shoves the ball at him like it's fresh out of the box from Dick's Sporting Goods.

"Fookin play, pussy boy."

I figure Lefty knows this is where the balling is, so he is here, like me, out of place.

Andie's half smile, or smirk, says she enjoys how she's dug under pretty boy's skin.

With only the index finger of each hand, Lefty holds the ball. He is standing out of bounds on the baseline. No teammate comes for the pass.

Finishing a slurp from her kid's juice box, a mom at the playground instructs her red-headed son not to "grow up to be like these losers." I hear another lady in a winter coat say to her, "I'm glad our husbands do morning spin classes with us."

"Point. No one fook-in scores," Andie reminds all of us on defense as well as the whiney ladies watching by the swings, "but us fooks."

"Get another ball," Lefty pleads bravely.

"Fook that, winners are waiting," Andie says without hesitation. "For fooks' sakes…"

Lefty stretches the ball away from his body.

"It smells," he says.

"No girlie. Your menstrual cycle smells. The ball stinks." Andie whacks the ball out of his hands and onto the court at his feet, quickly picking it up, taking two hard dribbles to the basket and laying the ball up… and in.

"Game," she yells, swatting the ball against the fence, stirring the hovering sea gulls into flight.

The ball wobbles back toward her. Andie pounds the top of the ball with her left fist. The ball bounces back up to hit the bottom of the rim . . . and back down on her unflinching head.

"Where are the fookin winners?" she yells, "Let's go, I want to be drinking by noon."

As I'm ready to high-five Andie, her carnivorous dad lunges between us on the court, screaming "we gots your fookin winners."

He hugs his daughter.

"Way to be tough. Fookin loved it," he whispers to her, "fookin love you, bro."

Lefty swaggers over to this odd, loving daddy-daughter scene. He starts to say something, but Pete stops him. "Shut the fook up. You pussy."

With his fist clenched and floppy hair drooped over his eyes, Pete pounds his right arm over the number 24, spitting, "You got n-n-n-n-no wood… you played Division 2 all right, but these D-3er's kicked your spoiled, unworthy ass. I know your coach at the University of the Sciences. Dipper Pauley, grand guy. You should give back the half scholarship or whatever you got."

Lefty slumps his head like the whining dog under the bench. He quick-steps to the street and his Cadillac Escalade, screaming loud enough for the mothers at the playground to hear, "Assholes … I started making $70,000 right out of college though." He spins away in his shiny white caddie.

"No fookin cursing near my dog," Pete yells at him speeding off, fixing his hair in the rear-view mirror. "For fooks' sakes… p-boy."

"No fookin cursing near my dad either," Andie yells, mixing with a laughing flurry. "Watch out Koonce. Lefty's a maniac behind the wheel."

Andie dribbles toward me, scissoring the very same puke ball on the way to my blank face.

"Good game," Andie says, as I stand numb on the court. "Good rotation on the last possession. You really must have played St. Anthony's lockdown *dee-fense* on Kidd-Gilchrist."

Mac rubs the top of my head like I am a kid who just missed a pop fly in Little League, as if he's forgiving me for shooting zero-for-whatever and getting beat on game point.

As the sun burns the top of my head, Pete squeezes into the middle of us five, like a coach in a timeout, and screams, "That's the way to bring the wood… and ya'll had to carry the n-n-n-new guy."

I am into sociology, but my dad says there is no money in studying people, just locking them up. He says I need a college degree to be a trooper. But being black, I don't have to score as high on the tests, I am told by my B's… so I can work on my game more and hopefully rise to D-1. Or use the reward money to buy onto a D-I team as a walk-on.

Now, thinking about it, maybe this "networking," as my dad calls my spying, with the law makes sense. Hell, the Brits want to write and do a documentary on this cold case, so I should be able to cruise under the radar asking questions to tell The Man.

Up next, I must face Andie's dad. He's tougher than his pit bull. Must be much smarter. The wandering mutt is licking the Puke Tree.

"We got Leyne now instead of p-boy Meags," Pete gloats. "We ain't losing again."

I want to cover White Magic, but he isn't playing. Actually, I want to have another fever dream. I want a thousand balls covering up every shot I missed in the first game. And will miss in this game. I want my earrings to be covered by a thousand black roses… and cover my real purpose down here.

Mostly, I hope her dad doesn't cover me.

Chapter 3

Pete struts up to me.

"I got Byrdie," he says without a hint of venom, as casual as if he is ordering a beer.

He dribbles the ball, crossing it over in front of him like the ball is on string, like a yo-yo. He pounds the dribble while square in my face.

"Hey, you must hate Isiah Thomas, too," Pete says sternly, switching into intense mode, as swift as his dribble. "He said Bird was only good because he was white. Can you believe that? Larry Bird was only good because he was white? He was only good because of the color of his skin, huh? The Pistons legend must be right since his middle name is Lord, right? Yeah Isiah Lord Thomas III."

He stabs me with the ball, pushing into my gut, spraying spit in my face with "shoot for ball."

Andie zips over to where her dad is testing me under the basket. She rescues me saying, "Winner's ball. We won, our ball. It doesn't matter some of you… three of you old guys are our pops."

The Grand Master stares me down, blocking out his baby girl's declarative plea.

"You fraidy to shoot?" he asks, grinding in my face hard, as intense as any coach I've ever seen, and I played for some maniacs in AAU ball. And Coach Hurley flat-out scared me into playing man defense against Gilchrist last year as a junior in the Group B North Jersey finals in Piscataway. Standing here, I want to say, there is a reason Gilchrist is going to Kentucky and I am a D-3er - like you. But I don't. "You fraidy?" I hear again.

61

Even Andie, after her passionate reiteration of "winners ball," chews on her lip. The twenty or so white guys around the court suddenly stop bragging about how much beer they drank last night and how much beer they will drink tonight.

Everyone at the court hears my pounding heart. Those staring can see my chest thumping.

Even the pretty moms and their kids on the swing sets listen to my every beat. The seagulls squawking above the bay, a block and a half away, add background beats to the thump of my heart.

A toilet flushes in a gray beach bungalow between the courts and the tennis courts. The puke guy, White Magic, stumbles down the ramp from the bathroom, holding his shirt, checking out a pretty mommy with a whiney boy.

"Helloooo there," White Magic sings.

Tripping at the bottom of the ramp, he braces himself on the shoulder of the crying kid.

I avoid looking at Pete's stabbing eyes. I focus on the lines in his forehead splashed by sunspots. He is challenging me to shoot. He pushes the ball harder into my gut. He isn't backing down. He somehow inches closer.

If I don't shoot right quick, I'm going to piss down *his* leg.

My head reminds me I played in big games at St. Anthony's all over the country, but my exploding heart tells me never this big of a game.

I yank on the ball like I do have onions while making blue-chip stock sure I don't pull the ball out of Pete's hands like I am defiant.

Sneering, he locks both hands on the ball. He

pushes me up the lane, past the foul line, back to the 3-point arc. He squares my shoulders, using both hands clasped on the ball. He sets me dead center facing the basket closest to the street. A jeep, with the top down, bucks to a stop. The driver stands on his seat. He hears my heart beat.

The wind blows to my right. I'll shoot a full half of a ball right. I golf with my dad, and this is how he instructs me to putt – either straight in, a half ball outside the cup or a full ball outside of the cup - depending on the break, of course.

I need to make this shot… actually, I need to hit the rim.

Sweat splats on my shiny new Nike Jordans. I don't know if the glob is from the mad man or my ruptured aorta. I really want to make this shot, but can't focus on the backboard let alone the front of the rim like shooting coaches drill with their "elbow above eye" commands.

Pete will gauge my eyes if I make this shot.

I shoot.

I can't even blame the wind as a factor for missing. The ball banged off the backboard exactly a half a ball to the right – smack where I aimed, clanking so hard it bounced back to Old No. 24 on one hop.

He stares at me. His eyes, though, are softer than before my concrete shot. He inches away. He can't hear my heart anymore.

"You should learn to golf," he says, "when you shoot in the cross wind down here, you got to aim a ball to the right with the wind coming off the ocean and a ball to the left if the breeze blows off the bay. The only time the wind comes from the south is during Hurricane season, and in that case just take the ball to the basket."

He sets the basketball on the foul line. Then stands over it. He makes a putting stroke with his arms.

"Just like when you're putting," he continues. "You must watch Tiger Woods all the time. That's how he does it. Well, before he putted his Norwegian wife."

He clutches my arm, turns me around and points to the basket facing the playground.

"Down the other end, the wind blows opposite."

"Even in a Nor'easter?" I ask, hoping for a laugh.

I chuckle inside my head with him telling me what's what with golf.

He couldn't even sneak on the grounds to caddie at some of the country clubs my dad plays above our home in North Jersey, like Ridgewood near the New York state border where old big money from Manhattan floats across the Hudson River and stuffs the locker room tip jars. There is real green in that club, not Shamrock green.

I've caddied up there since I was a kid. I probably bagged more cash as a caddie than Pete sacked in his life. When I carried two bags, the gentlemen pair tipped me $150 bucks for 18 holes.

He is a two-bagger. I've met a few two baggers on the golf course. Always guests.

I don't embrace labeling him, but Pete is what the caddie master calls a, double-divoter –

devilish Wall Streeters who expect you to carry two bags for the price of one.

Since I needed the caddie money to help pay for St. Anthony's, I knelt to the devil, carrying two bags for the price of one too often. My parents felt paying part of the tuition would be sweat equity, make me work harder. My dad believes no one will give you anything. "You must work and network for your life to workout," he says.

Although he lectured often on life, my dad never talked to me about Civil Rights. Once, when my uncle from Texas and his family visited the Statue of Liberty, I heard my dad "discuss" Lyndon Johnson and the cause with him.

"Our ball," the old man roars. "It's on."

I anchor in front of him, bellying up between the 2 and 4 on his chest, thinking he probably never even played mini-golf down the shore and he's schooling me about putting. I must cover him. Guarding him is weird. It's whacked to think of him as a player who needs to be guarded, with the rosacea on his red face older than me.

Andie pushes me to his side. "I gots 24," she says.

"I want him," I say, trying to sound brave, but knowing I sound more like the wimpy dog under the bench still squealing.

"We all cover our own dads down here," Andie says as the five old guys circle the 3-point line and our five anchor inside the lane. "As it was in the beginning. Is now. And always shall be."

My dad's out golfing now.

Mac nestles in front of a 6-4 guy – the long sleeve hacker. Mac's old man sports bushy hair, a barrier surrounding a mini-bald dome. No other of the old guy's hair hangs as long as Pete's mop.

My hands and toes unclench after being ordered not to cover him.

Mitch glides out to check a 6-1 guy who looks like him except he has thin blond hair. He spits in his hands, rubs them, and then shakes his son's hand, old-school style without any fist bumps or hand slaps, just a straight vanilla shake.

The court darkens, as if an eclipse. I look up for the end of the world, but sadly it's just a low cloud covering the early morning sun.

For the blessed few seconds of darkness, I couldn't even hear my heartbeat anymore.

With the sun back beaming, my toes clench up again. I notice that the dads are all about an inch shorter than their sons. If Mitch and Mac's pops are anything like Andie's old man, their dads must be so pissed their kids are bigger than them.

Let's play, I demand of myself, but I can't stop analyzing the tribe waiting to cannibalize us.

Meags is 6-7, so I figure he'll take the other 6-4 grunt and I'll take the 6-3 Cro-Magnon, who looks smaller because he is so jacked-up, like a linebacker in one of those Under Armour commercials, genetically engineered with HGH.

Guarding him will show I am at least tough.

"You got Mr. Mac," commands Andie.

Obedient as a first-grader, I strut over to Mac's dad, but I am silently confused since I thought the sons covered their dads.

"Nah, not that Mr. Mac, the other one," Mac says, pointing to the 6-4 guy that looks just like him and more like his dad with shaggy brown hair - except he owns a larger balding spot in the middle of his head. And he sports retro wire-rimmed glasses. "That's my uncle Matty."

"Take it easy on me," he says, reaching out his ashen hand to shake.

He isn't a double-bagger. The only way the Grand Whitey would reach out to shake the hand of a more athletic guy like me is to pull my hand in to draw a charge in a game. The grab-and-pull is a bull balls move D-3 type guys do all the time. They are floppers.

We shake hands. Mr. Uncle Matty says, "Hang in there, bro... just know, if you already don't, Pete would rather die than lose this game ... honestly, bro."

Meags waltzes over to cover the thick guy even though he is bigger and probably should've covered Mr. Uncle Matty Mac.

"You sure, Andie?" I ask, "I'll cover the shorter guy."

"Old Leyne would break your bony butt in half," Andie snaps, "making your balls earrings."

"Keep repeating their names to me," I whisper to Andie with a quivering half smile. "Ya'll look alike."

"Good one boyo. Now cover Uncle Matty," she insists. "Don't break his goofy glasses."

Uncle Matty shakes my trembling hand again. His grip is strong, although he is skinny compared to the other old guys his age.

"Don't snuggle too close to Uncle Matty," she says to me. "He's an entrapping mix. He's half Irish, half Italian and was half Catholic."

Feinting, as if he is diseased, I back away from him and pull my hand from his mason's grip.

As much as this pregame profiling sounds as harsh as waterboarding, I really do love this, sizing guys up before playing a pick-up game. No coaches. No refs. Just all pride and ... prejudice. I admit I think I am a better player than a D-3 guy. I know I am more athletic. No, athletic isn't just a code word used exclusively by ESPN announcers.

The Grand Whiteness is ready to throw the ball in to start this tribal war without spears. A kid in the sand playground beats his bucket with a steady thump, thump, thump...

"I feel alive again, like the Scots are getting ready to fight the Brits in Brave Heart," Mr. Leyne says to me and demeaningly adds, "Mel Gibson, a nonfictional movie when men were men."

"Or like in Macbeth," I suggest. "Bill Shakespeare, biographical literature when there was more truth in jest."

I can't read these older guys from their faces, or bodies. Not even who has a strong handshake. The big guy shakes soft. How? His boys shake hands like they are auto mechanic monkeys, especially the Iggy Pop skinny one.

Mr. Meags sets a pick on me, blocking my ass out like an overhead garage door dropping when the house security alarm breaches. Uncle Matty curls over the pick, reaches easily around me, saunters down the lane as wide as the ocean, and catches a bounce pass from Pete. He doesn't need to jump for an uncontested left-handed layup.

"One the fookin nothing," Pete barks as I am thinking how Uncle Matty packs a strong right hand shake, but still makes a soft left-hand layup.

What side do I force him?

"Get over the fookin picks," Andie barks to me as Mitch inbounds the ball quickly to her.

"Get the man who gots you," Pete growls and then mockingly adds, "Mighty Mac, you got Byrd Man even though he ain't covering ya'll."

This won't end until I end it. I know the law of the asphalt jungle: Buckets. Make buckets.

Pete's daughter sprint-dribbles to half court where her dad pounds the green asphalt with his scabby hands.

Although I need buckets, I don't want to cut to the basket like I should. I don't want to move without the ball. I don't want to set a screen. I want to watch this crazed man guard his baby girl.

This is more intense than Louisville playing Kentucky in the Final Four last March; the "2012 Bluegrass Bruising Ass Battle." For sure, this is more rabid than Pitino vs. Calipari meeting up in the national semifinal inside the Superdome.

I finally made the big time, I think.

This is real. I mean, this is insanely intense… there is no one watching, except for the "winners" and the other guys who have winners after the winners after them… and the women pulling their sleepy kids to the beach, sneaking some peeks… and the ladies at the playground pushing their toddlers in swings… as well as to be Olympic gymnasts one day.

Man, I am going to watch, too.

I slip under the basket, figuring I can slide from box to box in the lane and look like I am ready to break to the wing for a pass. But I don't want the ball. I will witness this disembowelment.

Andie rips a spin dribble with the ball in her right hand. Her dad reaches with his right hand, but not for the ball. He pushes on Andie's hip to slow her turn and then he stabs his left hand where Andie is hooking the ball behind her.

Pete pokes the ball to half court. He darts. I mean darts. I don't think I've ever used the word dart, but that's what he does. He darts right to the ball like it's the cure for the skin cancer he'll have before the longest day of the year next month.

Andie rips right behind daddy. She is too late. The slick, sick old man snags the ball.

Only Andie doesn't think so.

She dives. She swipes his right hip. The ball is in his left hand. He protects the rock like in the textbook dribbling drill book that my dad made me study the illustrations while potty training - his Red Auerbach manual.

Andie drills her old man so hard the ball bounces behind him. Andie crashes to the ground on impact. She bounces up. She dives once again for the loose ball. They're too consumed to hear my heart pounding like the bouncing ball.

Pete doesn't go for the ball. Instead, he blocks Andie's path. Andie intersects her dad's thigh and drops to the asphalt. He scoops up the ball. He stands over her like Ali over Liston, the ball cocked in his right arm at his waist.

"Got to WANT the fookin ball," he screams to the world. "WANT to bring the wood."

He dribbles hard to the basket. Our upright four don't follow him. He scores without jumping.

"One the fook n-n-nothin," Pete barks.

"That's fookin two," Andie says.

He heaves the ball to her, saying, "The first basket was too easy, Byrd didn't play any D. No one gives you anything in life. We don't want a free fookin point, especially not from a n-n-north Jerseyian.

"One the fook n-n-nothin," he stresses again, but louder, sending the seagulls flying off the bungalow bathroom roof and stirring the puke guy sleeping on the handicap ramp.

Andie doesn't flinch. Pout? Not a cowboy's chance. She picks up the ball, taps it against the pole holding up the basket, effectively taking the ball "in" herself since all of us stunned teammates are recovering down the other end of the court.

Andie pounds her dribble. She slings the ball below her knees from hand to hand. At half court, her dad simultaneously slaps the palm of his hands on the asphalt again.

Pete tilts forward, spreads his arms out like he's waiting to whack his daughter with a 2 x 4.

Andie does a stutter step dribble to the left at the white half court line that separates the daddy and daughter like North and South Jersey. She rips the same spin dribble to the right that she tried last time. This time she spins harder, somehow.

He slides to his right. He uses his inside hand

to slow her spin. He steps in front of his girl.

Damn. Man, he is Chuck Manson maniacal.

They both crumble to the asphalt. Andie splats on top of Lucifer.

"Get off me bro," he yells, "offensive fookin foul."

Offensive foul?

He's the biggest flopping flopper of all the non-athletic D-3 guys on the flopping planet.

Pete pushes his daughter off him. He pats her butt, saying, "nice try," before "our ball."

"Hustle back," Andie directs us, "play D."

He hoists the ball trophy-like toward the sideline, but one step before stepping out, he sneaks a quick inbound bounce pass to Mr. Uncle Matty, who streaks toward the basket like Pete will kick him off the team if he doesn't go balls out.

My man catches the ball at the foul line while I am still on the other side of the court. So is everyone else except, of course, Uncle Matty, Andie, who sprints back on defense and Pete, who races down on offense after throwing the ball inbounds.

Andie steps in front of Uncle Matty, trying to draw the charge after he makes two dribbles to the basket. He stops, though, bounce passes to Pete for an easy left-handed layup. Andie doesn't flop like her flopping old man. She stays standing.

"Two the fook nothing," her dad blasts as if none of us can count, even by his rules.

Andie picks up the ball, taps it again on the pole. The pounding dribble tightens her scowl. I drift back to the half court line to help her out.

Really, I've seen enough from the prodigious prick. This is unconscionable. Should I blindside pick his ass? Andie, though, wildly waves us all off. One dribble before half court, her dad says very softly to her, "Yo-yo me. Come on, Andie, you can do it. Yo-yo me like in the driveway."

Andie clenches her teeth tighter, dribbling right at him, stutter stepping, forcing him back two steps. Andie back-dribbles, surges one step, and swiftly crosses over to her left hand. Her dad steps up, but as she's coming forward, Andie dribbles with her left hand, protecting the ball with her strong shoulders and thick body. She pounds the ball real hard twice. Her dad steps back twice.

Pow. Andie back-dribbles and crosses over to the right.

She's created space. Yeah, baby! There is just enough space to pass to Meags.

Yeah, baby. She yo-yoed her yo-yo dad and got the ball across half court by back-dribbling and changing directions. I am frozen in admiration when I should be cutting, moving without the ball.

So is her dad, who masks a slight smile by moving his mouth, "Lucky fookin move."

Her pass to Meags is crisp like it needs to be, but he doesn't come to the ball and Mr. Meags reaches across his body, slapping the ball away. The prize bounces to half court. Pete grabs the ball and hits a streaking Mr. Mac for another layup.

"Three the fook nothin," Pete yells. "Four is a fookin shutout."

While running back to get the ball to inbound, Andie yells, "Since when is four a shutout?"

"Since fookin now. You're a college player now. Time to grow some hair on... up."

Andie taps the ball against the pole. She snorts her nose and spits on her hands, rubbing them like sharpening chisels. She dribbles right at her dad, right into his heart of darkness. She doesn't yo-yo him. Rather, as soon as she busts up to her dad, she crossover dribbles to her left hand.

Her dad squats in a really low defensive stance, positioned with his feet shoulder-width apart and his butt rigid. He's yoga low.

As soon as Andie crosses over, Pete pokes the ball behind her. He darts again to the ball. Andie dives on the outside of his scarred right knee. He steadies his feet, attacks the free ball, scoops and dribbles for the easy right hand layup.

"Fookin next," he yells.

At least I didn't miss a shot in this daddy-daughter civil war, this dysfunctional duel. The walk off the court means my path to freedom.

Us five losers stroll off together in a loose pack, none shaking hands with each other.

My left hand is sweaty from patting Andie on her back. She tightens the knot in her ponytail.

Pete struts over to where we're licking our wounds near the flagpole.

The ringing cell phone in the trashcan stirs me. Pete pulls out his cell. "Wassup," he says. He listens for a solid minute before replying, "No thanks bloke, oops missy, but thanks for thinking of me. Say hello to the Stones and your queen."

He lifts his phone triumphantly, announcing

he "found it."

"Who's tracking you?" Andie asks.

"Just the Guardian, the London tabloid," Pete says with the ease of making that last layup.

"For fooking what?" she huffs.

"They wanted to know if I would grant an interview for the *chilly* case this snoopy Adele-like dolly is doing on the Sea Isle cop in the coma," Pete says. "I should've told the lady I would talk to her for a *chilly* case of Guinness and Bass Ale."

"Fookin snoop dog," he says looking at me. "What type of zenless being would snoop?"

"How'd she get your digits?" I ask.

Pete edges purposely in front of me.

"Stay out of the sun here guys it's a long wait," he says, pointing to a shady area across the street under a tree where some kids are selling the smaller seven-ounce Gatorade bottles out of a cooler for $5.00 on someone's front lawn with a Penn State and a Villanova flag draped over the second-story decking. "Byrdie, of course, you can stay in the sun. You were bred to reflect it."

"Actually, black absorbs the heat and white reflects the sun," I say under my breath, but fearing maybe too loud.

With my head tilted down, I squeeze the tape on my earrings. I am *fraidy* he heard me. I don't want to end up like the cop in a coma over a meaningless basketball game with Neanderthals.

"You lads gots a long fookin way to go to the Final Four like us back in '81," Pete says.

"Mr. Duffy, we'll keep working intently and stay in the realm of improving each day," I say.

"What the fook is a realm?" he injects, "you just need heart like we had back at Ursinus."

Reaching both his hands toward me, he adds, "Run to the tomb," and then says, "I know you guys will bring the wood."

He squeezes the tape over my earrings, and then taps the top of my head with his generous compliment of "nice dreads, darlin."

"I thought my mini-dreads would look cool at the beach."

"Who has us fookin winners?" he yells.

I am lost in the middle of a Naked and Afraid ... and Nuts episode. I slump near the whimpering dog.

"Let's go man. We gots some drinking to do," Andie says to her pop. "You old guys are up."

He squeezes a line of juice out of a sports bottle at Andie, who opens her mouth and catches the stream like performing in a circus act.

Pete pats me on the head as if I am someone he likes - like his dog – not saying anything more about my silly dreads.

Chapter 4

Andie crouches against the fence around the court like someone told her Pete's dog died.

"Fook, we gots a three-game wait now," she says to no one in particular, but really to me, I know. "For fook sakes…"

There are 10 guys waiting to play, including the five guys who have winners. That's two games before we can play again – or a three "winners wait" according to Andie's math.

Andie slinks over to me, loosens her ponytail and says, "That's why we can't fookin get assed-out… fookin three game wait, fooooo-k.

"Sorry," she adds, "I'll stop cussing right after this game. I know it bothers your girly ears."

Pete blares, "Winner's fookin ball," not letting the new team shoot, or shooting for the ball himself. He swipes the bottom of his sneakers with each hand, wiping away the last game's sweat.

He dribbles the ball up the court while the other team still strategizes whom they are covering. Alternating hands, he smacks the ball.

"You got ball," some D-3 looking guy agrees as Pete throws an alley-oop pass to a wide-open Mr. Mac for an easy no-jump layup.

"One the fook nothing," I hear again like a reoccurring fever nightmare from our game.

Andie relocates her depression to the swings next to the courts. Two mommies move their infants over to the jungle gym. Andie watches the game as she swings. But she isn't going straight up and back. Instead, she just twirls in small backward circles.

The chains above her tighten.

"Fook, Hook, hope the old guys, the Lids win again," she yells from the swings, tying and tightening her knotted red ponytail, confusing me ... the Lids? Why are they called the Lids?

She keeps circling backwards until the chain tightens snug at the top, and then she spins around back to the chains straight again.

After a few more twists, Andie stops circling and stands on the swing. She stretches fully into some long backward swings. When the swing can't go any higher without flipping over, she reaches the top of her arc and does a flip in the air, landing on the ground standing.

The staring seagulls squawk with approval.

The game stops.

"She can still do that, man, just like when she was little," Uncle Matty says incredulously, wiping his glasses with his paint-stained shorts while standing down the other end of the court. "You taught her well, Pete."

The redheaded acrobat plops on the bleachers, the tension gone from her body. She strokes the wimpy dog. She reverts to being Andie, the same loosely likeable girl without a face who Tweeted me all nice when she heard I was going to Ursinus. Her Twitter photo is of the Townsends Inlet Bridge, which we crossed only an hour ago, into this warped world, with a sunset - or maybe sunrise – illuminating behind that rusting drab blue-gray structure.

My crossing over into this new universe started when she first tweeted me, saying we could be roommates. I tweeted back that I was black, thinking it would scare her away. Quickly, she responded, "you tweet white... I dig black music... the Black Eye Peas rock - just not like the Stones... we'll rap about it down the shore ..."

Pete would decapitate me right here if he saw the tweet about rooming. Not that double mixed roomies are even permitted by my D-3 college. My oddly named college that was started during the German Reformation, and is located on the Perkiomen Creek, below three towns called Zieglerville, Schwenksville and Trappe.

I like *this* Andie sitting next to me. Even more than... well even as much as I admire her as a player. She wants to win more than be liked, but it seems like she can turn off the psycho switch, unlike her dad, now guarding a helpless guy.

"They're old, but they're good," Andie says, "plus, they've been playing together forever. They know how to win. More than that, they play for each other. They care so much about each other that they'll do anything to win for each other. They think they... they're the best. Still.

"We need to become like them," she rattles, whipping me with her ponytail.

"We gots to bring the wood."

Be like them? Like her dad? No fookin way.

Black Jesus, waiting to play, is already sleeping while sitting on the swing Andie just dismounted. Hah, he falls. The brown mulch sticks to the drool on his ROCKIN CHAIR BAR t-shirt.

Andie worships these guys like kings, like King James himself, even though they haven't worked as hard to be as good as LeBron.

You would think the old guys, especially Pete, would understand how my B's ride me, especially now for going to a WASP college after playing for a white high school coach. And especially following that Fab Five documentary on ESPN for the 20th anniversary of the five freshmen – my old favorite Jalen Rose with his boys Juwan Howard, Chris Webber, Jimmy King and Ray Jackson – who invaded the Final Four in 1992 with unheard of long shorts and smack talk.

They must have watched. They must still be angry. Or angrier.

In the show, Rose said Duke recruited only black players he considered "Uncle Toms," specifically dogging Grant Hill, my dad's favorite.

I was called an Uncle Tom by some of my boys for choosing Ursinus, for coming down here this summer… nothing has changed even 20 years later.

I heard how Hill was so classy in his response. That must have infuriated the blacks that called him an Uncle Tom but was so helpful for me. He acknowledged the Fab Five was "a cultural phenomenon." He said he understood that young blacks looked up to them like he once looked up to the Patrick Ewing Georgetown teams of the mid-80's. Back when he was in high school.

He said, though, it was pathetic calling all Duke black players Uncle Toms. He was right on since Rose took a shot at all blacks from two-parent, middle-class families like mine. Hill said the stereotype was disparaging to his parents for their priorities of structure, hard work, education and commitment to their family.

And what surprises me is that Rose is an ESPN announcer now. He is working with the same white upper class types he knocked Hill for becoming. Rose certainly has changed his stripes.

So now, when Andie just said, "We need to become like them," I worry what my friends back home will think. And I worry if I don't "become like them." What will Andie and my new friends think of me?

Seagulls land near the playground on the bay side of the courts. One of the mommies just handed her kid some food scraps to toss. There is one blackish gull in the entire pack of white birds now pecking away noisily.

Andie flips one M&M toward the odd bird in the pack. None of the birds notice the red candy.

"I do think like Grant Hill and not Jalen Rose," I blurt to Andie. "How insulting and ignorant it is to even suggest former black players like Stanford coach Johnny Dawkins, Harvard coach Tommy Amaker and Nets general manager Billy King ever sold out their race."

"Bro, you are getting deeper than I thought," she says. "Just make some buckets."

Watching the black bird fight the white gulls for the crumbs, I think how Hill cautioned his 'fabulous five friends' to avoid stereotyping him, like so many people stereotyped them 'with their baggy pants and swagger.'

"Really, how many white people still think the baggy-pant look is ghetto?" I ask her. "I don't even wear my shorts below my knees."

"Still too low. Jack 'em up higher," says Andie, who's wearing longer and baggier pants than me covering her bruised knees, as she walks away from me and paces waiting to play.

Up walks a guy not much older than me. His brownish, blonde hair pulled back in a pony trail, dressed in an all-white work outfit with a large green trash bag.

He stops where the bunch of us waiting to play sit. He blinks at the empty Gatorade bottles under the bleachers.

"Hey, say hey to Mole," Andie says jovially, bouncing toward us, "he doesn't say much, but he's asking you to pick up the bottle."

"Sure, the bottles aren't too heavy for me," I say smiling.

"That's no fookin foul," Andie barks at someone who calls "ball" on her old man. "Play on, we gots a long fookin wait for winners."

With Andie's gruff voice weaving through the chain link fence openings around the court, a taller guy carrying his sneakers gives her a hug.

"Hi, Mr. Cola, how be the bird watching in Cape May *tis* morn?" Andie asks. "I'd like to live at The Pointe someday, all the way at the bottom of Jersey where there's nowhere to go but up."

"Epic," he says. "Not as good as the fall when it's migrating season south, but still epic seeing the eagles, hawks and falcons return north ... kind of like all us old guys returning to the courts this weekend every year."

This bird watching freak, with a ripped

"DENO'S RAIDERS" t-shirt, pats my shoulder. Pete yells over, "Hey Colanuts" while dribbling.

This professor guy doesn't look like Pete and his other boys. He is taller, about 6-feet-4. And leaner, more muscled. He also sports dark hair, parted crisply on the side. No sunburn. He owns the Italian good looks, not the blotchy, bloated look of Pete. He looks smarter, too.

Andie paces the length of the court. She strolls sideways so she can watch the game. Her lips convulse as she walks over to the water fountain. She spits next to the pedestal in the grass.

"You OK?" I ask her, not knowing really what else to say.

"Ok? Not half way to K," Andie says, "we gots to become like them."

"Why?"

"They win," Andie says. "They've won all their lives here... they're still winning here."

She splashes water from the fountain over her face, saying "I need to feel sweaty, like we're still playing" and then rattles "they've been in each other's weddings, all watched Villanova win the NCAA tourney in 1985 at the bar together, took us to hundreds of games at the Palestra to watch their buddy Fran Dunphy coach Penn, took us to bunch of games to see Temple because they think John Chaney is the best, right up there with Dunph."

"Your dad likes Chaney?" I inject with a telling surprise tone that I was hoping to mask.

"Yeah, he just loved the way the Owls played under him," Andie scowls, as if I'd asked a rhetorical question. "They protected the ball every possession, rebounded, and got back on defense. They'd think Coach Chaney was John Wooden himself if he didn't let his star players, like Mark Macon, take so many forced shots."

"What about Rollie Massimino?" I interrupt. "They must love him. He coached Nova to the national title in '85."

"Nope. Daddy Mass is Italian," she says, tossing the water cupped in her hands at Mr. Cola.

"They understood that Chaney wanted his best shooter shooting and his best rebounder rebounding and his best passer passing and his best defender defending… they've adopted the same down here," Andie continues seamlessly.

"Now that's the fook what we gots to do. Move the ball. Pick for each other. Open man shoots. We all can score. That's what they do."

Cola stands on the bleachers, pointing to the pack of birds. A bunch of white gulls try to pull the red M&M from the black bird.

"So, cool," Cola says. "You rarely see an Atlantic Puffin mix with Sea Gulls, actually they are really Bay Gulls."

"Funny Mr. Cola. I get it. Ba-gels," Andie says.

"No really, the white gulls everyone calls Sea Gulls are actually Bay Gulls," he says. "But we all know, in nature looks are deceiving…

"Really, it's strange why the Atlantic Puffin is here," Cola adds, pointing to the black bird with gray cheeks and white blotches underneath and its contrasting red beak with orange legs.

"The Puffin winters in the North Atlantic

Ocean, all the way up to Greenland, and returns to land at the beginning of breeding season in late spring," Mr. Cola continues as if he's teaching.

Andie offers Mr. Cola some of her mixed M&M's. She then flips one. He one-hands it.

"Maybe we should major in biology like Mr. Cola did at Ursinus. He is real smart and successful now," Andie says seriously. "He isn't being pushed out of his job like a lot of our dads here … and he lives in the coolest house at Cape May Pointe, under our state's southern-most Lighthouse and backed up to the bird sanctuary… and, most importantly, he's the only one of my dad's old teammates who could dunk."

"I'm half Italian, half Irish." he shrugs, offering me a handshake. "I'm Mick Cola."

He cracks the outer shell of a yellow M&M and pops the chocolate core in his mouth.

"Man, that Puffin is hungry," he says sympathetically, "now that's what happens when you're out to sea all winter."

"I'm out to sea, or at least it feels that way," I say to him, looking for sympathy from someone.

"Good for you," he says. "You'll return to your world fitter, stronger, and better, smarter."

I should be like Mr. Cola and know more about things, but I really don't know anything about Ursinus except the hoops team went to the Final Four in 1981… and, oh, J.D. Salinger went to Ursinus for a semester before transferring out.

Yeah, my mom thinks it is Cape Cod cool that I am going to the same school as the recluse who wrote the Catcher in the Rye. I won't have the heart to tell her I might pull a J.D. and transfer out - before even going - after meeting these old guys.

"Two the fook nothing," Pete yells, reminding me there is still a game being played.

Man, this is going to be decades before we get on the court again. Pete's dog whines next to me. About 15 guys – all wearing their suburbia bar league t-shirts from decades ago – wait to play. Each one of them sizes me up.

"Why don't we run on the court next to this one?" I ask Andie, who rubs sun block on her nose while pacing. "Why wait? The sun only gets stronger. You don't want to see me bake, do you?"

Andie tightens the cap on the sun block with a death twist, squirting the lotion under the lid and on her firm chest.

I ask again, "Why don't we run on the other court? It's open. We can play the guys waiting for winners."

Andie spits in her hands, rubs them together. "Should I wipe my ass or the disdain look off my face first?"

"Really, why wait?"

She head-butts me, lightly, and says, "I haven't played on that fookin court since 9th grade. It's for high school kids and dads who never worked on their left-handed layups. It's for girls. This is the court."

When I was younger, we played on an all-black court near St. Anthony's in Elizabeth. The older bros, the guys who never made it out of the city, didn't like us playing there. They pounded the catholic school goodness out of us, and hell into us even though we were black too. They said we were "Wannabe Uncle Toms" for playing for St. A's... and then did their coke and crack and created graffiti shrines to themselves on the metal bleachers splattered with torn plastic baggies.

They told us to play on the "baby black boy" court around the corner... and do more crack.

Andie presses her face against the fence while pulling on her right ankle to stretch the quad.

"Seven the fook to four," Pete blasts.

We are up.

"Fookin finally," Andie yells to the sea gulls, or to heaven.

Andie, Mac, Mitch and Meags had been stretching for the last few points of the game, while I just couldn't stop watching the old guys, the black bird and, truthfully, the mommies' perfect asses in the playground... and thinking.

I've been nurtured by a man on the Mount Rushmore of high school basketball, up there with Morgan Wooten, Ernest Blood and Speedy Morris, but these old guys here are over K2.

They call out every pick. They hedge and recover like a Bobby Knight video. They box out, even against smaller guys, like they are playing against the length of Syracuse. They call out "help" on defense so much you think they have six guys out there.

Strange, though, Pete isn't one of those guys who says, "good pass" after each assist. The old guys don't even point to the player who threw the assist like Duke and North Carolina does. I would've thought the old-school finger point would be first on their to-do list.

"It's as if the good pass is expected," I say to Andie without even mentioning not pointing first. "I mean a good bounce pass is expected."

"That's what good basketball players do," she says while strangling her sneaker laces tight.

And, in the games, these old guys didn't huddle up at the foul line when the ball went out of bounds and game plan. Strategy? Plays? Adjustments? Everyone already knew what to do.

Coach Hurley would admire these guys. He was a former probation officer in Jersey City for 30 years. He probably worked with a guy who got out of jail after assaulting a cop… like Pete.

As the five us huddle in the lane and the older guys circle along the 3-point line, Andie obsesses, "Move the ball, pick for each other and the open man shoots. We all can score. That's what the Lids do."

Lids? There is no lid on the basket for any of them. They keep winning.

With bruising eyes, as hard as one of my brick shots, her look tells me I'd better box out.

Her piercing laser widens my reality, punctuating how we were all so good at St. Anthony's that I didn't have to do all the little things, like boxing out on every possession, because we would still get the ball. Heck, we beat St. Patrick's by double figures when they were ranked No. 1 in the nation with Gilchrist and we were ranked No. 2 during my junior year.

We outscored them 23-5 in the fourth quarter, and I know I didn't box out once. I was leaking for some easy buckets.

"Everyone boxes, everyone checks their fookin man," she says as we back pedal for defense. She reaches out to me as I stumble.

Andie picks up her dad at half court.

She hand-checks her dad.

"Be gully," she barks back to us, using the street slang for tough that probably only I know.

Is she talking code now to me?

"Golly," I mock like a hillbilly, but under my breath.

On the first shot, Jimbo Mac blocks out his dad, Mr. Mac. The ball seems to hesitate in the air to watch when Mr. Mac just tosses him to the side, gets the rebound, puts it back in.

"One the fook nothing," Pete barks.

Mac pops up. He sprints down the court blank face, like he fell on his own. I know better to call a foul for him, but I want to... I don't want the ball, but get it. Uncle Matty dares me to shoot by staying off me two full feet. He doesn't chest me.

"Let him shoot," Pete screams.

I shoot.

I don't watch to see if my brick goes in because I know it won't. Instead, I watch Big Mac box out Little Mac. The dad drives him from under the basket to the foul line. Pete scraps for the rebounds and pushes for the fast break.

Uncle Matty snatches a bounce pass at the foul line, stops and pulls up for a jumper. "Go to the fookin hole," Pete yells as the shot bangs off the back rim and then violently off the backboard.

Mac boxes out his dad again, even harder.

White and red-sunburned limbs tangle. This time his dad can't push him away. Instead, he flings himself over his son's back. They both knock the ball free. They dive for the loose ball squibbing out of bounds. They both grab the ball simultaneously, sliding across the base line. They wrestle in a heap of scraped elbows and knees.

They grapple for what seems like a healthy two minutes. I watch like it is inside the two-minute warning of the Super Bowl.

Greenhead flies land on them. Two of the dads wander toward half court. They've seen this old-school session before.

"This is older than watching porn on video," a bored dad yells as I angle to the battlers.

Andie runs over to the water fountain, spitting next to it again.

Old Mac tugs the ball away from his son.

"Your ball, I went over the back," Old Mr. Mac says casually, as if they were wrestling in the backyard for sport.

Old Mac punches his son - playfully - on the upper arm, then rubbing the targeted spot.

"Now, that's the way to play tough," Old Mr. Mac says before humming an Irish ballad I heard the nuns sing around St. A's on St. Patrick's Day and then adding, "Your ancestors didn't fight Trevelyan, steal his corn for you to play soft."

I didn't score in the second game either against the old D-3ers. I couldn't have scored since Uncle Matt taunted me to shoot, giving me two feet cushion and helping on defense instead, shattering my confidence. And I thought he liked me as much as Mr. Cola liked the Atlantic Puffin.

"Let's go for a little drink me little loser lads," Pete exalts while tap dancing off the court. "The Lads and the Lids together again, perfect, like the Jersey Shore."

I say, *"fa'shure"* trying to sound like I often drink before nine o'clock in the morning.

Hauntingly, Pete looks at me as if I said Coach Chaney never got to the Final Four. He snaps, "The only thing for sure in life was the first time I... had sex with myself, I was *fa'shure* I was going to do it again."

"Aren't you Catholic?" Isn't that a sin?"

"A wee bit one... maybe... perhaps... yeah, now we're talking life stuff, indeed bro, life's just about managing your sins, and not getting too many of them before you die," Pete reasons. "It's better to die sooner than to keep sinning."

"If it's better to die than keep sinning, is it better to kill someone to keep them from sinning?" I ask only to be amusing, but gaining his attention.

"I'd kill myself right here if I wouldn't end up in hell. Gone. Done deal," Pete says. "That's me only real worry... and when the bucket fills up at night next to my bed. Then I got to get up and piss in the toilet. That sucks."

I am guessing he doesn't sleep with a woman. Andie never mentioned anything about a mom. I can't imagine him loving anyone but basketball... and his dog. And in a weird way, I think, Andie. I do remember he said he loved her at half court.

Pete picks up his dog with a definitive

"we're done," carrying this scarred-up and scared pit bull through a pack of about 20 or so now. He busts through them, many of whom pat him on the back, and keeps walking defiantly before stopping on a dime to say "hey coach" to Steve Donahue of Boston College, who I recognize.

Pete confers with Coach Donahue for five minutes. I want to say hello, but I am just a D-3 guy and won't waste his time.

Walking over to me, Coach Donahue shakes my hand.

"Hey, Nate, I want to wish you all the best at Ursinus," he says, looking much fitter than Pete even though I knew coach was younger than him at Ursinus. "I saw you play against St. Patrick's two years ago, you did a great job doubling up on Gilchrist.

"Ursinus is lucky to have you."

Man, I am floored.

Coach Donahue knows me! He pats me on the back and walks over to where Coach Dunphy and Fran O'Hanlon, the coach of Lafayette College, circle around with a few other guys, who looked to be around 60-years old... and look like they can all still play. They all listen to Pete, standing in the middle, telling a story that ends with all of them laughing and hugging.

I guess everyone meets here to play or to go drinking. I know this Camaraderie Classic, which they call the players "the chosen ones" starts with some play-in games for the new teams this afternoon. I guess lots of these guys here now play in the "CC." Still, they are here in the morning.

Pete hobnobs. Everyone seems to know him, which now doesn't surprise me. Everyone seems to like him, too, in a distant way of sorts.

"Come on Black Byrd, got to get moving," Pete says in a Austin Powers British-like accent. "Get it? That's a Beatles' song, Black Bird."

I start to peel the tape off my ears when Andie stares me down. I press down on the tape.

"Come on Byrdie, we gots some fookin drinkin to do," Pete hollers, walking to the street with the ball stashed under his bruised right elbow. "I'll drive the Lads."

Pete shoots an empty Gatorade bottle 25 yards into the back of the white pickup truck. The one Andie drove me into Jurrassic Park.

"He did it again." I say.

"Sit up front," he says to me while stopping to bust on White Magic, still a lifeless puddle on the ramp with his shirt off.

"Who? Me?" I ask.

"You didn't really think I would make you sit in the back bed," Pete smirks.

Andie slides into the middle seat up front, lifting-up the armrest and grabbing the red baseball scorebook on the cup holders. She hands me the scorebook to hold while she slugs down her warm Gatorade. She steals a swig of my bottle before handing me the half-finished yellow juice.

I sit halfway straight, strangely not knowing to feel ashamed or proud to be Pete's passenger, holding the musty book out the window.

"For fooks' sakes don't let Pete see you hanging his scorebook outside," Andie warns.

"He'd rather play on the girly court than lose The Book."

The book is from 1968, at least that is the date scribbled between the yellow cracks on the cover. There is a crusty yellow newspaper stuffed inside.

"He keeps the book in case he runs into the two kids from that team he *hasn't* seen since his first year of playing organized sports over 40 years ago," Andie says with admiration. "He always keeps the book in the truck just in case he sees Cooker and Koch again. I forget first last names."

I pull my arm inside, stuffing the holy book under the passenger side front seat.

"They used to put the little league box scores in the paper back then, so he saved the first time his name was in print," Andie says.

"If the book and paper are so important, why does he leave them scattered in the front seat of this old truck?" I ask, thinking my Little League trophies were trashed during our house move.

"For fook sakes, it's why he still wears the old No. 24 cutoff, it reminds him of his youth when he still had dreams in life," she snarls, grinding where her tooth is missing like she will bite my head off. "The faded green jersey reminds him of his favorite player as a kid, it reminds him to always play hard, and to always play the game with the love of his youth."

"Who is his favorite player?" I ask, thinking Rick Barry, who was No. 24 with the old Golden State Warriors when my dad was in high school. He was a white guy. I remember him because he shot free throws underhanded and my dad tried to teach me how to scoop it when I was shooting poorly from the line in 8th grade. But I'd rather miss free throws than make them underhanded like an old white guy.

Not hearing me, Andie yanks on her dad's old 24 jersey to hurry. Mac, Meags and Mitch pile in the back seat of the box-like king cab.

Pete hands me the dog with the sad eyes.

"Hold Scoob," Pete orders nicely. "Be gentle with him."

Pete named his pit-bull Scoob, like after Scoobie Doo? This hard ass guy names his dog after Scoobie freakin Doo?

"That's a cool name," I say, trying not to laugh, but really trying to get Pete to like me. "I used to watch the cartoon."

He floors it toward the bay, swatting greenheads inside the cab with both hands. He hooks his truck right onto Ocean Avenue. Spitting out the window, he decelerates in this three-way intersection with 8th Street and 3rd Avenue at the corner of the courts. The lives of Pete, Andie and I are all now intersecting for some reason.

"His name is Scuba, I call him Scoobs sometimes for short," Pete finally answers.

"Oh," I say after a pause, "sorry, Pete."

I can't believe I called him Pete again, but really, I am more scared I called his pet Scoobie Doo.

"SCUBA is his favorite acronym," Andie injects, breaking the short silence, "it stands for Self-Contained Underwater Breathing Apparatus.

"My dad is a diver."

On the causeway, we seemingly can reach out and touch the bay to our left and the ocean to our right as we approach the rusting Townsends Inlet Bridge going into Sea Isle. I glance at Pete with the sun reflecting off the bay behind him as he sticks his head out the window. He stops even though there is no toll this direction.

"Boo," he yells, stirring the guy with a blonde goatee and his feet up in the booth behind the cracked blinds reading an old Playboy magazine. "Wake the fook up. What's big today?"

"You are," the guy around Pete's age answers, spitting tobacco juice out the tollbooth's ancient window treatment and inside the pickup bed. Pete high fives with the toll collector.

With his head still out the window, Pete yells, "four and fookin ohhhhh… with Mean Machine."

The old guys, behind us in an apple-red Lexus, beep four times. I get it. The old guys won all four games this morning with Leyne.

At the bottom of the bridge, Pete screams "four and fookin ohhhhh" again while slicing a left turn into a dune park with plastic benches.

Jumping out, Pete darts to the back of the truck as fast as he sprints down court playing defense on game point. He jumps in the bed. He opens a cooler. He starts throwing bottle beers around to his old boys, as they creak out from the pimped-up wheels.

"You OK?" Andie asks. We stay in the front seat. "You ready to drink?"

"I don't think your dad likes, gets me." I

whisper, wondering how quickly she would agree.

"What the fook you mean?" Andie asks incredulously. "Your fookin kidding, right Hook?"

"Well, you explained about your dad's deal and the old guys, where they're coming from, but I don't think he gets where I'm coming from," I say, hoping Andie understands being a girl.

"Where the fook are you coming from?"

"You know."

"You mean your whole Grant Hill thesis, being a black guy who's looked at from other black guys like an Uncle Tom for playing ball with white guys?" she demeans as if asking a question.

She rubs my forearm and looks at her palm, acting like she is checking to see if the skin color flakes off. Andie rubs again. Checks again.

"Man, I get that, but let's face it, your ancestors had it worse than being called an Uncle Tom, so *book* the *fook* up" Andie accents in fake Irish. "Listen, my uncle teaches at the University of San Francisco and their football team has been undefeated since 1951.

"You know why?"

I knew USF was a Jesuit college, like Boston College, but I never knew they even had a football team. I knew they had a great basketball team with Bill Russell and K.C. Jones in the mid 1950's, winning back-to-back national championships, because Russell and Jones played for the Boston Celtics and my dad always talked about the great Celtics... from Russell to Bird.

"Nah, why?"

"They were undefeated in 1951 and Ollie

Matson was the nation's leading scorer. They were invited to a Bowl game. They didn't go bowling, though, since the Dons' two black players were told to stay home, they weren't allowed to play.

"San Francisco hasn't played a football game since '51. The Jesuits dropped the sport.

"What I'm saying is, black players don't have it *as* bad today, not like their dads and granddads did. So come down from your cross. And, I'm also saying white players like me and our new teammates have your black back.

"Here, have some M&Ms," she says, opening up her hand with the mixture of peanut and chocolate candy. "You'll understand better.

"And, I was only kidding when I asked you to be my roommate. You aren't dark enough."

Pete pokes his head in the truck and says, "Are you two done making out?"

"Fa'shure," Andie says, scaring me, as she answers Pete's ringing cell phone on the seat.

"Hey," she says with concern, holding the phone against her leg. "This British film documentary show wants to interview you for the police officer in the coma case. I'll tell the man to jump in the pond, like you told the Guardian. They do *chilled* cases, too. He says they are wildly popular in the United Kingdom."

"Nah," Pete says. "Ask the bloke when he can cross the pond for tea and talk?"

"The squeaky-voice dude said he is already here," she whispers. "This bloke said he interviewed the Sea Isle P.D. yesterday."

Song breaks out behind us. Mr. Mac hums

that Irish ballad from the courts I recognized.

The dads and their boys, the Lids and the Lads, belt out "it is so lonely around the Fields of Athenry… you must raise our child with dignity… ooh the Fields of Athenry where once we watched the small free birds fly…"

They hug like they are at a wedding, or wake, too, for them, arms tugging each other, especially Mac and Mac … as if they didn't fight for every rebound in the game like their brave Irish ancestors fought the oppressive Brits.

"Alright, I get the Scuba acronym, but what is Lids?" I ask as Andie hands me a Guinness in a can from Pete's stash in the bottom of the cooler.

"Think. It's easy, boyo," she says, smiling wide, showing the missing one tooth. "It stands for fookin Leftover Intellectual Dumb Scats – LIDS - it's our acronym for our dear dads. Endearing?"

"Scats?" I ask

"Yeah, I don't want to fookin cuss in front of me dad," she says opening my beer can for me.

Pete slouches on the rusting rail of the Townsends Inlet Bridge, he flips a faded blue Villanova baseball hat to me.

"Put it on," he says. "Don't want you to get a sun burn."

"Thanks."

"Give it back, though."

"Will do. Looks like it has a few years left in it."

"Indeed," Pete says. "Gots it in 1985 at the NCAA tournament East Regional final. Me boys here and *meself* drove down to Greensboro to see

Nova beat North Carolina to reach the Final Four."

"Sweet."

"Indeed," he continues. "Was the last time we all road tripped for a tournament game. Over the years, one or two of us wouldn't be able to make the NCAA tourney trip. Life. Kids. Wives.

"Back then, life was good. The Wildcats beat the Tar Heels... with Jay Wright as an assistant coach for the Cats and Daddy Mass.

"Jay's a grand man, never forgot where he came from, he comes down here when recruiting in July ends and drinks a beer or two with us at Twisties... man, what I would do to be back in 1985 with me boys... what I would do differently... what I would do to see Villanova win a national championship again... like back when life was good, when there was hope... when life wasn't a race to the tomb."

Chapter 5

With Pete driving and popping his head out the window to greet every bicyclist and pedestrian, we poke up Landis Avenue in Sea Isle. We arrive at "The Rock" to start "the next best day of our lives."

Even after playing war ball in Avalon, and hooligan drinking and singing below the Townsends Inlet Bridge, no Lid or Lad even talks about showering. We don't even towel off.

Pete leaves the truck running, and scurries to feed Scoob. We wait outside Pete's house, "The Rock of Ballbuster." That's what the old guys call the place even though Pete calls it "The Hut."

The home juts over the sidewalk at 39th and Landis Avenue. It's just three blocks from the main drag that brings you into Sea Isle. The two-story, yellow-brick square compound towers on a red brick foundation, which makes it seem like a fortress compared to the prevailing white or tan duplexes down here. The ones with the Penn State or St. Joseph's University flags draped over the deck rails.

The house stands right next to O'Donnell's Pub. Across 39th street there is another bar, Shenanigans. Figures. These two bars seem to flank Pete's house. I am surprised there isn't a basketball hoop on the high red brick chimney, which pokes from the worn shingled attic roof. I sneak around back to shake off the beers.

On the side of the house there is a pair of swinging white garage doors, but no hoop. Inside the fenced backyard, a two-foot white statue of

101

Jesus backs up to 39th Street. The inscription on the base reads, "have faith in the cross." It looks like it was hand carved with the bottle opener hanging around wooden Jesus' neck.

Andie crouches on the steps out front, picking at the tape around her ankles. I gently touch her shoulder with my left hand, pretending my balance wavers while climbing the steps, which are divided.

"There're seven steps on each side to the first landing," Pete says, carrying Scoob down the lower flight, "and then six steps to the second landing and the front door for 13 total steps.

"Fascinating, huh?"

I'm thinking 13 - Wilt Chamberlain maybe - when Pete informs, "There're traditionally 13 steps to the hangman's gallows, which is partly where the 'Unlucky 13' superstition derives."

"And, bro," Andie says standing up on one foot doing toe raises, "There are 13 loops in the hangman's noose, which is really unlucky for the person wearing it. Let's go drink 13 beers."

"Indeed, let's go wear a good soaking," Pete says. "Onward."

"Indeed," says Andie, high fiving her dad.

We march down Landis toward Avalon and cross the main boulevard. We stop in front of Braca's Cafe, a corner bar a half block from the promenade here in sunny Sea Isle. Pete turns the **CLOSED** sign on the door around to **OPEN**.

None of us Lads are 21, but I figure age matters as much as the Closed sign. Old Pete surely knows the bartender, the owner... and probably the cook and the guy who sweeps the floor... and the builder and architect.

Our mob wanders toward the bay, to the basketball courts on this main street going over the bridge from the mainland and into Sea Isle. This South Jersey shore town, just one exit up the Garden State Parkway from the courts, doesn't look as high rent as neighboring Avalon.

"No one plays in the morning at the Sea Isle courts," Andie says, answering the question I am thinking. "These courts start to see action late afternoon when renters had enough beach time.

"The old guys don't play in Sea Isle. They live here. They drink here. But, they don't play here. The games have always been in Avalon. Lately some games are breaking out behind the Acme food store around 62nd Street back by the bay on the way to the Townsends Inlet Bridge. But they're like the girly court in Avalon.

Pete turns around past the Sea Isle courts on JFK. With him strutting toward the ocean, the pack walks to the same spot he turned before reversing tracks, too. He struts back across Pleasure Avenue where the door to the closed bar is under a long green and white striped awning.

On this corner of Pleasure Avenue and 41st is the joint where the off duty black cop was drinking before he got knocked comatose last summer. Braca's Café, since 1901 it says on the cornerstone. The place looks innocent enough.

I'm hoping that I look as innocent. That no one thinks I'm down here to spy for the cops. My gaze drifts toward the ocean where the glare from the sand is blinding.

That's the whitest sand I've ever seen.

There is a menu on the outside wall, which intensifies my hunger. Andie pops M&Ms in her mouth, mumbling something about missing a 17-foot jumper, needing to protect the ball... her ball.

The menu, is as aged and cracked as the locals' faces. On it, printed between the "Sea Isle Sliders" and the "Braca Burgers" is the quote, "The whole-world is about three drinks behind," - Humphrey Bogart.

The doors open without a drum roll.

I'm standing out on this corner while the Lids filter in Braca's. I note that one block south, on 43rd Street, is the Springfield Inn. The sign's traitorous letters are orange and black, a blatant contrast to all the green and white down here.

"I need to get some air," I say hoping she joins me, walking toward the beach. Andie follows me as the last of the Lids and Lads flock inside.

A promenade runs along the grassy dunes on the beach and parallel to the ocean. A pavilion with benches juts out in the middle of the sand. The area is open, which allows a view down the promenade. North is toward Atlantic City where one block away I see a public bathroom.

This is where I will surely run to puke after a few more beers. I am not tossing in Braca's.

Looking south toward Avalon, I see the outdoor Carousel Bar next to the Springfield. Pointing, I say "my sister warned me not to get attacked by any cougars there," to an unamused Andie, who says "you're not their type... too old."

We walk toward the pavilion at the center of the promenade. It's near the steps where the white guy whacked the black cop. Well it *has* to be a white guy.

Right?

Approaching the steps, I can feel the breeze coming off the bay and I can see behind Braca's - Jondes Fudge is an obtrusive pink building with a bronze plaque, "The Sea Isle City Theater."

Next to the theater stands the Sea Shell condominiums, a four-story wall on the promenade. Didn't someone looking from a window or from one of the outside decks see the cop get ambushed? Isn't there a security camera?

An obligatory decorative lighthouse rises in the middle of JFK Boulevard near the promenade. A white lifeguard boat with square painted red letters "SIC" tilts away from the 30-foot structure with the blinking bulb. Across the street is an odd open lot before a covered theater stage emerges.

We wander back to Braca's. While pretending to look at the menu, I scan the area like a CSI guy here in SIC.

How oxymoronic... a bar on Pleasure Avenue is where the unpleasant Lids drink.

"Come on boyo, we're missing good drinking time," Andie says, "times as good as playing winning basketball."

The clock on top of the lighthouse in Center Circle at the end of JFK reads 11:11 AM!

Under the green and white striped awning, double glass doors lead into the foyer of Braca's. Pete holds open the door, allowing a view of the glass case on the wall filled with old pictures and newspapers. There is a photo of Bob Hope and a front-page headline screaming, WW II Is Over.

Over the door in stained glass are four words: "Celebrate Family Friends Tradition."

Before our beer is even poured, Pete holds court at the bar. The five Lids surround him. They all wear baseball hats inside here. None of them wore hats outside in the sun.

Our Mitch, Meags and Mac are right behind them, wearing lids too. Andie and I nudge over, hatless, but all sweaty like them, too.

At the bar, I plop on a stool. I'm tired. Half drunk. The older guys sit closer to the large TV on the left side. Or as Pete chides, "Nearer to the bath room, just in case, I got to puke from watching you guys play this morning."

"I know you're enthralled with our play," I say to Pete, feeling lubed up enough that I can start being me slightly and crack jokes.

"Enthralled is a Steven A. word," Pete says. "I'm not that smart. I'd probably say amped or juiced."

Maybe I'm trying to sound whiter than just being half white.

"I should call you Bir," Pete says with a look of revelation to me as the bartender starts sliding over-filled beers to us.

I figure it is a racial slap. I don't ask what it means. I wait for him to say, "Blackie Immune to Rebounding" or something similar. I am actually, even more intrigued how the bartender just starts dealing beers. He doesn't ask for ID.

Pete pats me on the head like a little leaguer in the dugout and says, "That's a good name for ya'll, Birrrrr," rolling the 'r' with amusement.

Every few minutes for the next hour at the bar, with Pete drinking three Irish Car Bombs, which Andie explains is a shot of whiskey dropped in a pint of Guinness, he jabs down to the end of the bar where us Lads sit with "how ya'll drinking going Bir? Hope better than your defense."

Andie and the Lads swallow their Guinness with the urgency of sprinting back on defense. Needing my senses, I switched to ice water.

Uncle Matty spills down to our end of the bar. Pete follows, thoughtfully unwrapping the paper from a straw and stabbing it my water.

"Easy on hydrating, Bir," Pete says, "don't over hydrate, as harmful as being over your head."

"Thank you, sir." I say. "I'm a straw man."

Prying between Uncle Matty and me, Pete squeezes closer to the bar. He stretches over the inside rail and snatches a white towel. He flips his hat off and rubs the towel over his thick hair.

"All the beer from the towel makes me think straighter," he says, laughing stupid silly while flipping the wet rag over the bar.

The bartender, a guy called Lynchie, slings the towel in a bucket with squeezed limes.

Putting on his hat backwards, Pete continues bouncing around, poking and joking. Uncle Matty pulls up to me. He orders another "mother's milk."

"Sure, you don't want one?" he asks kindly. "Pete's easier to absorb drinking. I won't say he's likeable, but he's tolerable when he's drinking…

but only if you keep drinking too."

I accept another hydration of "dark stuff."

"I've drunk lots of beers before," I say without impressing Uncle Matty.

"You don't say."

"Last summer," I continue, "we finished a Central Jersey Shore League game in Spring Lake and went to an outdoor pub with palm trees - Bar A. We pounded 16-ounce Natty Ice cans until the cops came. "

"Cops," Lynchie hushes, wiping the bar in front of me with a fresh white towel and placing an over-flowing discolored pint on a coaster. "Don't say that too loud in here, my man. Drink this lighter beer, my friend."

The bartender turns a shot glass upside down, saying the next one is "on him," pointing toward Pete, in the middle of everybody, smiling like he made the game winning shot.

"Cheers, Bir," Pete says lifting his pint glass. "Here's to us… the Merry Misanthropes."

Uncle Matty taps my glass with his, saying to Pete, you mean the "Misguided Mendicants."

We gulp more of this dark stuff. Pete reaches over Andie and taps my glass with his.

"Do you think it's ironic these pale white guys all drink this darker beer?" Andie questions, rubbing her forearm near a fresh scrape, either from this morning or arm wrestling her dad on a stool while I was talking with the bartender.

"The beer is kind of orange," I say as Pete nudges between us.

"Orange?" Pete says. "That's a Harp. And

yeah, you're right, orange like Andie... like the Asian-looking Jeremy Lin color, actually, even darker than the Knicks' Chinese or Taiwanese guard. Wish Andie played like the handsome Lin."

"Hah, Andie is darker than Lin," Uncle Matty says. "He's smarter, he is a Harvard man."

From my gaping mouth launches a stream of beer over the bar. Lynchie is quick with the towel. He wipes my spew from the forearm of Andie, who is smiling like a prom queen.

"Good to see you laugh," Uncle Matty says to me. "That's why we drink, it makes us old guys laugh... makes us forget... makes us remember."

"I thought basketball made you happy," I say feeling like almost one of the guys now, well, at least around Mister... Uncle Matty.

I struggle to stop calling these guys Mister like my dad's friends, although it feels unifying calling him Pete like everyone else.

Uncle Matty pump fakes his beer to his mouth like the pint glass is a basketball. He downs the brew, slams the empty purposefully on the bar, points to the trembling glass, taps his heart and points to the sky like he won an ESPY.

"Yep, the Merry Misanthropes don't hate life and people when we're drinking... and playing basketball," Uncle Matty pontificates. "But when we don't play ball and drink, we turn into the Misguided Mendicants... and then we do."

I nurse a sip. Uncle Matty taps my glass, signaling for me to "bond with another belt."

"I'm sure old Hook here wants to know what the fook is a Misanthrope Mendicant anyway," Andie says, sitting on her heels like Buddha a few stools down. "Byrdie hears you old fooks say M&M now all the time... oops, sorry Hook for me cussin."

"Hah, Byrdie will learn the way living plays out, when he's 30 years out of college and life sucks the life out of him with every blink... except for drinking and playing basketball," Uncle Matty says, "You'll be just like us... not like Mike."

I float down the far end of the bar, already knowing I won't be like Michael Jordan, but lamenting once again about my failure now while just trying to keep moving, trying to survive.

Andie hangs closest to the old guys and the madman, who stands next to an empty stool. About the ninth time he calls me Bir, Andie squints at me, saying with a half mouthful of dark stuff and half on her chin, "How ya doing, Bir?"

"What the *feck*, you too? Is he going to stay on the black stuff all night?" I ask, but don' care.

"Nah... just all summer," Andie says and quickly adds, "But Bir isn't a black thing, bro.'"

"Fa'shure," I say, not knowing for sure.

The dolled-up dinner crowd arrives in their snappy white outfits at 4 o'clock. We bolt like crowd-fearing monkeys at the zoo who don't want to be seen by more busloads of school kids after already having peanuts thrown at them all day.

Outside, Pete jumps an inch, at best, missing touching the top of the green and white awning by a foot or more.

"Still gots your ups," Uncle Matty quips. "Shame you never blocked Calipari's shot with those ups."

"Calipari *me* arse," Pete grumbles.

I am so loose that I want to ask Pete why he rags Calipari, but already knowing it's fa'shure because he recruits blue chip black players who stay one year and go to the NBA, taking up a scholarship from a D-3 kid who would stay four years and get his degree and go to Wall Street... and ironically work for my dad.

"Man, don't get started on Coach Cal," Uncle Matty says. "You will drop so many f-bombs you'll get bounced out of the Springfield before you piss behind the juke box."

The bartender from Braca's, Lynchie, follows us and begs, "Pete, I just got done my afternoon shift, I'll slip you a free pint tomorrow if you don't troll Calipari," but he doesn't listen.

"Matt, you just don't want to hear any fooks and fook this because you were converted by the Mormons and don't say fook anymore," Pete says. "I still can't believe you changed fookin religions after perfecting being a hypocritical Catholic like meself before even confirmation."

"That's OK, Pete, I will convert you soon," Uncle Matty bites back. "We'll move to Utah."

Pete swings the empty pint glass in Lynch's chest, saying, "Ok, Lynchie, I will oblige for two free beers tomorrow," before jumping, missing the awning and screaming "no more fookin Coach Cal talk, free beers after basketball... and church... tomorrow... fook-hoo... the night is on."

"Pete doesn't like Calipari because he played against him when he was in college," Uncle

Matty tells me.

"Yeah, Ursinus played them in the Randolph-Macon tournament, we were the only Division 3 team invited because we made the NCAA tournament the year before," Mr. Mac says real proud.

"It was us and Clarion State where Calipari played at the D-2 school outside Pittsburgh and Virginia Union, who had a 6-9 freshman monster named Charles Oakley, who later played with Michael Jordan on the Bulls," adds Mr. Mitch.

"Well, we beat Clarion in the first-round game before being hosed in the championship game by the home team Randolph Macon, which had walk-on freshman Greg Marshall, the Wichita State coach," Mr. Mac rattles like Pete's disciple. "Pete really outplayed Calipari."

"Yeah, he's pissed Calipari is making mega money and he beat him in college," Uncle Matty says.

"He's multi pissed because he saw Calipari at an organizational seminar about six years later, that's what Pete does, he puts on leadership programs, and Calipari was a guest speaker," says Mr. Mac. "Pete asked Calipari, who was coaching at UMass then, if he remembered playing Ursinus.

"Well, Calipari started bitching about the refs like they got hosed for about five minutes before he asked Pete, 'why buddy?'"

"Pete, just said 'no reason buddy' and walked away," Uncle Matty says.

The bay breeze washes my face as Pete turns left on the corner of Pleasure. The Springfield looms in sight, the orange and black letters signaling a change in drinking venues like white smoke pouring from the Vatican chimney.

"Later Bir," the bartender, Lynchie, says smiling to me, waving the white towel at us, now monitoring these misfits from the side door.

I don't care he is calling me Bir, too. I must have had ten tranquilizing beers.

We strut like pirates down Pleasure Ave. together. There are about 10, maybe 20, of us now.

"You know, I was at the Final Four a few years ago in San Antonio for the 24th anniversary of the Retired Irish Bounce-passers banquet," Pete introduces out of his wobbly ass. "You could walk the length of the River Walk drinking fruity margaritas outside."

Pete flings both his arms around the shoulders of Andie and me. He lifts his legs and swings, pulling down forcefully on me, at least.

"You know what was fooked up about the Final Four?" Pete asks, as if my thoughts really mattered. We resume walking, sniffing the ocean air filled with screams of kids loving life on the busy promenade, just a long bounce pass away.

"Kansas didn't win?" I say, not even knowing if the Jayhawks reached the Final Four

"Nah," he says, slurping from one of the Lids' "borrowed" beer mugs from Braca's. The glass chips when Pete bites the edge.

"Nope, no black people there," he says.

"What? There aren't plenty of blacks in New Orleans?" I ask, confused and thinking he means the site of the last Final Four. "All... most of the players are black. The ones *in* the game are."

"Yeah, but not *at* the game, not *in* the crowd," he says, stunningly indignant. "It was all whites, I'm sure it was that way in New Orleans, too. It was white as a bone in San *Antone.*

"A Caucasion Invasion. The boosters, teachers, professors, parents... the Irish Bouncepassers... everyone was astronaut white. The entire Alamo Dome was Apollo 11 inside. Except for the teams, and the school bands."

"So, enlighten us, why the blatant disparity?" Uncle Matty asks. "The meaning..."

"It means," Pete surges, "that college basketball exploits D-1 players. It's fooked up."

He tightens his forearm around my neck. With his calloused hands, he squeezes my shoulder. Does he know I know the cops think he did it?

"The irony was the Memphis band was all black and they were called the "Mighty Sound of the South," Pete continues. "The old South tried to keep *'dem* all down."

"How d-d-did they s-s-sound?" I stutter.

"Grand. Fookin grand," he boasts.

"The old man knows his music, too," Andie says, walking on the other side of her dad, getting a nice, approving nod from him.

"In the afternoon, on Saturday, before the semifinals, the Memphis Band played at the River Walk, all bunched in a crowd, a cluster of 50-year-old white dudes all wearing basketball gear from colleges. Everyone looked like an assistant coach. College basketball coaches are the only ones who still use fookin hair gel."

Uncle Matty reaches on top of Pete's bushy head with all his judgment stuffed securely, rubs his hair like he's messing up the tired thoughts, pours a little beer on his crown… and rubs more.

"Cool down, buddy," Uncle Matty insists, "you're forgetting names now, grouping people."

A white, square block of a compound, the Springfield, rises in front of us on the corner. Intimidating, like a prison, it is.

"Let's belly-up," Andie says as we stumble in the corner side door without paying a cover.

You can tell by their flat calves a lot of the men coming in the Springfield weren't players, but Pete and the bounce passing Lids still talk to them.

Some friends of Andie, Mitch and Mac enter the dark bar. They all look the same to me.

The Lids mix in with their kids' friends like Andie's M&M's concoction.

If they don't already know each other, it takes a half beer for the old Bouncepassers to find some connection to these young guys from their neighborhood, parish, school, or town.

Or their parents hooked up at one time down the shore.

Circled around a white steel support pole in the middle of the floor, the mixed group toasts their beers together. They man hug as if they have known each other since first communion.

The band, three short heavy guys, plop on stage behind the bar. They open with "Sweet Caroline" as if we are in Fenway fookin Park.

With their swaggering friends squeezing in the Springfield, Andie nudges me to move from the bar. We nest near the stillness of an unoccupied corner with an unplugged jukebox.

"I grew up in Drexel Hill with my dad," Andie offers. "My mom, she is Turkish, which is why I'm a little darker than my fair dad."

Truthfully, Andie looks much darker than her pale-faced pop. They both are really red. I think, she is like orangey, if that's a word, but when you are all-day drinking it doesn't matter, you can make up words like Pete calling me Bir.

"Pete and my mom aren't divorced, they just haven't lived together since I was born," Andie says. "My dad still loves her, I think, in a Christian way, at least. He's never been with another…"

Damn. No wonder the guy is "bar-bent," a made-up word I think Pete used at Braca's, describing his warped mind from drinking.

Pete hauls over two more dark beers. I still sip my first one. He slides to the wall side of the jukebox. A yellow stream flows out underneath.

When my embarrassment ceases and I return, Andie is stroking her hand around the scarred ears of Scoob on top of the jukebox.

A lady slips behind Pete in the corner, and knees him in the back of his knee. She's wearing Uggs with cutoff short blue jeans and a cutoff blue jean matching top, showing off her tan, skinny shoulders. Her brown hair is tied in a ponytail to the right side. She is very skinny and very pretty.

Pete re-arranges himself in front. He pours beer into his cupped hands. He rubs them together and swipes both gnarled mitts on his long-sleeve shirt before giving the beauty a double high five.

"Josey, my man," Pete says with a smile wider than the jukebox.

"Pistol," she says smiling with the brightest, savory set of teeth I've ever seen, straddling the stream on the floor. "Pistol Pete peeing again."

"Hi Dei," Andie says to the lady, who is even prettier than I first thought as I see her full face. And she looks younger than I first thought. She looks great, but must be in her late 40's.

Pete and the lady tap Corona bottles after every swig or two. They talk and laugh, screaming in each other's ears as the band, the Julio Brothers, play the opening chords of Sweet Home Alabama.

"Who's she?" I yell in Andie's ear.

"Old friend of Pete's," she says. "They met down here when I was a kid. She has a boy around my age. We all used to go to the swing sets in Avalon. We did this for years before we got too old for the swings and I started playing ball on the other court."

"She looks cool in warm furry boots," I say. "Her face is beautiful. Why does he call her Josey?"

"Why? He's Pete."

The band stops and I fear the lady heard me say beautiful once too often. Four seats open up at the bar. Dei sits in the far-right seat and taps the top of the seat next to her for Pete to sit. Andie sits next to her dad and I sit in the far-left seat. Dei buys us Coronas. Pete tosses the lime. We cheer.

"Pistol, tell them the story when you were in Ireland and did the Gaelic toast." she says.

"You tell them, darlin," he says.

"I'm from the south, well up until high

school," she explains, "so he calls me "darlin.' I just love the sound of the word, darlin."

"I love his Gaelic toast story, too."

"Tell us," Andie says. "Tell me again."

She enjoys a slow sip of her beer and starts, "Pete was in Ireland at the Tom Collins pub, the oldest in Limerick, with some real Irish lads. He'd learned a Gaelic toast and offered it to them, saying 'slainte... saol fada... agus feadfaidh tu bas... in Erin,' but trying to sound real Irish himself, he over accented each syllable of the toast, especially *Erin*, which means to 'your health... long life... and may you die in *Ireland*...

"The real Irish lads were impressed, but one guy Donal says, 'hey, grand toast but you just fookin wished we all die in fookin *Iran*.'"

Pete roars and pats the top of her ponytail. Pete and Dei talk and laugh, and high five for a few more beers. Andie and I listen. Dei looks at me, her beautiful brown eyes roll to the floor.

"How did you remember the Gaelic toast?" I ask, but don't think she hears me looking down.

"Oh, sugar, I have a bad habit of remembering interesting things," she says.

Pulling up her Uggs, Dei peels off by herself to the dance floor. Stayin Alive blares from the jukebox. She's alone on the dance floor with a beer in one hand and fist pumping the other.

Pete gapes at her spinning like a ninja as all the other ladies around her age seethe, knowing she is the real deal.

Dei is so good-looking she can pull off wearing Uggs in a bar in the summer, tie her hair to the side like a teenager at girl scout camp, and dance like she is an equal half mix of Uma Thurman and John Travolta.

"The Bee Gees are better now, well their old music is, than in the 70's when they were the biggest band in the world," Pete says staring at the dance floor. "I can't watch…"

The Springfield is spacious, but it isn't the Trump's Taj Mahal of bars. The place is uninviting inside for being a block from the ocean.

"You know why, Bir, they call these joints bars?" Pete asks. "I'm testing you."

I spin around and look behind me, acting like I am searching for any answer but really just checking out Dei dancing alone with her aura.

"Bir, back in the old days of our fine country, owners fitted iron *bars* in pubs to protect the booze and the money," he says, getting in my face like he is covering me on defense. "They needed the bars because all the Irish guys would get drunked-up and fight and try to steal the booze.

"Ahh, the fooking Irish," he says laughing, stepping away. "The owner of the bars didn't care if they shot the bartender behind the bars as long as they didn't get the money and the booze. Many a bartender died behind bars.

"Hey Bir, you know why I call you Bir, right?" he continues with remarkable easiness.

Pete inches closer to me. He backs off. He is floating, like his mind, going in and out and everywhere, now happy as can be. I am feeling good myself, so I figure I can try my joke.

"Hey Pete, shouldn't you and old Scuba be

hanging out at the Dead Dog Saloon?" I say bravely, feeling reassured while drunk how I can recite the perfectly politically incorrect name of the bar I saw on Landis Avenue near Pete's house.

Pete pushes me back a step with both hands. The shove isn't real hard, but it isn't playful. It would be enough to get him kicked out of a basketball game with real refs, but not out of this asylum surrounded by his Pavlovian posse.

He could pound me with a plank and the Mexican brother's in the band, none of the trio, would miss playing a beat for a Sea Isle second.

The pack of Lids and Lads circle us. Pete inches closer to me. Everyone can see my heart thump. No one steps in the middle of our chat.

Pete pushes his chin under mine, leaving enough space for a whisker.

"Scoobs isn't old," he sneers, "he's mangled because someone like your boyo Michael Vick did this to him. Made Scoob fight for food... his life."

"I don't even like the Eagles," I say.

"Tell him what the fook does Bir mean," Andie says trying to intervene, to save me from Pete, who holds his ground a chin hair away.

Dei waltzes over to the pack. Hovering outside the circle of jurors, she waves for Pete to go out on the dance floor. He spins and twirls and stomps like he invented dancing.

Chapter 6

Light. I see the light.

We are going to find food? Sleep? Right?

Fookin A. Smith this bar does close.

The lights are on and thirsty bouncers usher the really fooked-up folks to the open double doors. The sticky air tastes like a saltwater taffy, reminding me we haven't eaten since... when?

Andie places her calloused left hand on my shoulder, pushing herself up from the barstool. Standing, with her hand sliding slightly toward my neck, I think Andie tells me we are heading to The Rock, or is it The Hut? Her hand's warmth matches my relieved smile back at her.

Time to pass out, right? But I don't know. I don't know where we are going, or where this... this summer is heading.

Walking out through the twin glass doors, we stutter-step as the fresh air splashes us like chilly water from the morning bathroom sink. The swaying bright bar lights cast our floating shadows on the white concrete. The bobbing streetlights give a dusk-like glow. A cop car slows down as I try to adjust my eyes... my mind.

Across the street is Basilicus, some sort of Greek restaurant. Yeah, man, we are going to eat some grub. Damn, Basilicus is closed. I turn on my iPhone. I had shut it off at some point, somewhere to save some battery in case I needed to call my parents to save me. It is two minutes after two in the morning.

Pete dances onto the sidewalk. He tries to

step on his shadow's head, hopping from one foot to the other and waving his arms for us to dance with him.

With barely a burp, Pete and Andie and their boys just drank "properly" for 14 hours. I probably drank, with less success, about half that time. I stopped boozing for a good bit after my dog joke bombed.

Hope he forgives me… or forgets.

How can Pete go to church and not forgive? To metaphorize life on his level, it would be like only playing offense and not rebounding in basketball. He would be an incomplete Catholic.

"Boys, we're heading up, down to the end of the island," Pete says between erratic hops.

"He knows the owners," Andie says. "Time to do some more boozing in Strathmere. A place like you've never seen, called Twisties."

Strathmere? I am just starting to recognize some of the haunts in Sea Isle, like the Springfield and the red brick bank across the street.

There is an oasis ahead. A pizza place is open diagonally on the block. Pete shoots me the look like he forbids sobering food. He says he wants to "make up words that mean nothing."

Andie and I hold each other up. My right arm wraps around her hip. Pete doesn't see me touching his daughter. His eyes look blankly to the black sky. There is no moon. No stars.

"Then I see the darkness," he sings in a throaty voice, walking beyond the lights of the Springfield. "And then I see the darkness."

"My dad loves Johnny Cash," Andie

whispers as we wobble. "But I've never seen him wear any black. Just green t-shirts from the hoop leagues he's played in for 30 years, or the old gray Ursinus t-shirt, with white or gray gym shorts."

Pete abruptly turns and runs in place. He fitfully waves his hat, signaling for us to hurry up.

"He never has any pockets," she adds. "He carries around his wallet and cell and keys all balled up in that baseball cap he hardly wears."

With the cathartic rhythm of the ocean rolling at my back, massaging my mind from the darkness, I see a gold steeple rising a block behind the line of two-story shops across the street.

Are we at Notre Dame? Heaven? Or is Satan head faking us with a mirage? Is this hell?

Pete stumbles over the low bike curb. He zig-zags up to the Church on Landis Avenue. The sign near the steps says **ST. JOSEPH'S.** There is a handicap ramp along the side, on 44th Street.

"I do me best sinning just before going to the first mass on Sunday morning," Pete slurs. "This way the sin isn't too old and can be forgiven quicker, like the six second rule when a meatball drops out of the roll and onto the floor."

I glimpse at my iPhone. It is 2:22 in the morning. Pete drapes his arm around me. Wrapped in his other arm is Scoob, who appeared out of nowhere at the bar earlier, then vanished, I think.

"Bir, my man," Pete says, gripping the back of my neck like my dad did before criticizing me as a kid, "you're a fair to midling drinker."

I forgot he has been calling me "Bir" for most of our acquaintance. I had forgotten at other times, too. Like at Braca's. I think I forgot on the concrete deck of the Springfield, trying to ingest the sea air to clear my head of the fog. Why is he calling me "Bir" again… or is Satan calling me?

The player with the Villanova hat from the courts and a long-legged lady wobble toward us.

"Check out the stilts on that babe," Pete taunts as they lay down on the handicap ramp. "Hey Pinck, your girl could be a power forward."

With Pete hanging dependently on me outside the church, I ask "is my new name tribal?"

He pulls me with him and slumps against the handrail of the busy handicap ramp.

"You know, it's like Larry Bird, see," he tells me. "My man, you the Bird Man." He spits and hits the back of what looks like mini monument, like a granite tombstone. "Only you got no D. Get it? No dee-fense. Byrd with no D like in Bir. So, you boyo, are Bir."

"Got it," I tell him. Damn, no D - that's a good one. Especially since I'd been thinking Bir was a racial thing. Maybe it really is equivocal. There must be a meaning inside the meaning.

I don't even chuckle… if I laugh he'll probably stop poking me… if I laugh he'll know I know I don't play defense.

I'm thinking offense anyway. I shot badly today – yesterday. How bad will I shoot today – in a few hours?

The Church is puritan white. Intimidating, it is. There are some new red shingles patched inside the older faded ones.

I will need to return for confession. When?

At the front of the church, above the double doors, hovers a huge stained glass window of some sort. Between the doors and the colorful window is an enclave with a statue of a bearded man. Joseph, I figure, holding the Baby Jesus.

Below the two brown doors are stone steps. I plant both feet on each landing for balance as I hold the gray handrail in the middle and Pete on my right side. I count the steps as we climb.

Thirteen steps. Just like at Pete's house.

The stairwell is flanked with red bricks.

Pete tilts in front of the two doors, facing them, as if waiting for the doors to majestically open for us. He inches back. He cautiously turns.

I need to watch out... I am fading big time.

I try to focus my fading vision across the side street to Mary Anne's Pastry shop.

Suddenly, Pete spins. He taps on the door.

The ocean barely murmurs below the darks skies from a point beyond where we had been. I scan Landis Avenue, over Elements Salon - or is it Saloon? Another bar? One shop over is Giovanni's Deli. How did an Italian place open down here?

I fear I am spiraling in one of my fever dreams. Why am I here? What is God's plan?

Andie and Scoob lounge on the top step. I squeeze between them, leaning against her. Pete slumps on the other side of Andie.

He rambles "why church doors should never be shut... how God's House should always be open... I'm ready to close out." He leans over us and whispers the same sentiment to Scoob slumped on the steps, rubbing his pocked ears and saying, "Pal, we'll go out together."

Andie jumps up, startling Scoob. With Pete's head now leaning on my shoulder and her heels hanging over the top step, she does toe raises

"Got to build up my calf, both of them, if I'm going to dunk before Byrd does," she laughs, spreading her arms as if she is about to launch into flight. Looking like an angel... an orange angel.

Pete doesn't go to confession anymore, he told me at the Springfield right before the lights went on, but not because he doesn't "buy" the forgiveness of sins. Rather, he confessed to me he now feels he doesn't "deserve" to be forgiven.

"I ought to suffer," Pete professes, curled into a ball with Scoob on the highest landing.

He straightens up, amazingly transformed, suddenly composed and determined, from the cowering guy shrinking on the top step.

"I didn't earn to be in heaven with mom," he states, after a gasp, with unapologetic acceptance. "I've sinned, she didn't. I can't take the E-Z Pass entry to heaven just because God is so merciful."

A Sea Isle City black-and-white cop car with To Protect and Serve on the door cruises by with curiosity. The redheaded cop points his finger out the window like his hand is a gun. He then flips into a friendly Miss America-like wave.

Pete salutes. The cop offers a compassionate nod, as if saying, "get home safe."

Piously, Pete returns the sign of the cross, touching his forehead, chest and shoulders, folding his hands like the devoted nuns at St. Anthony's.

"Let's go fookin grub," he orders, "Jesus ain't here turning church bricks into bread loaves."

Food! I hop down the first step, then, take two at a time. I count all 13 of the steps again.

"God just might be good enough to take me before I sin more," Pete says, stopping on the seventh step with Andie holding his elbow. "He has taken enough of me mates lately. Perhaps... He is rounding up a starting five, put me at point."

"But your doomed to hell, remember? Never seeing your mom again," I remind him. Hey says, "Oh yeah... your right. Thanks Bir."

Andie holds my elbow with Scoob under her left arm. She tells me her dad is "just a little down since he lost another of his mates to cancer.

"Three of his old basketball buddies have died in two years," she whispers. "The latest one - Butch, with the Dick Barnett leg-kicking jumper - passed away the night before last... or is it two nights back now?"

Weaving down Landis - or is it up Landis? - we cross over 42nd Street, which is also according to the sign post named CHARLOTTE SAFRONEY STREET. Huh, one street with two names? Odd.

Why no Pete Street?

On the corner is a shop JAMAICAN ME CRAZY. Next door is another shop, "Its a Girlz Thing." I want to scream to Pete that he's making me crazy. I want to scream to Andie "This isn't a girls thing down here," when across the street I see two pizza shops right next to each other - Soprano's and Angelo's. How can two pizza places be next to each other? Only in Sea Isle... And two more

Italian place. How? Why?

Andie is bouncing with each stride between Pete and me. She says, "There is a little diner on the main highway, on JFK Boulevard. That's where we're headed."

"Not Twisties?" Pete pleas, leaning on her.

The blocks seem short here. Even while carrying an all-day drinking load. I look up at the JOHN FITZGERALD KENNEDY BOULEVARD street sign. I think, how fitting. This main drag stretching all the way from the causeway bridge to the promenade, through this warped Irish town, demanded to be named it after an Irishman. Not after another famous shaker of the 1960's with three equally recognizable initials – MLK.

Pete races Scoob the last half block. The chipped sign on the door says SEA ISLE SEATING AVAILABLE, with no break between the words.

"Hey," I say pointing to the sign, "aisle seating available. *Me* don't have to sit in back."

Pete plants Scoob on top of a newspaper box and leads us through the sloped entrance.

The Sea Isle diner seats only about 20 or so. There is a short line of a half dozen people waiting to be seated in the walkway. A tanned waitress with squinty eyes waves for us to sit right down at a table where three young guys, who are all wearing matching yellow Red Bull shirts, get up.

A thick man with a distracting bulbous nose struts right up to the table. He blurts out to Pete, "You going out diving this morning?" Then he rudely turns and sits one booth away while still talking, "Ocean's light, only two to four-foot swells out by the deeper, more lucrative wrecks."

Biting a piece of toast left on the front table, reaching over two 40-something ladies sitting in the booth next to us, Pete gives the intimidating looking man a high five. Then he rubs both ladies on their heads like they are his adopted puppies. One rolls her eyes. The other's eyes widen.

"Sit with us Peter," the wide-eye lady demands, sliding her skinny butt. "Com'n Pistol Pete." The defiant lady kicks her under the table.

Pete's shutters, showing no interest to the invite. He puts the hat holding his wallet and cell down where our amused waitress is waiting.

"Pistol? Man, I wish," he turns back toward the inviting lady, while our waitress clears away unfinished waffles and ham in front of him.

"I wish I was The Pistol," Pete insists, chomping on the leftover toast. "He is dead.

"Fortunate to exit early naturally."

The waitress grabs the plate in front of me that looks like someone puked on top of the stack of pancakes. Pete slings his arm around the shoulder of the girl. He pushes off her like a crutch, standing on a chair and screams, "Pistol was the maaaaaaaan. Maravich, the magic of No. 44." A few drunks at a table in the middle of the diner lift their glasses of water in a toast.

As I'm wondering why he doesn't wear Pistol's sacred 44 jersey on the courts, Pete plops down and sprawls across his side of the booth as if reclining in his living room with the remote.

"Maravich would've loved Drexel Hill," he says. "Back in the late 60's when he was at LSU, he would've traded his floppy socks to play in games at Aronimink Swim Club on Sunday nights in the Philly heat. I was a kid. It was heaven watching Jimmy Lynam, Herb Magee and Jack McKinney, and some of the other legends from the Hill, play against invading Big Five teams.

"Eddie Hastings brought the Nova guys over," Pete continues while lying on his back. "Howard Porter would come to play at Aronimink. He played a few weeks after playing UCLA in the '71 NCAA Finals with the grand Tom Ingelsby, who coached me at Ursinus and was from Springfield next to Drexel Hill, but played at Cardinal O'Hara, and married Eddie Hasting's lovely sister and Hank Simeontkowski… Fran O'Hanlon graduated the year before… and they had a black guy who was really good, strong… fook… man, I can't remember his name."

"How he can remember a guy named Seimenkowski from four decades ago, but not the name of the lone black guy on a Final Four team?" I ask Andie in my low Montessori school voice. "His name was probably Smith or Johnson, too."

"Hastings is from St. Andrews in Drexel Hill," Pete adds, sitting up straight as if this will help his memory. "They couldn't beat the St. Bernie kids, though, from our side of The Hill."

Suddenly, like a vision, I remember Pete said he attended St. Bernadette's until 8th grade.

"Back in the day, Jerry West came up from West Virginia and Artis Gilmore flew from Jacksonville to play at the *Great A* pool … Hastings, Ingelsby, Seimenkowski … and Villanova beat the

7-foot-1 Gilmore in the Final Four semifinals in '71, advancing to play Lew Alcindor and unbeatable UCLA.

"That's before Alcindor changed his name to Kareem Abdul Jabbar," Pete continues while popping back up, looking at Uncle Matty's table. "I still call him Alcindor. I don't believe in changing names or religions.

"How is that m... m... m... Mormonism going m... m... m... Matty?" Pete says, getting louder, slurring his words. "Is m... m... m... Mitt Romney recruiting you for the cabinet?"

Uncle Matty shrugs while wiping his glasses with the paper place mat. He balls up the disposable table setting and jump shoots it at Pete.

"You're a Mormon, I'm a moron, but you changed religion..." Pete ponders before turning back to us with "just because you change your name doesn't mean I'm calling you by that name.

"Hell, my grandfather never called Cassius Clay by m... m... m... Muhammad Ali.

"And what's up with m... m... m... Meta World Peace? He went to St. John's. How can Ron Artest change his name after going to a fookin Catholic college? I played ball in Turkey, I didn't change my name to Muslim. I even m... m... m... met a Muslim Turk girl and... the Islamic faith is one of the three great Abrahamic religions, I just don't know how you can change from the religion you were raised... from the faith God borne you...

"Enlighten me."

The two ladies at the next table flip their napkins over their unforked pancakes. Pete grabs one from each plate and stuffs them in each side of his mouth like Belushi in Animal House.

"They still got the wooden square backboards and probably the same rims, but no one plays there now," Pete mumbles on about Aronimink. "More kids play on the tennis courts. Can you believe kids play tennis instead of hoops?

"Hell, the women tennis players these days all look like fookin linebackers. They're so muscled up they look genetically engineered."

Another college-aged waitress hurries to our table, pointing her pencil at Pete like a sword.

Pete puts his finger over his lips, hushing "I'm fookin sorry." She says, "You must be him."

"I must, I'll have the butter milk pancakes without butter and milk," Pete says, poking her like the cracks already on her weathered forehead.

He bows and she pats his bushy head.

"For some shipwreck reason, girls dig his act," Uncle Matty grumbles loud enough for the paradoxical ladies at the other table to hear. "It can only be because he has all his hair and then some."

Sliding back down, Pete tells the waitress this is going to be the, "Grandest meal of his life."

"This is the only night I got," he turns to me, "gots to be my best meal."

Andie offers a sympathetic glance.

"Growing up, Pete played during the summer at the Jewish Community Center in Pennsauken. He played with a guy named Tommy Dove," Andie says. "Pete looked up to him so much that one summer when Tommy was red from head to toe with a real-bad sunburn, Pete went out the next weekend and got sunburn, too."

Using a knife, Pete scrapes off the burnt edges from another table's leftover slice of toast.

"Me dear mum drove me from Drexel Hill to Pennsauken back in the day…" Pete says, losing his thought "To play basketball against the grand Doug Collins and the unknown Lloyd Free, who is now World B. Free, from Guilford College

"The Dove passed, but he came back to see me in a dream," he continues while taking the first bite of my toast. "He flew into the room …"

Everyone listens, even the busy waitresses. The one with brownish-reddish hair who served us steadies Pete's hip so he won't fall into the table.

The thick Irish guy pulls a chair closer to Pete. Andie squeezes in next to me, across from her dad. She leans in closer to her pop like he is St. Peter himself in the Upper Room.

"My buddy comes back in the dream to a lot of us are in a room. Friends of his from way back are in the dream. He talks to us one at a time, but he never looks at the one he is talking to…

"He's sitting at a table, and everyone is like so relieved to see him. It's like he's back for good. He hands a piece of paper to each of us. I look down at my piece of paper. It's a report card. There are three categories on one side and four on the other. I can't read the categories. But there are letters next to each category. He has graded us on our lives. It was our report card of life."

The brutish Irish guy grunts, "What did you get Pete?"

Pete kneels. He puts his head down on the

table.

"Come on Pete, what were your grades?" the guy says, leaning closer.

"Gotta go," Pete says standing up. "You diving today?"

"Oh yeah. You?"

"Nah, got mass and then bas'kaball," Pete says, backing out the door, waving to everyone, and plucking Scoob off the Daily News stand.

I think we - Andie and I - walked home to the house we're renting across from the courts in Sea Isle. We rubbed shoulders for a long second or two while squeezing in through the front sliding glass door… that's what happened, I think…

Violently, Pete is shaking my shoulder and screaming, "Wake up, you're lying on Scoob." I am spread across the sofa of The Rock or The Hut, or whatever he calls his headquarters. So, we didn't go to the Lids' place. Did we even rub shoulders?

I see light, but no dog. The sun is up. I couldn't have slept more than a few fitful hours.

Andie flies down from the top bunk bed in the other corner of the living room. "The Top of the Rock," she roars as she rips a dozen or so jumping jacks and then 18 finger-tip pushups, "one for me age," she whispers as if a stock tip.

"Good thing we slept in our basketball gear, we're launching right to the courts after church," Andie says. "And fill up an empty Gatorade bottle with water. You'll need to hydrate like a fire truck on July 4th after all you drank, bro."

After drinking with her I guess I am a bro now to Andie, too. I also think the booze inside me is stirring up. I am getting drunk again just thinking. My earrings are gone. My dreads are cut.

The church doors are open. Pete does an air knock anyway. It makes Andie and me, smile. We sit in the back.

"Pete always sits up front at Saint Bernadette's," Andie whispers, "but here at Saint Joseph's he leaves right after communion. That's so he can get to the courts in Avalon by five of eight before the first Sunday game.

"The Saturday games start at 7 because the Lids don't drink as much on Friday since many don't drive down until later. But on Sundays 'they like to eyeball God' in case they have the big one on the courts."

Around us in mass are guys, from the courts, or from Braca's, or from the Springfield, or the diner, but not the Lids. I see Black Jesus limping up to the only open space in the front as Dads spread to the end of pews along his route. He sits next to White Magic, who looks like he's wearing the same shirt he puked on yesterday.

I am really not sure of things at first, until I stand up for the gospel reading. Then I can look a few pews ahead and behind and see most of the guys with hung over looks have their basketball high tops on and gym shorts. They look like they are going to play basketball. Or paint a house.

"These guys also do their best sinning on Saturday night," Andie says, nodding at her dad's people in church with their fingers already taped.

"They leave the bars when the lights come on and five hours later go to mass," a lady in front of me scoffs without turning around. "Like nothing happened. Like choir boys."

I have to start listening to the priest since I am sinning looking at this accurately judgmental mommie's ass in front of me. She is old enough to be my mom… and I can't stop looking at her ass.

I am pissed I'm even thinking this. I never thought like this before. Pete is fooking me up. Now I'm cussing. And I'm cussing in church.

Hell, I'm going to hell. I'm going to be Andie's roommate in college and Pete's roommate in hell.

Before digging this lovely mom any more, the priest, an Irish guy who doesn't seem much older than the Lids themselves, starts his homily by preaching about a little kid who threw up all over in church. "He was sitting in the second row and just barfed," the priest says with emphasis.

Everyone laughs like it's funny. You know how you laugh at something someone says when it is not funny just because they are in a position of power? Well, this crowd gives one of those laughs.

Anyway, the priest goes on to say how after mass he got the bucket and mop from the closet to clean the mess. He says he was mopping the chunks when an older Irish lady "suddenly swiped" the mop from him. He says he wanted to clean, but she wouldn't release the dripping mop.

"This is SIC," the lady told me.

"Yeah, I know," he says. "It's Sea Isle City.

"The lady barked back at me, 'No, it's Send in the Cleaner.'"

Everyone laughs, although he said nothing

funny. They laugh louder when the redhead priest with the comb-over describes the Irish lady as having gray hair, glasses and red cheeks. He says everyone knows a lady like that and they laugh real silly. Stupid silly. Hang-over splitting silly.

"What's so freakin funny?" I ask Andie.

"Maybe they're laughing at themselves," she says with her eyes latched on the pulpit comic.

The whole church is stuffed with either older Irish ladies like her or the smoking mommies in their white-hot mommy uniforms, like the one in front of me, who turns around when Andie says again, "They're just laughing at them fookin selves." I recognize her as the mommy with the kid in the stroller from the courts.

"Maybe, just maybe, they fear more than hell itself they'll one day look like the older cleaning lady," Catrina says.

The priest seems to enjoy making everyone laugh. He says he has a point to make still.

"The lady wanted to do it because that was her way of doing service and being charitable," he says. "But I told her that she would deprive me of doing my service for God.

"She said, 'Give me the mop.'

"I gave her the mop."

Everyone laughs like they are going to barf like the kid in this parable.

He finishes up by saying, "Wanting to do service is great, but you have to know why and who you're doing the service for."

Service? I try not to think why I am here. I don't want to think about my covert *networking* with the cop tomorrow. Or is it the next day?

As I am trying to think heavenly thoughts, Catrina turns around to shake hands for the Kiss of Peace. Her rack can't be real, too lovely. Her soft hands barely touch mine.

On the way down the 13 steps out of church, I say, "Now that was a sweet sermon by the preacher" to anyone who would agree.

I know Pete hears me even though he's already at the bottom of the steps, hustling to get to the courts.

"Hey Pete," the priest says, "I noticed you didn't laugh during the homily... you were the only one..."

Pete turns around, but doesn't step any closer to the priest.

"Well, Fr. Devlin...'

"You know, outside of church you call me Dennis."

"Well, we're still on holy church grounds," Pete says.

"Why didn't you laugh?"

A crowd circles around Pete and the priest. They stay about six feet apart.

"The story reminded me of my youth," Pete says.

"How?" asks Catrina, covering her kid's ears with both hands and her skeptical stare.

"Alice and Wonderland," Pete says to her. "You must've read your little lad The Walrus and the Carpenter."

Confused, she shakes her head sideways, her boobs slightly bouncing, beautifully.

"I did as a kid," the priest says. "What about it?"

Pete steps halfway to the priest. The circle of people squeeze in a half step as Pete says:

"The Walrus and the Carpenter were walking close at hand; they wept like anything to see such quantities of sand: 'If this were only cleared away,' they said, 'it would be grand!'"

Pete steps halfway closer to the priest, now only a foot and a half away. The circle tightens a half step, too. Pete continues:

"If seven maids with seven mops swept for half a year, do you suppose,' the Walrus said, 'that they could get it clear?' 'I doubt it,' said the Carpenter, 'and shed a bitter tear.'"

Pete leans toward the priest, saying "You see Dennis, wanting to do service is grand, and you do have to know why and who you are doing the service for... but some deeds in the past can't be cleaned up... never can be swept away."

Driving over the bridge at Townsends Inlet into Avalon, I look over and see Andie, Pete, and the ocean. It's like they are all connected.

"Boo," Pete screams as the toll collector pokes his head out with donut crumbs on his blonde goatee. They high five as Andie reaches out the window, giving him a handful of M&Ms.

"Boo... Boo... Boo... who the fook are you?" Pete sings like the Who song, hitting the gas and without paying the toll.

"Dad, what did you get on your report card," Andie insists. "You know from last night?"

Pete stops at the bottom of the bridge where

waves are crashing into the jetty rocks and splashing onto the narrow causeway.

"We gots the stiff nor'eastern wind," he says. "Got to aim your shot another ball out...

"Got all A's."

We pull up to the court at exactly five minutes to eight as a gust of wind blows more sand under the basket.

"I couldn't believe I got all A's," Pete says, "I'm such a sinner and I had all A's, I didn't understand."

Pete grabs a push broom with gaps of missing bristles from the back of his truck.

"But just as I started to ask my old friend, the dream ended. I think I should go now when I have all A's still, somehow. Or, I wish in life you could sweep away the past."

Chapter 7

Pete thrusts his broom forward at the sand with angry jabs. He is trying to sweep away the white stuff that blew onto the court overnight. But with every ferocious swipe more sand seems to appear beneath the broom.

The broom is missing half of its bristles. After each push, Pete stares at the sand which puffs into a cloud and floats away with the wind toward the back bay of this barrier island. When he looks down there is more sand. He brooms again angrily. His stare seems peaceful, but then he shoves and shoves again as in a panic. It's as if each swipe cleans away one thought, yet uncovers an even more troubling guilt underneath.

SUV's with license plate holders from different Philadelphia area colleges converge on the court, slam on brakes and park haphazardly.

"Hope these boys shoot like they park," I say to Andie as she tightens the tape on her ankle for the Camaraderie Classic.

"They don't," is all she says.

One guy drains jumper after jumper at the opposite end of the court from Pete. He finally misses one and turns around to get the bouncing ball. It is Tim Legler. I recognize him from ESPN, where he is an NBA analyst. I grew up watching "Pardon the Interruption" on ESPN, the talk show with Michael Wilbon and Tony Kornheiser. I love their interplay. "Legs" Legler can still shoot. I wonder what's his hook to these wannabees?

My dad once said that Legs played for

LaSalle, but not against his Boston University teams. He played in the late 1980's for Speedy Morris… who now coaches at St. Joe's Prep in Philly. Oh yeah, down here, basketball connects anybody that is anybody in their world like the Townsends Inlet bridge is the umbilical cord which connects Sea Isle and Avalon.

There are no refs for these tourney games either. The winners from yesterday afternoon's games play in the first round today. There seems to be eight teams of about six guys, maybe seven for the older teams. I am on Andie's team. The Lids are another squad.

At the other end of the court from Legs and his team, everyone who is waiting to shoot surrounds Pete. He is still brooming specks it seems that only he can see from the court.

"Hurry up, man," White Magic calls out to Pete. "We're jammed up waiting for you to post the odds on each team."

I rhetorically ask Andie, "are odds what I think it means?"

Pete heaves the broom at White Magic. He slides a Wawa napkin with writing on it from his pulled-up sock and hands the balled-up paper to White Magic, who yanks off his puke-stained shirt, sporting an attractive mane of hair growing down the back of his neck, with his other hand.

"Odds like in betting? Fookin-ay yeah," she spits and gives me the dumb-ass look. "No one's betting on our hides, so don't dump in your pants. It's always the same two or three teams in the CC Final Four."

She stops taping her ankles, rips the tape and throws the roll at White Magic, screaming, "What's our number?"

White Magic rips off a piece of tape and puts it over his mouth.

"He won't tell us… but, yeah, we're from The Hill. We fookin bet on everything," Andie says, reaching out her right hand as if to make a bet. I'll bet you the first pint at the bar today my dad brooms the lane again."

She uses her left index finger to make a slash over her right palm. I do the same as if we are making a blood bet.

"After waiting so long?" I say, scanning the basket where Pete has stopped sweeping. Warm-up shots start dropping through the net. "They'd shoved the broom up his Irish arse. Okay, the wager is on."

I hold onto the shake as Pete once again snatches up the broom. He sweeps under the same basket. Everyone stops shooting.

"Want to bet he sweeps one more time?" I ask Andie when Pete fires the broom at White Magic. I really just want to hold her hand again.

"For fooks' sake, Tim Donaghy is from Drexel Hill," Andie tells me as I reach out my hand to shake for another bet.

"You mean the disgraced former NBA ref who was caught betting on games?" I ask.

"His dad, Gerry, used to ref games at Aronimink," she says. "He learned to ref and young Tim learned to bet in The Hill.

"I'm sure people say betting on NBA games

like he did was wrong, like he was in the mob," Andie keeps going. "For fooks' sake, he went to the pen...

"That's what we do. We care about winning. I know we aren't bad guys."

Pete straddles the broom he retrieved at White Magic's feet, "flying" over to us like he is a witch in Macbeth ready to stir the pot.

"Enough with all the handshaking, grab-assing going on," Pete scorns, pointing the end of the broom at me throat, then down to my privates.

"We shook on a bet," Andie says. "No grab-assing goings on around here."

"We're getting deep," I tell Pete, giving my most serious look. "We're rapping about the morality of gambling. You knew Tim Donaghy?"

"Timmy went to St. Bernadette's, too, just like John Nash and Ed Stefanski, who both were Sixers' general managers," Pete says. "Not everyone from the Hill is Richard Nixon crooked.

"Playing the ponies, our code when calling in action, is embedded in The Hill's culture."

Pete sweeps the broom in the air around his head. He spins around, like Dei on the dance floor, with the broom as if brushing back the bay breeze.

"Can learned behavior as a kid, even though unacceptable by society, be accepted as normal by the kid when an adult?" I ask directly into the broom handle like an ESPN microphone, trying to soften my poignant question with humor.

"Like Vick and dog fighting?" Pete retorts.

He pauses for my answer before Pete says how "Vick said he grew up around dog fighting, which is why he did it as an adult."

Pete pushes the broom again, letting loose so it sails toward me. I duck with a chuckle.

"Young Timmy just got caught up in the culture. He had three kids. Mouths to feed…"

The first-round games tip-off.

About 12 guys are surrounding Pete now, squeezing in close and listening to him like he is Jesus at the Last Supper offering second helpings. His exudes an aura as if he is drunk again, but this time the stupor is on basketball. He just keeps preaching while guys fight over picks, box out, and deflect the ball out of bounds in the game just a few feet away. Both Pete and the game are as intense as the semifinals of the NCAA Final Four.

Both courts are being used for this tourney. I should bet Andie that Pete will only play on the frontcourt, but she knows as well how the organizer will have to placate his Irish arse and put him on center stage.

"You know Mike Daly from The Hill played on the Villanova team in '71 that lost to Alcindor in the finals," Pete is saying to the gang. "I blanked on his name last night. He didn't play one second in the finals. To this day, he is a loyal Nova guy, though. He texts Jay Wright with inspirational quotes, he keeps the alumni together, and he lost his minutes to an outsider. He's Drexel Hill gold."

Was Daly black? I think, but don't ask.

"He lost playing time to the black guy, I forget his name," Pete continues. "I forgot to tell you at the diner that the grand Fran Dunphy went to St. Dorothy's. He's a St. Dot guy. The Man Up In

The Press Box doesn't make them better than Dunph. Maybe John Chaney."

"Yeah, Chaney got Temple to three Final Eights," I say, edging into the pack of guys. "My dad's buddy, a cool Jewish guy called Dr. Z, believes what Chaney says is gospel.

"Indeed, his wisdom was grand," Pete says, "just like there were a lot of grand players from The Hill who were good guys, went to mass every Sunday, and so their drinking and gambling sins were wiped away. God forgives drinking and gambling, like refs overlook hand checking on defense in big games.

"I mean, you couldn't help but gamble on games growing up even though it's probably quasi wrong," Pete says. He checks the odds on the napkin. "No one threw a game. Everyone paid their debts. No way would you get stiffed."

"You had to pay. Everyone drank at Shields Tavern." Uncle Matty says. "You wouldn't get across City Line Avenue without your name being sullied up for not paying up."

"Indeed, Old man O'Dowling was a grand bartender," Pete says, slamming down the broom. "Grand like my man Lynchie down Braca's. We called him O'Dude. He would keep the bar open until everyone was done drinking."

"Yeah, he used to say, 'we never close, we only open,'" Sprout says from the pack, but I am the only one who seems to hear him as I'm boxed out behind a guy with purple-red blotched cheeks.

Everyone listens to Pete like he is delivering The Hill's own Sermon on the Mount.

"Blessed be thy O'Dude," Pete says, making a sign of the cross. The old guys make the sign of the cross, too. "Blessed be he who pours."

"Does this homily count, Pete, for mass?" Sprout asks. "Last time I was in church with your ass, you sneezed during the consecration at mass and instead of saying, 'excuse me,' you whispered, 'thank you Jesus for expunging the devil.'

"The divine expulsion, though, doesn't seem to have worked."

Pete pours some of his Gatorade in Scoob's mouth. He blows a snot rocket in the grass.

"I'm taking all action against Legs' team. Two pints at the pub of your choice that his squad doesn't reach the finals again," Pete challenges.

Half the Bounce-passers take the bet.

"Want a piece?" Pete asks me, looking down, smearing his snot in the grass with the broom. He is recruiting me to sin.

"Don't bet on the Sabbath," I say steadfastly, daring to hope he might laugh.

"For fooks' sake, it's not as if we're killing dogs like Vick," Pete says, "Fookin hell, on The Hill Timmy got more jail time than Vick and he didn't execute… extinguish life."

In April, last month, my dad advised me his state police golf buddy explained to him the imperativeness to cross-check the Bounce-passers in their comfort zone.

My dad called them "Medieval Misfits" and said point blank that Pete was the prime suspect. He said Pete was in the bar late that night and was seen in a concerned "discussion" with the poor coma cop, who was hanging with a white lady over near the gas-lit fire place in the corner of the bar where the tables were empty for hours.

My dad's state police pal told him there could be another impulsive attack. He feared Pete would never change, only spiral with more hate.

The cop and the judge knew my parents made enough money so I didn't qualify for any financial aid. They knew I always expected a schollie from my dad's boasts. They knew I didn't want my parents to foot for college after they paid so much for St. Anthony's - about $2,500 a year.

I thought that was a lot of money, but my dad pays that a month in country club dues.

My parents paid my $500 registration fee to Ursinus. Then, a few weeks ago, they paid the first month's tuition payment for September.

I suspect the heat is on the state cops from the feds to solve hate crimes. Particularly, after the Trayvon Martin case in Florida. Damn, a 17-year-old black kid gets shot dead and a white vigilante is holding the smoking gun. If laws can't convict this Zimmerman guy, they sure won't nail a guy down here who pontificates venom in plain view.

Pete and Matty argued about the Martin and Zimmerman case last night at one of the bars.

I laugh to myself how my dad called these guys Medieval. I think, Pete is only half evil.

Scoob lounges at my feet while I am spacing out on the bleachers. A plastic water bottle suddenly slams against the fence. Uncle Matty and Pete resume arguing about Trayvon Martin and George Zimmerman. It's as if they were still at the bar, ranting their bent-elbow evangelism on religion and race, basketball and babes.

My head spins from the booze and all the arguing. I need a break and some shade. I target the empty swing set under a tree already in full bloom. I lean back. The Atlantic Puffin is perched alone on the top branch. He is looking down at me.

I pull myself up and just sit. No swinging.

A blonde-haired kid with his shirt tucked in climbs on the swing next to me. A lovely blonde mom pushes him gently. She asks, "Are you OK?"

Looking over, I say "yeah" before I see her familiar face. Catrina. She's the hot mom I shook hands with in church a half hour ago. She shakes my hand again, telling me, "Tough one last night, huh? But you'll get used to it, playing down here." I nod, knowing I should say something, but don't.

"My husband plays," she says, letting go of my hand. "Well, my boyfriend. Hopefully we'll get married, we have a two-year old, but he wants to wait… until he can't get back on D anymore."

Upright on the swing, I stretch in a hurdler's pose, trying to act like I am over here prepping to play, not checking out the hot mom.

"I vowed I'd never marry again," she says, pushing her kid. "He's younger than me anyway, don't know if he's ready to settle… he's only 40."

Someone throws a ball at me. Since I am not really stretching, I hop off the swing and make the catch gracefully. I drop the ball, though, to act like I can't catch, which I know is what the old guys want to see. I am right. They point and laugh.

"I came over from church, picked up my

other baby from my mom's and dropped off my older kid to his dad, just to show my support, or really to get him jealous when another guy hits on me, it always happens down here," she spouts with her chest up. "They always throw a ball at the guy kissing up, knocking him off his pick-up rap."

I don't know if I should nod in agreement.

"Maybe not today, I mean about getting hit on. Sounds like they want to argue about the nice 17-year-old African-American kid Martin who was killed in Florida by the gun-toting, wild white man Zimmerman." She keeps speed talking. "That was way back in February and they're still arguing about it. I live in Moorestown, right outside of Camden, and a poor black kid is shot every other day there by another black man and no one cares."

Like the steady pace of the ticker scroll on the bottom of the ESPN screen, Catrina bends over with each return of her kid in the swing to push, giving a pleasing view to the CCers in waiting.

"The guy's as guilty as you are sitting under the Puke Tree. He pursued the black kid even though the cops told him to stand down. Zimmerman packed a 9-millimeter and anger. Martin carried a Skittles bag and a can of ice tea.

"Martin weighed just 140 pounds while Zimmerman tipped over 200 pounds. He had no criminal record while Zimmerman had beat a cop.

"You heard about the cop beating in Sea Isle last year? Do you feel safe?"

I shake my head up and down a few times and then sideways twice. "I do," is all I say.

Another water bottle slams against the fence.

Pete and Uncle Matty are still arguing. "I read this week Martin and Zimmerman…" Pete rants before suddenly stopping when Scoobs starts whining and whimpering. He kisses the dog.

"Martin pleaded for help before shots were fired," Catrina yells over toward Pete. "He made a cell call telling a girl he was being hounded by a strange man. The guy's guilty as your boy here is hung over. Stop arguing. Play ball so my baby daddy will see beach time with his deprived kid."

A muscled-up guy, yells from the court as his man blows past him, "The black kid attacked him, what was he supposed to do? Sorry bro."

"Supposed to do?" she bites back. "He should've turned the other cheek like Jesus. You make mass half of the Sundays. You believe a bit."

The muscle man picks up his dribble at midcourt and yells, "Hey bro, she's good looking and all, but she's more nuts than meathead Pete."

Catrina stops pushing their kid in the swing, fixes her top, steps toward the court and shouts, "Zimmerman had no bruises or blood from fighting, you're the one f-ed up in the head."

"Holy Muhammad and Moses, ma'am… take it to the bedroom, you two sweethearts," Pete screams. "Finish the fookin game."

"Are you OK?" I ask her. "That's so cool you feel that way about, you know, Martin and Zimmerman."

"Who? What?" she asks.

"You know, Martin and Zimmerman?"

"Oh, boy, I was just being politically correct," she says with an annoyed look.

"That's it?" I ask. "You sounded passionate."

"Yeah, I wanted to poke the old guys, real-good, too," she says. "And, I wanted to give you more time to check out my perfect boobs.

"Time's up. My girls are as fake as me."

Pete jogs over to us as Catrina starts pushing her kid again, affording me another blessed view of her two hanging gifts from God.

Pete picks up the ball at my feet. He spins the ball on his middle finger.

"Sometimes there are other factors, or another reason, or just happens," he says, kissing the turbulent air behind the whirling ball. "And this is tearing the country apart."

Pete pokes my nauseous gut with the ball.

"Tearing the country apart? You should talk… what you did… you no doubt…" Catrina says as if searching to change the subject, "you no doubt rooted for Rory McElroy because he's Irish over Tiger in the Masters… that's wrong."

"I feel the concept of death is wrong," Pete says, pushing her kid in the swing. "People are selfish… they cry for their loss… not for the actual dead person. It's not like Martin is in heaven eating English snap peas… we don't know."

"What are you talking about? Stop pushing my kid, you're still drunk."

"I mean, let me think… I mean, just this week in Missouri, a 13-year-old white boy was followed home from school by two black kids, who set him on fire on his front porch," Pete says. "Really, they poured gas on him, saying 'this is what you deserve white boy."

"The mother, Melissa Coon, really I can't make it up, her last name is Coon, is rightfully seeking her son to be a hate crime victim.

"Ironic, her name is Coon. Huh?" Pete says. "Now that's a hate crime... burning a coon...

"But she isn't going to get it... there're a lot of injustices... like how Kentucky does one-and-done recruiting, taking scholarships away from kids who earned the free ride... filtering down to Division 2 and then Division 3... spots are taking at the top, pushing kids out the bottom... maybe that 13-year-old kid's dad in Missouri deserved a scholarship and never got one... now he can't protect his kid... I wish someone would protect my kid when I'm gone."

Uncle Matty walks over with the two plastic water bottles indented by the fence. Like at the bar, I figure he is not missing a chance to get in a "deep discussion," but probably trying to protect Pete from himself. He pours a bottle over Pete.

Catrina's kid is wearing an over-sized "Play Like a Champion Today" Notre Dame t-shirt. She takes him out of the swing, knocking the bottles out of Matty's hands and says, "You guys are f-ed up. What are you talking about?"

She scoops up some mulch and throws the handful at Pete, spewing "you guys have no worries, no young kids to raise, you just talk bullshit, play basketball and get drunk... and then pose in church as if nothing happened at all."

"I got my own worries," Pete says, picking up the bottles. He opens the filled bottle and leans it toward Catrina's chest. He smiles and drinks the water, spitting out the last swig on the Puke Tree.

I slouch over, acting like I am too hung over to care that we dropped two straight games.

A youngish-looking man, maybe in his mid-30s judging by his slight belly, shows up. He nudges near Pete. He is wearing circular framed glasses which are perched high on his nose like windows into his green eyes. His striped red and blue tie squeezes his collared white shirt.

"You must be our man," he says decisively to Pete. He sports a leather satchel strapped over his right shoulder, which he shifts to his left hand.

"You must be Harry Potter," Pete says in a tone that somehow isn't condescending before adding, "Lovely purse, Lad."

"Actually, the name is Rathborne, Basil Rathborne, I'm the producer for a British TV documentary and I have some newspaper clips on the Sea Isle cop assault case in my bag. Actually, I'm a bit confused why there are so few articles. In England, there'd be a tabloid headline every day."

He extends his right hand, which holds a shiny blue business card between the thumb and forefinger. "You can call me Harry if you wish. I've read all the Potter books. I even still have tea with friends at the 9¾ platform on the underground tube stop where Harry goes through the wall and joins the Hogwarts Express at Kings Cross. My friends and I still play quidditch, actually in a league. We grew up with Harry."

"I once ate me fish and *quid*-wich at the Heathrow airport on a layover to Turkey," Pete says. "And wee bit odd isn't it, the 9 ¾ platform is actually between platform 8 and 9 and not 9 and 10 at Kings Cross?

"And, Harry, you would never cross me," Pete says, turning his head, and giving me a piercing look. "Would you, Harry?"

"Lovely and it is," Harry answers, sounding awkwardly polite while dropping his satchel. "And, no, I would never cross you. Are we on then for an interview, for the TV documentary?"

"Lovely," Pete says. "Indeed."

"When? Where?"

"Catch me at the court or at the pub."

Walking to his truck, Pete quotes George Bernard Shaw, or at least he says the words are from him, but I don't know what to believe.

"When we drink, we get drunk," Pete says rubbing his hand through his thick, wet hair. "When we get drunk, we fall asleep. When we fall asleep, we commit no sin. When we commit no sin, we go to heaven.

"So, let's all get drunk and go to heaven..."

Makes me think Pete believes he does have all A's and will go to heaven. Or is paradise here at the courts in Avalon and heaven in the bars of Sea Isle?

I reach to shake Andie's hand, whispering "let's get drunk and go to heaven ... on earth," but she slaps my hand away and puts her muscular arm around her dad, who is talking to the goofy Harry Potter clone.

"Harry, what did the Sea Isle police tell ya?" Pete asks, taking the guy's glasses and putting them

on halfway down his nose.
"To talk to you."

Chapter 8

My iPhone blinks erratically as I check the Google maps mileage to the Atlantic City Country Club in Northfield.

The bus ride back to Atlantic City on Monday is much different than just heading north.

My mind flashes back to after the games yesterday... we drank first at the Deauville in Strathmere, under the bridge going into Ocean City, where there was a life-sized wooden pirate carving, and Pete put Uncle Matty's rimmed glasses on the black-bearded statue while he wore Harry's circle glasses halfway down his nose.

Then we drank in the late afternoon at Twisties, a little red shack of a bar on the bay in Strathmere down a few blocks from the D'ville. Twisties used to be open only the week after Labor Day to keep the liquor license active. At least, that's what I remember Andie telling Harry, who said he loved the Stones while the jukebox was seemingly stuck on blasting "Gimme Shelter."

We then beat the sunset to the Carousel. I remember more now than I did before throwing a pint glass on the beach. I stood down-wind from Pete on the promenade and he was kicking off his "seaweed stench" sitting on steps with Harry. I heard Harry say while spinning his head around, "Of course the coppers have no video of the incident here, there are no surveillance cameras on any of these beach front properties. Don't you Yanks have crime everywhere?"

"Guilt," Pete said, "is a crime."

The air-conditioned bus keeps me from napping. Every swerve startles me, multiplies my anxiety of meeting my dad's lawman golfing buddy. He is a Jersey judge and the older brother of a New Jersey state trooper, who graduated from the police academy with another trooper stationed in Strathmere, where Twisties sparred me some shelter from Pete and his poking after we lost two.

My sister, Mari, texted me that she heard from one of her teammates how the local cops suspect that one of these old white guys whacked the black cop with an old wooden bat. Or at least something wooden that splintered. She said Sea Isle has its own police force, but neighboring Strathmere is so small it's under the jurisdiction of the New Jersey State Police. Since the Sea Isle PD doesn't have any fresh leads after almost a year so, the staties have stepped up their assistance.

Her teammate from down here told my sister that she read on Facebook how the black cop was dating a white girl and was at the bar with her the night he was attacked on the promenade in the center of town. He had left the bar alone. His zipper was halfway down. He was probably was going to take a piss and was ambushed walking down the steps onto the grass dunes of the beach.

This flows with what Andie had text me, saying how last summer a black off-duty cop was cracked over the head with a wooden plank, perhaps from one of the promenade benches, when leaving a bar in Sea Isle. She put it right out there to me, like telling all of Avalon, "gots winners."

This hate crime is why my older sister didn't

want me to go to Sea Isle for the summer, even though she knew I needed to play ball with the D-3 guys who were going to be my teammates in the fall. She didn't know of my *networking* role.

"Maybe they will even pass you the ball by Labor Day," she'd said.

She wanted me to try and become a walk-on at Fordham, where she got a Division 1 basketball scholarship. I know she thought that this little college less than an hour drive from Philadelphia would be as plaster white as Avalon.

Still, for me, Ursinus is the smart pick, even though I am a black Catholic going to a white Protestant college. Wikipedia lists Ursinus as a German Reformation-based school. The Catholic high schools in North Jersey recruit the best basketball players, Muslim, Mormon, Methodist … I will be the outsider now.

Ursinus plays Division 3, which means no athletic scholarships - all based on need. My parents weren't expecting to pay even a "wooden nickel minus a red cent" for me to go to college.

Knowing there is nothing else they can say, and hoping for the reward money, my parents now tell me the $49,000 tuition at Ursinus will pay off down the road. That is what they say at the kitchen table anyway. And they are satisfied I'll play in college, even if only D-3. I think that's important for my Dad, to tell his friends at work I am balling since he's been bragging about me since chucking up from the hip my first 3-pointer in our driveway.

I remember telling him about my first dunk, back in 8th grade. He was more excited than sealing a big money deal. Later that night, during a summer league game, a bunch of other dads congratulated me. My dad bragged his butt off.

The next day, my dad rushed home early from work, practically running over our cleaner, an Irish lady who comes twice a week, and banging the truck of our Mexican landscapers opening his new car door, and asked me, if I "dunked on someone's f-in face again."

I told him no.

Disappointed, he asked, "Why not Superman Son?"

"Well," I told him, "because we played on the 10-foot courts and not the 8-footers at the nursery school playground like yesterday."

I laugh... blanking how that poor Sea Isle City cop is still in a coma a year later.

My dad and I meet Judge Thomas Dewey at the golf cart shack. He has a thick head covered with tight blonde hair parted sharply on the side. He sports a thin blonde mustache without any gray, even though he must be older than my dad, probably pushing 60. He has a firm handshake.

I drive the golf cart with their clubs in the back while they walk and play. We stop to eat hot dogs slapped with yellow mustard at the turn.

"Hurry up, I want you to see the 'birdie rock' here at ACC," the judge, who is friendlier than I expected, tells me, "it's on the 12th hole."

The judge and my dad skip 10 and 11. The plaque reads: "bird of a shot" occurred in 1903.

"So, what is the origin of the word birdie," I ask kneeling before the rock bordering the 12th tee.

"The etymology," the judge answers knowingly, "has to do with the slang use of the word bird, which back in the day was used to describe something cool, something hip."

The judge scans the fairway toward the green and says, "A foursome was on this hole back in 1903 when one guy hit a shot inches from the cup. Someone called it a bird of a shot. He tapped in for one-under-par.

"And there you have it. A bird of a shot became birdie."

On the 13th tee, the judge said it was not only unlikely, but it was impossible that no one in Sea Isle knew anything about what happened. "Not in a small town," he stressed. Still no one has bitten on the $40,000 reward with even a tip.

He explained how the Cape May County Prosecutor's Office seeks justice for the cop. However, there are no witnesses. So, the prosecutor can conduct an investigation without a public trial by presenting the case to the grand jury. "The accused is not present, unless called as a witness," the judge said in a sand trap on 13.

"If guilty, he's too fast of a talker," the judge says about Pete, missing a short putt without a break. "In a trial, he would talk in circles and his way out of it under cross-examination. But there aren't any cross-examinations before a grand jury.

"He already consented to a CVSA and passed easily."

"A what?" I ask.

"The Computer Voice Stress Analyzer interview," he says. "His voice never wavered. Of course, he was the only one who filed the OPRA for the police report on the incident. He used the Open Public Record Act to learn what the cops knew about the incident before taking the CVSA. The Grand Jury is our ticket. He can't prepare."

The judge said the prosecutor presents the case to the grand jurors when there are no witnesses by using hearsay evidence, which isn't allowed in court. So, someone who didn't witness the crime can provide evidence.

"Also, any information obtained unconstitutionally or illegally can be 'heard and relied on' by grand jurors, even though that evidence isn't admissible in court at trial," he says.

"And even if the prosecutor knows of information that shows the accused is innocent, it doesn't have to be presented to the grand jury.

"So even if Pete didn't do it, one of his boys did and if stays silent, well," the judge says, picking up his ball three feet from the hole, "Pete is smart enough to know he would take the fall."

The judge explained to me how the grand jury issues a bill of indictment when finding probable cause that a crime has been committed and the accused is responsible.

He reasoned the grand jury is the only way to charge Pete with this crime. The judge said a decision by the grand jury isn't held by the lofty standard of proof beyond a reasonable doubt, which applies at trial to convict a criminal.

And unlike a trial, only 12 of the 23 grand jurors need to agree for a majority.

The judge also said they should bring Pete in

front of grand jury since he couldn't plead the fifth because he could be considered a public danger in a hate crime.

Under a grand jury, the judge said Pete wouldn't have his sixth amendment right to counsel either, which aids the prosecution.

The judge said Pete could be indicted by the grand jury by the end of the summer, if I help.

"We just need some evidence to present to the grand jury," he says. "Justice will do the rest. Will you do a consensual with him?"

"A what?"

"Give me your phone," the judge says.

He slaps what looks like a black magnet on the back of my phone.

"A consensual phone conversation with the suspect Pete could land you the reward money. He could incriminate himself. Here is a script of questions to ask him. Just call him and the detectives will have the conversation taped with the device I put on your phone."

"Is it legal?" I ask, hoping it isn't so I can decline doing it.

"It isn't legal in Pennsylvania," the judge says, "but it is here in New Jersey... the problem with a grand jury is leaks. Pete knows everyone."

Skipping the last five holes, my dad rents a car at the Atlantic City airport.

"I will return it at Newark Airport," he says. "I sold the boat in AC... need the tuition money."

Like he used to drive me to grade school each morning, he shuttles me back to Sea Isle. It is Senior Week for high schools. Andie and I don't have classes this week.

We stop at the Wawa in the center of Sea Isle. I buy a bag of chocolate M&M's.

I open the bag at the counter.

"Pour," he says, sticking out his hand.

I empty the bag.

"Hey, there's only one black M&M," I say.

My dad Googles M&M'S and on the official website and sees "Find the bag of M&M'S with all black M's and you could win $100,000."

"Maybe I won't have to call Pete now," I tell him.

My dad dials my phone as I sit in the Wawa parking lot where the bus dropped me off on Friday and where Andie picked me up ... from my previous life.

Pete answers.

"Hey Pete, it is Byrd."

"Hey."

"Hey, thanks for the fun weekend, I got your number from Andie."

"My phone still has mustard on it from the trash can so talk louder."

"Well, I was with my dad and he just had a few questions, or concerns."

"He should, he is your dad."

"Well, can I ask you a couple questions for him."

"He can call me."

"Well, he told me what to ask."

"Shoot."

"My dad is concerned about the cop beating down here last summer."

"He should be."

"Why?"

"Everyone should be concerned."

"Oh, do you know who did it?"

"No."

"Do you know why someone would do it?"

"There could be many reasons why, but none of them would be right, like taking a jump shot on a two-on-one fast break."

"Why does no one talk about it?"

"That's a good question for a kid not even in college. That's deep. We can talk about it someday, but I think people just want to go down river in life."

"You sure you're not working for the man... from England? Are you helping Harry on the documentary?"

Chapter 9

Glass on the beach shines like Dei's smile in the early Tuesday morning light. A glass. It is the pint glass I threw from the promenade Sunday night when skipping out of the Springfield. I wasn't able to swallow another sip after telling the brilliant dog joke… or was that Saturday night?

I am surprised none of the bendy old women or the few inflexible old men doing yoga on the beach didn't pick up the pint for their shelf. Why not wash the glass in the ocean?

There is one smoking gray-streaked blonde who steps around the pint glass. She gives the instructor, another hot dark-rooted blonde mommy-type a half hug. The group outlines a circle. The pint glass is in the middle. The class is only a block from the Springfield's outdoor Carousel bar where I confessed my sins into the pint glass for last call.

Looking down from the promenade, I can see these health freaks make a peace sign with their yoga mats inside the circle. There are probably about 40 of them doing their stretching next to an overflowing rusty drab blue trashcan.

With one clap of their hands, the yoga class bows toward the ocean. The sun's reflection bounces off the waves as if bowing back.

The instructor screams, "Anyone go out last night?" and then soothes by saying, "Be where you are at. Detox with each pose. Life's more about acceptance than balance."

The group chants "We are amazing... I am amazing."

Clouds blanket the sun's shine as the poses begin. The old guys, who squat on the mats next to the women in the tight black yoga pants, adjust their sunglasses above their eyes.

"Let go of the clouds and tap into our inner sunshine," the instructor shrieks. "Don't judge."

Her voice is so piercing a guy with an eye patch knocks over his two light blue water bottles.

"Damn, Tucker!" she screams, snapping her yoga pants out of her butt crack. "It's absolutely obscene to waste water."

There are park benches on the promenade branded with big white letters facing the ocean. They all say so-and-so sat here with a life's a beach type saying and the date they died. All the dashes in the dates look like Morse code, like the dead are saying something. I want to lie down on one, but the park benches seem like tombstones.

I need to throw some water on my face. I walk down the steps where the cop was beaten and onto the beach. I look down so not to seem like a perv staring at the yoga mommies when I bump into a metal detector guy in sunglasses. It is Mole. We both keep going without saying a word.

Like a high school field hockey coach on steroids, the instructor screams, "Water fills any container... no competition and no judgment."

She adds, "Feel the shell... we're all shells... we all look different..."

I see, peeking out of my right eye, the instructor admiring my healthy suntan.

"Hi there, you look different," she says to me, "your shell is different... would you like to share something? Anything? Everything?"

I am close enough to see the crossed tan lines in her feet from wearing flip-flops every day.

Without meditation, I respond, "Train yourself to let go of everything you fear to lose."

"Wow," she says. "That's very deep. Who shed that wisdom? Buddha himself... from the stars and peace of our past and present?"

"No," I say with a theatrical look skyward, "Yoda himself... from the Star Wars movies."

When the instructor says, "Drink from the energy of the ocean... let it flow into the rivers and streams of your life today... and everyday..." I know it is my time to flow since I want to embarrass, not enlighten her, telling her how rivers and streams actually flow into the ocean. That is what Pete would do as a public service.

I slow jog, trying to run off this lingering weekend, hundred-year-storm of a hangover from the middle of Sea Isle up toward Strathmere.

Each stride is shooting pain, a dagger through my pounding temples. The deep sand scratches my ankles. I wish I could fly away.

This run will take longer than planned. I definitely will be late, which is not right no matter how much I'd rather listen to the screeching yoga lady than meet my networking cop. As if Jason Bourne, the text from my dad this morning, "your run at 8" gave me the time and his advice "run the highest dunes" gave me the place.

What do I tell the cop?

I'll just let my thoughts flow... like the annoying yoga lady preached... yeah, I'll tell him we played Sunday in the Camaraderie Classic, losing against Legs, the NBA analyst for ESPN, and how I wanted to ask him if I could meet Wilbon and Kornheiser. That is what I'll tell him.

I pick up the pace of my run. I stop. I turn around toward Sea Isle. I look down. I stand in a gulley of hard sand formed by the retreating tide, alone in the crossroad of my life.

Why would the cop care about the Camaraderie Classic? About ESPN?

Maybe I'll tell him I played against a Division 3 legend by the name of Louie D. from Widener, who can still dunk at 50-something and only 6-1 or 2 at best. That is what I will tell him. He is a local… well at least Louie is down for summer weekends. Should all locals be suspects?

That's profiling. Right?

I will tell him Louie D doesn't need to play 'D' like me.

The surf rushes up the gulley. Instinctively, like stepping in front to take an offensive charge that will hurt, I spin around toward Strathmere.

I rehearse my tattletales.

I feel like puking again. Looking back, the gulley is washed away by a rogue wave.

My legs slow down as my mind races. I'm chugging up to Strathmere to see The Man.

I target a trashcan ahead to puke. Only a few steps away from my bull's eye, a plump sea gull swoops and snatches a pizza crust from inside the can while two skinny gulls dive in too late.

The rigid letters on the lifeguard stands tell me I am in Strathmere. There are no lifeguard stands with SIC. I sit on the dune. I watch the Army Corps of Engineers pump sand onto the beach from the ocean through a long, snaking pipe with the numb attentiveness of watching yoga.

A dude stands on the dune above me doing surfing poses. He can't be a cop. He sports a long black ponytail under his straw cowboy hat.

On my iPhone, the shuffle stops on Cold Play's "Clocks." I reflect on what Pete said when we drank a beer leaving the Carousel Sunday night, how "these sands will always be here on the beach even with the engineers planning and machines pumping when instead the Chosen Few, the ones on the clock, really should be throwing the sand back into the ocean."

Looking north I can see the skyscraper hotels and casinos of bankrupt Atlantic City. I also see that one dune seems higher than the rest. I walk the couple blocks to the dune, and run the sandy path to the top. I walk back down the path. I run the path again to the top. I need to puke. I lay in a gulley shaped by the wind on top of the dune.

The swishing of sand stirs me. A trooper tramps up and sits across from me in the gulley.

He has to be the trooper. But I have seen him before, I think. They all look the same here.

He waves his thick hand to the surfer dude posing a few blocks down the dunes. On his wrist is a wide black-banded watch. Its alarm starts beeping. He allows the penetrating beep to continue until stopping on its own.

Turning off my iPhone music, he tells me "the loud churning of the sand from the beach replenish project will keep us from being taped."

I don't know if he is kidding or not. Just like with Pete. Seriously, no one is even around to tape us. The surfer dude would need a satellite hook up to tape us, and anyway he seems already too spaced out to care about a cop in a coma.

Bingo. This trooper is the same thick Irish guy with the bulb nose from the drunken diner. I should have known his intentions Saturday night.

"Hey, buddy," he says. "What's up?"

He said, 'hey buddy' like we are. I'm only here networking. "How you been?" He then adds.

The cop is a block, obviously wide from lifting serious heavy weights when younger.

He stabs out his meaty hand with the strained watchband, saying, "My name is John."

Figures. His name has to be John. These guys down here all have the most common names, which must be why they lug silly nicknames.

"What, are all *youse* guys named after saints?" I say, using slang to fit his profile of me.

"What do you mean, youse guys?" he snaps. "I'm not one of them."

"Well, you're all about the same age, and… look the same, you know, respectfully saying, sir."

"I'm not that ugly, if I looked like Pete, I'd shoot myself right here," he says, tapping a gun – I guess – that is covered by a flowered Hawaiian shirt tucked into his tan cargo long-short pants.

He wears brown leather sandals, making me think maybe he is not one of those guys because Pete and the Lids would never don open footwear. His toes are twisted like the pipe pumping sand.

"You and Pete both go diving, too." I say, trying to go on offense and learn more about my aggressive accomplice. "Do you dive together?"

"No, actually, we're kind of competitors," he says. "We both dive the same wrecks off shore for relics. We both sell to the same dealer. I like to kick his self-righteous ass.

"What do you know about him?"

"But you already know him."

"I want to know what you know."

"I thought, was hoping, I was just networking? You know, for a job someday."

"No, you know damn well you have a chance to do more. You can deliver justice."

I look down the beach toward Sea Isle and the surfer man frozen in poses. It hits me to describe Pete just like I would describe that freak I'm now looking at... about 5-foot-8... overly dark tan... skinny, but tight muscles... wears dark sunglasses... black pony tail... cowboy hat... looks like he never shot a basketball...

This will be easy.

"Well, Pete... a solid man at 5-10... prototype point guard... in charge... the rock... unusually thick brownish red hair... everyone calls him for books to read... he makes up words..."

"I know all that. Tell me in detail about the last time you played against him. I saw the video."

"We didn't get a chance to play Pete and the old boys on Sunday," I say. "We lost to the guys from Drexel and Penn, really we lost to Legs and Louie D. I didn't feel too bad losing two straight since I did score a bucket in each game."

I keep small talking, saying I wasn't upset not playing Pete again because he would've won big. I say Pete seems like he once liked to be liked.

"Pete and his bounce passing posse beat the guys from Penn and Drexel and five other teams with guys from St. Joe's, the University of the Sciences in Philly and a talented team from Scranton with this Division 3 legend like Louie D named Hoppy, a white guy who I guess can jump."

I then tell him I heard Pete went to Scranton first, but got cut from the team and then transferred mid-year to Ursinus… but no one talks about it… he never talks about it.

He unbuttons the top of his flowery shirt when I say, "But like me, of course, everyone wants to know what really happened at Scranton."

He huffs, so I tell the cop he "listened to Pete at the diner like he was St. Peter."

"Did you know Pete is a big hockey guy, a big Flyers fan?" I continue as if he cares.

"It's only because hockey is an all-white sport," the trooper spats.

"Yeah, all those bounce passers from Drexel Hill think the Flyers are direct descendants of Erik The Red and the hockey playing Norse Vikings," I agree and then reflexively add, "But, yeah, why do they all play basketball then?"

Not answering, this thick Irish cop asks if I heard "anything strange from Pete, something out of the ordinary? Not Scranton over 30 years ago."

Where do I start? I've never heard anyone else pontificate like Pete, period. Again, I was around Irish people at St. Anthony's, too, but that's like saying all Irish priest are like St. Patrick.

"Does he talk about blacks, like is he superior? Tell me how," he demands.

"But he talks like he invented the bounce pass. These guys think Pete actually invented the knuckle punch. They don't think he started the high-five, but they really think he originated the knuckle punch. And then they followed him doing it, spreading the K-P around the world.

"Pete even says he knows exactly when it started - at the courts, of course.

"He was out drinking with this guy, Mole. He went back to the guy's 'hut,' as they call the rental homes down here, and on the walk back on the beach they saw this girl Pete said just looked like 'she fought 15 rounds with Mike Tyson and lost them each 10-8 on all three scorecards."

"She came back to the hut and Mole's friend hooked up with her. Pete said the two were in one room while six other guys slept packed in the other bedroom. The next morning, when the guy said he scored, Pete didn't want to touch his hand. When the guy went to give him a high five, Pete closed his fist and… the knuckle punch.

"Pete K-P with the Bounce-passers the rest of the morning at the courts. It was July 4th, 1999, the birth of the knuckle punch, he said."

The trooper pulls out some high dune grass below a Do Not Disturb the Endangered Dune Grass. He chews on the end of a stand of grass and throws the rest of the handful at the sign.

I tell him "never would you imagine what Pete did as the Halfway Healer."

The cop takes out his iPhone. He clicks on the recorder app and puts the phone back in his top pocket of his goofy colored shirt.

"Now this, boy, this is the dope I want to hear. What's a Half-Way Healer?" he asks as if I'm going to relay where the Holy Grail is buried.

"Really," I start to say, "a Half-Way Healer is what Pete does. It's who he is, I think."

I don't want to tell him HWH was just about drinking a beer while walking on the beach at night, then turning around when halfway done the beer, and while walking back, drinking the other half. Really that's the dopey deal, which we did last night.

Over the weekend with Pete and his mates, I heard a few of the guys tell me how much Pete has helped them, just talking on those short walks on the beach at night over the years.

That was what Pete was. That was what he called himself, a Halfway Healer, to me.

"Stop thinking and talk," the trooper says, whipping my cut mini-dreads with the dune grass. "Tell me or I will chop off your fro."

"On a walk Sunday night, Uncle Matty asked Pete to convert from Catholicism to Mormonism. Pete responded, 'you mean flop, like faking an offensive foul?'

"Matty and Pete had this religion conversion conversation more than all the beers they had 'dranked' together since they were kids boozing when going to concerts at the Tower Theater in Upper Darby... they saw David Bowie record 'Live at the Tower' there as 10-year-olds when Uncle Matty's dad, who was a Philly cop working the event, opened a side door for them.

"So, what the hell happened?" the cop demands, sounding madder than Pete at his worse.

"The next day Pete and Matty had their pictures in a crowd shot photo from the concert in the Daily News... they got their knuckles whacked by their third-grade nun Sister Theresa."

"What the hell?"

"Yeah the nun scolded them not for going to the concert but for 'abetting androgynous activity.'"

"No, bro, what happened with the Halfway Healer thing?"

"I don't know," I say, "I wasn't there."

"What? That's it?"

"Well, Matty came back in the Deauville smiling and put his glasses on top of the pirate carving head. They were only gone for 10 minutes or so."

"They could've went out and got high," he huffed, "or done some androgynous activity... "

I lean away from the antagonist. I look out over the ocean. The waves break right at the beach. I stare at the surfer dude in his distant pose.

"Anything combustible about him? About the others?" he asks as if I'm on trial.

I hold in my piss, rattle off what I know...

"Johnny Mitchell - Jimmy's Dad... only 6-1 or so, but a power forward, thick and strong... thin blond hair...

"Sim McManus... the dad of Jimbo and brother of Matty... a 6-4 center... likes to shoot outside... brown shaggy hair...

"Phil Leyne... a 6-3 powerful... linebacker type... a winner...

"Matty McManus... Uncle Matty... 6-4... brown shaggy hair like his brother, except a bald spot in the middle back..."

"You forgot Tom Meagher."

"He's just a part time player," I explain.

I'm not ratting out too much more info.

I'll just describe them like I would the surfer dude, because, well, I really don't have anything... anything but my opinions and stories of Pete. But, I am smart enough to know this cop wants some stuff. And I know my dad would treat the call to justice and rightful reward money equally, like me earning a scholarship.

"These older guys thought whoever got the most sleep-in life won, not the most toys. But they don't sleep down here. Not on Sundays either. They get up for church.

"Pete says Sundays are for 'life repair'... but honestly the whole prayer thing with these guys is confusing, to me," I ramble. 'They pray before pickup basketball game to win. They pray before they go to the beach so they don't get too much sun. They pray before they go out drinking so they get drunk enough, but 'not too drunk where they go up to Atlantic City to get hookers.'

"The prayer thing with them is like they pray not to sin too much. They don't want to do the 'big sins' as Pete calls them, but pray just to limit them to the little ones.

"Pete was putting on Uncle Matty's glasses and acting scholarly when I asked him what he meant at the Deauville about big and little sins. He told me he wishes he coined the Mark Twain quote from Life on the Mississippi, 'when we were kids we wanted to live a good enough life and long enough that God would let us become pirates.'"

I don't know how else to explain Pete. He seems to want to be good enough to be real-good, but bad enough to be only a bit bad.

"There's like this good and evil conflict in his head as intense as game point in a pickup game on Sunday morning at the courts," I say, "that lasts all day long and for every tortured minute."

"Don't get your psycho analysis," he says, "you're either a good guy or a bad guy. There isn't any other way. That's who you are, bro."

"Well, I know what you're saying, but these guys, well, Pete mostly, seem touched, different."

I'll try to explain why Pete swears.

"It's like cursing. These guys will say 'F – this' or 'F – that' a million times, but if someone says, 'God damn it' or 'Jesus Christ,' they freak on the guy, or lady…"

"They use the f-bomb not only as adjectives, 'like fookin great shot' or 'box him the fook out' or just 'fook you' and Pete uses it as an adverb, like 'that's a fookly beautiful pass.'"

The cop turns off his iPhone recorder, stands up, kicks the sand, "fook all that and double fook all this," mocking Pete and his boys.

He motions for me to rise. We walk down the dune. Our steps are measured in the sand, taking strides to the beat of the breaking waves. We stop at the line where the waves reach the dark sand of the beach.

"Your boy is a mother f-er twisted guy."

We half turn south toward Sea Isle, away from noisy dredging machines in Strathmere.

"My name's John Rage."

Walking with the sun beaming now on the side of our face and the ocean roaring to our left, the surfer dude runs from the dune, cutting us off, and dives into the ocean.

"The Kumbaya baby of hippies is taking his bath," he says with a laugh and adds sternly, "He scares the weekly renters. He shouldn't be living in the dunes. I told the SIC cops to run him."

A wave washes up on the trooper's sandals.

"Faa-uck," he yells, scattering some sea gulls. The odd 60's child is the only in earshot. There are no moms down here playing with their privileged kids in the shallow surf or just being.

Stepping back from an oncoming wave, I ask, "Who's he?"

Rage looks over to the ocean as the dude unties his ponytail and scrubs his scalp.

The cop pauses and says, "Life's loser."

Another wave washes over his sandals, leaving wet sand between his twisted toes.

"Why don't you run him then?"

"I'm not going to be the bad guy. Everyone loves him. He's harmless... not like your boy."

The dude bodysurfs a wave, popping up right in front of us. He is about half the size of the towering Rage. His tan is as dark as me. He makes the cop look as white as dune sand. He is slender with a taut torso. His face is wrinkly, making him look older than his body. His face says 50 something, but his body says 20 something. His yellow tank top says California Surf School.

"Nice ride Cal-holi," the cop says.

"Hey Rager."

The dude jogs over to a pile of clothes on the wet-dry line in the sand. He wrings out his tie-dyed tight t-shirt and slips on another colorful one just like it, but with long sleeves, and without drying off. He puts on dark sunglasses and a straw cowboy hat. He zigs and zags back to the dune.

"He's a leftover hippie from California who migrated east one summer decades ago to open a surf shop on Landis Avenue and never left," the cop says. "He attended Cal-Poly, developed some sort of surfboard polyester resin and made all this money.

"Now he doesn't have a job. He lives in the dune illegally. He doesn't try to work, except teaching surfing lessons, but young moms are too scared to send their kids to him and teenagers are too creeped to be near him."

I straddle the dark-dry sand line on our walk toward Sea Isle, hoping we stop soon.

"My dad says he sees this apathy with a lot of 50-year-old white men who were once athletes. How they're pissed blacks are making all this money and these guys can't afford to pay for their kids' college after dumping so much money into their Catholic grade and high school education," I say, looking closely at the cop for a reaction.

He removes his soggy sandals. He uses his thick hands to wash his crooked feet in the surf.

"They're pissed, but will never say it… how blacks are getting the money for college and their kids aren't," I say. "They're pissed because they feel their kids worked hard in sports and are passed over by *brothers* who didn't work as hard but have better genetics."

"They are pissed because their wives don't bang them anymore," he says. "They are pissed because their 401k's suck more than their wives. They are pissed because they can't play ball anymore. They are pissed because a black guy is President of the United States…

"They are just pissed. Pete is the Prized Pisser."

"I guess, in one of the bars, I'd heard Pete is a consultant or does leadership lectures. He can't be that pissed, not in public. His lifelong boys seem to love him."

"Only a dying dog could love him," Rage disagrees while splashing me. "I mean, who could be married to him? He's so intensely intense."

"I can see him all wired up since he mustn't get laid, or 'made' like he said to a bitchy lady about his age at the Springfield the other night. He said right out to her, 'you need to get made' and she said, 'what' like five times, any finally Pete said something like, 'you're so beautiful I'll be your house maid.'"

"Pete teaches leadership skills to company management teams," he says unimpressed with my play-by-play of Pete in action. "Pete works as a leadership consultant. He lectures at universities in Philadelphia area. Last winter he went back to

Turkey to do his thing, to preach nonsense. He played professional basketball in Turkey."

"Pete played in Turkey?" I ask, acting like I didn't know even though Rage was at the diner the night Pete slurred his words, his m... m...m's.

Don't let Rage see, I think, how much I really know about Pete.

"Yeah, he's actually friends, played ball with Leon Rose, who is Allen Iverson's agent, back as kids in Pennsauken," Rages says, "He helped hook Leon up with people in Istanbul. He helped arrange a place to stay for A.I. and all the logistics over there."

Pete would help Iverson?

"Iverson is like the poster boy for black guys that the Bounce-passers... envy," I accuse.

"Pete always said he admired Iverson because he plays so hard," he says. "A cover."

"Why Turkey?" I ask with fascination.

"Have you seen Iverson play lately?"

"I mean Pete."

"When he played there, he stayed one summer and Pete hooked up with a Muslim in Turkey. He married a girl from Ephesus, where the Blessed Mother last lived. Your boy is such a big-time f... f... f... messed-up Catholic. He probably thought marrying a chick from the Blessed Mother's town would buy his unforgivable freckled face into heaven."

"What happened to her?"

"Don't know... he probably whacked her... with a wooden... crucifix."

"Why?"

183

"How the hell do I know," he snaps.

"How could he marry a Muslim?" I ask. "They have dark skin too, right?"

"Don't know… his kid isn't Wonder Bread white… is Andie?" Rage pokes, well more rips.

"I wonder if he hates Muslims?" trying to prod this guy.

"Don't know either, but I do know Pete," he says. "And I like him, or used to … I mean, I first met him in Drexel Hill a few years ago at my cousins' surprise 40th birthday party. He didn't know anyone. The crowd was younger. The only reason he was there was his sister lives across the street. He was visiting.

"Well, by the end of the night he knew me. He knew everyone. He was dancing in the middle of the living room with this 50-year-old neighbor dude, Kevin, to the Black Eye Peas.

"That is the thing with Pete, I can't figure him out. I like him. I don't think he likes himself."

"Me either," I say, "I mean, I don't think he likes himself either."

The walk back down to Sea Isle will be torturous. I need a nap. I see flags about half way up the beach between where I am and the hazy high condos in the center of SIC.

I will nap under the flags. I will think there. I will get lost in my unconscious conclusions.

The American flag points to Sea Isle with the northerly wind behind me. The stiff flag is on a short pole rising from the wooden-wire snow fence weaving along the dunes. The flag announces the walkway from the ocean to the road.

Walking up the path, I face a brown sign carved in the shape of a seagull, nailed to a post. In the middle, over a heart shape painted the same drab blue as the beach trashcans, in shiny while lettering says BEACH OF DREAMS 2013.

The post tilts to the right, pulled from a hanging brass bell that could've washed up from the Lusitania. A rope with a bulky knot at the end drops from the bell. I don't dare ring it.

There are two low signs up the path: DON'T YOU JUST LOVE THIS BEACH! and HELP CLEAN THIS BEACH – BONZ.

Above me at the top of the dune, cracking in the wind blowing toward Sea Isle, fly three more American flags. Climbing the sandy hill, I keep my head up, seeing how the 12-foot white flag poles are staggered with the middle one set back farther from the other two. My neck aches and so does my mind, flashing back to the crosses at Calvary in a painting that hung in the entry hall of St. Anthony's.

Higher on the dune, beyond the flagpoles, shore stuff is scattered like a beach comber's yard sale, except everything is lettered with a sayings or message on it.

BONZ'S BEACH OF DREAMS is painted on the flat paddle of a white oar. A white buoy hanging with the black numbers 318 hangs on a nearby wooden pole.

An ash-colored clock with a dolphin on its face droops on a wobbly post. A sandblasted wooden model rowboat balances on top.

Sitting in the sand, a carving of a wood pirate wearing a tie-dyed t-shirt leans against a wooden table on its side with the white letters CLASS OF 57.

"Hey there," the surfer dude says suddenly standing up from his pirate's pose, scaring the piss out of me. "Welcome home."

"Hey man," I say while trying to catch my breath. "But this isn't my home, dude."

The dude reaches up his hand to give me a high five. I just wave and keeping walking past a square sign with a chipped corner and a white sailboat floating on the trashcan-blue ocean that says WELCOME!

THIS WAY TO THE BEACH BARS points a low rectangular sign that looks like it was painted on a quarter sheet of particle board left over from an old house remodeled recently.

In the center of this confusion and up front on a wooden post is a warped sign. Probably stolen from a bar. In carved, black letters is painted BONZ'S and below the sign reads WHALES TRAIL INN GREAT FOOD & GOOD SPIRITS.

"Hey, I'm sorry," he says walking toward me. "I didn't mean to scare you. It's just that not many people come up here anymore. Not like in the day. Not like when this sandy spot supported a house above, a place full of life."

"It's just nice to have company."

"I'm just passing through," I say, looking straight toward the bay.

"We're all really just passing through."

I keep walking past a sign showing two empty beach chairs that says HOME IS WHERE THE BEACH IS, but the word IS, is crossed out and WAS, is scrawled over it in black paint. Tilted at the foot of the post is a wicker lunch basket with its handle stuck straight up.

Two stacks of about a dozen white plastic chairs seem to be waiting for the party to begin.

"Come back anytime," he says, sitting on the one plastic white chair not stacked in two columns. "I'm always looking, ready for people to gather here again."

I take a few more steps before stopping in front of a pole with a black metal mailbox that has three pointed directional signs - HEAD TO THE BEACH and BED AND BREAKFAST and REM'S HOUSE nailed loosely to the pole.

There is a bent aluminum – well it must be metal since a SIC PD refrigerator magnet sticks on the arm - beach chair tilted next to the mailbox. I lift the chair with the tattered canvas for a seat. I need to sit. Under the chair is a broken wooden oar, well half of an oar. I reach to pick it up.

The dude comes over quickly, grabs it and stands the half oar behind a small decorative white lighthouse with a red roof. He leans on an old sailor guy with a blue-striped white sweater matching his blue jacket. The sailor is wearing a black captains cap. There is another white oar with the words WHALE BEACH painted on the face.

"Rest here all you want," he says. "Rest all you need my friend."

I don't sit, but stare at an ashen sign on a fence post with the white painted letters IF YOUR LUCKY ENOUGH TO BE AT THE BEACH YOUR LUCKY ENOUGH!

"The sign painter didn't go to Catholic school I guess. YOUR? The nuns would've made me write YOU'RE 100 times."

"Me too," he says leaning on an open newspaper delivery box, "but I didn't paint it."

There is a yellow faded newspaper inside. There is a photo of all of this stuff on the dune behind me. The paper is from March 6, 2012.

The headline reads "50 years later…"

The weird, wired guy comes over and shuts the mailbox.

"You don't have to read it," he says.

He recites: "The first paragraph says, "Colt and Dale Bonsall lost their home in the 1962 Storm from March 6-8, but continue to pay taxes on the property… the law forbids 'piercing of the dunes' by a dwelling."

Behind the newspaper slot box is the top of a yellow surfboard, broken in half, sticking upright out of the sand.

Behind the grammatically challenged sign is an old wooden water ski stuck in the ground with a round sign crossed by fishing rods that reads AN OLD FISHERMAN LIVED HERE WITH HIS BEST CATCH right next to a green bird feeder.

There is a long brown oar at the dune walkway entrance closest to the road pointing to the ocean. Below rises a wooden sign with the white words LIFE WITHOUT WHALE BEACH I DON'T THINK SO!

At the entrance to the walkway at the street is a yellow mailbox with the black letters "Dale A Bonsall." On the upright pole behind the mailbox is a carved wooden sea gull with the painted "WHALE BEACH" in white. The letters "OB" are painted where the eyes should be.

The red flag of the mailbox is up.

I open the rusty flap.

Chapter 10

I've been looking at the water tower, floating like a blimp, from the window of our rented house since the sun has been up. The tower rises on the other side of the main road into town. At the same time, I've been listening for any footsteps or movement downstairs. While lying in bed I stare out of the second-story bedroom window to see the words, SMILE YOU ARE IN SEA ISLE painted on the drab blue flying water saucer.

It has been only a few days since I talked to the cop, but I still feel anchored to the bed from the tension. I really want to be floating again, smiling and drinking with Pete, or with Andie.

Even what she wears makes me smile. And what she does. As I lay here, looking at the tower, she is jump shooting balled up socks at me while wearing girlie boxer shorts and a gloriously tight mid-drift white tank top.

"Let's roll," she says. "We *gots* to throw gear in the wash. Can't keep wearing your dirty socks, even though you don't sweat playing ball."

"I thought you said last night we're cleaning up *our* Hut this morning?' I remind her. "Not doing wash."

"Not after last night," she says in that sexy deep voice, banking a balled-up sock off the closed door and onto the bed. "We gots to get out of *our* room before our boys, wake. Gots to do wash now."

The house we rent with the Lads is a square two-story yellow building with two sets of 70's style sliding doors on the first floor. The main entrance door is oddly set to the left and not centered between the glass sliding doors where we first rubbed shoulders. The shower is outdoors.

Andie leans over me, her smooth hair dropping off her shoulders and blocking the view of her adorable little chest, as she strips the pillowcase off the flat pillow. She bends over, picking up a dozen or so pairs of rolled-up socks off the floor and last night's clothes. With each bend, the back of her tight thighs squeeze into a solid tube running from the crease of her knee up to her rising boxer shorts.

Our little block of a house is only a couple blocks in the middle of town from Pete's fortress.

"Right, then, I'll get moving." I say. "Could you please stop mixing up our socks?"

From the back alley-way I still see the hovering water tower, making me think of waking up this morning... and about last night. I stand between an old, tan-bricked firehouse - SIC 10 FD - and our concrete block building, looking up at the window of the room, and trying not to think of Andie. I look down and walk... to somewhere.

There is a choppy asphalt parking lot next to the block building. No one ever uses the space. Except sometimes Pete stops over and passes the basketball against the wall. He practices his overhead pass and bounce passes the most... all the muscles in Andie's shoulders seem to explode out of her tight tank top... she must've thrown the ball against the wall all day long while growing up to get so lean and tight.

Sometimes Pete backs up to the title company near the end of the block and throws longer bounces passes, as if he is starting a fast break. Once I saw him back up to the bank on the corner of Pleasure and throw long baseball passes.

Our house Number is 118. But the 8 looks more like a 0 so the other guys tell girls at the bar we live at 110. On the second story is a room with a window air conditioner. That is my room… where I keep my clothes.

Pete told Andie to give me the room with the air conditioner. He said North Jersey Catholics don't like the heat, which I always thought was the opposite stereotype, you know black guys don't like the cold, but I've learned to listen without hearing down here.

From the room, next to the window with the AC, I see Andie checking out my musings. She lifts up a pillowcase stuffed with socks.

I dribble a ball in the backyard over to the Sea Isle courts here in the middle of this lovely insane South Jersey ocean side town with the main street "named JFK Boulevard not MLK Boulevard for a reason," as Pete says every other time we walk across JFK.

The two courts on JFK Boulevard make like a T. There are double full courts running the same way of the island, north to south, parallel between the bay and the ocean.

On one side of the courts, closer to Central Avenue and the bay, is a playground with a swing set and bunch of sun burned kids sitting around.

The swings are empty. And still.

The mommies hover around their kids. Just like in Avalon. The mommies all look the same to me, like the ones in church. They all sport lovely shoulder length blonde hair. The shades of blonde, though, vary, just like the shades of red on their kids' sunburned shoulders… they don't let their hair just drop down, like Andie, over their faces… or tied tight into a pony tail tight like when playing basketball… or just hanging over the front of a tight white tank top in bed.

The ladies sport outdoor uniforms. They wear khaki shorts… no boxer shorts fa'shure… and a flowered t-shirt… no tight tank top…

Closer to the ocean, only a few feet away from the double courts, is a singular full court running perpendicularly. One basket backs toward the ocean, the other toward the bay.

Pete told me in the storm of 1962, "the ocean reached one basket, and the bay reached the other basket." He said the court never got wet and the old-timers played a game of five-on-five on the high ground while the rest of SIC bailed out.

This "legendary" court here is shorter. It is only 8 feet or so from the top of the key to half court on both sides. Two dribbles over half court and you are in 3-point range.

Pete said the court is just 48-feet long. Andie said it's about half the length of a regulation NBA court, which is fitting since these guys got about halfway to The Big Time.

The Bounce-passers don't play here unless they have been drinking and don't want to drive into Avalon for an "afternooner no shower happy hour." So, they will play a "get sober in sixty minutes" game here.

I think Andie would be fun to do wash with, like for our sweaty socks. We wouldn't even have to talk. We could just sit there and listen to the cathartic rotation of the machine.

Although it is Memorial Day weekend, few cars cross over the bulging concrete bridge from Route 9 onto JFK and into our quiet Sea Isle.

I shoot baseline corner jumpers on my own, not for practice and not for fun. I guess it is like Pete just throwing the basketball against the wall alone. There is peace to being alone with a ball... peaceful just lying with Andie last night – just really nice and meaningful holding her and not needing to do anything...

With each shot, I eye the house, hoping Andie comes out to play. Hoping to shoot with her now like every shot doesn't justify her existence.

I think about my new boys, the guys we all share beers – and socks - with from a large ice cooler we keep in the living room down stairs. They like their socks cold. This is the first time the cooler is empty, so Andie is washing all the balled-up socks that were lying in each corner of our hut... and I think of her.

I need to stop sinning... and think... of Jimmy Mitchell... 6-2... a perfect player with the looks to match... blond hair... good shooter, passer, but soft... always corrects everyone's English... went to St. Joseph's Prep, but grew up across the river from Philly in Moorestown...

Jimbo McManus... 6-5... out of control player... tough rebounder, defender... played at Camden Catholic... acts poor like from Camden, but really a Pennsauken kid... shaggy brown hair...

Tommy Meagher...reddish brown hair... 6-7... a shot blocker... works in summer collecting tolls on Townsends Inlet Bridge... Monsignor Bonner High School in Drexel Hill "where everyone plays basketball like a religion..." has a girlfriend back home...

This is their sacred ground. They played on these courts when too young to run games in Avalon with their bounce passing pops, whose stories are becoming as familiar as their faces... Andie's cheeks were soft last night. Her strong hands weren't balled up, but still the veins in her forearms popped... I need to pass like the Lids.

I shoot a quick layup going off the outside foot like Uncle Matty... Matt McManus... 6-4... brown shaggy hair like his brother, except a bald spot in the middle back... sometimes does 1,000-piece military history puzzles with Sim.

I flip-spin a ball on the block, catch it and post up, reverse pivot to face the basket and shoot like Jimbo's dad... Sim McManus, the brother of Matty... a 6-4 center who forces shots outside... brown shaggy hair... played at Camden Catholic... grew up in Merchantville, but moved to Pennsauken...

I drive hard to the basket and take a cross-over step, like Jimmy's dad... Johnny Mitchell, who the Bounce-passers say invented the "Euro step" in Sea Isle 30 years ago because he is only 6-1 or so, but a power forward... thick and strong... thin blond hair... played at Shawnee High School... grew up in richy-rich Medford... after Ursinus he moved to richer Moorestown…

Phil Leyne… 6-3 powerful… linebacker type… his two daughters' own a bar outside center city Philly in Gray's Ferry… don't really know much more about him excepts he backs into the basket, which I don't bother to try and practice as I would never want to score that way…

I stand on these courts and think of all these Bounce-passers… but mostly of Andie – how the back of her arms curve into her shoulders, how her long biceps always look curled. I look toward the ocean to steer my mind right. I drift over to the corner of Landis Avenue, to the shady Pavilion. A breeze from the ocean also invites me to sit on the marble white memorial to World War II guys.

Across JFK Boulevard from the main court is the post office. Pete still mails a letter every Monday morning before driving up to work. There is also the First Bank of Sea Isle, which is shaped like a lighthouse, the library, where beach tags are sold and La Costa, a bar with motel rooms behind an iron balcony and a sign saying, SUNDAY IS FUN DAY.

I am paying attention to details… some things to tell the cop… for justice… and to not sin as much while thinking, imagining of Andie.

"Bro, you smell like low tide," Pete barks, sneaking up behind me with his keys rattling against his phone in his hat.

"Well, you could… could you teach me how to clean up like you at church on Sundays?" I stutter, looking down to my untied sneakers.

"Can't," he says. "Bir, never help people

because you like being liked. They'll end up liking you and wanting more help. When you can't help them more, they'll push you out of their lives, you'll be gone like sand swept by the wind off the beach and washed into the ocean."

He pats my head. Scoobie licks my ankles. The old dog doesn't look good. I want to ask about him, but before I can Pete quickly adds, "but I'll show you how to keep sand on the beach now."

Pete runs through the red stop light. He crosses Pleasure Avenue as the automatic traffic voice activates, "Stop... Danger... Stop." and brakes in front of Braca's. I fear he is going to ask me what I did last night and then beat me up under the green and white-striped awning. I wait for the traffic voice to say "Go... 30 seconds... 19... 8 seconds" and fidget with Scoob crossing the street.

"It's important to always be honest, right?" he says looking into my twitching face.

I nod Scoob's head with my right hand so he doesn't look into my revealing eyes.

"I got to tell you something, no one knows this," Pete says.

I bend over to put down Scoob, not wanting to look in Pete's face.

"Back in the day, railroad tracks ran down Pleasure Avenue, right here," Pete says, tapping my head, making me look up, pointing down toward Townsends Inlet and then up toward Strathmere. "The tracks from the mainland crossed at Corson's Inlet, in between the Deauville Inn and Twisties and ran south to the middle of town to the Garden State Publishing Company."

"How do you…" I start to say.

"This town was built around a newspaper publisher, everyone, I mean everyone, worked there. Now newspapers are dying faster than, sadly, Catholic school powers St. Patrick's and your St. Anthony's… please stay alive Big 5."

"No, no way… my St. A's will never die."

"Check your history, the saints all die first."

"But, you aren't quite dead yet."

He peels off, looking back quickly as if to encourage Scoob. I lift the struggling dog. Pete sprints past the Sea Isle lifeguard boat in the middle of the roundabout under three limp flags.

He bounces across the promenade and past the pavilion to the steps where the cop was beaten… he jumps onto the beach, missing all the steps, doing a roll in the bright white sand, snatching two handfuls of the powdery stuff.

"And you thought white men couldn't jump," he yells into the wind blowing in his face.

He dodges past a napping mommy half his age with a toddler wiggling on her lap. A fit grandmommy type walks around her chair with a book, but doesn't look up from her paperback.

The kid wakes the dozing mommy, "There's daddy" pointing to Pete. The mother stirs and says, "Oh no, no he's a bad stranger."

Pete, looking back to Scoob and me, says loud enough for the grandmother to stop reading, "How do they both know?"

He sprints toward the ocean. An energized Scoob is right along his side, seemingly juiced by the fury. Pete crosses the line onto the dark sand and rips a full-frontal roll, like an old East German gymnast trying to fling over the Berlin Wall. He lifts both arms up. He starts wind milling. He runs into the ocean above his scraped-up knees. He hurls the sand from each hand into the ocean.

Or what little sand still left in each hand.

He bops out of the surf, crossing the line back to the white sand. He does another roll, scooping up two handful of sand. He runs back to the ocean, wind milling his arms and throwing the sand into a rising wave.

Scoobie's saggy butt faces the ocean. With his front paws, he starts digging the white sand, flinging the soft stuff backwards like trying to cover a load of poop.

"That's my boy, Scoober," Pete lauds.

Possessed Pete darts back into the ocean, windmills and heaves the sand, which blows back into his face. He howls. Seagulls scatter.

"Come get some religion," he says as a wave crashes into his back, dipping him.

He pops his head up, with eyes shut he yells, "Come in and get baptized my boyo."

Slower than crossing Pleasure Avenue a few minutes ago, I tiptoe toward this mad man. Scared like I was in front of Braca's, I yell to him, "I don't want to get my sneakers wet." I stand on the dark sand, stopping at the line where the waves retreat. Like a wave crashing at my feet, a sudden thought rushes over me. I can't believe he knows what I did last night.

Or does he?

"What are you doing?" I ask, knowing I'm

going to get a lengthy lesson in some insane nonsense I can't wait to hear.

I should just do this. I grab a handful of sand. Whip it towards the ocean. Of course, none reaches and falls on top of the dark sand. I can see the trail leading back to me, until a wave comes up to my Nikes and the white sand is gone.

Pete rushes toward me like a rogue wave, reaches out his hands spread as wide as the ocean.

"You're one of us... now," he says tilting his head to the amused sky.

"One of who?" I ask.

"I've started my own religion for people like us," Pete says.

"How?" I ask. "Like who?"

"Hey, Joseph Smith started the Mormons from some farm field in Western Pennsylvania where all the grand quarterbacks are from, and Zoroaster started Zoroastrianism in the Near East where all the grand religions are from, and Ken Kesey started the Merry Pranksters on the Left Coast where the grand Grateful Dead still lives even without Jerry."

He does another roll, grabs two handfuls of sand and runs back into the ocean, wind-milling the sand into the air.

I need to get him back on shore. He pulls himself out of the waist-deep water with Scoob barking madly.

"Yo, tell me what the religion is called?" I demand, knowing if he doesn't have a name yet for his religion, perhaps my Yo will bring him out for a lecture on proper English.

He runs toward me, does a roll in the white sand behind me and says, "yo... man, you talk like my man Stephen A. Smith using big words like capitulated, acumen and abomination describing a missed layup and now you say yo. What the fook? Be honest with your words. Talk your truest self.

"Your words are all you gots in the end. It is your word against The Man."

He runs toward the ocean, stops and blares, "My religion can be called the Merry Mendicants or Merry Monks or the Merry Misanthropes... it depends how you're feeling... you get to choose... religion is about you... like when Jesus threw the sand back into the Sea of Galilee...

"I thought he walked on the... "I start to say before he blurts, "for example, if you are feeling capitulated, you can call yourself a Merry Mendicant, or if the acumen at the time suits you, call yourself a Merry Monk or if life's just an abomination, just call yourself a Merry Misanthrope."

He wipes the sand from his hands into the ocean.

I know from studying medieval religion in high school that Mendicants and Monks were like cloistered dudes who prayed in castles and caves until they were eaten by a wolf or beheaded by a king, but I didn't know of Misanthropes.

"Yo," I start to say before catching myself. "Pete, what the f... f... f... heck is a Misanthrope?"

He runs back, does a roll, scoops up some sand and stops.

"Misanthropy is a generalized dislike,

distrust, disgust, contempt or hatred of the human species or human nature," he says like he is reading a dictionary. "A misanthrope, or misanthropist, is someone who holds such views or feelings...

"A Merry Misanthrope is one who is halfway hating and halfway healed... The Halfway Healers."

He turns toward the ocean and throws the sand from where we're standing. Scoobs does the backward fling thing.

"This is where my philosophy of Magnetic Reversion helps heal," Pete says.

Pete must know I have no idea what he is talking about.

In a way, I think he is testing his theory on me first before telling his bounce passing boys, but the Lids have already used these words, so maybe he really is trying to convert me...

"Magnetic Reversion is simply the things that initially bring people together ultimately drive them apart... for example, basketball brings us together, but ultimately it will drive us apart."

"What? Why?" I say, halfway hoping we will be driven apart by the next wave and not at all, ever.

"We're playing ball together now, with Andie and all, but ya'll will get so good that ya'll will play at higher levels, go overseas to Turkey, perhaps like I did, m... m... m... meet a girl...

"It happens all the time in life, especially in Little League or Youth Basketball... your kids play together and the parents all hang out when in third and fourth grade, but by the time fifth grade comes around when the players start to separate because of working harder, puberty and just genetics, the parents push apart like two attracting magnets. They don't drink together anymore.

"That's why the guys who do make their 8th grade basketball team and play on the same Little League team, they have to stay friends for life, like a tribe on Survivor Island… we're all we have, everyone else from the beginning is gone.

"Ya'll will see when ya'll a parent someday… by eighth grade parents don't even talk, except when one parent dies and they see each other at the viewing. Then they only trivial talk, though, they don't talk about what happened, they don't talk about Magnetic Reversion because it is irreversible for most… unless you're a Merry Mendicant, or Merry Monk, or a Merry Misanthrope… unless you're a Halfway Healer who practices Magnetic Reversion Reversal."

Pete hands me some sand. He could've shoved the whole beach down my throat because my mouth is so wide open.

"You see, throwing sand into ocean brings the ocean and beach together," Pete says. "This will ultimately drive the ocean from taking sand from the beach."

"How?" I can only say.

"Well, you do understand how the ocean and beach are brought together here?" Pete says without waiting for an answer. "They're one, as tight as the backs of two refrigerator magnets pushed together by opposite forces.

"But then the ocean takes from the beach,

like a friend starting to take from a friend when they become close. But then the beach can give up no more sand or else it'll be gone, like a friend can only help so much before being ostracized. It's just the way nature and life works."

Pete grabs two more handfuls after another roll, runs into the ocean and windmills the sand …

"By returning the sand to the ocean first, the ocean can't take, like a close friend or spouse plundering your soul," he says. "You're plundering for them already … but only partly.

"As one of our Halfway Healers now, you need to practice this Magnetic Reversion Reversal," Pete says. "There are problems in life that unite people like the ocean and the beach, but you don't really listen or hear them fully, or they'll drive you apart. So, you only listen halfway.

"You only heal them halfway."

"What happens if you can't heal someone even halfway?" I ask hesitantly with trepidation.

"Nothing you can do but S.I.C.," he says, "Send In the Cleaners... not Sea Isle City."

With his hand on my elbow, Pete guides me throwing the sand from my hand into the ocean, like a dad teaching his son how to one-hand bounce pass a basketball with topspin against a lonely wall. The white sand still lands on the dark sand and not in the ocean. The two-colored sands mix as one when the wave washes over.

"See. Doesn't that feel good?" he asks.

We head toward Strathmere. I kick the surf with each stride, but my head is up scouting for trooper man, or the surfer dude, thinking of an excuse for reversing tracks if I see them.

"Where we going? Uncle Bills Pancakes in Strathmere?" I ask. "Where all the girls are all white, wearing college shirts, and all with names like Katie, Meghan and Colleen."

Pete smiles on that dig, knowing he taught me true.

"What's your problem? I will halfway heal it," Pete laughs. "You sound angry when you should be healed... halfway anyway."

"I don't have any problems," I say, not daring to tell him the half-truth of anything.

"Well that's good too," Pete says. "Letting someone know who you are by telling them your problems is also saying goodbye. So don't start telling anyone anything or they won't be around anymore soon.

"But if someone needs to tell you something, just go on maybe a 10-minute walk at best - both ways - and pretend to listen to their problems. But instead of really listening, mix in your own problems.

"When you're done, say to them 'you're healed.'

"And, they truly are, they're healed because they realize their problems, not only aren't that big, but no one cares about their problems. They might pretend to care, they might listen, but they don't fookly care.

"They learn people only care about what you can do for their little problems."

I scoop up some sand, edge a little closer to the ocean. I throw. Half the sand goes into the ocean. The other half leaves a trail back to me.

"You're feeling better already. Aren't you, bro?" Pete says, patting my head.

"Is the beach here heaven for the Halfway Healers?" I ask.

"There's a half answer for that, but it'll require me to start getting deep," Pete says. "We aren't like Catholics where heaven is this mystical place on the mountain where you find the Zen. I believe like in the book Zen and the Art of Motorcycle Maintenance, the only fookin Zen you find on the mountaintop is the fookin Zen you bring there.

"So, we're already halfway there because the Zen is inside us. The other half is letting it go. But we do have a physical place, too, the Halfway Healers' Heaven is Hannibal."

"The movie?"

"For fooks' sake, no, in Hannibal, Missouri where Hook Finn grew up, it's heaven because he treated everyone as equal. He was the only one who treated the slave, Jim, as a person. His Aunt Polly and all the white folks who bled their knees in church each Sunday scorned upon Hook because he fished all day instead of going to church. But young Hook embraced the message of mass without going, by treating Jim as an equal.

"Hook had the Halfway Healers motto down when he said in Life in the Mississippi, 'now and then we had a hope that if we lived and were good, God would permit us to be pirates,' like I learned you the other night.

"You see, we truly want to be halfway good.

Truly, like pirates. You know, like drinking beers all day on Saturday and then going to mass on Sunday morning, looking at all the pretty moms and thinking about doing some good sinning."

Pete smears sand on my spinning forehead.

"You're baptized, bro," he says triumphantly. "Youse one of us."

I grab two handfuls of white sand. I windmill so hard I fall into the surf. Scoob rushes over and licks me. As the salt water mixes with the tears in my eyes, I see the blurry water tower. I smile. I am here in Sea Isle. Or, I'm halfway between Strathmere and Sea Isle… somewhere near Bonz's Beach of Dreams.

Chapter 11

The first Saturday of June, the Bounce-passers ride their bikes down to the Jersey shore as part of Kelly's Ride. They have been doing this for the last six years. The first five years were part of the official ride, but last year they biked from Pennsauken, which is on the Delaware River across from Philadelphia, to Margate on the Atlantic Ocean. This was their continuing tribute.

They Lids ride again today. I am riding with them, just two weeks and too many memories to remember after meeting them.

Andie drives us toward Philly. We will ride the bikes stashed in the back of the white pickup.

I guess we're meeting other riders halfway.

"You don't ask where we're going anymore. You notice?" she says to me. "You used to always ask what was the name of each street in Sea Isle and Avalon and what way we were going – north or south. But you don't ask where we're going now.

"I think you will start bounce passing, too."

Andie also wants to ride, but she needs to drive old scrappy Scooby back down to the shore to meet us. I am sort of surprised Pete doesn't put Scoobie in a sidecar on his bike. I better not think too loud. Scoob doesn't look too good these days.

We pull in the parking lot of LL. Bean, an anchor store at the Promenade of Sagemore. It's in the town of Marlton on the busy four-lane Route 73. Pete needs to "pinch one out."

"I'm getting knifed," he yells.

I get out to stretch my legs, and knock the

red scorebook right out of the truck.

"Watch the book," Andie barks. "Don't let Pete see the book on the ground."

The parking lot is covered with pollen from the trees. The red book cover is now whitish-green. I wipe off the pollen and shove the book, and the newspaper inside, back under the seat.

"Why does he save the old book?"

"The scorebook tells time," Andie says.

With Pete looking relieved, we drive across Rt. 73 to the parking lot of a spacious funeral home, Bradley's. It is in the middle of one of the New Jersey's highway system's unique left-turn constructions called a jug handle. I'm thinkin' it's like the dead can hop back on the highway of life.

The pack of riders from Pennsauken, which is up about 10 miles farther north on Rt. 73, must still be riding.

A hardtop MINI Cooper pulls up. Harry hops out of the toy car. The uber driver hands him his double-strapped satchel and parks under a tree.

"You still around, thought you died," Pete says surprised. "What did you find out, Sherlock?"

"That you were at Braca's that night," he says. Pete interrupts saying, "I already told you that."

"Yeah, I know, but before you cut me off like an ugly Yank I was going to say so were a lot of your mates," he says. "But they are loyal school boys in knee socks, they never say anything.

"They hold onto their secrets like booze," he adds, squeezing his satchel with both arms.

"Indeed," Pete says smiling, throwing a fake

jab at the satchel, "like at Hogwarts."

At the funeral home, we meet guys with pet names like Vogde, Zup, Murt, Olse, and D, who are around Pete's age. None wear tight bike pants. Rather they wear cargo shorts that look like they have been worn to cut their lawns. They all wear various shades of green t-shirts from previous Kelly's Rides. Pete wears his old No. 24 shirt.

Harry tells me the ride with these guys is about 55 miles. They all sport decent road bikes like Pete's. I'm riding an old 10 speed with a rusted chain. Pete said I am too young to need a good bike and "the ride will build up your legs since youse the only black guy in the Western Hemisphere who can't two-hand dunk."

Our first stop is 14 miles, I'm told by Harry. "I figure they break so they can drink," he says. "You know, tea time for the Teetotalers."

It is only 9 in the morning and Pete says we average about 15 miles an hour while riding. So I guess we'll be at the tipoff bar by 10 … with about 40 more miles to ride. But Harry says we will loaf.

More middle-aged riders from parts unknown converge at the first stop. "Chauncey's" occupies a corner of open fields on Route 73.

"My butt is already singing," I say to Pete.

"Get used to it, you'll be sitting the pine this year in hoops," he says.

Chauncey's bar is dark. Harry is sitting in the corner with the uber driver, who holds his satchel. There are a few more biker guys sitting around on stools here than are actually riding and it's only mid-morning. The lady bar tender has giant "yaboos." Pete told me early in the ride that she would. He said he feels uncomfortable with Andie when they are around her "Godly gifts."

From out of the darkness near Harry, some bull of a man approaches Pete.

Damn, man, it is John Rage.

"Hey Pete, I'm sorry," John says.

Man, I really did not tell the cop dude anything about Pete and he is busting him right here. Right in front of all his buddies and the bartender with the big ones, whom I know Pete wants to hug so bad.

"I'm so sorry Pete," he says again.

Pete gives him a white guy, half man hug, but hard, saying "Rager, let's throw one down."

He drags the sympathetic cop over to the bar, then leans over and gives "Sugar" a huge hug.

"Hey dar… how ya been Sugar?" Pete gushes. He is sweet-talkin' the blessed bartender!

"Dandy, now that you and your old buddy are swapping spit, hugs and beer again together," she says sliding an approving glance at Rage.

"And one for me little buddy over here," Pete says, pulling on my arm to place me between him and the cop. I don't look at Rage until Pete turns to kiss Sugar's hand.

Three pints arrive. We hoist "cheers" to each other. The Three Drinkin' Desperados.

Sugar bops around the bar, her boobs bouncing like basketballs, and sits on Pete's lap, bellowing out "so good to see Pete's still gots his bring the wood shirt… how big is your penis again, Pete?"

"Just six inches," Pete shrugs, lifting his beer to toast the air.

Sugar points to the two on his shirt saying, "yeah two inches sulking" and then points to the four saying, "and four inches happy."

"That's right," Pete roars, "a grand six inches, total."

The beer tastes as smooth as Pete's humor.

"I'm really so sorry Pete," the cop says again. "I just had to come up and say hey."

"Hey, OK, Rager," Pete says.

Rage studies the floor. I check if he packs cuffs on his belt, but I can't see behind him since Pete has us all snugged in so close.

"Pete, I used to dive with you and ride bikes with you and drink with you but I stopped. Had to, the drinking was killing my marriage," he says. "I'm sorry, I just stopped calling you and coming to the boat to dive...

"Rager, grand to see you," Pete says, finishing his beer. "Was good to see you at the diner, though we didn't really talk... not like this."

"Two more, Sugar, make it three," Pete orders softening his voice, looking at my half beer.

"Pete how do you do it?" Rage asks. "I mean, I blew you off, out of my life. And I showed up at the diner, that night and you welcomed me back then, and now after over a year since that night we drank at Braca's... you act like... I... Judas... has never been gone."

Pete swallows the foamy beer. He bangs the empty glass down playfully and says, "I believe in the Stoneosophy of life, you know Keith Richards' philosophy, 'you were there, now you're here.'"

We ride on, whirling toward the entrance to Atlantic City Expressway. The speeding SUVs filled with lovely mommies and their more perfect kids zoom down to the shore, slowing in front of us to snap cell photos of a strange sight, a 20-foot statue of a boy in suspenders with mouse ears and a straw hat in front of Mr. Bill's restaurant.

On the narrow shoulder, Pete pulls up to me, nodding to the AC Expressway, and over the traffic's streaking roar, he screams, "Did I ever tell you about the time…"

I shake my head "No" and slow down to hear him better.

"When I was a kid, my buddy Boo got a car before all the rest of us."

"Who?" I ask.

"Boo," he screams.

"Boo?"

"Yeah, the toll collector on the T.I. Bridge."

"Boo? I thought you just yelled 'boo' in the booth to act like you are scaring him," I say.

"What? Do you think I'm goofy? That's his name, Boo, short for Boucher. He's a fookin frenchy."

I nod my head up and down as the traffic whizzes by without hearing Pete's story.

"Boo's dad said he could only drive local, around The Hill," Pete continues. "But the first night bust down to the shore. We're drinking beers and forgot his dad worked on the Atlantic City Expressway taking tolls. We pull up to the toll booth and there's his dad… the toll collector."

The shoulder gets narrower. The asphalt is bumpy and littered with little stones, or pebbles, going through Mays Landing. The town is country small. A sprawling desolate factory sits vacant in the middle, at a T in the road. The drab bluish-gray building could pass for a mothballed battleship. Slowing down because of the choppy road, I say to Pete, "Harry told me at Chauncey's how you said you didn't 'jive' with the coma cop."

"Indeed," Pete says squeezing his handlebars and pushing down while bouncing over a pothole, "I didn't dig his game."

The Palace is an outfitter for canoes and kayaks. Pitchers of Guinness are $5 – per the outdoor menu board.

The bar nests on the Great Egg River, and also serves pizza. The Bounce-passers aren't bothering with grub, though. My stomach isn't ready for food after seeing John Rage, who didn't drive down here to meet us at the second stop. Yet.

Pete is already 'Stoneosophizing' at the corner of the bar when I limp out of the bathroom. His big five buddies - Phil Leyne, Uncle Matt McManus, Johnny Mitchell, Tom Meager and Sim McManus - flank him. Just like on the basketball court, Pete is always in the middle of the action and his loyal teammates are right by his side. Only now he is drinking, roasting and toasting.

"To River Religion," Pete toasts. "We're on the river drinking to our universal religion."

"To Pete, who's saving us all," says Uncle Matty, raising a pint of a lighter colored beer than the other four.

I converge again at a bar on Uncle Matty, knowing he found peace in the Mormon religion, hoping he might pour some reasonable seriousness on the origins of the River Religion and the connection to the Halfway Healers.

Uncle Matt rips a $10 bill down Hamilton's face. He gives half to the bartender. "The Halfway Healers are here," says the lady with her frizzy burnt red hair pulled back. "We need some more scotch... and scotch tape."

In hairy hands, she hauls over a pitcher of Guinness with the half of the bill rolled up in her mouth like a cigarette. She fake-puffs the bill.

"Pete calls his basic belief... well he bases his core beliefs... on what he calls the universal River Religion," Uncle Matty says to me.

Before I get too confused, I swig the pint he pours me for brilliance, like I am one of them needing both. I sip an orgasmic good soaking for a few long seconds, before saying to Uncle Matty, "I thought his religion was called the Halfway Healers, or the Magnetic Reversionists, or the Merry Mendicants, or the Merry Monks, or the Merry Misanthropes."

"Exactly," Uncle Matty says. "You're one of us now."

"He baptized me, tackling me in the ocean."

Uncle Matty pumps his arm like he scored game point. He nudges toward Pete, rubs his thick hair and taps each cheek, saying, "Good-job f-in up Byrd man. No one will ever believe anything he says about you."

Uncle Matty rips another $10 in half. He

comes back with two more pitchers. Drinking right from the pitcher, I suck down the bottom half of the first one. "Next time use no hands," Pete says.

"The River Religion is his theory," Matty says, pointing out the double window to the river, which snakes behind the Palace. "Pete says life is simply like flowing down a river. It's the religion of his Halfway Healers, Magnetic Reversionists, Merry Mendicants, Merry Monks and Merry Mad Misanthropes... did I miss anyone?"

"Just the Mickey Mantles," I say, looking on the wall of a picture of the Yankees great No. 7, who my dad swears was greater than DiMaggio.

"Hah! A religion for the heavy, old, angry white guy drinkers who used to play sports," Matty says with a smile. "Call me Matty Mantle."

"His River Religion philosophy of life is truly wise, though. He preaches to always continue paddling up and down the river, meeting people, making friends, and gaining experiences. And when you're old, just wade down river one last time, stopping in, saying "Hey" to the people you met who are still around... to the friends who kept you... and revisit some of those old experiences.

"Maybe tell some stories. Once down the river, find a place where all those people you met and friends you've kept will adventure down the river to say hey or maybe just stay... or maybe to just properly say bye-bye."

"I do see the wisdom, though I'm not ready to go down river to the end yet," I say intrigued.

"Yeah, he lives it," Uncle Matty says. "During tough times, and man, he's had his bite of them, Pete says life's more like an ocean crossing, not a river, where rough seas will knock some people overboard, but you don't ever want to throw anyone overboard during high seas, or rough rapids in the river, because of how they treated you or what they did... or didn't do.

"He stresses, though, you can't let the life-suckers pull you overboard either by doing something to hurt you.

"Pete feels the only worse deed in life than throwing a friend overboard into rough waters, is to toss them into calm seas just to hurt because they can, which you see bloody life-suckers do.

"He teaches it's better to fall overboard yourself than toss a friend. He believes you just paddle to shore and either the friend will return and get you, knowing they were wrong, or you just patch your own life raft, and when you're ready, get back on the river.

"Always, I remind him of his Stoneosophy, get back on the river in life... you were here on the river of life... now you are back on life's river."

Matty and the hairy bar lady carry over two pitchers. The werewolf bartender tapes two halves of tens together, but both are Hamilton's nose side.

"Forgiveness," Pete says, biting down on Matty's pitcher, swallowing a swig no hands. "I need the cleansing of forgiveness, like leaving the confessional as a kid still thinking dirty thoughts about the girls waiting in line, but feeling lighter."

Matty snatches a taped $10 from the furry mitts of the lady bartender and rips the bill in half again, saying, "You can't patch a torn friendship, relationship or battleship like money, you can only forgive, forget and forge ahead… Pete taught me so in the first book of his River Religion."

Harry, like the sneaky fast butler in Mr. Deeds, appears suddenly, plops down between Pete and Matty with a pitcher of the dark stuff.

"Didn't know you partook. Or is it partaken in King's speech?" Pete says.

"I'm not driving," he says, nodding to a new uber driver with his feet up at the next table.

"Right, you are flying fleet on your quidditch broom," Pete says. "I'd like to learn."

"If you tell me why you didn't like the black cop," Harry says with equal poignancy and courage. "The poor bloke in the coma."

"In quidditch, did you ever play against a guy, like in your league now, who played at a higher level when he was at Hogwarts with you? And that guy still thinks he is better than you because he played Division 1 and you only played Division 3? And you have been beating his ass so bad in recent years he stops playing against you? But still thinks he is better than you? Does that ever happen in quidditch? Or you think he thinks."

The next 15 miles fly by, partly since after four pints, the numbness reaches my feet on the pedals. I also know I'll "hear me some more Pete" as Uncle Matty said, leaving another torn ten-dollar bill at the accommodating river bar.

The third stop on this pilgrimage to their Mecca, called Margate, is Testa's Good Guys Pub.

"Good guys?" I say about this corner pub farther south in Mays Landing. Then slumping off the bike, I say to Pete "Why not grand guys?"

I aim right at the can. The entire inside is wooden-paneled and adorned with hundreds of black and white sports photos. The bathroom door doesn't shut all the way and I can see Pete's already sitting out there under a photo of Ricky Marciano and Joe Walcott. I can tell while standing up and pissing that the photo is Jersey Joe. The Rock's fist is halfway through Walcott's jaw. My dad was an Ali fan. He said white people like this photo since it's this Boston guy, even if the Rock was Italian, bashing a black man.

Inside the bathroom, there is a duplicate photo of Marciano pounding Walcott.

"I guess they really like the Rock here," I say to Pete as he hands me a pint.

"Yeah, there are two photos of him crushing Jersey Joe," Pete says. "Did you know Walcott was from Merchantville, right outside of Camden? His real name was Arnold Cream."

A black guy named Cream getting creamed by a white guy… just creamy.

"Did you know it was 25 years ago last month Al Campanis, who roomed with Jackie Robinson, told Ted Koppel on Nightline that black people didn't have the mental faculties to be managers in baseball?" Pete says, not asks.

I didn't know any of this. Who would?

I did like talking race with Pete. He did, too, and continued. I also feel protected by him here like an outlaw biker gang protects its own.

"Campanis, who was the Dodgers general manager at the time, said blacks had to pay their dues and manage in the minor leagues, saying 'better known black players have been able to get into other fields and make a pretty good living in that way,'" says Pete, adding he just reread this on the toilet at The Rock from his old Sports Illustrated magazine "potty pile" stack.

"Koppel said it was 'baloney' and argued how lots of black players would love to be managers.

"Campanis said he didn't believe it was prejudice. He said he truly believed that blacks 'may not have some of the necessities to be a manager or a general manager.'

"Campanis ranted on how blacks didn't have the 'smarts.' He said, 'they're outstanding athletes, very God-gifted, and they're very wonderful people, and that's all I can tell you about them.'"

I swig a long dripping of beer. So, does Pete. The slower pack of our biker group filters into the sports bar filled with history lessons.

"Blacks were smarter than whites," Pete says. "That is the irony."

I swallow the rest of my beer.

"Slow down, brother Byrd, we have a few more miles to Margate," Pete cautions.

"You're going to get our ass kicked in here," I say. "Well at least yours and mine."

"You really should read the book 'Guns, Germs and Steel,' by Jared Diamond. He is in the news of late because of the success of the genome project," Pete says. "I read a lot about the project, to get information for my leadership lectures.

"You should also read Steven J. Gould, a Harvard sociological biology professor, and E.O. Wilson, who wrote the 'Social Conquest of the Planet,' but first read Diamond… he is a gem."

Pete laughs at his own joke.

"You shit diamonds," Mr. Meags says to Pete, getting up and walking to the can.

After a long, soaking swig of beer, Pete is dead serious again.

"We're, I mean whites, are all descendants of about 10,000 black people who were actually pushed out of Africa 50,000 years ago because they were weaker than the stronger blacks.

"These 10,000 black-folk migrated mostly north to colder Europe. Diamond proves this by archeological and anthropological findings, but mainly through linguistics. He traced the origins of the five predominant languages of Africa and how and where they evolved.

"By doing this, he not only proved whites came from blacks, but were the inferior blacks who couldn't fight or weren't smart enough to stay in the warmer climate of Africa."

Old man Mitchell and Leyne squeeze in tighter to our corner of the bar. Uncle Matty points to the photo of Marciano blasting Walcott. The other McManus says he has to go to the bathroom because he wants to relieve "his dripping rock."

Wiping his glasses with a moist bar rag, Uncle Matty looks puzzled at his smeared specs and recites like reading, "The blacks who were weak migrated to Europe, their skin pigmentation turning lighter because of the cold, where they eventually enjoyed the advantages of guns, technology, literacy and political organization."

"Yeah, Diamond wrote how Europe developed these advantages due to food production because Africa didn't have the needed domesticated animals for farm work," old man Mitchell says as if he studied under Diamond.

"And Eurasia had native cows, sheep, goats, horses and pigs while Africa had wild buffalo, zebra, rhino, hippos and giraffes that never have been domesticated," Leyne adds.

"So, European's colonization of Africa had nothing to do with the differences of whites being smarter than blacks," Uncle Matty concludes, cleaning his glasses. "Pete opened our minds to all this … it had nothing to do with intelligence, but due to difference in geography and biogeography, particular on the different axis areas, like the gap between baselines on the basketball court, along with different animals and plants."

"Yet even with all the inherited advantages, it still took Europeans nine wars and around 175 years for their superior armies to subdue South Africa," Pete says, grabbing Uncle Matty's glasses and putting them on, smiling silly like he is dumb.

Uncle Matty snatches Harry's glasses and puts them halfway down his nose. Harry pulls out another pair of circle specs from his open satchel.

"I was wondering what was in the satch," Matty says. "Thought might be mug shots of…"

"Just my spare specs, there are no newspaper articles on the cop beating," Harry interrupts. "I was wondering why your Professor Pete never asked to read them when I said I had clippings, and why everyone is so loyal to him. But you guys particularly. The Sea Isle cops have no witnesses or leads for the beating of the black officer. No one is talking, you gents don't say boo. Why so blindly loyal to your wizard?"

"You mean," Matty says, putting Harry's glasses in the empty satchel, "loyal like Harry's Griffindor House at Hogwarts?"

The ride to the fourth stop is endless. The traffic is thick. My pedals don't float anymore. But now that I know the old white guys knew I was from stronger and smarter stock, I couldn't stop out of fear their concession would be reversed.

Ahh, the Magnetic Reversion... I need to ride faster, now. Smarter, too.

I fall off my bike at Juliano's, which is in Egg Harbor.

"Ahh Juliano's," Pete screams riding into the storage shed in the corner parking lot.

Both sprawled on the asphalt, Pete tells me Juliano Cabos was a top Peruvian guide. He says the Cabos family leads trips to Macchu Picchu.

"How do you knows this?" I question, helping him to his feet. "I heard from Andie how you went on a Catholic mission to Guatemala, but never knew you visited Peru."

"Thanks for the hand, but I didn't need the help... I treated meself to hike the Inca Trail to Macchu Picchu after serving a week in Guatemala with Sending Out Servants out of Christ the Light parish in Cherry Hill, down South Jersey," he says. "I had a religious experience, connecting my religious beliefs in the mountains during a home visit in LaPeurta above the village Santa Cruz del Quiche... enlightened, I celebrated on Picchu."

I sit back down on the flat asphalt between our bikes, folding my legs like Buddha's student.

"I always had a problem when I was a kid of how the nuns said only Catholics could be saved, that we could only go to heaven? Why wouldn't God love a Lakota Indian in the Black Hills of South Dakota, like Dei, who lived a spiritual life and worshipped the Great Spirit?" Pete says, sitting next to me, but not like Buddha.

"The Lakota taught the wise Phil Jackson," Uncle Matty says, pulling up on his bike about the former coach of the Bulls and Lakers, and has the most NBA titles. "He was half Lakota and he even got Dennis Rodman to read his book, Sacred Hoops, about the circle of life and basketball."

"Selective salvation always troubled me. When I was playing ball in Turkey, I met a guy, Emrah, who escorted me to the Blue Mosque, the Grand Bazaar, the Bosphorous and the Topkapi Palace, home of the lucky Sultan and his harem."

I wanted to act a little smart so said, "Yeah, Istanbul used to be Constantinople."

"We visited the Kariye, a 7th century Catholic church that was turned into a mosque when the Byzantine Empire ended with the conquest of Constantinople by the Ottomans... a fresco of the Birth of Christ still coated the ceiling.

"I asked Emrah why the Muslims didn't paint over the Catholic scene and he said, 'the Catholic religion is a great religion, like Islam, and it's in some ways greater since it is older.

"It hit me as if the frescoed ceiling fell on my head. Emrah felt the two religions worshipped the same God. He felt Mohammed and Jesus were both prophets, I realized, of each of our God.

"Now, I feel Jesus is the Son of God, but I don't know how God manifested himself to other people, like the Muslims or the Lakotas, who weren't taught by nuns with steel yard sticks.

"Then, I'm sitting in the mud of an adobe hut in the Guatemala mountains in a home where the family never saw a white face probably, or at least a red face like mine. There were about 20 in the family and not even the men were more then 5-feet tall. I must have looked like a molten giant.

"On the wall was a photo, so I asked the translator, who asked in Spanish to a family member who spoke the native language of Quiche, who was the man in the photo? A woman, around my age wrapped in a petite colorful dress, said in Quiche, to a Spanish translator, through an English translator, that the man was her dad, who taught her as a child how God was inside of everyone...

"That's the defining spiritual moment of me life's search for God's inclusion. Here I was on top of a mountain above the rain forest in Central America, and a lady my age who never left the top of her mountain, told me God is in everyone.

"So, through two translators the message of God in everyone was clearer to me than through all the well-intentioned nuns of my youth... and so I figured if God is in the Mayan Indians above Guatemala, He must be in the Lakota Indians above the Black Hills and in the Muslims above the Bosphorous... and the sun-worshipping mommies in Sea Isle.

"I was on a revelation roll, so I floated with the cirrus clouds to Peru... for more religion."

Climbing the uneven steps into the bar, he said the famous explorer Hiram Bingham hired the Cabos family in his search of the famed Lost City of Peru as guides and how you can still employ the Cabos family in search of the Lost City.

I used my iPhone to search Wiki and see if this was true. Sure, enough the Cabos family are guides in Peru, specializing in taking tourist on the Inca Trail. Except they didn't start until the 1950's while Bingham made his discovery of Machu Picchu back in 1911... and his name wasn't Juliano, but Juvenal Cabos...

Putting my right elbow on a cracked coaster, I settle next to the bar for the next parable.

"Hiram discovered Machu Picchu and what I find interesting is the remains of the old Incas showed back then they were just about five feet tall. Well, a hundred years later, the people of Peru are still five feet tall.

"Just like the Mayan Indians in Guatemala. The two cultures haven't changed physically in hundreds of years, perhaps thousands. Why?" he asks. I place my chin on my fist like The Thinker.

"You're a good foot taller than the Machu Picchuians, why do you think?"

Taking a gulp of beer to get up the courage, I instead ask, "Do you think it's unfair, that I'm taller than Machu Picchuians?"

"No, it's unfair to you because you could never be a jockey… you are too tall, but a Machu Picchuian could be a basketball player, Spud Webb was only 5-foot-something and he won the dunk contest."

Chapter 12

My dad finally has a son.

"Yahoo," as Pete says when good and drunk about anything good. So, I say, "Double yahoo!" The words echo off The Rock's walls.

The U.S. Open is on TV. My dad and I, with Byrd of course, can watch golf on TV for hours without talking. Byrd is always with us.

"McElroy needs to lay up here," Byrd says emphatically, looking at my dad, who nods in agreement. "He doesn't need to reach this green in two, it's a par-5, he can still make a birdie."

"You're a birdie," Pete says. "How do you know the game like a scratch golfer?"

Byrd stands up and holds the remote down like a golf club. He turns in a full backswing, rotates his hips and holds the follow through.

"It's in the hole," he says, dropping the remote and strutting to the TV with both arms up.

"Why can't the Open be like the Masters? Enough with the fookin commercials," Pete says.

Byrd picks up the remote and points the controller to the TV. The red number 44 pops on the screen. The channel changes to the Black Entertainment Television. Red 44 keeps blinking.

"BET baby," Pete yells. "The magic of 44… did you know when Villanova played in 1985 in the Elite Eight, the Wildcats had played in 44 previous NCAA games and they won by holding North Carolina to just 44 points… Nova went on to beat the evil empire Georgetown for the championship by making 44 baskets – 22 free throws and 22 shots from the field … ahh, the magic of 44."

Pete laughs as satisfied with himself as he's ever laughed. Maybe his laughter is as content when pissed drunk at the Springfield with Dei.

"You know," Pete says, sustaining his smile like the blinking 44, "didn't know you knew."

"Know what?" Byrd asks oddly.

"The magic of Nova's 44," Pete states firmly, his laughter ceasing. "*Whad* you think I was asking? Who whacked the black cop?"

"Why was Georgetown evil?" Byrd asks quickly, defiantly. "Because the coach was black?"

"Hell, in the 1830's, the Jesuits of Georgetown sold their slaves to pay off debts and to keep their sacred school in business," Pete scoffs. "The slaves, 300 of them, had mostly converted to Catholicism… they were sold by priests, the point guards of God, to where there were no Catholic churches in the Deep South.

"Villanova delivered justice," he declares.

His throaty laughter resumes when Byrd says, "Have you ever notice how the BET channel never has commercials for white folk?"

Through the open door, the Lids run in rapid succession like the blinking 44, dashing to silly Pete on the sofa. "You ok bro?" Uncle Matty asks. "Thought you might be having the big one."

"Nah, only if Woods misses this putt," Pete says. "Gots some Tiger action to pay for losing another leadership seminar in September."

After Woods misses the short putt, my dad huffs over to the cooler in the corner. Byrd stares… at me. "Spraying the infield," Pete says as he flips beers to everyone as Byrd stops looking at me. He first delivers a beer to each of his Lids.

We still haven't beaten the Lids in basketball, including earlier this morning. We are scoring more against them and Byrd is actually hitting the rim on his shots – he doesn't miss against anyone else – but we can't beat them yet. I think by Labor Day we will take the Lids down.

My dad flings another brew to all saying, "drink up, the fastest two gets the last two."

Pete and Byrd win.

I notice my dad doesn't say fook as much, or hardly at all, since he's been around Byrd.

Pete slips up with stories more than the cussing, I guess, around me he forgets things, and says stuff about, like, having a blow-up doll. All the old guys refer to it even by name, like the doll is real. I don't know if he has one, but they all call her... it... Bianca. One time I heard Pete say he "packs Bianca" so he wouldn't sin. So maybe he does have... it.

"Hope the Open goes to a playoff tomorrow," Pete says as Tiger drains a lovely putt.

After Webb Simpson birdies two-straight holes on the front nine, Pete declares, "The Open rightfully does a full 18-hole playoff. The way it should be. Always got to go full, all in for everything ... bring the wood."

Byrd pours the bottled beer into his pint glass and licks the foam from the top. He steals a glance at me as Pete begins to speak.

"Another 18 holes on Monday, I pull for the playoff every year, since Mike's Seafood has

Mussel Monday." Pete says, wanting to stay down. "The only spread better than Mike's Mussels is Mike's half-price mussels on Mondays."

"Maria's mussels," Byrd says with a silly Pete-like grin, 'easier to chew."

"You like Maria's because it's a half block closer to your hut here… you lazy arse," Pete says.

"Well, that too," Byrd says real serious. "You know us colored folk, *we'd being* always looking for *dem* easy ways."

"I'd heard," Pete says, matching Byrd's seriousness. "Or I read it on Ebony online."

"I've heard enough nonsense," I finally say. "I'm not grab-assing around watching golf all afternoon. Dei invited me to take a surfing lesson down Strathmere this afternoon with her."

"Can I go?" Pete asks boyishly. "Really, I always wanted to surf."

Dei lives in the Spinnaker tower nearest Strathmere. I wave to her up on the sixth floor from the promenade. Her furry boots rest on the railing. She grabs them and taps the bottoms together. The sand floats off the soles and onto the promenade below, drifting onto three unknowing walkers wearing shiny black motorcycle t-shirts.

"How come you're not with your boys?" she asks, carrying her furry Uggs while gliding smoothly over the sand dune in white socks.

"Watching golf."

"Know the feeling. My hubby is out golfing again today," she says, slipping into her right boot. "That's why I'm taking up surfing. I need something to do before drifting to Happy Hour at the Springfield. Unless goodness itself moves Happy Hour up from 3 o'clock until noon."

"Looks like I'm going to need stuff to do in the afternoons this summer, too."

"What happened to Byrd? I like him," Dei says hopping around me on her right leg to miss a wave creeping toward her socked foot.

"After the bike ride to Margate three weeks ago, he can't be separated from my dad. Byrd's now under my dad's wonderfully warped wing. Just like the Lids and the rest of us Merry Misanthropic Mendicants.

"Byrd says he's just going down river now, even sounding like worldly Pete. He told me how he forgets being black around him... when my dad was passed out sleeping in the bed of the pick-up with all the bikes on the ride back down here.

With one boot on, Dei bends and digs out a clam half exposed in the wet sand. She opens the shell with her pretty teeth and slurps out the clam.

"Of course, they're *boys* already, your dad doesn't care what color you are... anyone is... only if you box-out in basketball and at the bar...

"Hmmm, I actually never assumed Byrd even thought about color around him as an issue... I'm really tan... well, in a week or so, by July 4th."

"Ya, fook, my dad's favorite golfer is Tiger Woods. Not Rory McElroy or Graeme McDowell or Padrig Harrington, although he likes those Irish golfing gods, too and roots for them to beat everyone ... everyone but Tiger, of course."

"He likes Woods because as good as he was, he grinded for all 18 holes better than anyone on tour," Dei says, holding the clamshell while slipping on her other boot. "He didn't care about him hooking every white, black, and Asian models with a pulse wanting some. That's Pete… just be the best you can be and then outwork the 'loafers.' The other stuff, he says, you answer *only* to God.

"Outwork them all… and outdrink them. Work hard, play hard, and pray harder. Bring the wood. That's his mantra. His motto. His madness," Dei continues to recite, pulling her hair into a loose ponytail on the right side of her lovely face. "I thought Byrd knew."

Dei's ponytail bobs sideways quickly like she just got the after taste of the clam. She splits the clamshell into two halves.

"We're all fooked-up," she says talking into one half of the shell with the other up to her ear.

She pokes her arms in the air and spins.

"On Saturdays, for the last 10, 12, 15 years, I sit with Pete while my husband golfs. We listen for four hours to the Julio Brothers, three guys from Mexico, play Southern Rock."

"That is," I say convincingly, "is normal."

"Not me. Born in South Dakota. Half Irish … half Sioux. Adopted. Raised by a family in Charleston, South Carolina. French Huguenots. Girlfriend, that's fookin not normal."

"Yeah, you are so pretty, but you swear like a dude," I say. "Pete says you're so pretty you make the waves stop in the ocean from breaking just so the awed breakers can look at you longer."

"Awww. Sweet. He said that? He's never said anything nice to me except … he calls me his most half-Irish friend."

"And darlin," I say. "He calls you darling."

Dei holds a half clamshell over each eye.

"The sand is kicking up," she says.

"You should wear sunglasses."

"Never, blocks my soul. My eyes are the openings," she tells me, wiping some water from her eyes. "Tell me a secret about our Pistol Pete?"

"I can't."

"Tell the shell," she says, handing me one of the halves. "Tell the Great Calm of the Clam."

Reassuringly, she holds my hand with the shell up to my mouth and the other to her ear.

"One night at Braca's bar, maybe the first time he ever took me there, the first time I met Lynchie, Pete told me he was confused. How his parents, my grandparents, were Vietnam War protesters and loved life, everyone... except 'war-loving' politicians... so my dad wondered how his grandfather didn't love everyone... like..."

"Jesus?" she asks into the clamshell.

"No, my great grand poppy," I say as she puts the shell back to my mouth.

"He was a pro boxer whose only loss was to a buster who went on to fight Joe Louis. But, Pete's grandfather stopped watching pro sports in the 70's, saying the games were 'too fast.'

"His grandfather was Irish-Catholic. He went to church each morning before working 8 to 8 each day at a machine shop in Philadelphia. The 12-hour days - 20 hours of overtime each week - paid for the original Sea Isle house, the one that washed away in the 1962 storm everyone talks about down here like it was Hurricane Katrina.

"As much as my great grandfather loved sports, he couldn't watch games with Pete, his only grandson. He felt his grandkids wouldn't be able to make the pros with so many 'athletes.'

"Pete said his grandfather was the grandest guy, but he couldn't understand how even though he loved boxing, he wouldn't watch Muhammad Ali fight. How he still called him Cassius Clay.

"Pete boasted proudly how his grandfather did root for Joe Louis against Max Schmeling.

"I think it was only because Louis was American and Schmeling was a Nazi, Pete confessed that revealing night at Braca's."

Trembling, I hold the shell to Dei's mouth.

"The scar I have running down my right cheek is from being slashed with a knife on the Indian reservation in the Black Hills as a teen ... by my controlling drunken birth father. That's why I was adopted. Sent south. For safety. Freedom.

"My real parents were left-over hippies. When not high or drunk... or beat down by life, they were wonderful. They named me Destiny."

"Ohhhhh, Dei is short for Destiny," I say.

"Perhaps," she says, returning the half shell to my mouth, cupping the other still to her ear.

"The week after the bike ride, on the walk to Twisties, out of nowhere he just wondered aloud why God created earth, and why not go straight to heaven? 'Completely passing Go?'

"Another time, Pete philosophized if he wouldn't have been better off aborted, or miscarried, so he would enjoy eternal life rather than destined to sin in this life and be damned. But then, I thought, why didn't he think if he was aborted, then I wouldn't be here. And then sometimes I think it be better if I wasn't here...

"I know he always wanted a son. Now he has half of one."

Dei brushes my knotted hair with her tender hand. I've never been touched so affectionately ... well, except by Byrd."

"I always wanted a daughter," she tells me, putting the clamshell up to her mouth and looking out the side of her beautiful brown eyes to me. "I do think of you as my girl."

She holds the shell up to my mouth again.

"Last Sunday, on the walk to Twisties, Pete said how - since he missed mass earlier in the day - he offered to die on the spot to God. Right there on Pleasure Avenue. He knelt-down in the middle of the street, asking God to take him. Already, as punishment, he didn't play basketball on that Sunday morning. Instead he double-shifted drinking all through Sunday night.

"Uncle Matty told Pete he could *celebrate* mass at night instead of offering his soul right there on Pleasure Avenue, which only incited Pete more to martyr drink with his sympathetic Lids."

"And make up compound words that don't mean anything," Dei adds. "And make everyone else at the bar jealous. The Lids are lifetime friends. Not playground parent friends."

"I know Pete has a lot on his mind," I say into the shell. "He says in the game of life he has lost. He thinks he can only win in basketball. Pete wonders why he can't have a normal marriage … with my mom gone. He said life makes you drink your own bone marrow.

"He promised, singing like Mick Jagger, he wouldn't be a 'Beast of Burden' on anyone…

"Beast of Bourbon," Dei laughs into my shell. "He only does whiskey. He'll be a burden."

Using my left hand to hold her hand onto the shell wrapped by right hand, I continue freely, "Last summer, on one of our twisted walks to Twisties, as he tried to spit on the low-flying sea gulls, he said how he tried to be a good guy. But after not getting any nobber for years - that's his word he uses in front of me meaning a woman…

"I know," Dei injects, squeezing my hand.

"Oh, well, he said he broke down. Hooked up with a stranger lady. Said happened just once. A decade ago. Said did it far *fairly* from here. But said distance don't matter… said he's still doomed 'to run double-nickel suicides' in hell forever."

"Didn't know." Dei loosens her grip.

"That's when I first heard about Bianca," I spew like confessing my own sins. "Uncle Matty and Sim McManus, Phil Leyne and Johnny Mitchell, especially Mr. Meags, all bust on him about Bianca."

"Yeah, Bianca, they say, is a blow-up doll," she says. "At least he has one friend who isn't at least part Irish."

"Pete joshes, I think, back with them, saying 'Bianca loves him for who he is … and isn't,'" I say. "Sim asked if Bianca's last name was Jagger, 'the skinny singer of the Stones.' Pete said her last name 'wasn't as hard… it was 'Malleable.'

"I have to admit, naming a blowup doll Malleable made me laugh, even though it was my dad saying it. Byrd liked the name, too, when I told him the story recently. Actually, Byrd knew what malleable meant. He really doesn't just use big words to show off.

"And cute," I whisper into the shell.

"You saw Bianca?"

"No, Byrd is cute," I say.

"Of course, he is… and she is capable of being extended or shaped," Dei says.

Dei kisses the shell and whispers into it, "My turn again. I'm embarrassed South Carolina still flies the Confederate flag."

Suddenly, she skips her shell into the flat ocean. The shell dances over a wave, on the backside of a breaker for six hops before sinking.

"Now what's your sex secret," she says to me as innocent as asking someone their favorite color of Uggs, pressing the other half shell securely against my quivering lips and fears.

"I have balls," I blurt with shocking ease. A wave washes over my worn sneakers as I add, saying for the first time how "I was born with internal testes."

"Balls, you got me beat," she says as if I told her simply I had hair under my arms. "I just have web feet. That is why I wear these boots."

Dei eases the shell from my limp hand and skims my insecurities into the dark belly of a breaking wave.

"No one will know your secrets," she says

239

with a soothing brush to a lose-strand of hair over my eyes. "Our secrets."

"We all have secrets," a voice from behind says solemnly, scaring me.

"Hey Cal-holi! Holy fookin shit. You scared us. We're walking down for our surf lesson," Dei says. "Do you know Andie?"

"I know of her," this older guy with long black hair in a ponytail says. "But hey, that's why I'm walking up here, to let you know there are no *rideable* waves today. Another day… perhaps?"

"You're so nice for walking up to tell me," Dei says. "But the waves are good for sending secrets… you're still an a-hole for scaring us."

"I'll make it up to you guys with a free beach lesson," he says.

For the next hour, Cal-holi shows us how to stand on a surfboard in the sand. He rubs Dei's furry boot tops like a lap dog every time she pushes off too slowly to stand up.

"Faster jiving sister fanny," he sings.

We repeat over-and-over again. We practice pushing, hoping into a surfer's stance and then holding the pose as Cali-holi rocks the board.

I invite both Dei and Cal-holi to Twisties.

"I need to be back when my hubby returns from golf. That's his only rule down here. He finishes on Saturday's at 7, which is perfect because it's the end of Happy Hour at the Springfield, but on Sunday's he's back at 3 to watch a golf tourney on TV, so I gots to roll."

Using her perfect teeth again, she opens-up another clam and slurps it down. She hands one shell to Cal-holi and the other half to me. Cali-holi walks up toward Strathmere. We turn to see him whisper into the shell and skip it into the ocean. I hold onto my shell as we walk down toward the center of Sea Isle. Dei holds my other hand.

I watch her tap the bottom of her boots from her perch in the Spinnaker. The sand floats gently below onto a pack of skinny runners. She waves to me with her two sandy white socks. I whisper into my shell and skip it into the ocean.

The pack marches to Twisties.

"Onward," Pete commands.

"Indeed," Byrd agrees.

The pack morphs around Pete depending on what story he is telling. Some of the Lids want to hear some stories over. The Lids circle around Pete to hear him better and to be closer to the flask he occasionally packs. Byrd drifts from one side of Pete to the other keeping one eye on me, I think.

The pack's malleable shape includes the Lads, listening to Pete tell another story about someone's grandness or his own guilt over something. I am not close enough to hear, rather keeping an eye on Byrd. I do hear old man Sim McManus tell him to "shut the fook up and just spit on the sea gulls."

Silently mouthing sorry, Pete talks louder.

Byrd drapes his arm around my dad. They both down their beers before crossing Landis Avenue, where cops patrol as if the street that doubles as Ocean Drive was the Mexican border. Pete makes a left and says we should check out who is playing ball. "Drinking can wait," he says.

Pete stops at the War Memorial at Veterans Park by the Sea Isle Courts. He stands under the flags of Jersey, the USA and POW-MIA, makes a fisted salute and says, "Prayers for our Protectors."

He taps the "Basketball Only" sign on the fence at the courts, saying, "Of course basketball only. What else would anyone do here? Scrabble?"

We face the Lads' boxed rental home. The one right next to the red-orange building that the Lids say should be my "home locker room."

"We should take the Sea Isle City lifeguard rowboat from the roof of the Curran Family Real Estate building and paddle down river in life," Byrd says. "It's only one story high. And it would be a great-story. Us Lads need some stories like Pete and his bounce passing old boys."

When the straggling Lids all walk onto the basketball courts on JFK, Pete is holding court.

"You know about Rodney King," Pete says.

The younger guys, the Lads - Byrd, Jimmy Mitchell, Jumbo McManus and Tommy Meagher - none of them ever heard of Rodney King.

His beating by the Los Angeles police in 1991 was caught on video and sparked riots when the four white officers who beat him with nightsticks were acquitted. I know of it because Pete talked about the injustice of it all for years.

I know now that Rodney is dead. Police found him in his swimming pool last Sunday.

"Rodney King, Martin Luther King and The King, Elvis, are all goners," Pete says, running around the jump ball circle at mid-court.

No one is playing. The court is his stage.

Squatting like a coach in a huddle, Pete suggests drowning like Rodney is the way to go.

"Pete's hoping to die," I say to Byrd. "Fears he's going to sin more as he ages."

"I thought melanoma was Pete's exit strategy," Byrd says.

"Pete says, 'imagine how happy I'd be if I was really happy' when peaking on a good load.

Pete tells our pack standing here on JFK Boulevard in the middle of the middle of Sea Isle, how "King's beating after a high-speed car chase changed the dialogue on race in America."

With stretched hands, Matty flaps his arms.

"Follow the Gull," he says, flapping faster.

He leans like a wound seagull, points to the sign on Landis Avenue. The Follow the Gull signs dot Ocean Drive through all the shore towns as if points on a time line. You can follow the gull from Atlantic City to Cape May on the O.D.

"The race narrative in America won't change," he adds, now flapping the wings of his glasses, "just the names... follow the gull to Twisties... and let's get twisted."

He wants to turn off Pete. Uncle Matty calls his frequent strategy "Diffusion with Confusion."

"Hustle up, we're going to miss the end of the Open," Matty says. "The Tiger train is rolling."

"We can watch the playoff tomorrow," Pete says, "with mussels half-fookin-priced."

The pack crosses JFK and walks past the Heritage Surf Shop on 37th street, then past the Pirate Island mini-golf on 32nd. We split in two small packs, talking and laughing until we all bunched up at the lone traffic light on 29th Street.

Uncle Matty presses Pete's floppy hair like a traffic button. The light changes.

"Works every time," I tell Byrd, nudging closer to him, rubbing shoulders with each stride.

By the time we see the next 'Follow the Gull' sign, Pete revs up his unfinished lesson of the day.

"The four LAPD'ers, Briseno, Powell, Wind and Koon, yeah Koon, were indicted on charges of assault with a deadly weapon and excessive use of force by a police officer," Pete says.

"But following a three-month trial in the white Los Angeles suburb of Simi Valley, three of the officers were acquitted of all charges. The jury, which sat no black members, deadlocked on one charge of excessive force against Powell, so a mistrial was declared.

"King said last year on the 20th anniversary of his beating that he's forgiven the officers who beat him, saying 'yes, I've forgiven them, because I've been forgiven many times.'"

"Sounds like … "Uncle Matty begins to say when Pete finishes, "Yeah, like our Jesus."

Pete stops to water the weeds in front of the Dolphin Motel across the street from the dunes. The dunes look higher from street side. The growth is wilder, too. No houses are built on the ocean side from here to Strathmere.

Cali-holi waves, standing near a shiny diver's oxygen tank leaning against the mailbox at Bonz's Beach.

"Hey Cali-holi. What can't you mix your

own oxygen?" Pete yells while pissing on the shell of a turtle in the weeds. "I even mix my own air, and I'm not the brilliant business wizard like you, or the brilliant basketball coach like Calipari."

"What mix do you use, Mr. Wizard?" Cali-holi asks.

"Trimix 10/20/70," Pete yells, adjusting himself, "consisting of 10 percent oxygen, 20 percent nitrogen and 70 percent helium."

"Man, how do you remember?" Cali-holi says mockingly but Pete answers to show off.

"Simple to remember, it is easy man, I thought you were the science guy, the wizard," Pete returns the mock. "October 20, - you know 10/20 - and it was around 1970, the day Jacqueline Kennedy married Aristotle Onassis, ending any hopes of a return to Camelot... so 10/20/70."

I walk over to say hey to Cali-holi, to soften the sting from Pete's barbs.

"The marriage was actually in 1968," the surfer hippie says softly to me.

There are about a dozen wooden steps to the top of the dunes. Over the years, when the wind blows from the east, the beach sand is pushed up against the stairs so half of the stairs on the beach side are buried.

The wind barely blows this endless Sunday.

The walkway across the dunes is battered by the years. The crossing isn't wide enough, or sturdy enough, for all of us. Still Pete stops in the middle, backing everyone up, to "check out the tide." Pete could pee in the ocean from this perch. You can almost touch the surfers. You can almost touch the bay, too.

The narrowest strip on the island is here across from the Dolphin Motel on 9th street. I sit on the wooden rails above the dunes. It's high tide. The ocean and bay are so close, divided only by the length of a basketball court. Pete could cross in six dribbles, well seven at the most.

Even with the tide high like this, the ocean and the bay look so peaceful. As if they are not only getting along, but actually liking each other. Sure, Ocean Drive divides the ocean from the bay, but from the top of the dune, each one seems to be minding its own business. They don't seem to need to be divided by a concrete two-lane road.

I know, though, they are only a storm away from thrashing against each other. Another Storm like 1962 and they both will be raging. There will be destruction. People's lives will change. The world will watch. There is nothing anyone can do.

Then, after the storm, The Army Corps of Engineers will pump more sand onto the beach again to keep the ocean and the bay apart. The intervention works, at least for the time between storms. Then the ocean and the bay will collide again. I spot an empty swing slightly swinging on a porch up at 10th street.

"I can't figure out tides," Pete says. "Where does the water go?"

Inside of Twisties, the NBA playoff game is on the corner TV. The middle-aged blonde bartender with "B-ball yaboos" barely squeezed inside her pinkish-orange "Get Twisted at Twisties" tank top changes the channel to golf seeing Pete.

"Tiny," as Pete calls the blessed bartender, smiles at Byrd when she pours his pint.

Yeah, my dad's enjoying more than Father's Day with his new son.

I am glad Byrd isn't my real brother though... he's good looking and light skinned. The prissy college girls will like him.

Actually, our skin is about the same color... and I have some of the same plumbing he does... but he doesn't know about my equipment. It's not like you can feel my onions... only my dad and my girl doctor specialist up at Cooper Hospital in Camden know... and my mom, of course, but she's not around... and, oh yeah, now Dei.

My dad can't tell Byrd straight out. Fook, Pete makes up words so he can avoid talking straight. Like "Brewskaball," which after a few too many beers, becomes "baskbrewall," and somehow people know what the fook he means.

From a stool under the TV, Harry turns and points out to me that the newspaper article on the wall that says "Gimme Shelter" is always playing on the old jukebox here. Before playing the Stones again, Harry tells me his 30-day assignment to scout the *chilled* case is up and he is leaving.

A lady with a lumpy nape pumps her toddler's fist to Mick. She is standing in front of a black and white photo on the wall of a locomotive engine puffing across the bridge into Strathmere.

Harry stands. He plays the next song.

"41 Shots," Bruce sings.

I hope we don't do 41 shots here.

"This is the only Springsteen song my boys

and I knew growing up," Byrd whispers, leaning closer to me at the bar... checking out Tiny.

"You listened to a drinking song about doing 41 shots?" I ask, looking at his reflection, watching his eyes off the windows behind the bar.

"No, Sugar, 41 gun shots. The 41 shots the four New York cops took at unarmed Amadou Diallo, the Guinea immigrant... McMellon, Carroll, Murphy and Boss..."

"A cop named Boss," I say. "Seriously?"

"Serious enough to shoot him in a Bronx ally, not far from Fordham. My mom still reminds my sister of the case since she is right there at the Rose Hill campus," Byrd says staring into the bay.

"Diallo had only reached for his wallet ... but how were they supposed to know? Still 41 shots ... the cops were acquitted."

"The song is actually called "American Skin," Pete says over our shoulders. "Listen to the words. Always listen to the words. Words matter."

No one in Twisties sings along.

"41 shots they cut through the night... is it a gun... is it a knife... is it a wallet... this is your life... it ain't no secret my friend... you can get killed just living in your American skin..."

"If your life is worth living," Pete says, lifting the stool, smiling at Harry and then faking to crack him over his stuffed head, "you would rather be tried by 12 than carried by six."

"Tell me then, since I'm leaving tomorrow, did you whack the cop?" he interrogates snarkily.

"You mean like how Voldemort killed Harry's parents?" Pete asks without impertinence.

"You got a spell over everyone," Harrys says. "The coma cop talks more."

"You mean like a Petronius?" Pete says, wiping Harry's lenses with his sweaty shirt.

"I'm gone," Harry huffs, leaving his satchel on the bar.

We are all getting good and gone. The beers are flowing as free as Gimme Shelter again.

Looking out the screen door, past the rusted metal tower with a windmill, there is this secretive town's only traffic light... a blinking yellow light.

The blink-blink... blink-blink... blink-blink... syncs with my heartbeat.

A kid across the street screams, snapping me out of a peaceful trance. He gushes seeing a carload of cousins. I guess they are related since the two mommies look identical like Barbies.

My family is done watching golf. The Open is over. There will be no mussels on Monday. My family roars when a dude walks in front of the award ceremony wearing a Peacock hat and the announcer says, "enjoy the jail cell pal."

"Now that's a really *colored* dood," Pete says in his drunk Irish to Byrd.

Pete connects the winner, Webb Simpson, to O.J. Simpson and to the jail cell.

"They both got the same last name, but their lives are a bit different, Webb and O.J., now," Pete says softly without his odd Irish twang.

"I think Pete's afraid of screwing up his life like the Juice did," I say to Byrd. "I think that's why something so dangerous like scuba diving is his hobby."

"Or screwed up… he and John Rage both are diving again, but not together, though," Byrd says. I guess he knows more than me. "They've been diving the last couple of weeks for a German U-boat, a wreck 40 miles off Atlantic City."

"I know, Pete dove and saw the sunken Nazi sub U-869 off of Brielle in Central Jersey," I tell him. "Did you know he almost died? Came up to fast and almost got a bit of the bends."

"Don't tell me that," Byrd says.

"Yeah, when I yelled at him about being careless, Pete just said to me 'there gets a point in life where you need to want to live again,'" I tell Byrd. "Being on the edge, losing everything he's got makes him want to live again, I hope."

"Perhaps, that's why he deep sea dive again with Rage," Byrd says trying to be reassuring.

"He likes that Springsteen line, 'some guys, they just give up living and start dying little by little, piece by piece,'" I say. "He says Springsteen was influenced by the Catholic religion, too."

Pete plants himself at the corner of the bar next to a really good-looking Italian guy and his beautiful wife. It is Jay Wright, the Villanova coach, under a white baseball hat and with a few days growth of beard. The three of them just talk, and look out the back window to the bay where boats slowly motor by, keeping the wake down. I know it is Jay and Patti Wright because they've been coming to Strathmere for years, and she is a South Jersey girl from Bishop Eustace Prep, but none of the drinkers here notice and the Lids leave Twisties' royalty couple in peace.

Not Pete. He edges closer to Jay. Asking Tiny for the pen stuck in her cleavage, he scrawls on a paper napkin while talking to Coach Wright. He draws three X's with three O's, and then marks a zig-zag line, saying "he's the one with the ball off the inbound pass." Pete draws a straight line and then three dashes, saying "he dishes to the trailer for a 3-pointer . . . bang."

Politely, the Villanova coach folds the wrinkled napkin, tucks it inside the brim of his hat.

"Is that *the* Coach Wright?" Byrd asks before adding incredulously, "Pete is drawing up a play for a D-I coach... for a Big East coach..."

"You know, after failing to play more than one year in the Turkey pro league, Pete coached as an assistant at Afyion University, where he met my mom, a student from Ephesus, who is really pretty. She came over to the States, but felt guilty about me … and went back to Afyion."

"Guilty about you?"

"Ahh, yeah, she got pregnant before they were married," I spit out.

Hearing a "poof" over my shoulder, Harry pops over and puts his arm around me.

"Hey, it's the butler from Mr. Deeds," Byrd says. "The sneaky fast Emilio. Pesky too, bro."

"I couldn't leave yet without trying one more time, you know, sometimes talking about what someone did eases the guilt," he says to me.

"He already told you what he knows," I say.

"Did you know these chilly cases never go away," Harry says looking at Pete place the pencil back in Tiny's top.

"Huh?"

"Britain has a long love affair with them, dating back to the "Brides in the Bath Murder,' who drowned his first wife in the bath tub a century ago last year. He drowned two other wives … it took a couple of years to nab him before he was hung in 1915.

"His name was George Joseph Smith… "

"You mean like Joseph Smith the Mormon?" Pete interrupts, putting Harry in a headlock. "Blasphemus."

Byrd pries Pete's arms apart.

"Did you notice most of the middle-aged women wear like tennis skirts in the bar," Byrd says as Pete points to his empty glass, getting the attention of the other bartender. "Low enough to protect showing their ass, but high enough to get a rise out of the old guys. They are halfway teasers.

"Not the other bartender," I say, trying to force Pete into some bar banter with Harry. "She's all in ... she brings the wood."

She is younger than Tiny and not as big. Maybe mid-30s. Her brown hair flows to her ass.

"She must have been an athlete," Byrd marvels. "Her tanned legs are long and not much thicker at the top than above her knee. Her cutoff blue jean shorts are high enough where you see the back of her thigh melts like lava into her ass.

"Can't really tell where her butt begins and her thigh ends," Byrd whispers to me. "It's like life's perfect middle ground."

"Are you talking about Legs?" Pete asks while she hands him dark beer in a frosted mug.

"You mean the hoops player from ESPN? Byrd asks. "The great shooter... "

"No, my bartender with the lovely... hair."

Now, I plan to let my hair grow down to my balls, stroking a strand as I down this beer, my thoughts blinking like the yellow light, listening to Gimme Shelter as my dad, Pete, makes up names with his arm around Byrd after drawing up a play for Coach Wright, thinking of my own wrongs and twisted fate here celebrating Father's Day once again at Twisties... wanting to look like Tiny and Legs... wanting to visit my mom in Turkey... wanting to bring Byrd to meet her.

Chapter 13

My mom begged me to come home and visit. I hung my sneakers there for a few days and then drove down with my dad to meet the Lads and the Lids at The Pic, which is about halfway between our house in North Jersey and my new home down Sea Isle.

The Pic-A-Lilli Inn, a taproom in the middle of the Pine Barrens in the heart of South Jersey, looks like a log cabin. A little like the one in which Abe Lincoln was born, only with metal beer kegs stacked on the side porch.

My dad wanted to get there early because he didn't want Pete to leave without him.

Google Maps lists The Pic at U.S. 206, Shamong. Route 206 is a two-lane state highway running north and south. It divides the pines from the cranberry farms near Hammonton, runs through Trenton and Princeton and weaves for 30 miles to the Raritan Valley Country Club where my dad golfs in a league on Wednesday nights.

While waiting on The Pic's front porch, my dad and I read the history of this bar, which seems to jut out of nowhere in these coniferous clustered woods. The menu posted next to the door claims to serve the "world's best buffalo wings."

"These have to be Pete's boys," my dad says as two gray vehicles, a Range Rover and a Land Rover, appear out of the grainy shadows cast by the tall needle trees in the early morning sun. Sure enough, the Lids and the Lads spill out of the shiny SUVs driven by Catrina and Dei.

After she drops off her passengers, Catrina peels out so violently that the stones in the parking lot pepper the porch like bullets. Rocks almost hit Dei and her furry boots as she -ances away from her flashy wheels with the open sunroof.

"Hey, ya'll," she smiles with her blinding teeth brighter than the sun sneaky over the trees.

"Morning," my dad says. "Morning Miss.

"Gots to go," she says, pulling on the cabin's bolted door before scurrying around back.

We were all supposed to meet here at 6:15. No Pete still. I flip the bolt lock up and down.

"I'm acting casual," my dad says.

"No… cool," I correct him like Pete would.

Reading from the posted menu, my dad says, "Gene Autry and Will Rogers used to visit" as a white pickup truck hooks a wild right turn off 206 into the parking lot. Pete jumps out with the engine still running and Scoob whimpering. Squeezing his legs and the dog, Pete hustles behind The Pic, howling like a wounded wolf.

"But don't be too cool," I instruct my dad as Andie bounces over the railing onto the porch.

"This is my casual dad," I say to her.

She gives me a knuckle punch and says, "My casual pop invented the K-P," with an unusually nervous laugh, and then shakes my dad's outstretched hand.

My dad tells her she has a strong handshake when a black van pulls up nest to Pete's running truck. A black man gets out. With Scoob wobbling behind them, Pete and Dei emerge from the woods, wiping their hands on brown pine bristles, to greet him with hugs and a handshake.

"Use protection, boys... I gots extra sun block if ya'll need some mo," Dei says. She smiles mischievously and waves to us as she drives away.

Pete herds everyone over to the side door of the van. He doesn't take time for introductions. My dad says to anyone who'll listen, "Did you know Gene Autry and Will Rogers use to come here regularly?"

"Never met those cowboys!" Pete says.

Pete stops my dad from getting in through the side door of the van. He says, "*Youse* have to sit in the back of the bus with your son." I open the front side door and point for my dad to sit in the middle. I say to Pete, "But the van's color is black like us and not white like *youse*."

"Good call," Pete says with a one-huff laugh, offering my amused dad a high five.

The four bounce passing Lids and the three Lads with Andie pile in the back four rows of this old black cargo van. The two dads shake hands old school-like. Pete hops into the driver's seat and flips his truck keys to the black driver.

"Thanks Willie," Pete says, turning the key to the engine. The dog is on his lap. "Boys, Willie played at Middle Township for the grand Coach Feraco, who we played against when he was at Franklin & Marshall College.

"Willie brought the wood when he played."

My dad stretches out in the front seat next to Pete. I'm on the other side of my dad. I hold my knees, cupping them anxiously as if I'm sitting on the bench waiting to be called into the game.

Us Frontseaters have to raise our voices over the rattling and whining noises coming from the engine. Pete's borrowed black van, well the radiator squeals like a whining puppy. However, Scoob is now somewhere in the back seats.

"My dad played at Boston University under Pitino," I say louder the second time.

"Hi boys, Thomas Byrd here," my dad says, turning halfway around and waving his left arm to the Backseaters.

"Good to meet you Tom," Uncle Matty says with a welcoming back slap. "This is our escape north from our existence south each year."

"Do you call your mommy mammy?" Pete asks my dad. "Tom, can we call you Tommy?"

"Well, Pete, I prefer Thomas. But you, Peter, can call me Tommy. Just not Tom."

"We'll call you what you want," Pete says, possibly joking. "You're our stowaway. Stay still."

"Still as wearing my fresh starched levis in a coffin," my dad says with mocking obedience.

"Yeah like a harrier iced in a tub, man," Pete sings piously, "or someday on a twenty *dollor* bill."

"Nathaniel told me ya'll go to Boston to escape..."

"Our lives," Uncle Matty finishes for my dad. "We don't go for Independence week end..."

"But because it's the weekend after the NBA draft," Pete now finishes. "We go to lament another year without getting picked by the man."

"Yahoo, it's on," Andie screams out the window, "fookin 4th of July weekend."

Scoob has worked his way forward, climbs

onto my dad's lap, drooling on his golf pants.

Pete playfully elbows my dad's shoulder, advising him, "Don't worry, you can tell all your right wing, conservative NRA friends who will blow off three fingers today blasting fireworks they'll be reconstructed since Obama Care will cover their medical expenses."

During the ride up the New Jersey turnpike, my dad reads the notes I had texted to his iPad. He glances back at about every mile marker putting sleeping faces to my descriptions.

"Andie Duffy... she's about 5-9... really red hair, but darker skin than her dad... played high school ball at Archbishop Prendergast, the sister school of Monsignor Bonner called "Prendy.

"Sitting next to Andie is Jimmy Mitchell," my dad says to me. "He looks 6-2 even seated."

He looks down again and reads the notes on Mitch: "Precision player with the blond hair looks to match... Nate said he thinks he wants to be a priest, but can't tell his dad... good shooter, passer, but soft... went to St. Joe Prep, which is probably why he always corrects everyone's English... grew up across the river from Philly in Moorestown, which is 'rich like Rumson'...

"On the other side of Andie, by the open window giving us a whiff of the approaching Meadowlands air, is Jimbo McManus," My dad tells me after reading his notes and turning around. "Shaggy brown hair... 6-5 out of control player... tough rebounder, defender... Nate says he thinks he was abused as kid... Pennsauken kid who played at Camden Catholic..."

Turning back, my dad whispers, "That's Tommy Meagher sitting in the row with two of the dads, the Lids." He scrolls down. "Reddish brown hair... 6-7 shot blocker who says, "no beer past that point" when blocking a shot and in the bar when he is empty and a stranger walks by... Monsignor Bonner High in Drexel Hill 'where everyone practices basketball like a religion.'

"Was I casual enough?" my dad asks me.

I pat him on the head, like Pete does to me.

My dad doesn't like dogs, but he strokes Scoober on his lap and ignores the puddle of drool.

"Hey Pete," my dad says, initiating small talk. "I hear you went to Monsignor Bonner?"

"Yeah, it was an all-boys high school back then, Archbishop Prendergast was the girls school on the same hill," Pete says. "We were so poor I would cut holes in my pockets on Christmas morning so I had something to play with... while thinking of the girls from Prendy."

"Still must," a squished Tom Meagher yells, "cut his pocket, never pays for any brews."

"Yeah, *twas* a special place," Pete says. "Bunched up Irish kids with *holy* pant pockets.

"Our lovely mothers used to sew the miraculous medals of the saints inside our school jackets and when we fought in the school ground at lunch, all the medals would drop all over the recess yard... we had to find our medals before going back into the building, we were always late getting back from lunch and the nuns would whack us... but we had our medals... we would tell our moms we took the medals out of the jacket from their stitching to

260

hold while the nuns beat us… our moms would sew them back each night... *twas* a special place, indeed."

"Did you know John Cappelletti from Bonner?" my dad asks. "I know he won the Heisman Trophy playing for Penn State back in the early 70's…"

"Na, knew his younger brother, Joey," Pete says solemnly. "They made a movie about him…

"I knew Tina Fey, though," Pete adds, his voice rising above the whimpering Scoob. "She lived in the next town, Upper Darby, where Louie D's from. I knew her before she wore glasses."

"Nothing surprises me about The Hill," my dad says. "Who else do you know on TV?"

"For fooks' sake. Are you just trying to make conversation?" Pete asks, "huh, Tommy, or can I call you Terry? You don't have to chit-chat for old Pete's sake… even though *me* driving."

"Why would you call me Terry?"

"Didn't you play at Boston U. – aren't they the Terriers?"

"Makes sense to me," my dad acquiesces.

"You will like the Roisin Dubh," Pete says. "Although only the locals refer to the perfect place by the Gaelic name and everyone else calls the bar, The Black Rose."

Pete tells my dad they don't drink on the way since 10-years ago when they were all spruced up real-good. They "were real, real gone," and he made some bad decisions. He is not remembering details or many names, but he is still telling the story as if he was in court speaking to the judge.

"I once met this girl named Evangaline in Boston," Pete says as if a line from a country song.

I thought he was going to finally talk about a woman, but he suddenly changed course and started relaying about the guy they met who was responsible for the "Beat L.A." chant at the Boston Garden. He said it was after the Sixers beat the Celtics in Game 7 of the 1983 Eastern finals.

"I do remember the chant since I was at Boston University at the time and it was classy and cool," my dad says.

"We bought the guy shots all night," Pete boasts, centering his self in the story.

The Lids are passed out-like asleep in the back two rows, not listening to Pete grab-assing with my dad. Pete still turns around and talks to his boys as if they are awake. I look, too, but it's hard to distinguish them with their heads leaning on each other's shoulders and young Meagher's.

"He doesn't seem to mind at all," my dad says, pointing to Meags. "Or at least he isn't saying, 'no beer past that point' like when he blocks his one shot a game."

"So, three of youse dads all played college basketball, too," my dad continues.

"Duffy, Mitchell and McManus played at little Ursinus," Uncle Matty says, suddenly waking. "As seniors, they went to the Final Four in 1981. A freshman on the team was Steve Donahue, the Boston College coach.

"He's supposed to meet us at the Black Rose," Pete says. "Stevie D will show… for sure."

"I know," my dad says.

"How did ya'll know he's going to meet us?" Pete asks, genuinely confused.

"No," my dad says. "I know about youse guys back at Ursinus. "I got the scouting report on ya'll from Nathaniel."

"Let's hear," Pete says.

My dad reads his iPad: "Pete Duffy... a solid man at 5-10... prototype point guard...

"You're driving the van like I heard you ran the offense back in college and now at the courts on weekend morning," my dad ad-libs. He continues to read: " . . . he is the rock ..."

"Figures your name is Peter," my dad says before reading: " . . . thick brownish red hair... everyone calls him for books to read... makes up words... doesn't shut the fook up to steal one of his words... doesn't like the black... cop in coma."

"Go on," Pete nods.

"Leaning on young Meagher is Johnny Mitchell," my dad says. "He's Jimmy's dad."

He reads: "...only 6-1, but a power forward, thick and strong, not like me... thin blond hair... good guy who took care of his mother, Mary, when sick... tries to speak French to act worldly... played at Shawnee High School... grew up in rich Medford, but not old money rich like Moorestown... after Ursinus moved to Moorestown... technical writer or some techy-type job for Lockheed-Martin."

"By the window is Sim McManus," my dad says, looking back. "The dad of Jimbo and brother of Matty."

He reads: "6-4 center... likes to shoot

outside... brown shaggy hair... teased by Johnny Mitchell for not 'banging boards or broads'... played at Camden Catholic... grew up in Merchantville, moved to Pennsauken... works as a sports writer for the Post-Courier.

"Nate told me Sim tries to act smart too, which I think is funny, how he talks biology to girls, recites the five phases of mitosis at the bars," my dad now says. "Metaphase, anaphase, telophase, prophase... and...

"Prometaphase," Pete says, "but you didn't have the phases in order, prophase is first."

"Right," my dad says and then continues to read: "... about 6-4... looks like an ape with broad shoulders shaped and ripped like a bunch of bananas... his jaw juts out so far it looks like he could open coconuts with one bite... 'smells like the sweat twisted off of Byrd's socks,' is what Nathaniel said Pete said about him... a cat used to follow him home from kindergarten, so he 'must have always stunk,' Pete said."

The van already smells as we pass Giants Stadium, or MetLife as it's called now. My dad does analytics financial work with MetLife in the city, but he still calls it Giants Stadium.

"I can't believe the Super Bowl will be there next season," my dad says. "I should rent my house out to the rich folk coming from the south."

"You must like the Giants, living in North Jersey here," Pete says.

"I do."

"Well, the Jints sure do win when it counts," he says, nodding to the stadium.

"Yeah, winning Super Bowls is all that counts," agrees my dad.

"Who's your favorite all-time Giant?"

"Willie Mays."

Pete roars. "Good one bro, yeah the old baseball Giants. The Polo Grounds is a housing project, huh?

"How about your favorite New York Football Giants?"

"I don't really have one, like the team," my dad says. "If I had to pick, I'd say Jason Sehorn. Did you know he was the only white starting cornerback in the NFL over the last 15 years?"

"I didn't notice," Pete says.

"The law of large numbers really doesn't support how only Sehorn played corner," my dad says. "You would think just by math alone there would be another Sehorn.

"I think white kids who are good athletes aren't put at the cornerback position in youth football and certainly not in high school," he adds.

"You are very hermeneutic."

"Thanks, I believe in living in harmony," my dad says.

"*Hermeneutic*," Pete stresses, "study of methodological principles of interpretation… I'm a numbers guy, too, specifically 24 and 44."

"Oh, you mean like elucidating the Bible?"

"Exactly," Pete concurs.

"Or, the Civil Rights movement."

"Exactly."

"I think equal opportunity doesn't mean equal results," my dad says. "I think that's where the civil rights movement got it wrong. There shouldn't be equal numbers, only opportunity."

"Like Sehorn playing corner?" Pete asks.

"Exactly," my dad agrees with a single nod.

"Yeah, the Jints won what, two Super Bowls, with half-n-half corners," Pete says. "Amazing they could do it at half strength."

"You know your NFL," my dad compliments. "What's your team? Wait, don't tell me … the Packers, the Green Bay Packers."

"Yup. The old Packers."

"Not the Brett Favre-old Packers," my dad says, "you talkin' 'bout the Vince Lombardi-old Packers. The winning isn't the only thing, winning is everything Packers."

"Right on, the first sporting event I can remember watching was Super Bowl I – Packers against the Chiefs," Pete says. "Still got an old Packers jersey, but I cut the sleeves off since it was too tight as I got older.

"Probably," Pete turns to my dad, "you had to do that to your pants… when you hit puberty."

The Lids, who "escape north" to the Black Rose every summer but pack us Lads for the first time, are snoring like Rip Van Winkle on steroids.

Pete peeks at my dad's phone and asks, "Any more scouting reports?"

"Yeah. Way in the back of the van are two friends of the Ursinus dads," my dad says and then reads: "Phil Leyne… 6-3 powerful… daughters owned a bar outside Philly… high school basketball coach… big-time gambler… 'His face looks like Bird's ass,' Pete said about him.

"And by the window is Matty McManus," my dad adds and reads: "Uncle Matty... 6-4... brown shaggy hair like his brother... a tax collector... sometimes does 1,000-piece military history puzzles with Sim instead of going to Happy Hour at the Springfield."

Pete keeps checking the rear-view mirror.

The traffic on the turnpike is as crowded as my troubled thoughts about Pete... spying on him.

Tommy Meagher, from the back of the van, pleads to stop at his relative's pub, The Old Tavern in Union Square, "Please Pete, me gots a terrible thirst. Sometimes Frank McCourt drinks there... you can talk fondly about Irish misery."

Pete doesn't bite.

"Not enough time," Pete insists. "Wouldn't stop if the author and the former Dodgers owner, Frank McCourt, were both there and offered to pay for our Escape Road North ... we got to meet up with *me* friend, Auggie Saint Claire.

Pete pulls up to a parking garage around the block from Grand Central Station. I had thought we were driving all the way to Boston, but really I never asked. We park the van on the level below the street, past a freshly painted black and white sign: USED CARS SOLD HERE.

I shake hands with his friend, wishing Mr. Saint Claire, "all the best." I thank him. Everyone else scrambles to the exit sign where green arrows point to the tunnel to Grand Central.

Pete takes Uncle Matty's sunglasses and puts a leash on Scoob, following the dog onto the train. He tells the conductor, "Scoob are my eyes."

On the train all the talk revolves about basketball, beer… babes. Uncle Matty pokes Pete, saying, "We might run into your tangerine squeeze Evangaline." Even Andie chimes in with a joke how Bianca is "so holy she turns wine into water."

The Black Rose is a pub right out of Dublin's central casting, completely cozy with Scoob snoozing on the step here in the pretty and prestigious Faneuil Hall section of Boston. Everyone inside looks red, drunk and redundantly Irish already. Arguments and hugs spread equally around. Pete bashes "the man-made evils" of his own Catholic religion, which he says is the main current of his River Religion.

My dad questions some of his statements and tenets with Matty chipping in regularly.

"I went to college up here, Catholic too," my dad professes to Matty, who winks knowingly.

"Yeah, I knew I wasn't the only one who wants Pete to shut up on the priest sex scandals," Matty says. "And I was only raised Catholic."

Pete doesn't see patrons squirm around him since he's watching Scoob "drop deuce" in the middle of State Street.

There are at least a dozen Irish pubs in this fancy section of Boston. But this bar is Pete's favorite. He told me when we were taking a leak in the crowded bathroom downstairs. There was an old-time cigar machine against the wall, making me laugh to myself by thinking that not only is Pete old school, but he is up in smoke. He said we are here at the Black Rose for a toast to Roisin Dubh' and his, as well as his mates, ancestors.

Now, waiting outside the bathroom, leaning against the wooden and glass cigar case, is Coach Donahue of Boston College.

"Yo Bonzo," Pete says, pounding Donahue on the chest so hard I thought the cigar glass would break behind him.

Upstairs, I feared I was going to break Pete's voice box when, for about five minutes, he rambled about his lineage. When he paused for a refill, I retreated to a window where the sun shined on a quiet table, away from all the breathing.

Not wanting anyone to come over to talk, I read the parchment placemat: "During the civil disobedience in Ireland in 1848, the following nine men were captured tried and convicted of treason - John Mitchell, Morris Leyne, Pat Donahue, Thomas McGee, Charles Duffy, Thomas Meagher, Richard O'Gorman, Terrence McManus and Michael Ireland."

"But before passing the sentence," the place mat read, "the judge asked if anyone wished to say anything, when Meagher spoke: 'My Lord, this is our first offense, but not our last, if you will be easy with us this once, we promise on our word as gentleman to try to do better next time... and next time sure we won't be fools to get caught!'"

The judge sentenced them all to be hanged – 13 loops of the noose - until dead. However, the mat said a "passionate protest from throughout the world forced Queen Victoria to commute the punishment to banishment to Australia."

Pete walks over, puts a pint on the placemat and recites almost word by word what it says next:

"In 1874, word reached the astounded Queen Victoria that the Sir Charles Duffy, who had been elected Prime Minister of Australia, was the same Charles Duffy who had been banished 25 years before.

"On the Queen's demand, the whereabouts of the others banished with Duffy should be determined and the following was discovered…

"Thomas Francis Meagher," Pete bellows for the entire bar to hear, lifting his glass in a toast, tapping his glass with young Tommy Meagher, "Governor of Montana.

"To me Uncle Tommy," Tommy Meagher shouts. "We shall drink to him back in New York, too, with me other relations."

"Terrence McManus," Pete continues as the Lids and the Lads circle our table, tapping pints with Uncle Matty McManus, who turns and taps glasses with his son Jimbo, "Brigadier General, United States Army."

"Patrick Donahue," Pete adds, putting his arm around Coach Donahue, "Brigadier General United States Army."

I think is coach Donahue really related to this Patrick Donahue on the place mat, the one who Queen Victoria banished to Australia?

"Morris Leyne," Pete says, saluting toward Phil Leyne, who's leaning barely up against a nearby post. "Attorney General of Australia, the office of which Michael Ireland succeeded him."

"John Mitchell," Pete says, fist pumping Johnny Mitchell, who taps his pint glass with his son Jimmy. "Prominent New York politician, the man was father of John Purroy Mitchell, Mayor of New York at the outbreak of World War I."

Dozens of others in the bar crowd around my table now. As I stand and steal a swig from Pete's pint, I admit this is fascinating. Even if none of them are actually related. A coincidence?

"And to Richard O'Gorman, Governor General of Newfoundland and to Thomas D'Arcy McGee, Member of Parliament, Montreal Minister of Agriculture and President of the Council of Dominion of Canada..."

Pete concludes stoically. "May everybody someday find their ancestors as well... and properly toast them."

Hoisting Pete's glass with him, I see the TV above us showing MSNBC and the press conference covering President Obama, who just approved gay marriages.

"Do you have any famous ancestors? Pete asks my dad, sitting down at a table with him under the TV. I edge closer to hear.

"Just James Byrd," my dad says, taking a long draw, allowing the beer to give more courage. "He was murdered in Texas back in 1998."

"Yeah, three white boys drug him for three miles... tied barbarically to the back of their speeding pickup truck," Pete says.

"Byrd didn't die until his head and arm was severed ... the killers sped another mile... untied him from the bumper at a black cemetery in Jasper Texas.

"Those white devils weren't exactly Jasper the friendly ghost," Pete says. "Sorry... didn't know you were related... really, really sorry."

"Me too."

"James Byrd and Matthew Shepard have their names on the Hate Crimes Prevention Act signed by President Obama in 2009," Pete says. "Hasn't prevented hate... recently, a kid in his 20's from Katy, Texas was charged under this federal law for punching a black man as part of the fooking game knockout.

"And poor Shepard was the gay kid tortured and tied to a fence to die in Laramie, Wyoming," Pete continues with his encyclopedic knowledge. "He was born in Casper, Wyoming... the ghosts in the white sheets aren't friendly there either."

With her face even redder, Andie hugs two beers in one hand and puts her left arm around me.

She shoves the beers to me and hugs her dad, saying "Thanks for bringing us to The Black Rose... and adding precisely the proper mix of lessons and lunacy for us Lids."

I curl my arms around Andie and Pete, hoping my dad, who is talking with Coach D, doesn't see me.

Pete calls Andie his "little black rose." He hugs her, he brushes my arm off her shoulder, and then he says to her, "I love you . . . even more than this beautiful bar."

"We are going for a walk," Andie says to her dad with a wink. "See you in the morn."

The door of the tavern has bars over the little window in the center and has a black rose above the thick trim. On our way out, Andie turns and says, "Byrdie, here, he's *me* little black rose."

"Like a black rose," Pete yells to my dad still talking to Coach, "there's beauty in darkness."

The next morning, we bunch up on the train back to New York. Taking off her headphones, Andie nods for me to sit alone with her, away from the Lids and my dad. They are sleeping anyway.

"You know middle ground?' she asks hesitantly. "Like Legs... her ass?

"Oh yeah, a little bit," I say, thinking of the bartender in Twisties. Or was it the Springfield? Braca's? I think quickly back to Andie's taut ass.

"Bro, after last night I need to tell you how on a trip to Turkey, Pete informed me I was one the fookin lucky half percent of girls born with internal testes. He told me how my mom and him were torn what sex to designate... they chose Andie in case I was really an Andrew... so they split up... Pete feels like he failed as a dad, too.

"So, without my mom, and not knowing anything about girls, Pete raised me. I always had short hair. I played on boy's teams until I was 12-years-old. The Lids just called me a tomboy. After he told me this, I grew my hair.

"After seeing you look at Leg's lovely ass, I will grow my hair even longer... down to my ass."

In New York, we learn that Saint Claire's wife sold the black van to a scrap yard for parts.

Waiting for New Jersey Transit, my dad hasn't had his fill of Pete. Holding Scoob, he starts a conversation saying, "Hey Pete, did you know the first Super Bowl wasn't even called the Super Bowl? Did you know at halftime, the all-white

University of Arizona marching band played with the all-black Grambling College marching band?"

Pete answers with a staccato burst: "Indeed, bro, the new NFL wanted to show unity with the merger of the two leagues, the NFL and AFL. Also with the Civil Rights movement of the day… one of the songs the bands played together was called Waiting for Robert E. Lee… I still have a video tape of the game… and the halftime show of the Arizona band which closed with an O.K. Corral skit… the lawmen were outfitted in white and were shooting at the bad guys dressed in black."

Chapter 14

I am relieved Pete isn't still here with us in church. He left mass during the homily.

I know Pete knows we did the deed that night in Boston. He knows Andie and I hooked up. I don't want my relationship with Pete to change.

How, though, can it not?

I know he knows because he joked he got lucky too, spending the night with Bianca, who he says he packs away for every road trip because he "can't trust her alone at home with knives."

After mass, Andie opens the door to the confession box and enters. I close the door. The wooden seat in the opposite confessional without a priest invites my butt. Words aren't needed.

Feeling lighter, I count aloud the 13 steps I manage in descent. Each step returns more guilt.

Andie bounces, taking two steps at a time, looking more agitated than the perfect-haired priest, who chastised the congregation for getting to mass late and then ranted about the evils of homosexuality with equally angry venom.

Pete is going down. I feel his despair hanging on me, as heavy as his defense guarding me at the courts.

While looking for him, I see the light bulb is missing in the old black lantern on one side of the church. The statue of St. Joseph holding baby Jesus still looms above the entrance, but there is no sign of Pete. He left shortly after the horrible homily, looking like he was going to puke – just like he did the morning after we came back from our "walk" last weekend in Boston outside of the Black Rose.

On this overcast Sunday morning, Pete had slept in, passing on basketball after 7 o'clock mass. So, instead, we went 9 o'clock mass.

We walk by the rectory with the Blessed Mother statue in front. There is still no Pete. We walk to the Giovanni Deli across the street where he recovers with a ginger ale. The soda helps him burp during the entire walk home while humming the last song from mass, usually a sad Irish ballad.

We pick up the pace past Elements Salon, where we don't look in the window because Pete would not be getting a haircut. He cuts his own thick hair. We poke our heads down the block where the Basilicus Restaurant isn't open yet.

We walk back across the already bustling Landis Avenue, filled with kids holding their mother's hand with one and holding their whole future with the other. Some kids run away from their moms and halfway across Landis. Some of them turn around and go back. The others bust ahead, hustling to get to the beach in case it rains.

We cross the street. Perfect people wait outside of Mary Anne's Pastry's. No Pete. We walk up the block toward the bay and toward the yellow parish building with the one-way parking lot lanes. One way - seemingly like Pete. We trudge toward the dull yellow brick gym that's been changed forever into an auditorium. Changed forever... like me.

One block over is the bright yellow "Twin Gables" house "circa 1887" which seems like a place Pete would like to sleep. The two gables divide the roof unevenly. Strange.

Andie and I pick up the pace down Landis, past the church and to the shade-tree park on the corner. Andie darts over to the Knights of Columbus wooden cross, cleanly inscribed "Life is God's gift - In loving memory of the victims of Abortion. - Eagle Scout project."

"Pete once slept at the foot of the cross," she mumbles. "He wanted to repent before mass."

The air seems as still as her gaze … except for sporadic piercing shouts by the lovely mommies to "get back here, dammit, and hold my hand - we're crossing the street!"

Behind the cross, we see Pete's feet. His Chuck Taylors with the star on the side are untied.

"Unless he left his legs there, "Andie says, "Pete, is there, too, under the cross."

Pete is lying down with his head up and resting against the back base of the crucifix.

"Let him sleep," Andie says, patting his head. "He looks so foo… peaceful."

She sits on one side to block the unsightly view of her dad by the lovely mommies dragging their perfect kids to the 10:15 mass. I sit on the other side, blocking the other unsightly half of Pete. With my back to Andie, I lean so our shoulders touching lightly. This gives me a better view of more lovely mommies who either skipped mass, or aren't Catholic, or who don't need God before dragging their screaming kids to the beach.

"You can always tell the mommies who go to mass," Pete told me before explaining how "they aren't as tan as the other lovely mommies."

With Pete snoring, I think not having her mom around, life must seem half empty to Andie. The older guys, the loveable Lids, are like her family. Being around the Lids, though, surely isn't the same as a mother's love. They think of girls not much differently than betting on a horse race.

Uncle Matty and Sim think of particularly lovely ladies as either hitting the exacta or trifecta or the "damn daily double."

For the McManus men, a babe is an exacta if she is good looking and nice. She is a trifecta if she is pretty, nice, and her dad has money. She is the "damn daily double" if she is good looking, nice, her dad has money and she can make a great lunch - preferably a bologna or salami sandwich.

And the Lids don't call girls a "10" or say, "she's hot" like normal white guys, except sometimes when around Andie. They guess the age of ladies at the bars by saying the number a player wore, like calling her a "Pete Maravich" if they think she is 44, or a "Magic Johnson" if they think she is 32 years old.

The old guys think and talk of aging women in basketball terms. Pete will say 'she's a slam dunk," or a "long 3-pointer" if he digs her.

Funny, but surely not surprising, Andie, actually thinks of everything in sports terms, too.

For her, if something is good, it is a "double off the wall" or it is "in the back of the net" or it is "a fookin first down." If something sucks, it is "a line drive double play," or it "hit the fooking post" or it is a "fookin fumble on the goal line." However, she never talks about girls in these terms. Actually, she never talks about girls.

"We really need a double-off-the-wall day," she says, looking down at her dad, who is now curled up behind the cross like a newborn.

In between two ripping snores by Pete and trying to sound positive like him on the courts, I say, "I can feel a line drive in the gap coming."

One drop of rain kisses his forehead. Andie is right. This is shaping up now to be a "triple down the line" morning as Pete jumps up again. He swipes the rain off like he is getting out of the shower. Like it is perfectly normal to leave church and sleep outside the echo of the priest.

When it rains here, all the lovely moms and their perfect kids, who surely will get scholarships to Division I schools, march up to the promenade.

The Lids, who don't go to mass, like the now "Meditative Mormon," as Pete calls Uncle Matty, meet at Pete's place. They watch old Notre Dame football videos when it's raining on weekend mornings.

For the last couple of weeks, Pete has been saying that we are going to the Deauville Inn down in Strathmere to see this "cool Conklin cat," a sports comedian from Philly who's on the radio. So, I'm hoping this morning that watching Notre Dame tapes will wait until the next rainy day.

Still, we slug around Pete's house on another rain day. But Pete, himself, doesn't stick around to watch the ND videos. He goes scuba diving with Rage. I doze on and off, spread out on the floor, using a pile of socks as my pillow.

Andie nods off, too. Eventually, when the

Lids slowly leave, we both crash separately on cushy chairs by the open window

The rain bounces off the sill as I awaken. It cools off the thick air.

I had the fever dream again: I shoot the basketball... down 64-62... from half court... going in... thousands of other basketballs come flying out of the stands... no one sees mine go in... crushed under the bottom of the pile... I look for my ball... instead there is Pete... in his scuba gear... his mask fogs up...

We lug Scoobs with us to the Deauville Inn. We are meeting some of the Lids there for late afternoon brews. Andie drives slowly, pumping the brakes in the middle of blocks. She drives with one eye looking out the window at the houses across from the beach. We go from 19th street in Strathmere just after a stretch of empty dunes, past Dolphin Beach where the ocean and bay are divided by little more than just us. Andie pumps the brakes at Whale Creek Marina and at the Gray Gull House then drives past the trailer park, past Mildred's Store and past the drab blue library, where there should be a book about Pete.

The Deauville's back windows frame paddle boarders on the bay.

"Watch... the paddlers never cross under the bridge," Pete says, sneaking up behind us like Harry. "They never cross where the bay actually meets the ocean on the other side of the bridge... where the water is rough, where life is lived... and it's low tide..."

A spirited chorus of seagulls, clam-down on

a sand bar in the middle of the bay. A plane towing an advertising banner for "Mike's Mussels Monday" putt-putts overhead, barely moving. A dozen lifeguard boats bob along in the flat water on the other side of the bridge, rowed by young kids, perhaps aspiring lifeguards. The noise of a single jet skier interrupts the squawking of the seagulls and the peaceful putting of the plane. You can't hear the smooth strokes of the paddle boarders anymore or the heavy oars of the lifeguard boats splashing in the blue-gray water

Pulling up on the outside deck, past the host, Pete points to two older people getting out of a golf cart. Their wrap-around sunglasses are flipped up on their obviously dyed hair. Pete says, "They don't cross under the bridge either."

Already, on stage, Conklin spoofs on Gerry Sandusky.

Earlier in the week the Louie Freeh's report on Paterno came out. It basically said the Penn State coach looked the other way when his defensive coordinator was abusing young boys on campus at the football facility.

"You're never too old to fook up your life," Pete says to me, handing me a beer. He is wearing a scuba mask flipped up on top of his head.

Rage, sitting at the corner of the bar near the pirate carving, yells something inaudible, but he looks angry, like he's defending Paterno and knocking Conklin.

Pete perks up during the middle of the skit and yells, "If Paterno was black, he would've been lynched, and instead student rallies are held for Joe

Pa in State College."

The afternooners pour into the Deauville, but Pete and Rage behave like the bar is the Rock's living room and they are watching Notre Dame videos.

Conklin's act is funny, though maybe not as funny as Pete looks. Pete is still all red and tired from drinking all last night, puking at church, diving with the ranting Rage and now drinking with his scuba mask on top of his head.

"Conklin's a Philadelphia guy, too," Andie says. "Pete doesn't care when he mocks him."

"Why?"

"Conklin went to Cardinal Dougherty, which in 1970 was the largest Catholic High School in the country," she says. "Now the north Philadelphia school is closed."

"Seems like Pete isn't the only one left behind by time," I say, trying to get a reaction from Andie. She pops some M&Ms from the back pocket of her basketball shorts into her mouth.

Pete leans against the large pirate woodcarving, which is about his height. He looks like an old salt. He puts Uncle Matty's glasses on top of the wooden statue.

Conklin starts spewing one-liners: "Pete likes dog more than people – he says the food cost less on a date and they kiss longer... Pete would turn down an invitation to the Resurrection if he didn't have a front row seat... Pete said he would take any guy on his team if he could help them win... even Pontius Pilate, but Pete said he'd rather take Barabbas... Pete was a catcher at Monsignor

Bonner High School, after losing by a walk-off home run to my Dougherty team in the Catholic League playoffs he laid over home plate so it couldn't be tagged for the winning run, the ump had to drag him off the plate, but Pete didn't care since it was the only time in high school he ever got laid."

Pete pushes the comedian to the side, takes the reading glasses off the pirate, and gets up on stage.

"Conklin went to the Apple store to buy a phone and this genius looking guy, or maybe it was a girl, asked him if he wanted to buy the black phone or the white one?" Pete pauses and holds the frames of the glasses as if he is thinking. "Conklin asked does the black phone run faster and jump higher than the white phone?"

Rage stumbles over. Spilling his beer, he leans and says, "See what I mean? He did it."

"Fooking stretch, he just said if Paterno was black he would've been lynched," I say.

From the jukebox blasts The Who.

"Pete must be The Who's last freak," I say to Andie.

"If my dad had a choice of being Pete Maravich or Pete Townsend, he would take Townsend," she says in a disappointed tone. "There is no magic in life left for him, the magic of 44 is gone, even though he still wears floppy wigwam socks like the Pistol ... and the surfer dude Cali-holi across from Dolphin Beach."

"Why they call him Cali-holi and not Cali-Poly, like where he's from?" I ask.

"Because he's so holy, get it?"

"No."

"Bro, he gave away all the money he made down here pretty much to help locals flip their homes into money-making side-by-side rentals, the police build a new station and the fire department to get new trucks," she says. "Then a new resin was developed...

"He's out of luck."

"You mean, he's beached," I say.

"He's such a good guy," Andie adds. "People say he's the anti-Pete. My dad even says he likes Cali-holi more than his own self, but not more than basketball and The Who, and he doesn't hang with the guy."

Outside the paddle boarders on the bay still paddle. They don't cross under the bridge. They paddle in a cozy circle... not paddling down river in life... upright as stiff as the wooden pirate.

Chapter 15

Pete squeezes the ball, pressing with both hands and elbows out wide, rocking back and fro.

A young kid, maybe 12-years-old or so, follows the basketball – his ball – to midcourt.

"Excuse, m… m… m… me sir," the white kid stutters.

"Pull, boy."

"Please."

"You, boy, got to want it."

The kid pulls. His tight LeBron jersey stretches.

"Just give him the ball before you're rightfully arrested," Andie says.

"Someone has to learn him to hold on to what's important in life," Pete says. "Nothing's more important than the rock at the courts.

"Who's going to learn him, when I'm gone?"

"Where you going?" I ask.

"Boy, we're all going."

Pete releases the ball.

The rock rolls to the other court. The kid follows the ball, not picking it up. Another kid wearing LeBron's Heat jersey picks up the ball.

Pete patrols over to the two kids. He shows them how to follow-through on the shots.

"You got to change your shot to play with the big boys," Pete says. "Don't chuck 'n duck it. Get your elbow above your eye on the folo… and always bring the wood."

There is no wind to change my shot now.

The usual crew gathers, arriving like clockwork with the typically hot early morning July sun. The Lids, except for Uncle Matty, joust each other, serving barbs from the bar last night.

They haven't seen each other for five hours.

We all prepare to play in our own way. Pete taunts kids. Andie tapes up. I pretend to stretch.

Andie snugs the tape, making a figure-8 around her right ankle. She can't pull any tighter... she would if she could.

Pete dribbles the ball high above his hips, unlike his usual pregame rapid routine.

He told Andie and me on the slow drive through the low marine fog from Sea Isle down to Avalon how he is 'supremely' worried about Uncle Matt, whose mother passed away from breast cancer earlier in the week. All the Bounce-passers went to the funeral up at St. Bernadette's Church in Drexel Hill, a Lids reunion in the hood, where she was a teacher. Pete said I could go, saying to me "my lawn needs cutting."

I blew it not going to The Hill for the funeral mass. Rage wouldn't let me break the networking session Tuesday, saying "they don't need you at the Mass of the Resurrection, if she was a good lady, she'll go to heaven, if she was bad, she'll be babysitting Pete for eternity."

"Would they attend the coma cop's Mass of the Resurrection?" Rage had asked me. "They don't even talk about the poor guy."

We meet every Tuesday because the cop didn't want to chance one of the old guys being so hung over from Sunday's drinking he would not make it to work and hang around Sea Isle until late Monday. He doesn't care Cali-holi sees us on the dune, saying, "He doesn't have any friends to tell."

The networking logistics works out fine. I keep telling Andie and the Lads I'm running in the soft sand up to Strathmere. They never ask to join me every Tuesday and Thursday for the workout, but instead do dribbling drills behind the house or practice bounce passing against the sidewall.

The ten-block stretch of high dunes between the bay and the ocean where there are no houses is still secluded even in the middle of the summer. No one uses this path where the highest dune opening meets the street even though there is a Port-O-John.

Rage thinks the family will pull the plug on the cop. He told me he is afraid the case will then just die. My dad thinks he wants a promotion to lieutenant from sergeant and the $10,000 pay bump before retiring in the fall at 24 years on the job, not even hanging on until 25.

There's urgency, I think, now with the pressure from Rage to pin Pete. Justice he repeats.

In the seven or eight meetings down Strathmere with Mr. John Rage, I don't think I told him anything he didn't know about Pete. He actually told me more about Pete.

And he is diving with him again.

During one meeting, I asked Rage about deep sea diving. But he really didn't tell me anything I couldn't figure out. He said they both like getting away from people and hunting for the past, so they started diving a few years back as a once-a-month hobby. But then they started finding history. Pete got competitive. They started diving more, trying to uncover the past, beat each other.

They stopped diving together after the cop was beaten. Just started up again a few weeks ago.

Last Tuesday, I told him, Pete says "it's easy to play basketball when the shots fall."

But I wouldn't just tell him what Pete said. I would translate the meanings, like it is always easy to play basketball when the shots fall also means it is easy to live and be nice to people when life is going right, like the job, kids and wife are all clicking well. I told Rage that is the way he lived. When things didn't go right for Pete, like in a meaningless pickup basketball game down the shore or in the middle of real life, he was at his best, using all his life lessons to be at his best.

Rage recorded every word on his new white iPhone. Always. But I could tell he didn't like my translations. He would fake throwing his phone into the ocean when I started analyzing.

At least Rage didn't press me much. He listened when I told him Pete wonders why players today don't pose together on cards like Mickey Mantle and Willie Mays did. Any white and black issue allowed me to stall... and Rage to record.

Pete said with "all the great Hispanic players in baseball, there aren't many white and black all-stars to pose like the real M&M – not Eminem the rapper."

I told Rage how I don't see how that is a racist statement. There are more Dominican players than ever in MLB. Turning double plays in the streets is what they do down in Santo Domingo.

Even I know this.

I remember playing Little League as a kid in the mixed neighborhood we lived in before moving to leafy Rumson. A Hispanic kid was put on my team and he didn't even know what glove to use. He didn't know what hand he threw with or anything. But my dad gave him a right-handed glove and the kid went to second base and started turning double plays like he was Robinson Cano. We all laughed, especially the parents, both white and black, who said it was like the movie Airplane where missionaries gave basketballs to black guys in Africa and they immediately reverse dunked.

Anyway, the Hispanic kid batted left-handed. We never knew if he threw lefty, too, because he was so good throwing right-handed.

Rage stayed stoic mostly when I told him what I knew about Pete, but I knew these stories weren't incriminating Pete a lick.

I told him how he used to shoot free throws naked in his Drexel Hill back yard as a kid... to put more pressure on himself to get back into the house quicker so his mom wouldn't see him... and how he made 100 in a row one time in the rain.

And like how he would say to ladies at the bar "let's just get naked and say words that don't matter" just to scare them away so he could talk baskosophy with his old boys...

Always, in the beginning of my rat session, Rage asked me if Pete said anything race related during the week. Of course, he always did, as much as he dribbled during a pickup game.

But the stories were like the kid Hispanic

baseball player… and like Pete said more than once "how he used to wonder how can anyone really enjoy life when you know you will die at the end. But then he saw his mom die and felt her warm spirit float away" and how he said that while holding her head "life suddenly made sense, that it was the end of your spiritual journey, that it was up to you to get to know God better, up to you to become your own spiritual vessel."

Rage never seemed impressed how I could quote Pete word by word. He always wanted to know more what he said about blacks and whites.

One session, when the clouds were dark and low, Rage asked if Pete ever used the N-word.

He never did, which made Rage oddly look disappointed when I told him. I did tell him Pete thought it was lyrical and lovely how Mark Twain used the N-word in Huck Finn. He said it was local color, how the use of the word was historically real. How Pete said the use of real words and how'd people spoke at the time, is owed to the reader by the writer.

And I told Rage how Stephen A. Smith used the N-word on ESPN more than once.

I told Rage how Pete went on one of his moral compass soliloquy soapbox, saying "he's jealous of blacks because they're so fooking grand in basketball and how he feels guilty that he's so fookin grandly jealous."

Rage perked up when I told him this, but his interest waned when I stressed he hated being jealous – not hated blacks.

He asked me if I thought Pete wants to beat

blacks in basketball because they are black. Rage rarely asked me what I thought, so I remembered this. I told him no way, how Pete is "just envious of blacks in basketball because we're good."

I told him, "Twisted, but for Pete, it is like wanting a lady he meets at the bar, how he prays not to want her because it is wrong, but he is really not into the prayer, like saying the prayer with the same meaning as he did when his mother was passing. He says the prayer not wanting the woman 'isn't game point intensity' and so the prayer is 'just a bunch of wasted words.'"

Andie's ankles are taped.

I know we think we have a chance to beat the old guys without Matty, since he does the tough stuff Pete loves in the center of the court.

Tommy Meagher's dad is down for the weekend, so he steps in for Matty. Old Meags isn't as tall as Tommy, but he is thicker and a good 6-5.

Pete always says to me to "take the fight to the middle of court, Byrd, just like in life," during games, even when playing against me. After the game, he says to me always "you want to play in the middle, live in the middle, paddle to the middle of the rough waters... even though the middle man harbors the most guilt."

Mr. Meags must be loaded with guilt since he plays in the middle every possession.

Of course, we lose again.

We must be about 0-for-10 against the Bouncepassers this summer. After missing my first 10 shots in that first game, I am starting to make some jumpers, just not enough.

While we sit, bathing in our latest loss to the Lids, Uncle Matty pulls up in his shiny silver jaguar. He shakes old man Meags' hands with a "way to fill-in," and gives the white bro hug to all his old boys. He pats the heads of us young guys.

"I'm sitting this one out," Pete says as he walks with Matty over to the swings. They each sit for a few minutes before coming back over.

In between games, I ask Pete what he said to Uncle Matty and he immediately starts telling the story of hiking in the high Sierra's last July on the third anniversary of his mom's passing away.

"Two nights before my mom passed away, I didn't know she was going, I was in the hospital room alone with her except for the TV, which was showing the PGA Pro-Am golf tournament from Lake Tahoe.

"My mom and I enjoyed a family trip there a few years back, spent a lot of time talking about life while outside sitting on the picnic tables, intercepting the coolest of breezes.

"I told her I would take her back to Tahoe when she was out and she reached over and patted my face, like she used to do when I was a kid. She rolled over away from me. I didn't know then, but I did later, she was saying goodbye.

"A month later I went to Tahoe. I was taking her spirit back with me. Before I geared up at the REI in Sacramento, I went to the Jesuit Church for Sunday night mass. I didn't know why I went since I had a lot of food packages and water treatment pills to buy for a week solo hike in Desolation Wilderness to climb Mount Tallac and look down upon Lake Tahoe, ... with my mom.

"I guess my mom's spirit was alive in me since she always taught me to be open. During the homily, the Irish Jesuit priest talked about being open minded because in the news that week was a controversy of Catholic schools not being open to the President speaking to their students because of his stance on abortion. The priest talked about the importance of being open minded on issues like homosexuality even though you disagreed. He said Jesus used the Aramaic word "ephphatha" – to be open – in Matthew's gospel when he told the blind man to open his eyes and see.

"So, by being open minded, going to church because of my mom, I learned a word for my core belief of being open minded," Pete says. "I had the word ephphatha – when I tell the story about Sir John Franklin, whose epitaph said he perished of rigid thought – for my leadership lectures."

"Oh yeah, ephphatha," Uncle Matty comes over and says, "I'll tell Byrd who Franklin is.

"Sir John Franklin led an expedition across Canada in the mid 1800's to find the Northwest Passage to the Pacific Ocean. Of course, there was none and he had to winter in northern British Columbia, near Alaska," Uncle Matty says. "Well, it was there that he and his 168 men died.

"Franklin and his men died of starvation and deprivation while the Inuits around him thrived. You see, like his epitaph said, he died of rigid thought because he didn't accept the way the Inuits lived and instead died. If he was open minded, they would've lived - ephphatha."

"And he was a knight, old dead Sir Franklin was," Andie says, leaning into the lecture.

"Indeed, Andie, you've heard this life lesson more than once," Uncle Matty says.

"But I never heard the story about my grandmother and you hiking in Lake Tahoe," she says to her dad.

"Well, I guess I was feeling sorry for myself and I didn't want you to ever feel that way when I'm good and gone," Pete says. "I felt like there was no one left to please with her gone, so I didn't care if a bear ate me up in Desolation Wilderness. But then my mom showed me... how I was meant to go on... at the time.

"I remember the exact spot when it happened, I needed a break around noon so I decided to rest near Katherine Lake for an hour. Then I would hike all afternoon to get to the base of Mt. Tallac to make it up the next day. I found a grand spot about a couple hundred yards off the trail. It was a cove, surrounded by trees and this one giant sequoia at a small opening. I went inside the cave-like structure and slept for an hour. The grandest, best rest of me life.

"Refreshed, I reached where I wanted to camp. In the morning, I summited Mt. Tallac, with my mom's spirit. But, I was still depressed even though I was on top of the mountain... until I hiked the four miles back to the cove, the exact spot where I rested the day before.

"I planned on resting for an hour there once again. But I couldn't find the spot. I was on the right trail, but the opening wasn't there. As I got closer, I saw that an eight-foot wall... of something... had blocked the opening.

"It was the giant tree...

"The sequoia, which had to be 200 and some years old, had fallen right over the spot where I slept just 24 hours earlier. The tree had to be 75-feet tall. If it fell on me, no one would've found me. The enlightening spot was off the beaten track a couple of hundred yards. And even if anyone knew I was there, they would've found nothing but teeth and toes.

"I stood and stared at the tree for 15 minutes, realizing that the whole time my mom had been with me, telling me it was not my time to go, telling me to keep marching on."

"Eph... fookin... phatha."

Pete springs up quickly, like today he is meant to be the most alive that he has ever been, and jumps over to Uncle Matty, who is squatting against the bleachers behind us.

"I know you're hurting, bro, without your mom here. She not only taught religion at St Bernadette's to so many of us, she more importantly taught you to be open minded about religion when you were studying the Dead Sea scrolls in college," Pete whispers these words to him loud enough for me to hear as I edge a few feet closer and fake like I am stretching.

"She wants you to keep marching on, to keep teaching others, to keep showing how to be open minded to God... not to race to the tomb."

Matty's head slumps showing his balding spot widening more. His glasses fall under the bleachers. Scoob scurries under the bench and brings back the specs to him.

"I remember how you were confused that Judaism, Christianity and Islam each traced their ancestors to the prophet Abraham and their practitioners worship the same divinity - the God who made Himself known to Abraham," Pete keeps preaching, standing on the bleachers.

"Yeah, these faiths are known as Abrahamic," Matty says, sounding a bit like his old self. "The Dead Sea scrolls help to show Judaism and Christianity emerged from the same religious tradition of ancient Israel - both identified themselves as the children of Israel and not as Jews or Christians."

"Exactly, you accepted other religions, you Mormon lover," Pete said. "Fookin ephphatha – be open baby. Love the Mormons, Jesus does."

"Yeah, but I can't even spell ephphatha now and you want me to live it," Matty says, wiping the grass off his glasses.

"How can you dispute the Dead Sea Scrolls? They're the oldest existing copies of the Hebrew bible, written when Judaism and Christianity was formed," Pete says, sounding like his old self, questioning his life-long friend.

"Listen to you Pete," Matty says, defiantly, really sounding like his old self now, "you went to see the Dead Sea scrolls exhibit at the Franklin Institute, you bury Sir John Franklin's legacy… and you said you 'weren't sure the Ten Commandments were real' and now you're preaching to me…"

"Only said that about the Big Ten because I

personally don't think, rather I don't agree that man and woman should marry, it fooks up their friendship. That's all, I buy the other nine," Pete says laughing and rubbing Matty's balding head.

"I liked your story about ephphatha," I say, finished my fake stretching.

"Thanks, me dear mom taught me to be open minded," Pete says as if he was always open-minded about being open-minded. "She taught me to think, to read, how to talk …

"I had a speech impediment. My mom didn't want boys to mock me in kindergarten. I didn't care, I figured as-long-as I was good in basketball, no one would care how I talked.

"She spent years with me on the porch working on pronunciation. I would sit on the swing on summer evenings while she spent an hour teaching me how to say my TH's, L's and M's by showing me where to place my tongue.

"I still couldn't do it, but she still worked with me. I told her life was unfair. She shushed me and said, 'no one promised you a rose garden.' Finally, a doctor diagnosed me as needing an operation to snip the part of the tongue that holds it to the bottom of the mouth. It was too long and I couldn't control it.

"That's a shame you got it snipped," Uncle Matty says, wagging his tongue at Pete, "Bianca would like you more."

"She loves me enough," Pete says, blowing a kiss at him.

"We still did the speech exercises for a year, even into the summer after kindergarten, sitting on the swing I learned more from my mom than how to speak… she read me the entire Encyclopedia Britannica, except for the volume M-N because I used it as home plate one night in the backyard and left it out in the rain.

"A year after her passing, I went back to the house. The new owners took down the swing. But there were still the two holes in the ceiling where hooks for the chains hung.

"When I close me eyes while diving, I'm sitting on the swing on the porch… and playing basketball down here with Andie and you Matty… and youse young guys, Byrdie, and me old guys playing against each other… as if life's indeed a rose garden… making time swing back and forth… like me mom's here and gone at the same time… I still see our old porch swing… swinging."

Chapter 16

Time swung by the summer, ripping right through the end of July and all of August. Like Pete leading a fast break on the court or telling another story, or making a new friend or meeting an old one, either at a bar, or at the courts, or at Wawa. We played ball on weekend mornings in Avalon. Drank the rest of the afternoon and nights in Sea Isle. I continued to meet with the cop every Tuesday. The same cycle every week, like pregame layup lines. Still, we couldn't beat the Lids in basketball. I used the word "ephphatha" every chance I could.

Nothing seemed to change.

Pete and Uncle Matty discussed intellectual dilemmas worthy of Nobel Prize consideration. One discussion rising to particular masked brilliance was when the clock in a game hit 0:00.

Pete argued the side that the 0:00 was an event in the game, just like at 0:01 and 10:01 was an event. Uncle Matty theorized the game was over at 0:00 so it wasn't an event in the game because it couldn't affect the outcome of the game. They even took their discussion to writing dissenting opinions on the subject and emailing the New York Times and Britannica.com.

Yeah, nothing changed.

Except that over the summer my drinking improved more than my basketball. My relationship with Andie grew with each dribble and drink. So, did my admiration for Pete.

I certainly didn't tell John Rage any of my feelings on the last Tuesday we met before going away to Collegeville here. I just told him the normal, routine, what-we-did stuff and the Pete Parables, especially all the ones I couldn't stop thinking about. Like how the first Saturday night in August, we grinded the 10-mile run on the beach in Sea Isle City.

The annual race raises money for the SIC lifeguards. But Pete knows everyone, of course, so all of us young guys and even the Lids ran for free. Indeed, a good deal. Like free pints everywhere he goes, Pete even gets into charity events for free. And he gets all us in, too.

I actually should've been paid to run. Each stride was so tough. Brutal. I was "saggin and baggin" and "dragging onions," Pete told me.

I thought I was in running shape from all the basketball down Avalon and the runs to Strathmere, but the charity event was a killer. Like getting elbowed by the Lids trying to get a rebound with every stinking stride.

The run started on the promenade in the middle of town. We had to cross over the bright white soft sand to run on the dark hard stuff, which slanted downward from the beach to the waves.

Most of the runners were women. More than half were "fine, fit and fifty," as Pete says, "with finer, fitter and thirty-something daughters."

We endured this killer crossing of the sand dunes three times. First transverse was on the way running up for two and a half miles to Strathmere. Then the couple thousand of runners turned around at an orange cone with a red flag used by the lifeguards and ran back down toward Sea Isle. Then we crossed over the soft white sand again, back on the crowded early Saturday evening promenade. I felt like I carried a crucifix on me back crossing the white sand since I sank deeper with every step. But I saw Pete ahead grinding, more determined with each stride to cross from the soft, white sand to the hard, dark sand, and I believed I could make the crossing, too.

We stopped at the outdoor bar, the Carousel, at the Springfield, and Pete jogged over to the corner of the bar where some of the Bouncepassers were seated. Dei dashed right over. She wore her furry boots, brown bikini and electric smile, looking beautiful, waiting for Pete.

"Hey fellas, don't have any time to talk," Pete had said, sitting next to Dei. "On the clock."

She popped up and sat on his right side. She handed Pete a pint of dark beer waiting for him, still frosty as if she knew exactly when he stopped every year during the run.

"You want one Byrd?" she'd asked, showing a smile that stops waves from breaking.

"Yes, ma'am, please." Later, I told Rage, telling him I really said ma'am, but wanted to say darlin' or sugar.

"Hey, I hear you and Andie are going out," she had blurted in front of Pete and the Lids.

I downed the beer she handed me and edged closer to the Lids. They stared at my thumping heart with one eye and at Pete with the other.

"Pete," she'd whispered. But I could hear most of the words since I focused on her every syllable. I was acting like I was listening to one of the Lids talk about the game that morning. "I'm so happy for you and Andie. He's a grand guy, 'lovely,' like you say."

"He's playing a much better all-around game... I just want Andie to be loved," Pete did say. "I can live with all his turnovers, but he has to box out every possession, not when he wants."

"He'll learn," Dei had said.

"Thanks," he'd said. "You're the only one that gets me."

"Bianca does, too," she'd said.

The rest of August was hot and forgettable. I wasn't around Pete as much. There wasn't much to tell Rage about since in the middle of the month I left with the Ursinus basketball team on the Italy trip. We were over there for 10 days... Andie gave me her longest hug ever in front of the Lads at New York's J.F. Kennedy airport.

Jimmy, Jimbo and Tommy and of course myself all missed her. She flew to Turkey to see her mother while we were gone. She never called me. Not once. She later said she was too busy reading all the weekly letters from Pete that she found stacked under her mom's Quran.

Each night, she texted us all about Turkey... how there is no letter 'w' in Turkish so women sounds like vermin ... how the toilets in public bathrooms are built into the ground and girls just squat... how she visited Kariye – a 7th century Catholic church that was turned into a mosque. That was when the Byzantine Empire ended after the conquest of Constantinople by the Ottomans. However, out of respect for Christianity, a fresco of the Birth of Christ still remains on the ceiling...

She texted how street pretzels were shaped like a giant "O." How the Turk Mehmet Ali Agca shot the Pope. About the Monastery of St. George where visiting Popes throughout history stayed, including John Paul II, who forgave the shooter Agca while visiting him in prison . . .

Andie texted us a mixture of history and hysterics like in Pete's stories each night, but nothing about her mother. Instead it was stuff like how children on the street around the Grand Bazaar sold tissues... yeah single-sheet tissues.

I saved all of her texts to read each night instead of studying while here in my Old Men's Dorm. I learned more and laughed more from her texts anyway then from school. Stuff like how Turkey had small elevators and how they bathe after sex and how the Aya Sofya, the former Catholic church and later a Muslim mosque, is now the most visited museum in Turkey, including recent visits by Pope Benedict XVI in 2006 and President Obama in 2009. Pete would've been proud of her learning... and teaching.

No, I told Rage, she didn't say boo about her mom. None of the Lads asked either.

I texted her about Italy, but I couldn't remember many details. I was thinking of her and Pete mostly while over there. When visiting the statue of David, I couldn't stop wondering if Sea Isle would ever put up a statue of Pete. I texted her about Lazlow Toth, who attacked Michelangelo's famous Pieta with a hammer, acting cool like Pete remembering faceless names. I texted her "and people think Pete is bonkers"

I texted her on how we played three games in 10 days in Italy. How we saw all the usual holy sites, but since there was no commentary from Pete I didn't really remember anything. I couldn't wait to get back to Sea Isle, and I texted her "how much I missed her M&M's and Possessed Pete."

When she returned to JFK, I opened my arms wide to give her our longest hug ever, but she just high-fived my right hand and slapped my left.

I didn't tell Rage I was going to Sea Isle from Ursinus after just a few days away at college. But for some reason, fearing he had seen me down there, I called Rage on the Tuesday after Labor Day and told him about my first weekend back. I told him I needed a quick escape from my new world with ivy walls and without sandy sidewalks.

I told him the trip refreshed me soul like a good session of Magnetic Reversion, throwing sand into the ocean and making up words that don't mean anything.

I told him the pilgrimage was strictly by chance that we went down Labor Day weekend. How we sat in old Braca's and watched the Notre Dame game in Ireland against Navy. Lynchie wore a faded gold Catholics vs. Criminals t-shirt. Pete poked fun at his end of summer haircut. The beer was beautiful. The conversation soon turned into an argument about former Notre Dame coaches Charlie Weis and Tyrone Willingham.

I told Rage how I purposely stoked the argument by asking "if Weis would've been fired a year earlier if he was black and if Willingham would've been fired a year later if he was white?" I sat back and enjoyed it. I knew once the discussion started, it would be a grand one.

But I forget what side Pete was on in the discussion. He didn't like Weis, so I guess he argued Willingham was better, although I remember him saying Ty played too much golf and didn't recruit. Funny, I remember thinking, he cited how the black guy played too much golf.

Anyway, what I remembered most, I told Rage, was Pete bragging about how the Irish fought in the Civil War, and about how he transitioned smoothly from Fighting Irish football to the Irish fighting in America. He said the 116th Pennsylvania brigade fought fiercely in the Battle of Wilderness in 1865.

I remember saying to Pete how *righteous* the Irish were against slavery. Pete winced, then winked, telling me the Irish just hated the English more. He said skin color had nothing to do with it, or slavery. Here I was learning more from Pete drinking beer and watching football then during a whole week at college. He did say the Irish were also against free blacks, but only because both were the lowest on the social scale. He said they competed for the same jobs. He said the Irish felt the only advantage they had was the same skin color as their bosses. He said the blacks were bigger men and worked real hard, too, like the Irish. And the women worked like men. He said they were pretty too. He said the Irish still hated the English landowners more and that is why they fought fiercely against them.

I asked Pete how he remembered all this. Was it from school? He said he didn't learn it in college, but reading afterwards on his own. And then he said, "You remember what you want to remember, like all white guys me age know Babe Ruth had 714 home runs, but they don't remember Hank Aaron broke his record with 755."

Rage sounded more pissed than usual. So, I told him what Pete said about his friend who was the last white family to move out of "Polack Town" in Camden. Rage was interested.

I told him how Pete said this tough polish guy they called Doberman, like the dog, lived with his old parents in this part of South Camden once filled with Polish immigrants.

The parents were in their late 80's and Doberman lived with them. He was in his 50's. His parents refused to move. They had raised their family in the house. So, Doberman stayed with them, to protect them.

Pete said the parents died a few months apart. He said Doberman decided to sell the house. He moved out. Pete said the tough, squared jawed Doberman looked sad telling him the story.

So, Pete said he asked him if anything strange occurred when he left the house for good. Doberman said no. Pete said he kept pressing him for anything out of the ordinary that happened.

Pete said, as if a light clicked on, Doberman told him when he shut and locked the front door and walked down the path, the old oak tree he used to play on as a kid fell.

He said he had to step and climb over the tree

trunk to get to his car.

I told Rage how Pete said it was more than symbolic how the tree fell when the last white family moved out of "Polack Town." Pete said it was spiritual symbolism. Rage didn't care.

Rage said he didn't learn anything from my latest rambling about Pete. He said I didn't have to meet or call him anymore. He said Big Brother was messing with his pension and retirement salary since the economy sucked and he couldn't walk in October now. He was pissed, saying how society failed him and how his dad was able to retire from the New Jersey State Police at his age and all this angry stuff I didn't want to hear.

He told me the Cape May County Prosecutor is still planning on using the Grand Jury to indict Pete. Rage said he should be indicted by the spring, by the time Pete starts playing basketball again in Avalon.

I told Rage I would call him in a few months, saying Pete said the Lids are headed to our first basketball tournament over Thanksgiving weekend in Charleston and how I might hear something to help.

At the end of September, I went with Pete and Andie to hear Steve Colbert speak at Fordham. He jokes around about serious stuff much like Pete does. I think I learned more from Pete than I did in all my Western Civilization classes in the first semester at Ursinus.

Pete likes Colbert, too, but I knew why we really made the long trip to the Bronx.

To get there we met him at Hamilton

Station, took New Jersey transit to New York and then took the Metro North past Yankee Stadium.

I met with my sister when Pete stopped in at the women's basketball office in the basement of Rose Hill Gymnasium. He wanted to talk with his old friend the coach, Stephanie Gaitley. She grew up in Ocean City and her husband Frank is from Drexel Hill. So, Pete, of course, knew them both as kids playing pickup games down the shore and on The Hill.

I told my sister not to tell our parents that she saw me. We were standing on the steps of the administration building where U2 played "Beautiful Day" on Good Morning America at Fordham. I didn't want my sister to meet Pete. She wouldn't get him. She would like Andie, though.

I made small talk, like how the leaves were changing already. Then I told my sister how I always thought Andie could play D-I and wondered why she didn't. I told her how I think Pete wanted to be around her, almost like he wants to protect her from the big world and keep her in his own little world.

But I didn't want my sister to think I was bringing someone around to compete against her for playing time. Plus, I think about Andie's built-in natural physical advantage, which is probably unfair.

I rejoined Pete and Andie at the Seven Rocks of Granite statue outside Rose Hill Gym. Vince Lombardi was one of the famed offensive linemen. Pete tapped the plaque of Lombardi then Pete tapped his chest with his right arm. He is like a rock too, and so he should.

Thankfully, the transfer talk never came up in conversation, at least in front of Andie and me. I took them both to the steps of the towering stone administration building in front a sprawling grassy square to show them where U2 played.

"It's a beautiful day," Pete had sung out, getting the attention of dozens of students walking across the lawn. "Good morning, America."

Before I had left her, my sister told me to "be careful with Andie."

Back at Ursinus, while we were walking to the Wismer Cafeteria one morning, I noticed that Andie didn't have any socks on. It was early in October and it was already the first cold day of the year. I told her to live like the Inuit and wear socks because this wasn't Sea Isle. I told her to be ephphatha, to be open.

Our first regular Ursinus basketball practice started the same night as the first Obama/Romney debate. Pete came up to school to take us out after practice and the debate was on the TV at Da Vinci's, a restaurant in Collegeville. But Pete paid no attention to the TV. He talked a lot about Leonardo's subtle painting techniques.

And he wanted to know about each-and-every dribble from both of us, in between the Leonardo commentaries.

He came up again a week later to take us out to eat after another practice. This time the dinner at Da Vinci's was on the same night as the Sandusky sentencing. But, again, Pete paid no attention to the TV even though it was something I knew he cared very much about. Instead, he grilled us on each drill and dribble in practice.

Really, having him in our faces again was more than good. Andie didn't say much about how she was doing. But I heard she was killing it. She already was starting, or earned a starting job.

I did most of the talking, telling Pete how Jimmy, Jimbo, Tommy and myself were all pushing for more playing time.

"We're coming up big for Coach Small," I told him, making my only joke of the night. Of course, I was referring to our coach, Kevin Small, but my levity shot didn't make Pete laugh, dropping at his shuffling feet with untied sneakers.

I didn't see Pete for the next few weeks. Not until after Super Storm Sandy hit the Jersey shore. Sea Isle wasn't spared, although it wasn't whacked as bad as Moonachie in central New Jersey, where my family vacationed.

Andie mentioned Moonachie to me. Maybe Pete told her it was hit bad. I think Pete called her every day. I guess he didn't want us to worry about Sea Isle. But we did. He was down there for a couple of days to help anyone who needed help. He was taking time off from his leadership lectures to various Philly businesses and colleges.

The Sunday after the storm, during a day off from basketball, we asked Pete to pick us up and take us to help rescue Sea Isle. Of course, he did. He picked all five of us up. We drove in in his pickup truck along with Scoob.

We drive north as far as we can, but Landis Avenue is still closed at 30th street. There are piles of sand on JFK as high as a 10-foot hoop. Then we plow up toward Townsends Inlet, but only poke as far as the Coast Guard Station on 81st where the one glass backboard is cracked.

Still we play a quick 3-on-3 game. For the first-time I am on Pete's team. So is Andie. Ha, playing with Pete and Andie is, to quote Pete, "two-bagger lovely."

Of course, we win, scoring game point on my backdoor bounce pass to Pete.

We stroll up to the beach, all six of us with Scoob. We all grab two handfuls of sand and whirl them into the ocean. The lightness of Magnetic Reversion of the past just isn't there, though, at least not for me. I am angry at the ocean for attacking Sea Isle.

Scoob barks madly as Pete yells, "Long live the Magnetic Reversion Revisionists."

Andie screams, "Long live the Merry Mendicants too…"

Mac follows with "Long live the Furry Merry Monks…"

Mitch trips as he hails, "And may the Misguided Misanthropes live long as well…" He doesn't seem to know what to say, so he just lets the sand fly and turns awkwardly toward us, shrugging, "To *Ur-anu*s, the father of Ursinus."

We all laugh for the first time since seeing Sea Isle all beat up. I don't laugh as hard as them.

I throw a scoop, screaming, "Long live the Happy Huguenots… I mean the Halfway Healers."

With the heat on high, Pete speeds back toward the bay, behind the Acme basketball courts.

That's where a lot of the college players had started to play late last summer. The good players aren't going to Avalon as much. Instead, a younger group of guys play on the side-by-side baskets in the middle of Sea Isle back by the bay.

At a four-way stop sign on the corner, Pete stares like he is paralyzed. He doesn't drive through the stop sign for a good few minutes. We just all sit there in the middle of the road. All thinking, I guess, just how much nature hurts harmless people. What good are storms?

A siren pierces the still air. It is noon.

Pete never called these courts by name, but we knew them as the 64th street courts... or the 62nd street ball fields.

On the block behind the courts rises a row of old houses over the bay. They are battered. The street is named SOUND. We can hear seagulls dropping clamshells on the back wooden decks, breaking them open for lunch.

The last home on the left, a blue house on 60th Street facing the bay, sinks in water halfway up its front door. There is a carved wood sign on it reading CASTA DA LISA – 1907, which Pete does not translate. This is the first time I can remember Pete not knowing what something meant. He didn't even try to make up a meaning, even though he seemed to know so much about Da Vinci.

Instead, Pete said the sign reminded him of Italian food. We continue to drive past the Sea Isle Inn on 63rd and the Acme on 62nd and Marita's Water Ice on Landis without talking.

We don't open our mouths until we reach

Lou's Dogs, where the sign BEST BUNS WEST OF MADRID, BABY is hanging tilted.

We stop at Wawa in the middle of town to stock up on Gatorade. Pete wants to walk on the beach as far as we can past the barricade at 30th. Scoob stays in the truck with a pouty face.

Smiling, Dei floats up behind Pete at the counter and knees him in the back of the knee.

"Hey buddy," they both say at once.

They high-five.

"Sea Isle is broken," he says.

"Oui," she says.

"Oui, Dei, you speaking French on me now?" Pete says. "Just say yes."

"Oui," she says. "I was raised in Charleston by French Huguenots, remember?"

"Remember I told my Oui story at my mom's funeral," he says.

"Yeah it was touching," she says. "How you were reading the French girly magazine Oui at the newspaper store after church in Cape May one Sunday morning when you were 16 and you whispered to your brother to come 'check out *que*' and your mom came over and smacked you with the magazine and said, 'two years of French in high school and you pronounce 'oui' as '*que*.'"

"Oui," he says.

Dei joins us on the recon walk up the beach.

None of us figure we will get past Whale Beach. At 10th Street, near the Dolphin Motel, the dunes are gone. The ocean and bay meet once again. The outgoing undertow crashes into the waves as if they declared war.

Cal-holi is sitting on the dune across from us. A kayak floats across the washed-out beach. He waves his straw cowboy hat. Dei blows a kiss.

The last house on 10th street stands high on pilings and looks fine. The empty swing swinging on the porch isn't damaged either. It swings peacefully back and forth like nature lost.

We fill up on dollar dogs at Wawa for the drive back to Ursinus. We basically all sleep, except when Pete stirs us on the winding and twisting Schuylkill Expressway. He points to the river below and says in a commanding tone, "If you get knocked off the road or bounced from your raft in life at Ursinus, you can follow the river. Just see the rocks in the water and just keep going downriver, boys."

Andie doesn't ever mind being called one of the boys. But for the first time it bothers me. I almost say something to Pete.

Last month at school, a real smart looking guy in our biology class with Doctor Small, no relation to our coach, was digging on Andie. He even asked her to a Frat rush party during the October Harvest Moon festivities for Sig Rho. Andie said no. I took her out to eat at the Collegeville Inn that night, using my own money saved from graduation on an endless smorgasbord.

The weather is unseasonably warm for the middle of November. Pete takes us to the airport where we meet the Lids. The old guys are jacked to watch our first game like it is the Final Four. They are wearing their summer stuff, looking like they are ready to play a pickup game, and making me smile like Happy Hour at the Springfield.

"Interesting, your first game is in Charleston, where they accepted all religions but Catholics," Pete says, sounding like we are in Braca's. "They were big on the French Huguenots... I always wanted to be a Happy Huguenot, but I chose to be a Merry Mendicant."

Pete purposely makes me smile. I know he knows I'm feeling heat from my St. A's friends for not starting in D-3. They are playing D-I.

Pete bounces around like at Twisties when teasing Tiny and Legs. He is going to our game even though Andie is playing in a tournament at Randolph-Macon in Virginia this weekend. He is missing her first college game. I am thinking he doesn't want to put pressure on her... or maybe be doesn't want to see his kid playing D-3.

Dei is going to Charleston, too, to see us play. Her husband won a golf mini-vacation. They are on a different a flight out of Philly.

"Wish Dei was on this bird with me," Pete tells me in the long security line while kneeling on one knee. "Wouldn't care if crashed in midair if Dei was sitting next to me..."

"Why? Would you hold her hand during turbulence?" I poke him, tapping the top of his head with my knuckles.

"Would be good to die... just to hold the hand of Dei just once," Pete says still kneeling and looking at the worn carpet.

While waiting to board the plane, Pete sends out his first Facebook post. I call his page right up, feeling proud he is on social media now since I talked him into taking the dive into this century. I am his first friend - even before Andie. His post is "anyone wanting to play me in Words-With-Friends - I only know four-letter words."

When I refresh his page, a new status update reads "wondering while waiting in line to board plane why me the worse dressed flier at the airport... and the only one after going thru security who forgot to put their shoes back on."

Looking down, I can see his high-top converse sneakers. I am not sure they are on the right feet though.

Already five people friend him up, including Dei.

"I have a starting five on Facebook," Pete screams out, spilling his beer on the dog cage next to him. The dog owner doesn't complain.

My teammates sit in the front of the plane. I sit in the back with Pete.

The "flying waitress" as Pete calls the flight attendant, scowls at him, probably for carrying his beer on the plane. She is wrinkly and even worse she is snarly. She commands everyone in the two rows sitting near the rear emergency exit to "pay her their full antenna attention."

Pete closes his eyes and points his index fingers up above both ears.

"Sir," she barks, "I need your attention for the safety of all on board."

Pete says nicely, "I'm not flying the plane, dear, but thanks."

"Are you willing and able to help passengers through the emergency exit if there is an emergency landing?" she asks.

"Of course, I will help… and if by chance we have a safe landing as well."

She snarls at the passengers within earshot, which is half the plane since she employs a Catholic school-like teacher's "my way or the highway" penetrating voice.

"Can you lift 50 pounds?"

"With which hand?"

She clearly doesn't know what to say before settling for "both hands… sir," in an agitated but in an impressive restrained voice, managing to sound polite.

"Yup, with both hands I can do 98 pounds, but me right hand can only lift 46 while my left hand 52 for some reason and me right handed."

"Sir, can you can lift 50 pounds… will you assist needy passengers in case of an emergency landing?"

Pete gives her the double thumbs up.

She seems a bit amused. Southwest flies humor free, too.

"I need verbal confirmation?"

"Indeed, yes… but only if I'm not sleeping and survive the crash. I honestly won't be able to assist anyone unless they wake me up upon crashing… and I would struggle lifting 46 pounds even with my stronger left hand… if dead on impact… or with me arms severed on landing."

A half hour into the flight she returns, waking Pete again with a question.

"What would you like to drink? Sir," she says smiling nice and sounding like she likes old snoring Pete with drool on his unshaven chin.

"Just a coke, thanks, Sarge."

She leans over me real close to Pete's face, the bill of his cap keeping her from getting closer, saying "Sorry but my ears are already clogged because of the altitude."

"Coke," Pete says, "for me bloke… he may be broken but at least he is not Bir anymore."

Pete can't put the seat back because we are in the emergency exit. Worse, the last lady in the middle seat across the aisle starts talking about the government shutdown.

Pete asks me loud enough for the pilot to hear, "Wonder why she's bitching about money so much since she didn't have to pay for air fare?"

I am thinking he is going to make a social security joke or some cut while asking with experienced trepidation, "How do you know that?"

As both aisles in front and behind us as far as I can see out of the side of my eyes stare at him, he says, "Everyone knows on Southwest - to over 70 destinations - bags fly for free."

The flying waitress stops arranging bags above a well-dressed black guy. She bends over to Pete and "shushes him."

"The poor lady is just cranky because she's returning to Charlestown to spread her mother's ashes over the harbor where she swam as a kid," she says solemnly.

Through his headphones, I hear Pete listen to a Simon and Garfunkel classic, Bridge over Troubled Waters. Across the aisle, the well-dressed black man watches a violent cop-and- robber type action movie on his laptop.

Pete snores loud enough for the black guy in the knotted tie to look over, no doubt disturbed by missing a few shootings on his screen.

When Pete wakes up, we are in Charleston.

"Man, we're floating in the deep south now," Pete says loudly with his headphones still over his ears. "Fitting, it was 50 years ago this fall the Mississippi football team allowed its first black player in 1962.

"It wasn't until a few years later that Alabama had one."

He says to the black guy across the aisle as we get our overhead bags, "I heard the story when Alabama's first black player ran back a kickoff the first time he touched the ball and old Bear Bryant turned to his assistant coaches on the sideline and said, 'that Injun sure can run.'"

The well-dressed black guy ignores Pete... I don't have the time to tell him it is just Pestering Pete, but wink at the irritated, but composed man like saying "this crazy white man is harmless."

The flight attendant grabs Pete's shoulder.

"Can you help the lady in the middle seat across the aisle with her overhead bag?"

"You mean the one complaining about the government shutdown?"

"Yeah, she's here to spread her mother's ashes, remember?"

Pete reaches up and grabs a blue bag with brown leather handles. He hands the bag to the cranky lady.

"Thanks so much," she says smiling. "Mother sure feels a lot lighter."

The sharply dressed black man freaks. All Pete's black talk didn't bother him, but sitting under the lady's dead mother does.

"Man, that's just, like 13 years, bad luck you brought me," he says, storming off the plane. "You bestowed evil on me?"

"Do you need a ride?" Pete asks the lady.

Coach needs a volunteer to ride with Pete since our rental van is crowded with the luggage.

At the Dollar Rental Car counter, the customer ahead of us is none other than the well-dressed black man. He acts like he doesn't see us.

The mid-sized rental cars, however, are parked next to each other. He has to see us. He puts down his bags. The guy pops his trunk.

Pete pops our trunk. We all put down our bags as the well-dressed black guy turns to us with his arms out, as if to hug.

"I'm sorry," he says. "I was just spooked."

The lady and the man hug.

I need to get with my team so I just start tossing the bags in the trunks.

They get done hugging and Pete gives them both a half hug.

Pete drives the lady to her hotel across from the harbor with old cannons in the park pointing to the sea.

I open the trunk to give the once cranky lady her bags.

The blue bag with the brown leather handle, the one with her mother's ashes, isn't inside the trunk.

I must have put her mom in the well-dressed

black guy's car trunk.

We won the second of two games in Charleston. Pete fared better. He was two-for-two in getting drunk, making friends and having "the best day in his life."

The well-dressed black guy returned the ashes of the mother to the Dollar Rental, where Pete and the cranky lady were waiting. They must have all had a good laugh since the two strangers sat together at both of our games in Charleston.

Dei always sat to the right of Pete. At half time of both games, Dei and Pete went for walks. They returned each time with M&M's and a newspaper in time for the start of the third quarter.

Pete told me they walked 10 minutes to a corner with a vendor where they could view the state capital. He said he wanted to check each day to see if they "still flew the Confederate flag."

He said he wanted to be there at the capital just in case it was the day Charleston abolished the "Civil War worship."

"It's not even the state flag," he'd lamented to me. "It was raised in 1961 on the 100th anniversary of the Civil War... it stayed up as a protest to the Civil Rights movement... it's not even the state flag..."

I had asked him if he was able to hold Dei's hand on one of the walks, but he only said, "It's not even the state f-f-f... flag."

He showed me the New York Times Op-Ed page and the first item with Pete arguing the side that the 0:00 was an event in the game while Uncle Matty theorized the game was over at 0:00 so it wasn't an event in the game because it couldn't affect the outcome of the game… with Pete equating the debate of 0:00 to life and death… and how a good person can still impact others when the game is over and he is "good and gone."

Chapter 17

Andie won both her games in the Randolph-Macon tourney, beating Virginia Union and Clarion State. They didn't play the host Yellow Jackets. Pete didn't lament about missing both games, poking me how he only watched games below the "Mason-Dixon Line," but not taking the bait since R-M is below the M-D.

I am still not sure why he skipped Andie's two games, especially since he often wears the yellow-black striped bumblebee shirt of Randolph-Macon that Andie gave him as a gift. Pete joked how he looked grand in prison stripes.

Pete didn't seem to really care as much about anything over the Thanksgiving and Christmas break. Only about Notre Dame playing Alabama for the BCS title. He scored Andie and me tickets to the national championship football game in Miami through a South Jersey guy. A guy nicknamed Notre Dame Harvey, who is known by Pete from being a basketball ref.

I am pumped we are going to the Bama game... I mean Notre Dame game. We will be together, which is all that matters to me, especially since I think the Tide is going to roll big.

We have a break from games of a few days between semesters, so seeing the Irish works out for both of us. Maybe Andie and I will become more than friends again.

Yeah, we are going to watch big time college football on South Beach, baby. I can forget about being 4-4 this season after losing just four games in four years at St. Anthony's.

I am bummed a bit because I'm not starting, But not too much. My bros back home don't seem to care. They are consumed watching ESPN. I play about half of the game, just like Jimmy, Jimbo and Tommy. The college games against the Swathmore's and Haverford's and Muhlenberg's and Moravians of the D-3 world aren't nearly as intense or insane as playing against the Lids.

Andie is undefeated and kicking butt, but Pete seems more interested in our games. He comes to the Saturday afternoon home double-headers and goes to most of her away games.

At halftime of her last game before Christmas, an easy win over Immaculata, Pete borrowed my library card and left. He returned with a hardback book, laid it in my lap, and asked me, "Have you ever read 'The Rise of the Colored Empires' by this man Goodard?"

I pointed to the cover and corrected him, "The author's name is Stoddard." However, he was already deep into reading the New York Times. It turns out that he had snatched the "do not take" copy from the library and I don't think he even listened to me.

Then Pete asked me, "Have you ever read the report by William H. Frey of the Brookings Institution? The Times says Frey reports that for the first time in more than a century white deaths in the United States exceeded white births.

"In 30 years," he told me, "the white majority in the U.S. will be gone just like the old American Basketball Association with the red, white and blue basketballs."

"Now that would cause a real stir in this country," I said to him, tapping the cover of the book he had given me to read.

"Or level the playing field," he says.

Our flight is to Orlando even though the game is in Miami. Pete says he knows a guy who can drive us south. We don't ask Pete how he knows "Otis" would be here. He just does. Otis flew to Florida to just hang out with the Notre Dame fans. He doesn't have a ticket to the game.

By early Saturday afternoon we are drinking at The Village Grille in Lauderdale by the Sea. Andie and I tell stories to each other from last summer in Sea Isle. There is a "Go Irish" Guinness sign in the window. We haven't taken our first piss yet when a real Irish-looking dude walks up to us and says, "If Notre Dame wins tomorrow, we are going to party tonight."

The words are written on the back of his shirt – right above "Notre Dame Harvey, Grays Ferry, PA." I scream, "Who the fook is Harvey."

After our first piss, Andie says to me, "You notice how all the people wearing blue and gold shirts and hats, the ones with smiles wider than the ocean here, don't even say hello to each other while walking around… they all say, 'Go Irish.'"

"Harvey arrived for the BCS Championship game with 40 family and friends," Pete informs us. "Harvey's devoted subway alumni branch, which are mostly Irish Catholic like himself, have attended Notre Dame games for over 30 years now."

Pete calls it "Harv's Underground Railroad." They call their trips "The Pilgrimage."

"We're pilgrimaging with Harv," declares Pete, He genuflects in front of Harvey without spilling a drop of beer. Harv buys us a round.

The beers keep flowing like the ubiquitous "Go Irish" greetings. We still have-to drive to South Beach, where Pete is meeting up with his former Ursinus teammate Mick Cola, the cool, smart guy who taught me about the Atlantic Puffin and could also dunk.

Perhaps, since ND Harvey is a South Jersey basketball ref, Pete asks him why there're always three white NBA refs in every NBA game, "all real fit, who only go up to the armpits of the players. Yeah, with hair slicked back like all the good-looking white coaches, like Riley, Pitino and me fookin friend Calipari."

Harv is listening without really hearing.

A real Irish-looking dude with a "If Notre Dame wins tomorrow, we are going to party tonight" t-shirts sticks his head in the pack and says, "How come black people don't go to ice hockey games?" he slurs and then adds, "If white people didn't go to NBA games there would be a presidential outcry" before downing his beer.

"Good point, brother," I say. "Go Flyers!"

A balding guy with a gray ponytail and a green t-shirt with the Blessed Mother on the front and the words "I don't know if Jesus favors Notre Dame, but I know his Mother does" hands Pete and Andie a beer. Pete gives both pints to me.

"We need two more brews, bro," he says to

the guy as he pats the head of the Blessed Mother on the t-shirt reverently.

"You know," he adds, taking a sip from my beer, "the NFL scouts should just add an inch to the vertical leap of the white guys at the Combine next month just to make it fair."

Pete turns to me and says, "Don't you think so Obama?"

I palm the top of my pint and pull the glass away from him.

Pete adds, with his arm around me, "Hey Obama, you're an antiwar supporter and you give away free health care too."

I say, "No that would-be Jesus."

Harv needs to see the Notre Dame pep rally at South Beach at 7, so he invites us to squeeze in the rental van with his wife, and the kids. Pete packs a cooler from somewhere of "roadies."

On the way down, Pete gets a call from Cola, who tells him he won't be down until tomorrow – Sunday.

Now we don't have a place to stay tonight.

Before Pete is even off the phone, it buzzes.

"Damn, the phone scared me," he says. "I thought it was me defibrillator going off again… or the Sea Isle cops calling."

He reads the text.

"It is my old friend Mary Devlin," Pete says. "She says her husband and son are in South Beach now partying. I will text her back to see if we can stay with them."

We don't even have to wait for the text. Andie and I smile at each other, knowing we will be staying on the floor or sofa or a closet somewhere with the Devlin dudes.

"How 'bout that?" Pete sings. "Danny "The Dood" Devlin is down here. His brother is the priest in Sea Isle, Fr. Dennis, who preaches about doing service and good deeds.

"I have to tell the preacher his bro is doing a grand deed, indeed."

"Ya'll have to tell The Dood the Alice in Wonderland parable," I say, hoisting my roadie.

The traffic into South Beach backs up to the interstate exit ramp. After crawling for a few miles, we have to get out to piss. We all water the palm tree in front of a pink house with a dolphin fountain in the front yard. Andie uses the backside of the tree away from the street.

The Harvey van pulls away from the curb, heading east on the main street toward the beach, beeping wildly. It slowly edges into the traffic, moving without care through the night air puffed with excitement. The Notre Dame band is playing. The famous fight song echoes from the beach with the wind adding to the symphony of the brass… of the day… of life again with Pete and Andie…

We search for the Devlins somewhere in the Deco District flooded by a sea of green t-shirts.

While we are waiting in line to get into the Clevelander, one of the packed bars on the beach with Samba music blaring, we meet up with the Devlin son, Colman. He tells us that he started following the Irish when he was five years old.

"Can't they turn down the Sambo music," Pete says to a muscled-up doorman in a pale suit.

"Samba," I say. "Samba, not Sambo, bro."

"Oh, my bad," he says, patting the doorman's chest and rocking his hips like the girls on stage... but looking like he has to drop a dump.

Colman says his Notre Dame love has something to do with his dad's dad. He asks if I'm going out with Andie, but quickly apologizes.

"It is cool," I say. "So is Pete. I know there're guys down here for the game who would no sooner admit their daughter dated a black guy than they would admit she was a lesbian."

The next day, I sit with Mr. Cola for the pregame stretching. The stadium is empty. We both see the Golden Domed Lads are doomed. The field looks like a see-saw, with the smaller Irish being teetered in the air helplessly by the Tide.

With ND getting crushed by Bama in the first quarter, Pete slurs, "The Irish are getting hammered like me on a rainy *nooner* at Braca's."

At the halftime of the massacre, Pete says "Alabama uses a whiteboard in the locker room and Notre Dame uses an old school black board," adding "the Irish think they can write faster on the blackboard at halftime."

"I wish we could start the game over... and life," Pete anguishes. "Perhaps, though, there's no Magnetic Reversion this close to the equator."

Since there are no highlights of the game for a Notre Dame fan to talk about, Mr. Cola asks me about my courses. I tell him how I surprisingly now enjoy biology, but add "maybe just because I can help Andie with her homework in the class."

Andie hugs me, and then elbows my ribs like

she is boxing out without spilling her beer.

"Mick," he says to call him, explains to us that the sand here in South Beach isn't like the beaches in South Jersey.

"The sand in Sea Isle is more quartz," he says, "In Florida, the sand is more coral and more calcium based, which is better for growing grass."

Pete says he needs to smoke grass to watch the second half.

"You smoke now?" I ask him.

"Nah, but thinking of starting... Mercury, Venus and Saturn are aligned over the tips of one of the three pyramids of Giza, forget which one, but anyway seems like the perfect time to start."

The morning after the game is horribly hot. Even in Mr. Cola's air-conditioned hotel suite. I wake up early on one sofa. Andie snores on the other. Pete drools on the floor. I stumble down toward the luring call of the crashing waves.

At the edge of the beach the large floppy leaves on the palm trees float in a soothing breeze.

Last night, while leaking against a tree next to a bathroom, Pete said that these thin palm trees with bushy tops looked like "ragamuffins."

A mother with blonde hair tied in a red scarf and two kids with the same hair and wrapped head-to-toe in Notre Dame gear all scurry toward some swing sets, which are under a group of large palm trees. She boasts in a Southern twang how "her Bama-bred boys are bigger and faster than the Irish..." telling the pair of identical boys "to pull harder on the chains of your swing to go higher."

I scoop up some sand, clench both hands,

and jog toward the ocean about a football field or so away. As a wave inches up to my feet, I whirl and throw the sand back to whence it came.

The sand blows out to sea with the westerly wind. Not back in my face.

Perhaps, there is no Magnetic Reversion this close to the equator.

Or perhaps it is because the sand in Sea Isle is more quartz while in Florida it is more coral and more calcium based ... or perhaps it is because the wind is blowing out, making me wonder why I didn't think of the obvious initially.

Chapter 18

When the old guys played here, the old oak was famous, stretching from the sideline to the goal post right behind the back end-zone.

Even non-football folks knew of the Ursinus College tree.

Over the last few months, a half dozen or so people asked me about the tree. Actually, as many people ask me about the tree as inquire about J. D. Salinger, who went here for a few months in 1938. He wrote a column for the student newspaper called "The Skipped Diploma."

Often, I wonder if life is skipping by Pete...

I just had to teach myself more about the old tree. Especially since I knew the Lids would be asking about the former natural landmark when they came up for our game today against Moravian - Uncle Matty's alma mater.

It seems like centuries ago that I was waiting for Pete and the Lids... but the day was only yesterday, while the rest of my British Literature class plodded through "Ulysses," I googled up on the old tree.

After reading about the tree I returned to "Ulysses." Then, right smack on page two of the James Joyce classic, I knew I would have to bust a move like Leopold Bloom, to venture on my own odyssey, to escape my caged life.

Just like Pete preaches "middle" in basketball, I figured I would position my loser butt right smack in the middle of life.

The Ursinus Tree, as sturdy and strong as it

was, couldn't last forever, which made me realize that Pete, as strong as he is, wouldn't be standing forever either. I didn't know what Andie, who doesn't study bio with me anymore, would do after college. But I decided then how the first day after senior year, I'd go to Dublin. Maybe relocate…

Yeah, by the time the Irish writer first introduced his character, Bloom, I knew my path would lead to Dublin. As the plot of the book unfolded, Bloom began walking around the capital city of Ireland… an escape route that he traveled in one good day. Then I knew my future would have me traveling for at least one good year. I needed only to get to Dublin by June 16, also called "Bloom's Day" - the day the Dubliners recreate the walk around the city by Joyce's hero.

The fallen Ursinus Tree also reminds me my basketball days will be over after college. Except for bounce passing down in Sea Isle, of course. I am not even starting in D-3, so the chances of playing pro ball, even in Turkey, are about as slim as me bony calves that can't make me dunk.

The professor asked if I was OK. I apologized for daydreaming, saying "I'm confused only… how learning literature and history gets me more pumped than playing basketball now."

I am getting excited, thinking of how I will set sail to Dublin. First, up the East Coast, then to Newfoundland, over to Greenland, and then Iceland. Finally, over to Ireland. Reversing Saint Brendan the Navigator's journey to freedom.

It will only be for a year. Pete will approve.

The Lids are already lit up. They are high on

just being here at Ursinus. They didn't need a pit stop for roadies on the way.

As urgent as having to piss, they want to visit the site of the "end zone tree" even though the February air is biting, like Pete's comments about my shooting during the first time at the Avalon courts, and even though the tree is gone.

"C'mon little bro, let's go see the old oak tree," old man Mitchell says when the Lids gather outside my dorm room. "I haven't seen it since puking on the roots the night before graduation."

"And during graduation," Pete says.

"You graduated?" Matty asks Mr. Mitch.

"Yeah, he graduated, and Ursinus wasn't started as an all-girls school like Moravian," Pete says with Andie next to him.

"At least my college is in Bethlehem," Matty says, "named after the birth place of Jesus."

Hedging for a moment from the verbal jousting, I announce my plan to walk around Dublin on Bloom's Day, trying to impress how my life will blossom and spread with interest more than playing ball while gauging Andie's reaction.

"Actually, it was a Sycamore tree, the tree outside the end zone," Andie says oblivious to my shot to make her jealous and plea for me not to go.

"Gone," Andie continues as I wait for her to say good-bye to me before she says, "Too late see the tree. *Syc-no-more* is good and gone…"

"What do you mean the tree is gone?" Pete asks incredulously, as if Scoob had suddenly died. "Generations of family hugs, team photos, wedding pictures, I imagine, were blessed under the tree…

and some killer keggers, too."

"Just fell on a windless night… but a seedling taken from the tree was planted at the east end zone spot in Patterson Field," she adds quickly, "however, when they put the new turf field down a few years ago, the sapling was moved somewhere else on campus, I think, well no one knows where."

Pete huddles us around him, like he is going to call a play… or dish out roadies.

"I was at the house in Ephesus where the Blessed Mother spent her final days," he whispers. "Some believe her last nine years."

Slipping to the back of the huddle, I google Ephesus quickly. Indeed, from the cross, Jesus asked John the Evangelist to take care of his mother. And John wrote the Book of Revelations on the Island of Palmos, off the coast of Ephesus.

"That word means to be open. Right?" I ask, wanting to impress Andie how I paid attention to Pete's hiking story about his mother's spirit above Lake Tahoe and his own fallen tree parable up in the desolate high Sierra Mountains.

"That's ephphatha, but good try," Pete says, "like your jump shot, a close miss."

"Like the Halfway Healers," I say, "just trying to get it half way right."

"Like being a half dude," Andie says, sounding the crickets on the walk to the treeless field.

"Like… like the trees at Ephesus around the house of the Blessed Mother, "Pete says, breaking the stone silence. "They're halfway alive."

"What do you mean, halfway alive?" I ask,

fully into all this halfway stuff.

Pete whips out his iPhone, punches in some letters quickly, and as he does this, he tells us Ephesus is also where a Catholic Council was held in 431-AD where all the rules of the church were adopted after the Council of Trent in Turkey.

"That's interesting," I say, trying to loosen up the talk a bit, even though I miss these talks so much. "That's cool, Jesus showed up at the Council of Trent and gave us all these rules like not to eat meat on Friday in Turkey."

"Good one, Bro," Pete says, patting my St. A's ski cap. "You can make mock all the Catholic man-made rules, and I agree with you that the Catholic faith is a very hard religion to live in, but I tell you what, it's a grand religion to die in."

At the spot where the old tree once ruled campus, where the Bouncepassers puked more than once, Pete showed us a picture of an ancient stone house in Ephesus on a hill surrounded by trees. The closest trees were ashen white on the bottom four or five feet and the top of the trunk was brown with branches of green leaves.

"I've tried to read about those trees and found no info anywhere," Uncle Matty says, picking up a wayward lone leaf, ripping it in half.

"I was there, Matt," Pete says. "I saw them. They're dead on the bottom. They're miracle trees. They're the Trees of Life, like in the Book of Revelations, written by John the Evangelist, who's buried in Ephesus... I was at his tomb there too... it was John who raced against Peter to Jesus' tomb... did they run because they believed Jesus had risen or did they race to the tomb because they needed their disbelief... their doubts of the resurrection proven wrong?"

"Wasn't the Blessed Mother buried in Bethlehem? How would she have returned there if John the Evangelist died in Ephesus?" Uncle Matty asks, "I mean, that's where the gospels say Mary's buried, right? You Catholics need to get your religion history right like us Mormons."

"Right, I know the Blessed Mary isn't buried in Bethlehem, Pa., at Moravian College," Pete says.

"All I know," Andie says, "is I want to bury Moravian College tonight."

"Don't race to your tomb if you want your doubts in heaven proven wrong, "Pete says, tugging Andie's ponytail, "but race to your tomb because you believe."

I'm hoping not to get killed in front of the Lids in the first game of this doubleheader.

"It's nice to see the men and women playing," Uncle Matty says, "in a doubleheader."

"You got to co-exist," says Pete. "Like in Istanbul, the coexistence of the Grand Bazaar and the modern mall shows Eastern and Western Ways can indeed co-exist."

The Moravian basketball teams, both men and women, carry books in one hand and sneakers in the other departing the bus at Helfferich Hall.

Pete paces. He is ripping off facts rapid fire, even faster than a good drunk afternoon at Braca's. He is about to watch Andie play with a "bunch of suburb girls" in college and he doesn't know what to say but "there's more to life than basketball...

"The Grand Bazaar in Istanbul is over 500 years old," he continues with only me faking to listen closely. "Traders packed their camels and traveled from throughout the vast Ottoman Empire to sell their goods on the muddy banks of the Bosphorus Strait that divides Europe and Asia.

"Shoppers still come to the Grand Bazaar. There're over 4,400 small shops.

"Istanbul also has malls, which boasts every modern store imaginable.

"Fitting, since Istanbul served as a gateway between the East and West for Alexander the Great, a great man... he was over 6-foot-4 tall."

Pete stops rambling and looks out of the side of his right eye at me. When he sees that I am really still listening, he resumes, "Istanbul and Turkey still serve as a gateway between the East and West. As an Islamic democracy. Turkey is vital to connect the Western Democracies and the Middle East Islamic countries."

Somehow Pete will connect Turkey to race, religion or both... using the Bosphorus Bridge.

"Istanbul is not like in Indiana," Pete says. "Where ESPN's Colin Cowherd just, or recently, claimed the reason attendance is down, even though the Pacers are up, is white folks don't want to go to see all black players in games."

"Sounds like your grandfather lives in French Lick," Uncle Matty says, "They probably call Muhammad Ali still Cassius Clay like he did."

"Yeah, Indianapolis isn't like Istanbul," Pete says. "We celebrate Black History this month in America and we still don't cross our own bridges in this country that divide whites and blacks while they're more diverse and accepting in Turkey, where the Bosphorus Bridge connects the East and West geographically and philosophically."

"Maybe it is because we don't bathe after having sex, like the Muslims in Istanbul," Uncle Matty says.

"I guess you never bathed then," old man Mitch says.

Their Sea Isle rap-fest has landed here at Ursinus, probably where they started talking this way to each other. Someday, sadly, the talk will be gone like The Tree.

The old guys are at their fun-loving and fearsome best now. I want to stay with the Lids, but I have to leave all the shore talk to get my ankles taped for my game.

"Shouldn't you be going?" Pete says. "Don't you need to get your ankles taped before the game? Tell Pam the Trainer me said "howdy.""

I want to play like a St. A's player should, but really I would rather be in the stands sitting with Pete and listening to what he says about my game and listening to the stories he would tell.

We won.

"You looked good out there," Uncle Matty says kindly to me in the foyer of the gym where the United States Field Hockey Hall of Fame is located. "Not as good as the girls holding sticks though in those pictures from back in the day.

"It is so cool that you wanted to go to a college that is known for a girls' sport Petey."

"I couldn't make the field hockey team,"

Pete says, putting his head down in mock shame.

We hustle to The Flat, where Pete and the Lids started and where now the senior players live, to drink a beer before Andie's game.

Two beers later, right off the opening tap, Andie dives for a loose ball and bangs her head. She bounces up. We've all seen this down the courts in Avalon. So, we all know she isn't hurt.

The basketball court here at Ursinus is synthetic rubber and soft with the big black U outlined in gold and red in the middle. The court is also used for practice by the field hockey team.

"The Sixers used to practice here before moving to Franklin & Marshall College back when we were here," says Pete. "The Sixers were going to pay for a wood floor, but the field hockey team had so much power, they kept the rubber.

"In Turkey, we practiced at a University with a rubber court in a basement," Pete adds, "there was also this shorter 3-point line for kids."

"What were the games like?" I ask. I really wanted to ask about how he met Andie's mom and what happened, although didn't dare to go there.

"There were music bands playing during games," Pete says. "The refs wore orange shirts. I played for EFES Pilsen of Istanbul. We wore blue uniforms at home. The blue and the orange looked as strange as the advertisements inside the key. It was all about making money. The games were on Sky Turk TV in the Euro League, but they needed to make as much coin as possible, probably to pay for us Yanks, so ad space was sold on the court."

"Yeah, like the NBA isn't about making

money," Uncle Matty says. "Charity ball …"

"Well, in the NBA, the fans don't stand and clap in the last minute of the game for the home team," Pete says as Andie draws an offensive charge. "The fans, though, none of them looked like they had ever played. They all were rich, well-dressed businessmen."

I look around to see if there are any ethnic groups sitting near us who Pete is about to offend - or defend, depending on the side of the debates with Matty he picks - so I can give them the wink.

The Helfferich Hooligans, up in the far corner, under the 1981 Final Four banner, scream wildly for Andie after she dives through a player for a loose ball and pushes it ahead for a layup.

"Back then in Turkey, it was like America is now, where grand black players aren't from the city any more like their dads had been," Pete says. "Like Grant Hill's dad, Calvin. The black dads from the NBA of our day have all made money and moved to suburbs where there are lots of trees and few basketball courts."

A double nickel is on the way for Andie, who already has, like, 10 of each – points, rebounds, assists, steals and drawing offensive charges. Her anger spills all over the rubber court, bouncing around as if her dad were covering her.

"When we get back to New Jersey, we need to visit the tree in Marlboro where the Blessed Mother sightings were," Pete says, seemingly not impressed with Andie's killer outing. "We need to see the tree since we didn't get to see the old oak tree here at Ursinus."

"Sycamore," I say as Andie dives for another loose ball.

"Well, it must be half oak," Pete insists. "I know it isn't half alive like the trees in Ephesus."

Although he is overbearing even by his standards, I need to be fully alive like Pete. My Dublin scheme injects an anabolic bounce in my life much more than any rubber court here can.

"Why do you still think the Catholic religion is so grand to die in?" Uncle Matty asks as we hob-nob near the field hockey Hall of Fame after the game for Andie. Pete and a young kid have a catch with a field hockey ball.

"Because we believe… we know we're going somewhere, on the rest of our spiritual journey," Pete says, pointing to an old black and white photo of some team with girls holding sticks and skirts down to their knees, "I hooked up with that girl… in me dreams… passing on for us Catholics is like going on a European vacation… a Scandinavian cruise."

Maybe when I come back someday to Ursinus there will be another tree growing in the end zone. Maybe they will plant a ragamuffin palm tree.

Maybe I will forget the game today, put it all behind me when the clock hit 0:00.

I didn't do much in 21 minutes, except allow my childhood dreams to bleed out on the synthetic court.

"Don't worry about not looking good on the court," Pete says as we walk back to The Flat for photos and roadies. "Just about winning, which you did, so you look good Bro."

Chapter 19

Pete reminds us through a Facebook post that this is the last year of the Big East Tourney. So, naturally he plans for the pilgrimage to New York at the end of the first week of March.

We lost in the first round of the playoffs to Muhlenberg. So, I am not missing any games by going to the Big Apple with Pete and the Lids. Andie has a second-round playoff game at Scranton so can't go with us.

For some reason, no one talks about, Pete doesn't go back to Scranton.

The Lids have been going to Madison Square Garden for the tourney since 1985 - two years after graduating from Ursinus - when Villanova, Georgetown and St. John's of the Big East all made the Final Four in Kentucky.

Pete said they are "grand fookin luck" since Villanova won the national title in '85.

Uncle Matty picks me up at 7 in the morning outside of the 7-11 on the Main Street corner of the campus. We meet Pete at the 30th Street Station in Philadelphia 40 minutes later. Pete couldn't pick me up because he had a leadership lecture at Drexel University next to the train station the night before. He stayed over at the Penn Towers so he could get "properly lubed for the last Big East quarterfinal round."

We take the 8:08 New Jersey transit to the Hamilton train station. It's between Trenton and Princeton where we meet the other Lids at 8:42. I know the times because Pete keeps repeating them like he is barking orders at the courts during a pickup game.

In Hamilton, Pete informs us that before going to New York, we first must stop in nearby Marlboro. Pete wants to see the "Blessed Tree." He paces in the parking lot waiting for everyone.

Lynchie is the last to show. He wipes Pete's forehead with the white bar towel, which he hangs back over his shoulder.

"Back in 1989, a Joseph Januszkiewicz began reporting seeing visions of the Blessed Mother near the blue spruce trees in his yard," says Pete slapping his arm around Lynchie, who wears his Catholics vs. Convicts t-shirt from the Notre Dame-Miami football game in 1988. "The visions began, like, six months after he returned from a pilgrimage to Mediugorie in Yugoslavia.

"The visions occur at 9:28, so we have, like, 46 minutes to get there. Over 8,000 pilgrims have gone to his yard."

"Yeah, even though back in 1993," Uncle Matty says, while whipping Pete's back with Lynchie's towel, "the Diocese of Trenton ruled nothing 'truly miraculous' happened."

Still, despite the Church findings, we are pilgrimaging to the "Blessed Tree" on the Thursday morning of the Big East tournament. Pete won't be denied. He says he needs to pray.

He hunts down a taxi driver. We pile into the mini black van. The guy under the turban says he knows exactly where the tree "rises and spreads." He tells us the Marlboro Tree is a giant black willow that has been certified by the New Jersey Forest

Service as the biggest tree of its species in the state.

"It is over 150 years old and over 75 feet tall with a 20-foot circumference," Pete adds, wrapping Lynchie's towel around his head.

The "Blessed Tree" looks even taller and wider.

No one else is here. We don't see a vision at 9:28.

The five Lids join hands and circle around the tree while I take the picture. I post the team photo to Pete's Facebook.

"What I love about you Catholics," Uncle Matty says, "if the Blessed Mother Herself came right here in a vision right now and said there was no God, you wouldn't believe the Virgin Mary…"

Pete brings back giant Garden soft pretzels with the second round of beers. We are midway through the first game of the afternoon session. There is a time out so I can watch a replay on the big overhead scoreboard. I see there is just 9:28 left in the half… I close my eyes… I see Andie.

Pete heckles one ref like he knows him.

Tim Higgins tucks in his stripped shirt, fixes his pants, looks over to the scorer's table and then turns to the crowd as Pete yell at him again, "Yo Timmy, the guard can't hand check like that." Then Higgins calls a push off - an offensive foul – on the Villanova freshman guard, Ryan Arch-something, He was using his right hand to clear space for a shot.

"Damn, Huggie… youse refs have the God Syndrome," Pete barks. "You just called the offensive on Nova because I yelled… I didn't even bet who wins."

In between the afternoon double header and the night double header, we leave the Garden to drink at Mustang Sally's. I welcomed the walk of a block or so in the cool New York night air. But Pete changes his mind and says we are drinking at Mustang Harry's, a block farther away on 7th Avenue in the middle of Manhattan. That is even better by me.

"Boys, let's drink up silly at Harry's," Pete says. "I don't want to talk to women tonight at Sally's, so we'll drink at Harry's. It's the fookin Big East tourney, baby, the fookin last year."

We plop at the bar next to a group of women standing in a circle. They are as tall as Pete. They swing to the corner of the bar. We flow into their space like spilled beer on the bar. The buzz is back. The piano is playing. I am alive again, like at Braca's, in the middle of Pete's stories, surrounded by the Lids yelling, "Yahoo, the night is on" every time another friend walks into the swinging doors.

On the TV behind the bar, I see Doug Gottlieb, a college basketball analyst, on the set with TBS pro guys Charles Barkley, Kenny Smith and Greg Anthony. Before the game, Pete announces to the bar that Gottlieb is "is the token white guy on the set."

Two of the four ladies, who moped to the corner of the bar, look down at us and laugh. The other two give Pete approving looks.

Up on the screen, Gottlieb says the same about being a "token." He seems to be joking.

"Gottlieb is going to catch holy high hell," Pete says. "I can speak the truth in a bar around friends and lovely ladies, but he can't say he's the 'token white guy' on TV. What's he drinking?"

Pete is right, of course. The tallest of the ladies starts talking to Pete. She tells him just how "right he is, love."

At halftime, Barkley defends Gottlieb, saying he was "just joking" and for "knuckleheads tweeting to lighten up."

A taller, handsomely dressed black lady edges next to Pete, positions her elbow at the bar like she is challenging him to arm wrestle.

He immediately starts telling her where he is from in "lovely Philly" and "there's a long line of father-son duos from the Big 5" like what he sees on the Kansas bench.

"Yeah, there was Tony DiLeo of La Salle, and his son T.J DiLeo playing now at Temple," Pete says looking in her dark, serious eyes. "But it goes way back. There was Bruce Moore and his son Eric Moore both playing at Penn. There was Curt Fromal and his son Steve both playing at La Salle. There was Mike Kempski at Saint Joseph's and his son Michael playing for the Hawks."

The long, tall and handsome black lady looks at her expensive shiny watch. She taps Pete's shin with her pointed pink shoes.

Pete continues, "Yeah Vince Curran played at Saint Joseph's and his son Vince played for the grand Fran Dunphy at Penn. And there was Buddy Gardler, who coached Steve Donahue at Cardinal O'Hara, who played at Saint Joseph's and his son Chris played on Hawk Hill, too. And Matt Guokas, who later coached the Sixers like DiLeo, and his son

Matt… they both played at Saint Joseph's.

"Any of those father-son duo's have any color?" the lady whispers in a deep voice. "They all sound like Irish and Italian names to me."

"No. Well, Dane Watts played at Penn for Dunphy when Donahue and Fran O'Hanlon were assistant coaches and his dad, Stodie Watts, played for Temple." Pete says. "They were both black. Actually, they both are still black."

The black question sends Pete - as smoothly as his crossover dribble down the shore - back to 1963 when "the Loyola of Chicago Ramblers played Mississippi State in a conference tournament game, but not the Big East."

Naturally, Pete continues as if he is telling her where the Fountain of Youth is in St. Augustine – because he has been there. I heard him tell Dei this story over the summer in the Springfield, saying how she looks so young… but now I am rambling like Pete.

"The conference had to move the tournament out of Starkville to East Lansing Michigan, defying a state injunction to stop the game since teams from Mississippi were prohibited from playing '*interfaced teams*,'" Pete says. "Yeah, interfaced."

He continues telling the interesting lady all this. She pulls the white towel from around his neck and rubs the top of his head.

"And Loyola was coached by a guy named George Ireland," Pete says.

"How fitting, an Irish guy with an interfaced team," she says.

"He took them to the Final Four, where Duke's Art Heyman got the MVP and didn't make the final game.

"Man, honey, that was 30 years ago, Sugar," he says. "Good how race relations in this country don't still lag... not like me beer gut and ya'll tight butt."

"Times haven't changed," she says sternly, making her deep voice deeper, making her not only look like a Division I player, but sound a bit like one, too.

"Yeah, you're right," Pete says. "I was just poking to see how you think."

She pulls her bar stool closer and taps his shins... quicker. Pete speaks louder.

"Just this month, finally, the Memphis city council renamed three Confederate-themed parks, including one named after the first Grand Wizard of the Ku Klux Klan," Pete says. "The council, with three members amazingly abstaining, finally changed the name of Confederate Park to Memphis Park, Jefferson Davis Park to Mississippi River Park and Nathan Bedford Forrest Park to Health Sciences Park."

"Forrest, a Confederate general and cavalry leader, had a park named after him, and he was a slave trader before the war and the KKK's first Grand Wizard," Lynchie injects, taking back his towel.

Tapping his shins with both pointed pink shoes, she confronts him about being singled-out by society, ending her short rant about being black and a tall woman with, "what do you really know about being an outcast?"

"We Irish know about racial profiling too," he says. "I was in London last year, celebrating St. Patrick's Day in Trafalgar Square, and waiting entry into a British Pub, I was pulled out of line by the Bobbies and patted down from teeth to toe.

"The Brits racially profiled me, I looked like an old IRA soldier to them," Pete says. "They were just protecting their people – and me – so naturally I wasn't offended."

She wipes her eyes with Pete's bar napkin while resting one of her shoes on his knee.

As if his blotchy red nose, scabbed forehead, floppy hair and a mouth flowing like a public toilet with stories didn't ring the alarm to stay away, Pete pisses his pants at the bar.

She takes Lynchie's towel and puts it over Pete's wet crotch. They start talking about transgender athletes. Pete says you can spot them on the basketball court because their forearms look like an auto mechanics arms.

"Like mine?" the lady asks, putting her elbow back on the bar, challenging Pete to arm wrestling right there in the middle of Manhattan.

Pete tells the lady how "about one half of one percent of all girls born in God's unwilling world are born with hidden testes." He says for every 200 girls born, "one has nuts."

At times like this, I think Pete is nuts. The lady grabs his hand and smiles, pushing their hands between her legs. "I'm one of them."

He pulls up his hand quickly, like someone is stealing his beer. I hear Pete whisper to her how he knows a girl with hidden testes, which why her "mum returned to Turkey."

"You have to protect her…"

I am not shocked. I saw this coming.

Still, I consider myself not a bit on the homophobic side, even though I always saw myself marrying a hot Sea Isle mommy type, but I am feeling really weird now, falling for Andie.

I fell for a girl who has nuts.

This is all nuts. Pete needs new pants. It is only six o'clock and he is pissed drunk with pissed pants talking about girls with balls. The second game of the double header is at 7.

Uncle Matty waves the white towel to flag a cab. The lady wants to go with Pete, but tells Matty it'll cost $100 bucks. Reaching to use her scarf to dry the front of his pants, she asks, "Is your Pete is a great man?"

Pete slurs, "Peter the Great was a grand man. He was 6-4. People looked up to him."

"Our Pete is even grander," Uncle Matty says as Pete falls against the cab door.

"I'm real, real gone," Pete starts to sing, "I'm like Van Morrison and Jim Morrison gone… man, I wish Byrdie could shoot like Gonzaga's Adam Morrison…"

Matty helps Pete into the cab. He tells him we will meet at The Social, a club owned by their friends, the McKee brothers, who will let Pete sleep it off upstairs until we get there.

The cab takes off. We all go back in the Garden to see the night double header. The lady waves her scarf walking away; clearly, she never met anyone as strange as Pete… and she has balls.

I can't enjoy watching the game. It is not that I am not a D-1 player… I'm worried about Pete. I know he is Division 3 tough, but… I've seen him drunk, but I never saw him pee himself. I know he doesn't drink during the workweek either, so it is not like I miss any of his drinking outings. He knows when to piss by the jukebox at the Springfield or behind The Pic.

Uncle Matty says he's seen Pete much worse – at the Final Four in San Antonio when he was so hung over Pete fell asleep in a jail cell touring the Alamo and missed Saturday's semis.

"Me too," Lynchie says, "one night at Braca's… that night…"

At half-time we decide to go. We hustle out into the chilled night air and bright streetlights to catch a cab. Matty flags one down. The door opens for us. Pete says, "Get the fook in… the Blessed Mother visions in Marlboro are at 9:28 - at night."

We squeeze on the train filled with happy shoppers and content young couples stuffed with love and lasagna, zooming back to New Jersey, chasing a vision not seen on Facebook.

Chapter 20

The light above the trolley tracks is out. The tracks running up the hilly street in front of here just dim into darkness. The tracks roll past the corner of the last street light, going somewhere before being gone.

Andie's season is gone, too. She lost in the Sweet 16, so she has been done for a few weeks.

We play a lot of Ping-Pong at school. After she beats me every game, like 21-12, Andie gives me a high-five. I try to hold her hand each time.

The intramural softball games keep getting rained out and the teams aren't even co-ed, so I don't even sit on the same bench with Andie.

We are each going somewhere, perhaps like the trolley here... into darkness.

The tracks reminded me of how we all fell asleep on New Jersey Transit last month and missed the return stop for Marlboro, going all the way to 30th Street Station. We never saw the Blessed Mother vision, but it was a great night anyway. We were together. We were one.

Hopping the turnstile because his train ticket in his front pocket was soaking wet and didn't register, Pete smiled because we were one. He told me the word Catholic means union.

We are all together again, the Lids and us Lads, fittingly on April 1 - "April fookin Fools Day," says Pete, here at the Small College basketball awards banquet on the renovated campus of Philadelphia University.

The coach of Sciences, Dave Pauley, is a

lively host. He seems to be old friends with Pete. He looks a bit like him with the full blooming head of red-brown hair turning gray. He jokes that since it is April Fools' Day, he has asked "the biggest fool he knows to talk."

Pete is the guest speaker. After the dinner, before he speaks, I stand alone with my unspoken words outside by the trolley tracks. The lonesome one-car train putts by with no one aboard. I think about what Pete said before he fell asleep on the train to see the Blessed Mother, how "you're never on the ride of life alone because Jesus knows what it's like to be a man... just keep floating with the current and life with Him flows."

Pete talks about leadership to companies. That is his job and so it sounds like he will talk about being leaders to the coaches here. Wonder if he will tell some of his life theories ... or how many parables, really.

His old Ursinus coach, Skip Werley, is being inducted into the Sam Cozen Small College Hall of Fame tonight, and Andie is receiving the Small College Freshman of the Year award, for the women. Wearing a purplish-pink tie, Pete basks in the middle of it all, like pickup down the shore, like drinking beer in a bar, like telling stories in a New York cab with piss all over him to a lady with big forearms who will love him for money.

John Rage roams around at the banquet for some scary reason. I had stopped calling him early in the season. I don't know what if anything is up.

As I worry outside, under the dark streetlight, half hoping Rage pops out to tell me its over, the indictment was a true bill, I hope the audience will accept Pete's ontological being – he is what he is. But Rage doesn't take the bait of me being alone now.

I guess, I hope, maybe he just wants to hear Pete talk about leadership. Rage could learn from him. He only thinks about his retirement.

I am fearfully curious to hear, of course, where the investigation stands. I won't ask him here. I don't ever want to talk to him, really.

Pete dressed conservatively in a tweed jacket with patches on the elbow, a blue oxford shirt and the odd colored tie. He looks like someone who tries hard to look good, but wants to look like he doesn't try.

He starts by saying it was a "dream to sneak in the Palestra as a kid on Saturday morning when the custodian left a window open... and then to play there in the Catholic League championship and hear John McAdams' voice over the public address, calling my name on the same court where West Catholic, with no starter over 6-2, upset mighty Overbrook in '53 with Wilt Chamberlain."

Unloosening his tie, Pete gulps down his water from the glass on the podium.

"He called my name just like he did Kenny Durrett, Harold Porter, Corky Calhoun, Mike Bantom and John Baum... my dream back when I was a 10-year-old kid sneaking in as Penn's janitor, Dan Harrell, held the side door for us St. Bernadette kids at the Cathedral of College basketball... Now it's an honor to be speaking at the Sam Cozen Small College Hall of Fame."

Pete winks at Coach Pauley and says, "An engineer from Villanova, a physicist from Penn, a mathematician from Temple and a mystic from Ursinus were asked to name the grandest invention of all times… as grand as the Palestra."

"The Wildcats engineer chose fire, saying it gave man power over matter.

"The Penn physicist chose the wheel, saying it gave man power over space.

"The wise Owls' mathematician chose the alphabet, saying it gave man power over symbols.

"The Ursinus mystic chose the thermos bottle."

Pauley says what everyone is thinking, including me, when he scoffs, "What are you drinking, bro?"

Pete steadies himself with both hands on the uneven podium.

"Why a thermos bottle?" the engineer from Nova, the physicist from Penn and mathematician from Temple all asked at once, he says.

"Because the thermos keeps hot liquids hot in winter and cold liquids cold in summer."

"Yes -- so what?" they all said.

"Think about it." said the Ursinus mystic, "that little bottle… how does it know?"

Huh?

After a few silent seconds… slight laughter.

"How do you know how to be a leader," Pete asks, not waiting for the joke to settle.

More of the crowd starts to get his humor, I think. Some politely laugh, turning to each other.

"The big question in the leadership field is…

are leaders made or are leaders born?"

Rage stands at his table, looks sternly at Pete and says, "At our esteemed State Police Academy, leaders are first chosen, then they're made and then they're proven. We live leadership. We don't talk how to be leaders."

"Leaders are indeed made," Pete says unflinchingly, but lifting his empty glass to his mouth. "This isn't like a kid asking his coach how to become a Division I player. And we all know the answer is to choose your parents wisely...

"With any successful leader, they've had learning experiences that were difficult. Nelson Mandela endured 26 years of hard time experience, imprisoned on an island where he could see the mainland of South Africa.

"He used the experience to learn the language of the lynch mob who jailed him."

Rage stands again, looks at me, and says, "What do you know about... leadership, Pete?"

"There is a deep history of countries training their leaders," Pete says unflinchingly again, putting down the glass with thud. "I don't develop leaders, I teach others how to develop leaders, but thanks for asking, I welcome the open dialogue... ephphatha... countries develop leaders for the military. They don't assume military leaders are born. They believe leadership skills must be learned and practiced.

"In business, some might say Bill Gates was a born boss, but the truth is the CEO of Microsoft logged thousands and thousands of computer experience hours before ever stepping between the

Ivy walls of Harvard."

"So, did the Unabomber," Rage yells.

"Research proves it takes about 10,000 hours to become an expert," Pete continues. "No one's born an expert, not even Ted Kaczynski."

"Except, coach John Wooden," Pauley says.

"Indeed," Pete agrees, bowing. "The Wizard of Westwood, Prince of Pauley Pavilion."

Rage, who is still standing, walks to Coach Pauley. I hear him say, "How many beers did this guy buy you to talk about leadership?"

Pauley responds tersely, "mash potatoes."

"Just think how many Big 5 assistant coaches who have evolved to be head coaches in the last couple of years," Pete continues, obviously trying to pull the minutia of his speech together for a basketball audience. "They learned the trade, put in the 10,000 hours. They learned to be leaders."

Just when Pauley seems like he is going to give him the hook, Pete does what he does best and starts dropping names.

"You have Pat Chambers going from Villanova to the head job at Boston University to Penn State. Dan Leibovitz from Temple to Hartford and John Gallagher went from St. Joe's to LaSalle to take over at Hartford," Pete sputters, sounding a little rattled talking in front of so many coaches here he admires, like Pauley.

"Randy Monroe from La Salle to UMBC. Mark Macon went from Temple to Binghamton and Joe Mihalich went from La Salle to Niagara.

"Paul Hewitt went from Villanova to Georgia Tech and Matt Brady went for Saint

Joseph's to James Madison and Monte Ross went from Saint Joseph's to Delaware.

"Our Ursinus buddy Steve Donahue went from a Penn assistant, to taking Cornell to the NCAAs and now is at Boston College. Gil Jackson also went from being one of Dunph's assistants to Morgan State, and Fran O'Hanlon went from the same Quakers staff to Lafayette, and Fran McCaffery went from Penn to Siena to Iowa.

"Joe Jones went from Villanova to Columbia and Billy Lange went from the great Jay Wright's staff to be the head coach of Navy.

"So, the 10,000 hours can put you in position to be a leader, or teach you to be a leader, but that doesn't m... m... make you a leader."

Pete is sputtering his words more, talking faster than ever. In this audience he admires, the coaches - well some of them – begin to talk aloud.

"The first test of leadership," Pete evokes, "when looking behind you, are people following?"

Rage yells out, "I'm leaving, anyone following?" The cop shakes hands with Pauley and then walks to the podium to shake Pete's trembling hand. Pete spits... in his hands, rubs them. Then he reaches under the podium. I fear he will pull out a pint, but he lifts-up a book.

"In the Book of Five Rings - the 5th chapter is forget everything you learned and just be... m... m... Musashi said to be a leader 'do not show fear in the face of your enemy'... in the end, you may too be a Samurai warrior, who were buried standing up.

"If you're going to go down, be a leader and

go down standing up."

The applause is polite for Pete. I've never seen him so serious, so shaken. I try to clap, too.

"If you fall, fall on your back... "Pete says flopping backwards and screaming from the floor, finishing with, "Because if you can look up you can get up."

Pete slings his right arm around Andie and clutches her trophy with his left.

"Dad, take the trophy with you," she says, "you grinded through your speech with Rage ragging you."

"Yeah, it was like life," I say, "when life is unfair, you keep going and that's what you did in your speech... now do it in life."

With his head down, Pete says he wants to take the trophy on the trolley into West Philadelphia for a beer, "like the Stanley Cup."

The tracks split the middle of the road, where Pete wants to be in life, but life keeps pulling him to the sides. He wants to play ball in the middle of the court, where the action is, where the game is won, but he isn't winning.

Pete says he wants to ride the trolley by himself and with the trophy. He says he will meet us at a bar in Upper Darby, "near 69th Street and the Tower Theater, where I once saw Tina Fey as teenagers and where I saw the Stones in 2002 play a cover of Philadelphia's O'Jays 'Love Train...'"

We all plea with Pete, how it would be foolish to take the trolley through West Philly, the hood, where he would be racially profiled, just like he was in London on St. Patrick's Day trying to get in the English Pub.

But he says he wants to take the trolley through West Philly to bring back memories of West Catholic using four players to cover Wilt ... past West Philadelphia High with Gene Banks winning the national high school player of the year before going to Duke in the mid-1970's, when he would go to the Speedboys' games and watch Joey Goldberg coach, thinking someday he could coach in high school like the 'little white guy'... with his whole life ahead of him... always denying the realization in 9th grade that he would never play Division I basketball... and where he could take the train through Powelton Village, where former Philadelphia mayor Wilson Goode bombed the Move Compound when he was just two years out of college in the mid-1980's and thinking the world was fair...

"You know all the occupants of the house on Osage Avenue, every one of the black liberation group, took the surname of Africa?" Pete says, spewing facts like reading an old copy of the Philadelphia Daily News. "The leader was John Africa. And did you know a black mayor bombed the row home, killing 11 people, including five kids..."

"There were only two survivors... an adult woman, Romona Africa and a kid named Birdie... really Birdie... but the name was spelled with an IE and not a Y like you bro."

A trolley rumbles by as Pete speaks, heading west where he wants to go. He lifts Andie's trophy to stop the trolley. The driver must've thought he was just lifting the trophy and not flagging a ride.

"I want to go back to when I had my whole life was ahead of me," he says. "When the realization of not playing Division I basketball was not yet fulfilled."

We tell him how wonderful his leadership speech was and how more educators need to hear his message and not just business leaders as he stares at the empty trolley tracks.

I speak up and say, "Pete, maybe you should go to counseling."

"I'm fookin smarter than counselors."

We all understand he really just wants to take a train, where he can just go straight and go forward, not worrying about being knocked off his raft, not negotiating curves of going down river.

"Sometimes Pete," I say, "don't you have to swim against the current to get to the other side? Sometimes isn't Jesus on the other side waiting?"

As stumbles on board the red train, he doesn't look back to us, like he really just wants to take the train straight to heaven, to see his mom again, and not have to keep sinning and make ranting speeches in front of guys he admires and an unrelenting state trooper doing his job, wanting to nail him... and not have to keep sinning.

"Pete, wait," I say. "I read about Ontology last semester... you are who you are... you aren't like the Who song 'Who Are You.'"

The train passes the last dark streetlight, past a playground court where young kids are playing the game Knock Out and not basketball... and not doing homework.

The inside light of the trolley casts a shadow in the back window of Pete holding up Andie's trophy, with two hands, like hoisting Lord Stanley's Cup... or a communion chalice.

Chapter 21

Pete struts up to me, just like he did a year ago this Saturday morning at my reincarnation.

"I got Byrdie," he says this weekend before Memorial Day at the Camaraderie Classic on the Avalon Courts, the birth place of my new life.

Over the winter, the playground was completely renovated. I don't know if the courts were damaged in Super Storm Sandy since we couldn't cross the Townsends Inlet Bridge. The causeway was washed out on the Avalon side. Sea Isle and Avalon were disconnected like Strathmere and Sea Isle were above Whale Beach.

I didn't notice the courts had changed until walking to the fence where the playground is now. I had my head up, looking to see if my Atlantic Puffin friend made it through the rough winter.

The trees are gone except for the Puke Tree.

Maybe the other trees were ambushed by the storm. All the extra nourishment from White Magic puking on its roots saved the old tree.

A few saplings without leaves surround the courts, standing brave and bare like they don't know how to grow yet.

The old basketball courts were relocated for the expanded playground. I guess. The new courts squeeze between the tennis courts and two sprawling new turf lacrosse fields.

And there are three courts instead of two.

Pete and his bounce passing Lids, who survived another winter, shoot on the first court where a sign-up sheet on a clipboard is chained to the fence under a TWO GAME LIMIT sign.

There are now six NBA-sized square glass backboards surrounded by a 10-foot high green chain fence. The courts are fully enclosed. You have to enter through a small gate with a padlock.

With the backdrop of the tennis court's fence green slats, looking like Fenway Park's leftfield wall, Pete rips through his routine. He dribbles the ball, crossing over in front of him like a ball on a yo-yo. He doesn't stop pounding his dribble until he taps my nose with his forehead.

"Hey, you muss hate Sergio Garcia, he *juss* made that chicken joke about *Diaga*," Pete says sternly, breaking out his fake Gaelic from winter storage in the attic.

"You mean," I say, "what the Spaniard, who always finishes second behind Woods, said recently? About how Tiger would order chicken for everyone since the defending champion picks the entrée at the Masters' Champions dinner on the Tuesday before the golf tournament?"

He shoves the ball, pushing it into my gut, and says, "Shoot for ball."

Instead of staring him down, I look around again, seeing how all the trees are gone except the Puke Tree... how the dew sparkles on the plastic grass of the lacrosse fields.

"Did you know St. Andrews in Scotland is the birthplace of golf?" I say. "Andie should be able to golf there for free since she's named after the saint, if you would take us."

Pete inches closer in my face. His floppy hair is in my eyes. The number 2 and 4 of his cutoff shirt press against my collapsed lungs.

"Did you know St. Andrew was martyred on a diagonal cross, which is why the flag of Scotland has the saltire as the country's heraldic symbol," Pete says, one-upping me with his knowledge. "Did you know the confederate flag has the same diagonal cross? Ole' William Porcher Miles, who taught at the College of Charleston, you were there, designed the South's flag… that's still flying above the capital in South Carolina and on shiny 2013 pickup trucks in America."

Andie, chewing her mixed M&M's, walks between us and says, "Winner's ball, we won, youse was late getting here, our ball."

"No, youse shoot for ball," he demands.

The 20 or so bounce passer around the court ramble about how much beer they drank last night and how much beer they will drink tonight.

The kids and moms at the swing sets, which now face the bayside of the basketball courts, stare at this black and white VHS videotape in front of them on how basketball was played back in the day. Dozens of seagulls squawk. Scoob whimpers.

The sparkle of the lacrosse fields hold my gaze as he commands me to shoot. He knifes the ball deeper into my small intestine. He isn't backing down. If I don't shoot, I am going to piss down my leg soon, like Pete in New York, wetting the boxers Andie washed for me last night.

My pride reaches for the ball… a year in college makes sure I won't pull in defiance… I'll accept the ball like he's offering me a beer…

I step back and pull on the ball. Pete tightens

369

his plumber-plier hands. He pushes me up the lane past the foul line, all the way back to the 3-point line. He straightens my shoulders with channel-lock grips. He plumbs me dead center.

I am going to make it. Fook him.

The wind blows to my right. I aim about a half a ball right.

I shoot.

I can't even say the wind was a factor in making the shot. The ball just banged off the backboard – not where I aimed – and in.

As my ego twists through the net and then rolls under the basket, I feel the warmth from him, solace that Pete must have felt when holding his mom's head during her last breath on earth.

"Your ball," Pete says. "Yahoo. It's on."

"Give the old guys the ball," Andie says. "They ain't getting any younger. Their days ruling down here are f-f-f-fading… like Pete's Who."

She picks up the rolling ball and my bouncing emotions under the basket.

"Why don't you all just f-f-f-fade away… talking about your g-g-g-generation," she sings.

She hands the ball to her dad.

I face Pete. I'm ready to cover him.

Andie pushes me to the side with her hip. "I got Pistol Pete," she says snarling like last May.

"I want him," I say, trying to sound worthy.

"We all cover our own dads down here," Andie says, repeating the Lids' rule. "It's been that way in the beginning, is now and always shall be."

"World without end. Amen," I add.

My dad is out golfing somewhere now.

Again. Like last year. Like next year.

I walk over to Uncle Matty Mac.

"Take it easy on me," he says smiling, reaching out his hand.

We shake hands real hard, like men. Mr. Uncle Matty says, "Hang in there, this will be great for you down here all summer playing ball against us… again."

"Just know, still, Pete would rather die than lose this game… at least, I think, little bro."

Pete checks up the ball to start WWII. We didn't beat the Bouncepassers once last summer.

Phil sets a hard pick on me. Leyne laughs.

Uncle Matty curls over the wall with his shoulder down, easily losing me, goes down the freshly painted lane as wide as the ocean, catches a bounce pass from Pete as if he is throwing a handful sand into the ocean… doesn't even jump for an uncontested left-handed layup.

"One the fookin nothing," Pete barks.

"Fight over the fookin picks," Andie wails as Mitch inbounds the ball off the fence to her.

"Get the man who gots you," Pete growls, "Mac, you got Byrd Man even though he isn't covering ya'll… or anyone."

Andie dribbles quickly to half court. Her dad pounds the new tan-colored asphalt with the palms of his hands, as if banging war drums.

I don't want to cut to the basket like I should. I don't want to move without the ball. I don't want to set a screen. I just want to watch Pete play Andie… again.

"This is more intense than Louisville and the

crazed Pitino winning the NCAA title in March," Mole yells from the new bleachers.

Pete's dog curls under the bench and whimpers, balling up like a witness not wanting to watch an ensuing crime.

Man, I am going to watch Godfather II... knowing the sequel was better... bloodier, I fear.

I softly cut under the basket, figuring I could box out and look like I am ready to break to the wing for a pass.

Andie uncorks a spin dribble with the ball in her right hand. Pete reaches with his right hand, but not for the ball. He pushes on Andie's hip to slow the turn down and then he stabs his left hand where Andie is hooking the ball behind him.

Pete pokes the ball to half court. He darts, and I mean darts, right to the ball, his Holy Eucharist, like it is the cure for the skin cancer he will soon have... before the Grand Jury...

Andie squeezes behind the reincarnated devil, but too late. The sick man snatches the ball.

She dives, swiping Pete's right hip. The ball, in his left hand, is protected like the dribbling he drilled in the lot outside our Hut last summer.

Andie drills him. The ball drops behind Pete. Andie hits the ground, but bounces up with the loose ball. She dives once again.

Pete blocks Andie's line. Andie collides into her dad's butt... wobbles as Pete preaches, "Got to want the fookin ball."

He dribbles manically to the basket. Andie straightens up, chases him like WikiLeaks stole her identity.

The older Pete Duffy scores easily.

"Two the fook nothing," he barks.

I pat her butt – athletic like – as she picks up the ball, taps it against the new pole holding up the basket, effectively checking the ball 'in' to herself as the rest of our Lads play with their fig leafs down the other end of the court.

Andie dribbles, charging with the valor of a Braveheart clansman to half court where her betrayed knight protects Hadrian's Wall, pounding his hands on the court like the last Big East Tournament in a packed Madison Square Garden with Tim Higgins missing calls, and the other refs "acting like God and determining people's fate."

Andie shakes with a stutter-step dribble toward the fortress at half court. Pete slides to his right. He steps in front of... his hopes... and fears.

He is nuts. She has nuts. This is nuts.

They both crash to the asphalt. Andie lands on top of her fallen father.

"Get off me bro," Pete yells, "offensive fookin foul."

Pete pushes his only reason for living off him. He pats her on the butt, saying "Our ball."

"Hustle back," Andie screams, "D up."

Pete fakes checking-up the ball to Andie, throwing a quick bounce pass to Uncle Matty, who streaks toward the basket while I am still trying to figure out why this is still less a basketball game and more of a bare-knuckle brawl after all we have been through together.

My man catches the ball at the foul line while I am still on the other side of the court. So is everyone else except of course Uncle Matty. Andie sprints back on defense, stepping in front of him, trying to draw the charge after he made two dribbles to the basket. He stops and bounce passes to Pete for an easy left-handed layup.

"Three the fook nothing," Pete broadcasts as if none of us can count after a year of college.

Andie picks up the ball, taps it again on the shiny pole. She charges as if she is about to declare "freedom" to her oppressor.

I drift back to half court, maybe to help her out.

Before she storms half court, he says to her, "Yo-yo me, come on, Andie, you can do it, yo-yo me like in the driveway… in the good ol' days."

Clenching her teeth, she dribbles straight into the heart of darkness, forcing him back two steps. Then, Andie back-dribbles a step, crosses over to her left hand, and hesitates as Pete steps up, but as Andie tilts forward, she dribbles with her left hand, protecting the ball with her strong right shoulder… Pete steps back… Andie back-dribbles and crosses over to the right.

She created space on Pete's Congo River, enough to pass him and throw to Meags.

"Lucky fookin move," Pete says.

Her pass to Meags is a clothesline like it needs to be, still Leyne stretches across Meags and slaps the ball to half court, feeding Pete, who bounce passes to Mac for a gimme.

"Four the fook nothing," Pete yells. "Fookin shutout. This game doesn't wait for the clock to strike 0:00."

While running back to get the ball to inbound, Andie groans, "Since when is four a shutout? We switch sides of the court at four."

"Since fookin last year, remember you're a second-year college player."

"Fook that," Andie says, tapping the ball against the poll.

She dribbles right into the narcissism at half court and crosses-over dribbles to her left hand.

Pete hovers really low... as soon as Andie crosses over he pokes the ball behind her. Andie dives, slamming Pete hard on the outside of the right knee. The Humvee holds his ground, gets the ball, and dribbles out of his trench for the easy right hand layup.

"Bonus bucket, fookin next," Pete yells.

Like last year in the first game, I didn't take a shot.

With our heads down, the five losers walk together to the bleachers and the crying dog. None of us shake hands with each other. I pat Andie on the back, hoping Pete sees me touch his daughter affectionately.

Pete waltzes over to where we stand near the new flagpole.

Sneaking up behind us is Harry, without his glasses.

"I forgot my briefcase," Harry says, returning Pete's sweaty hug.

"I thought you were here for a quick quidditch?" Pete laughs.

"Don't play anymore," Harry confesses. "I'm moving to Los Angeles. The chilled case gig is up. Starting over. Needed to say hey."

"Basil, me boy, it's grand to hold onto the past, just put what made you in your satchel and lug the memories - and the molding - with you," Pete says, swaying in front of me, tapping my nose with his sweaty forehead.

"Stay out of the sun here guys, it's a long wait," he says and pointing to the old Puke Tree adds, "It's shady... and you can always lean on it to stop you from shaking... so maybe you make some shots next game.

"Byrdie, of course, you can stay in the sun. You were bred to reflect it."

"Actually," I say, "white reflects it."

Chapter 22

The Townsends Inlet Bridge is up, pointed skyward like its broken black-and-white striped traffic gate. I have never seen the bridge up before. On the rock-reinforced causeway, which stretches all the way back into Avalon, idles a long line of Jeeps and Jaguars. The Jeeps have their tops down and the Jaguars have their air-conditioners running even though it is May. With nowhere to go, Pete shifts the truck into park and climbs out. He lies down on the jetty that juts out between the backed-up road to Sea Isle and the raging ocean. Scoob flops beside him. The inlet is lined with white caps rolling over water more green than blue.

The crashing waves throw a spray over him but he doesn't flinch. He is as stoic as a good Catholic being dosed with holy water during Easter mass. A seagull bombs a splattered mess on his right shoulder.

"The birds are telling you that you shot too much this morning," Uncle Matty quips from his silver sedan stuck behind us.

Pete removes his sneakers and dives off the rocks. Matty jumps out and rushes up, screaming, "Come on man, no one swims here."

Poor Scoob barks wildly.

Andie and I squirm in the truck. We don't get out, though.

Suddenly, Pete's head pops up over the rocks. He climbs back out and picks up Scoob with one arm and his sneakers with the other as casually as stepping out of a backyard shower. He plugs one side of his nose with two fingers and blows a snot rocket into the air like he is aiming for the sea gull that bombed him. He blows another snot rocket out the other side and then lies down in the back of the pickup.

Matty climbs into the bed of the pickup. He stares at Pete and screams only, "What the fook?"

"Holding my promise to the Green Knight," Pete says, "Sir Gawain kept his vow, returned to meet his fate a year after chopping off the Green Knight's head, now I must meet my fate ..."

"Dood, you read to much, remember too much from English Lit," Matty says. "Sir Gawain and the Green Knight is just a fable. This is life. Hell, the Green Knight picked up his head and walked away after Gawain axed him ... "

The bridge is finally lowered and the cars in front of us cross. The ones behind us start beeping.

Matty jumps back out of the truck, saying, "We won't wear green sashes for you like the Knights did for Sir Gawain when he died." He walks over to the driver's side door and winks. He screams out over the beeping horns, "Just saying we won't wear a green sash for him will keep Pete around awhile, keep him wanting to beat ya Byrd."

Even after our freshman year, with a season of playing college ball - yeah, I know it was only D-3 – behind us, with the Lids getting a year older, with life beating them up another winter, with their wives hating them, with their bosses pushing them out the door for younger workers, with their kids moving away from them, with their 401Ks not OK, and with the Magnetic Reversion with friends in full force against them, they still beat us.

The last game was no closer than the first, either. They beat us by the same spread. They beat us the same way.

Really, I think, in a magnetic reversion way, Pete wanted us to win. I think if we won, it would have proved that his leadership methods, his teachings, his drinking with us, his whacky and wonderful ways worked. Indeed, to his mind, a win by us would have validated that he should have received a reward for coaching at the small college banquet last month. Or coached in the Final Four along with Calipari and Pitino, who won the last two national championships.

What seems to work against him, it seems, is us young guys really didn't want to beat him as much as we thought we did. Yeah, like Magnetic Reversion. With more effort, I know I could have fought over the pick Phil set on me. The one that allowed Uncle Matty to curl and make the left-handed layup making it "one the fookin nothing." I could have even slid under the pick...

I wanted to beat him so bad and now I don't. We wanted to beat him so bad and now we don't. We like it when he wins, when he is Pete, when he is fighting the Green Knight inside him.

I think we don't want to steal from him the one thing he wins at... and always won at... in his life. The rest of life beats up on Pete and the Lids, but they can still win down at the courts in Avalon. So, to them, anyway, life is good.

Anyway, he never would just let us win. Even if he wanted us to win so he could prove his crazy methods right, he never could *let* us win.

The drinking will pick him up.

I slide over, taking Pete's place behind the wheel. I put the truck in drive. Andie puts her hand on my shoulder, as if to guide me, holding on for a long second before I shrug her hand off me.

As the truck chugs toward the tollbooth, Andie pops her head out the rear-sliding window. "You guys are the winners again."

Pete pokes his head in the back window. "Winners?" he objects. "You can't choose to have winners without first not choosing to lose. First, you got to pay the price, to answer the challenge of the Green Knight, to earn your sash."

Pete stands up in the truck bed, yelling "Boo" into the tollbooth. He high-fives Boo, who has cut off his blonde goatee. The white and black traffic gate on the bridge remains broken.

Twisting, Pete manages to stick his head in through the driver's side window. He yells into my ear, "Choosing not to lose to us is as simple as shaving in the morning. You have to change your attitude when playing us. Be malleable, me young mates, change your thinking, choose not to lose."

"Malleable like Bianca?" Boo says as a horn beeps on the other side of the tollbooth.

The quote on Braca's outside menu hasn't changed. "The whole world is about three drinks behind," still dishes the wisdom of Humphrey Bogart between the Sliders and the Braca Burger.

The War is Over newspaper is still in the glass case, but the Bob Hope photo is gone.

Inside the bar, all the Lids are asked to

remove the hats they had just placed on their sunburned, scabby heads.

"The Shrunken Heads are here," I hear one new bartender moan to the unwelcoming hostess.

The glasses hanging above the bar, the little lights and shades on each corner of the bar, and the flat screen TV behind the bar doesn't upset me as much as the young hostess telling Pete and the Lids to remove their baseball caps

Feeling like White Magic, I go into the bathroom where the sink is new and fancy to puke. There are swinging doors now on the one stall, which used to be wide open, like now some people are too good to be seen taking a dump.

Pete and the Lids circle the bar. The new bartenders, wearing tight black collared shirts, ask us 'kids' for ID.

"They'd be college kids, just got done playing ball," Pete objects, "they don't have their purses on them."

The bartender, not much older than us, shakes his head defiantly as three older ladies, dressed nice with hair that doesn't move, order a lemon drop Martini, a Cosmo and a Manhattan Jack Daniels with a tight twist of lemon.

They aren't the type of girls who wear hooded athletic sweatshirts and furry boots into bars. There is no Lynchie smacking Pete over the head with the wet damp towel. Scoob is refused a seat at the bar.

"Where's Lynchie?" Pete asks the brash bartender who looks like he never made a jump shot, definitely not a left-handed layup.

"His hours were cut," is all the guy says, scurrying to serve the ladies.

We leave without a sip. No draft beer any way, just bottles.

Leaving, the thirsty Lids put on their hats as the Fleetwood Mac song "Dreams" starts playing.

Pete sprints toward the beach, jumping over the stairs where the cop was beaten and doing a roll over the grassy dune. He throws two handfuls of sand back into the ocean. He walks backwards, staring at his footprints being washed away by the ocean. He turns and walks toward Strathmere, jumping an inch or two over the approaching surf like a little kid… Andie and I follow.

The afternoon yoga class on the beach, the hung-over mommies' matinee, chants as a group. The Lids slouch on the steps below the promenade where the cop was whacked. They obviously have chosen to watch the hot yoga mommies and not walk with Pete. Scoob sniffs around their feet.

"You all are just looking for some camel toes," Pete turns and screams to his boys.

Pete weaves between the umbrellas on the beach where Dei is camping below the Spinnaker. She pulls her feet out of the sand and slips on the furry boots. They go for a walk toward Strathmere. Andie and I follow a block behind.

After 20 blocks, the beach fades into desolation. Ahead, only sand, Pete and Dei.

"No one really worships the sun here because the catamaran sailboats use this stretch and parents don't want their kids getting sailed over," Andie explains. She is smiling wide enough for me to see her missing side tooth.

"There're no cats out because there is no wind," I say all nautical, as if I'm Shackleton.

"You sound like you grew up here, at least in the summers," Andie says boasting.

About two blocks behind Pete and Dei, we see them holding hands.

We freeze.

"Did I ever tell you my mom still cries over my equipment issue?" Andie whispers. "Pete still sends her a card with money every St. Patrick's Day, the day they met after a game in Afyion."

"Does Dei spell her name with an 'ie' or 'y'?" I ask awkwardly, not sure what to say.

"That would-be D-i-e," she says, spelling out each letter, "like in death, or D-y-e would be like a fake color... D-e-i like in ... destiny."

Andie and I take baby steps, following the hand-holders for a block before turning around.

While not saying anything, we run back to the Lids who are sitting on the dune with Scoob. We sit there for only about five minutes, maybe longer, maybe a lot longer, before Pete walks up.

"Let's play ball," Pete says, whipping me over the head with a strand of dune grass.

Uncle Matty stays. "I'm doing yoga instead of balling." The other Lids say they have stuff to do this morning.

The three of us, and Scoob, drive around the fake lighthouse in the middle of the circle and head up JFK, past the courts on the left. Pete makes a sudden left on Central Ave. He drives about 20 blocks, stops at the blinking stop signs behind the

ACME, and checks out the game.

The beeping SUVs with empty bike racks weave around Pete.

No one moves without the ball. One guy posts up. He is open and doesn't get the ball. There are no cutters through the lane. A young guy with long gym shorts and low socks dribbles outside the arc with his head down, does a cross over and a spin dribble without getting anywhere, launches a fall-away 3-pointer.

The ball bangs off the backboard and goes in. The guy turns to a man practicing his invisible golf swing and a kid leaning on his lacrosse stick on the sideline waiting to play, and pounds his chest as the other team pushes the ball up the court. He is still pounding his chest when the other team scores.

A siren blares from the municipal building behind the courts. I guess it is noon already.

Wearing a hooded gray sweatshirt and with her furry boots in her hands, Dei comes up behind Pete at the Springfield, and knees him in the back of the knee.

"You want to go for a walk again down Strathmere?" he says to her.

She puts her boots on the empty stool next to Pete and gives him the middle finger salute.

"Your... really fooked you up," she says walking away to the dance floor barefooted.

She dances by herself, with the jukebox blasting the Bee Gees 'Stayin Alive" and everyone in the Springfield looking at her... but Pete.

"Dei's right, as always," Pete says to himself. "Like Hook Finn, me need to light out for the territory ahead."

"Where you going?" I ask with one eye on Pete and the other on Dei. "Why so soon?"

"We're all going soon... Yellowstone Park is a caldera... the last eruption was over 70,000 years ago give or take a few... we're due for a blow... we'll be as gone as Dino the Dinosaur."

The piano player, "McMann Himself" is playing at Busch's. The grand white building with red shutters looks like a bed and breakfast barracks for soldiers, but it's an old restaurant in Townsends Inlet boasting on the marquee "McMann Himself" tonight. "That means he will do his famed Phantom of the Opera set," Pete tells us finally smiling.

The bar crowd is older than Pete, less mobile than Scoob.

Before McMann starts, as he stands behind the piano, he asks Pete what he wants to hear. Pete murmurs "Stairway to Heaven...

"The Zen Leppelid classic is the proper piano piece to lift me spirits," Pete says instead of Led Zeppelin. "Bring the Zen... McMann yourself... Bring the Zen... baby face."

"I thought you were going to tell me to bring the wood," McMann says oddly to him.

The piano player, who looks like he never shot a basketball either, opens his arms swimming inside a fluffy shirt, as if he wants Pete to hug him.

Pete stands and bows, but doesn't approach McMann, rather he stands on the bar.

McMann sits erect and plays while Pete starts singing, squeezing every word with a crackling voice. The old timers howl with every bad note and sip their stale drinks rising by the melted ice. Everyone around the bar is roaring, except Pete and meself – I am feeling Irish and drunk, but not happy.

Andie ties her red hair into a ponytail on the right side like Dei.

"Pete's telling us something with this song, I know it's a classic, but what I'm saying is … I don't know if he plans to stay around much longer," she blurts.

"I thought this McMann was supposed to play Phantom of the Opera songs?" I inject, thinking about how much more Scoob sleeps in the truck these days… that Pete hasn't been drinking in the afternoons as much, but he has today… how he is only himself when he's drinking these days.

I hear him comment to an old timer in a blue sweater next to him something about the boat he owns for diving needs repairs and how he doesn't have the extra cash to put into "the tub" anymore since he doesn't have as many companies and colleges calling him for leadership lectures…

I turn to look at the old timer … it is Koonce in his Penn State sweater… his little dog with the Penn State sweater snuggles in his lap. "Ahh, lad, you don't have it so bad," Koonce says to Pete, "Not as bad as the unfortunate coma cop... I hear the man isn't doing any better… there are whispers the cop's struggling family will pull the plug… I hear there is a lot of insurance money just waiting… I hear the insurance company wants to close the case…"

"You hear, well," Pete says and then sings, "for an old guy knock, knock, knocking on heaven's door."

McMann sings with no worries. His voice is angelic.

"How does a guy sing that good?" I ask Pete as he stares into his pint.

"Good?" he answers. "You mean well."

Koonce's news has me thinking. Like with Andie... I wonder what is up...

Then I hear the singer with the sweet voice and wonder do people really have built-in advantages at birth? Are their lives predetermined? Do people even realize they use those inherent advantages because of their sex, whether it is a tall girl basketball player with strong forearms or a hooker in New York with a deep voice and strong forearms, being not what they appear to be?

Is McMann Himself so popular only because he is a man singing Phantom of the Opera with this angelic opera voice? Would the act work if he were a woman?

At least with the color of your skin, the appearance is real, I think.

There is no hiding what you look like.

Pete pontificates much more lately about genetic engineering and how gene therapy can someday routinely inject steroids into rich white kids whose D-3 parents want to begin equaling the playing field with genetically superior athletes. There will be no steroid test to catch these papered-up parents. No one will have to lie for a lifetime like Lance Armstrong and deny using steroids. No one will have to live a lie because the genes themselves will naturally inject the body with the juice of a better life.

The playing field will be even for guys born to be Division 3 athletes.

The bar picks up. The old folks sing along with McMann Himself. Pete rambles, telling me how he is going next month to see the Rolling Stones "50 and Counting" concert in Philly and how he wishes he could keep going strong like Mick and Keith.

A speaker blows out next to us. The angelic voice is suddenly distorted.

I think how Pete seems overdriven, and how his distorted thinking has affected me, and how I am thinking all over the place, looking for the truth... wanting to talk to Dei...

Slurring, Pete harps about the Stones "still rolling" and my shots still missing at the courts and how Sandusky is going on trial... and then switches to basketball again.

"I couldn't let you win today," Pete says, putting his arm around me. "You had to earn it, bro, sort of like how the teenage Australian Aborigines cut their stone spearheads.

The bartender unplugs the distorted speaker. I hear Pete clearly.

"Years ago, the English learned it took three generations to take the fight out of the countries they colonized," Pete says. "The Brits not only make the best music..."

He tells me the English were able to stop the Aborigines in Australia from fighting back and resisting colonization after just one generation, "only 20 years instead of 60."

I think how Pete said blacks were superior and everyone came from Africa and how it took the Europeans "with their guns, germs and steel" still over 100 years to colonize South Africa, so I am figuring the same reasoning would extend to Australia, at least in Pete's story.

"What the Brits did was watch the Aborigines' customs and traditions. They studied their culture," Pete says, staring at me in the eyes like I better remember every word. "They saw that once a year, the elders of the tribe and the men would steal the innocent 15-year-old boys one night and all the women and the girls would feign horror, but they, the female folk, knew what was happening, what had to happen.

"The men would take the boys into the outback for five days. They would teach them how to hunt, how to fight... and how to be men. Then on the fifth night, they would take them to the Sacred Stone, the place of their ancestors, where the boys had to chisel their stone for the spear they would soon get... the spear that would not only symbolize their manhood, but be a tool of their role as men in the tribe, as hunters, as protectors.

"It took hours for the boys to carve out the headstone, or spearhead. Their hands would be stripped of flesh and full of blood, but they would keep carving away...

"When they were done, the boys got the spear, tied the headstone proudly on top ... and marched back to the village as men.

"The women and girls would hug their boys - now men - showing them new respect. They knew their boys were now men, fully allowed to go on hunting parties, fighting parties, and to start a family.

"This is," I am thinking between gulps of beer, "really cool, but why is Pete telling me this?" McMann Himself leans over his shoulder listening and not playing. He is obviously interested in hearing this, too.

"You see, the Brits saw this sacred tradition and they realized immediately to break the boys from becoming men, all they needed to do was..."

McMann Himself leans closer, almost putting his head on Pete's shoulder to hear.

"The Brits would take the 15-year-old boys to the Sacred Stone, carve the head stone for them and tell them they are now men. After one generation, the boys were used to being given their manhood. They didn't have to earn it. They broke the boys as easy as horses in a corral. Yes, the Brits did, in 20 years."

"Brilliant," I say.

"In this country, boys used to earn their manhood through sports, but now coaches can't correct players, they can't hit outfield fungoes to them in little league for fear the ball might hit the fookin kid's noggin, and high school basketball coaches can't ask their players to take charges out of fear their boys might get hit in the nuts...

"Even the Catholic Church gives away manhood," Pete says blessing himself.

Koonce sets his toy dog on the bar in front of Pete, as if he wants pooch to hear the preacher.

"Back in my day, when you were confirmed,

becoming a soldier of Jesus Christ, you were symbolically smacked on the cheek," Pete continues. "The slap was a physical reminder that being a Christian would be filled with pain.

"Now the Bishop doesn't even tap the candidate... the church hasn't for the last 20 years, and we have a society of 40-year-old men who are still boys, playing video games, living at home with their parents, hanging out in their man caves, laughing at themselves being mocked on Miller Lite beer commercials, needing to pay a loser like me for leadership lectures, not getting up early to play ball at the courts... we failed our boys.

"So, you see, I can't let you guys win at the courts, you have to earn it... have to carve your spearhead on the basketball court against us..."

"I hear what you say," I nod. "Makes so much sense."

However, when Pete says, "none of you can menstruate or bear children so you need external pain," I hug Andie, who must have heard this talk many times before. I feel for her... and for Pete.

I also wonder, though, how fair is it to girls like my sister, who don't have ingrown testes firing them up with natural steroids like a bodybuilder, how fair is it for them to compete against these "girls" in high school. I know my sister plays against girls in college with thick forearms... who might be naturally juicing.

I wonder what Pete thinks about this... about how these girls have an advantage over natural girls. Of course, I will never ask him.

McMann sits down at our end of the bar. He

talks music again with Pete, who tells him he knows Allan Slutsky, which just excites the guy.

"Slutsky, also known as Dr. Licks, was born in Philadelphia and now the Grammy Award winning arranger, producer and music historian lives in Cherry Hill," Pete says. "He attended Temple before studying at the Berklee College of Music in Boston. I met him years later at the Black Rose in Beantown. McMann looks interested.

"I didn't know that. But he wrote the book Standing in the Shadows of Motown profiling the life of The Funk Brothers bass guitarist James Jamerson," McMann says with a lick of his lips.

"I liked the Funk brothers. This unknown group of musicians played on more number one hits than the Beach Boys, Beatles and the Rolling Stones combined," Pete says.

I find it less interesting how Pete is putting the anonymous black musicians above his beloved Brits than I do realizing at this moment why he doesn't talk to women at the bar - he is afraid they will like him. He doesn't want to be liked. I don't think he thinks he deserves to be loved.

Makes sense. He told me how12 years ago he hooked up with a good-looking lady, a little bit younger than him, when in Boston, and how it was a mistake. She didn't even know his name. She called him her "Black Rose" because that is the bar they hooked up in, and because she told him he was gloomy and blooming at the same time.

"I like how they did it for the love of the music not to make a name for themselves," Pete says about the Funk Brothers. "Like a good basketball team."

McMann puts his hand on Pete's shoulder. Pete stands, getting the hand off him real-quick without making it too noticeable.

"I like how you've expanded your music knowledge," McMann says, "since the last time you were here two summers ago, when you were down about Andie not getting a D-1 scholarship."

The piano plays again. Pete sings along to a Doors song, "When the music is over cancel my subscription to the resurrection."

Pete and Koonce squeeze together tightly. They are whispering. They don't want me to hear what they are saying. I put my head down on the bar, acting like I can't hear. But I do.

"I could go to jail for telling you this ... but I've been on the grand jury meeting once a week over the winter... I think you will be indicted for the cop beating... how could you do it?"

I must've fallen asleep like an old timer at the steamy hot bar...

Again, I had the same dream, the one I got as a kid when I got the fever. I had the ball. I took a few dribbles, crossed half court, and launched the ball to the basket.

On the flight to the hoop, I could see the scoreboard... down 64-62... the gym was packed... everyone was standing... there was a roar when I took the last dribble before the shot.

A hush.

The ball was going in the basket. I won the game for my team. I could see the ball going right in... then, later than ever, sailing from the crowd came thousands of basketballs… everyone who was watching threw a basketball at my basket… even the refs… all the balls hit the basket as mine did… no-one could tell my ball went in…

I want to tell everyone mine went in, but I was covered with basketballs. No one could see me…

Right at my face at the bottom of the pile was my ball. There was a black rose on my ball. I waited for the white rose to show… it didn't… and then I saw Pete's face with the black rose in his mouth… this time not breathing as the scuba mask fogged up…

And then the church emptied down the main steps and into a funeral possession… past kids with sunburned noses still from the summer, mommies holding their hands telling their boys not to grow up like Pete… and daddies with balding heads, not like Pete, holding their boys' other hand, whispering loud enough to encourage their kid to grow up just like Pete…

The dream seemed real as we paraded up Landis… the old guys and the young guys mixed upfront… Andie slouched somewhere in the middle… I moved closer to her… I held her hand… None of the hundreds, who couldn't fit into the church and were spread on each side of Landis Avenue, could see us holding hands…

The hundreds joined the procession… they all wore green sashes…

We walked past Raffa's deli-grocery on the corner of 43rd… past the white beat-up house flying a new Irish flag… past Welshie Steak Hoagie shop...

With heads slumped, we walked past Lou's Dogs and the best buns west of Madrid, baby sign... up to the Sea Isle courts... past the VFW, firehouse and police department and ambulance corps where flags were flying half-mast...

The procession hooked back by the bay ... past Carmen's Has Crabs in the middle of the block and Mike's Seafood and Maria's on the corner and the Lobster Loft across the street ...

We walked back to the middle of town, straight down Landis Avenue, past Sea Isle Ice, past the Twin Gables house and the empty town hall and Atilla's Gym... past the Yacht Club of Sea Isle City, past 69th-70th street, the one block triangle house with the New York Times and Philadelphia Daily News honor boxes on the corner with Pete's picture on the cover today...

We bravely walked past the row of old houses on the bay at Sound Street, which were battered by the super storm... past the Townsends Inlet Civic Center, where a meeting is being held to name the basketball courts on JFK after Pete Duffy...

We go past the Coast Guard Base, where the basketball courts were filled with young kids playing in the Pete Duffy League... past Busch's where McMann himself sang Standing in the Shadows of Love...

I floated up to the front door, banging the red bell with my knuckles... waking up soaked in sweat.

Out in the parking lot, I am on my feet

walking, I am in the cool air of Busch's gravel lot, hearing the seagulls squawk above the bay, looking up for Puffy, seeing Pete pissing by a car in the parking lot. With tears in her eyes, Andie sobs, "Best friends don't do this to each other."

A Sea Isle cop pulls up in his "to protect and to serve" car. "Yo Pete, you can't be going here," the redheaded cop says without a hint of anger.

Pete continues pissing as he stumbles to the back of the lot.

"I know there's no jukebox in Busch's to piss behind," the cop says laughing.

Uncle Matty darts out of the darkness behind the barrack-looking bar with square windows. He runs toward Pete. He locks his right arm around Pete's neck.

Huh? They never hug.

Uncle Matty squeezes. This is not a hug.

He twists Pete in a headlock. Pete bends at his waist. Matty clenches tighter. Pete doesn't try to fight out of the hold.

"C'mon Pete now," Uncle Matty says through tense teeth. "You had enough to drink. You got to go home now. You got to stop drinking so much … you don't have to fight the Green Knight tonight."

Pete drops to his knees as cars line up in front of Busch's on busy Landis Avenue. The dinner crowd trying to get into Avalon to the nice restaurants is backed up. The bridge must be up again.

"You're right," Pete says. "I'll stop... before lighting out for the territory ahead... on me race to the tomb."

Chapter 23

Outside of the Wawa, Pete hops on a bike with a surfboard strapped to the side rack. He makes loops in the parking lot packed with high school kids starting their summer, going to the left on the same side of the board's weight. He pedals in circles until a kid asks for his bike.

"Watch it, you can't go straight on that thing," Pete screams to the kid as he pedals easily between a parked Wawa delivery truck and a Sea Isle Ice van.

"Pete isn't going forward in life as he did leading a break on the courts," I say to Andie.

"He doesn't demand to 'fill the lanes' on the break to us Lids anymore," Andie says.

"He doesn't bring the wood," I say.

I thought he was bouncing out of his flat line by going to the Stones' concert with the Lids the following week. After his "feeling sorry for meself" speech, he was saying how Keith and Mick are inspirations to be playing and doing now as 70-year-olds what they did as teenage kids. But the last couple of weekends down here all he talks about is going hiking the Fourth Week of July back in the Sierra Mountains to "celebrate" the fourth anniversary of his mom's passing.

I am worried he wants to join her. I think he wants to swing on the porch again with her.

I want to tell him his whole life is ahead of him - like he tells me when my basketball isn't going well. I want to tell him Michael Vick redeemed himself... in case Pete did beat the cop. I

399

want to tell him society forgave Vick, that he earned the forgiveness by doing his time and then coming back to the Eagles and working hard, saying the right things, being repentant most of all.

If we were drinking I could tell him how forgiveness and redemption is the message of Christianity, how religion is not about fasting from eating meat on Fridays, but I know Pete knows this. And Pete isn't drinking anymore for me tell him what he already knows, anyway.

Pete drives a few feet up onto the Townsends Inlet Bridge. Throwing the gear into reverse, he backs the truck off the rusting bridge.

"No ball today, don't want to … can't bring the wood anymore, let's go to Dover, to the Monster Mile," he says. "To see auto racing. To see six-foot men who can't dunk fly around the race track in cars that are the grand equalizer between genetic differences."

On the other side of the road a shirtless teenager is pushing his bike up the incline onto the bridge. He whistles at a well-developed girl about his age trying to pedal up behind him. She is groaning with every revolution of the tires.

"Even Danica Patrick competes with the best of the boys," Pete says. "The rules in NASCAR are designed to make all the equipment equal – the amount of gas, the thickness of the tires, the same white dudes wearing identical jumpsuits in the pit crews.

"The only difference is supposed to be the talent and judgment of the drivers… that's the way it should be."

Pete stops at the foot of the bridge, backing up traffic, and watches a girl with straight black hair down the middle of her back ride all the way to the tollbooth up top. He bursts out of the truck and claps. The boy with the crew cut blonde hair and without the shirt is only halfway up the bridge. Pete peels off his No. 24 shirt, kisses the cutoff, flips it to the boy. The bay breeze blows his sacred shirt over the rusty rail, into the choppy inlet.

The kid made no attempt to catch the jersey.

Pete watches the tide pull the shirt out into the ocean. "Onward… to beyond," he yells, turning around.

He kicks off his untied "Chucks" and the old sneakers land in the bed of the truck.

"Let's get blitzed on donuts at Blitz's Market," he says as we drive by the store on 86th Street.

"Hey, we can celebrate faith, hope and love," Pete adds. He drives past Trinity Church on 85th Street with its sign out front: 90TH ANNIVERSARY OF FAITH, HOPE AND LOVE.

We slow down to 15 miles per hour going past the Coast Guard Station and the water tower on 81st Street. The engine breaks the silence, revving back up to 20 all the way down to the Sea Isle Inn on 63rd Street, and then dropping back to 15 mph. I fear what Pete says lately. I try to listen to him without hearing.

We putt-putt into the center of town before Pete says mockingly, "Yo, lets join Attila's gym… Attila the Hun is more fun than me these days."

Passing the Sea Isle courts on JFK, I see

there are now only two courts instead of three. The courts run parallel to JFK now. Pete looks straight ahead at the bridge going out of town.

He says we can go watch the new Philly Hoops League, "another professional league for guys who can't make the show," but explains that this one will involve former Big 5 players.

Andie is sitting in the middle holding a tired-looking Scoob. She spits right past me and out the window. Scoob seems to be aging in double dog years. Pete's thick hair seems thinner. His red blotches seem redder. He looks to be aging in regular dog years.

"Let's do something Scoob can do," Andie says.

We putter all the way back to the Townsends Inlet Bridge. We park next to the Jitney, "a little shore bus for shoppers and drinkers," says Pete. He is standing barefooted on the broken concrete curb.

"The jitney loops from the bridge to downtown, trying to promote shopping and drinking in one continuous circle of commerce," he adds.

We turn around.

We go to Lefty's house, the guy from the courts, and take fishing gear from his shed without asking.

"Why don't we go out on your boat Pete?" I ask. "I never saw your equipment."

"Yo bro, there's a girl around," he says, sounding a bit like his old self making sexual innuendos from my words. "I'm not showing you my vessel."

At Pier 88 on the bay, he stops in front of one fishing boat, leans over, and lets the minnows out of the container in the water. He passes two slips, hops on board, and pulls out a pad from underneath the captain's seat. The red Little League scorebook slides onto the boat deck under the throttle.

"Here, put me bible in the truck," he says, handing over the sacred scorebook to me as he starts writing on the pad. "I was just doing some remembering."

When I come back from the truck, he still is writing on the pad as he checks the gauges on the air tanks. I didn't even open the scorebook to look at his life because I didn't want the old newspapers stuffed inside to blow into the bay.

He sits backwards in the captain's seat facing us. He puts his scarred feet on the instrument panel and continues to write as he says, "Donald Crowhurst, a British businessman and amateur sailor, died while competing in the Sunday Times Golden Globe Race."

"Didn't know," I say.

"Crowhurst entered the solo round-the-world yacht race in the late 1960's in hopes of winning the cash prize from the London paper to save his failing business.

"He hit rough seas and secretly abandoned the race. Yet he still called in false positions. He was planning to re-enter the race in the Atlantic Ocean while not completing the circumnavigation of the globe and circling the world.

"But, he changed his mind," Pete says, ripping off the top sheet of paper he alternately wrote and scribbled on, stuffing the crumpled ball under the captain's seat, "and disappeared...

"Years later, when his boat was found on an island, evidence showed he went nuts, bonkers, insane... he couldn't live swallowed by his past... and so he executed himself."

With Pete's "Chucks" tied together and draped around his neck, we drive back through Sea Isle just listening to the engine. We drive down Landis Avenue, past the Catholic church where Pete prays and pukes on Sunday mornings and past the empty courts at JFK before he turns around at the circle with the lighthouse in front of Braca's. He drives back toward his boat on 88th, past Busch's, which has a For Sale sign under the red fire bell out front, where Pete says, "You know, they carried Bobby Sands' wooden coffin through Belfast, down Falls Road lined by over 100,000 admirers, before laying the Irish hero to rest in Milltown Cemetery... with all the bells ringing in town."

After a few more blocks of listening to sea gulls, we pull into the lot below the Townsends Inlet Bridge. We park next to the Jitney again.

"Hey Loopy," Pete says to the old driver who is reading the advertisements in the weekly newspaper. "Easy on the left turns tonight."

Loopy smiles mindlessly.

"Why don't you make a right turn once on your loop downtown and back just for a change? The rest of the town's changing."

The once blue rail on the bridge is now a more rusty-red. Specks of blue paint dot the white sand underneath.

"The bridge was built in 1940 when FDR was president," Pete says. "There was hope back then, before the start of the Big One. Hope, like when JFK was president. Hope. Camelot was real.

"Now the bridge is rusting, dying, like me… and me Lids… and Scoob… and your dreams…"

From the foot of the decaying bridge, he whips his tied sneakers into the bay.

Pete doesn't slow down going past the tollbooth to high five Boo.

"That was the only goatee that looked good on an old guy," Pete says. "Can't believe he cut it off. How is he going to get nobber now?"

There is a No Fishing sign here under the bridge on the Avalon side.

Putting on a pair of flip-flops that somebody left on the rocks by the causeway, Pete says, "This is the spot where fisherman are catching boat loads of striped bass in the fall. They fish off the rocks and not in a boat and don't worry about the intrusive sign like the summer shoobie fishermen do."

Lately, Pete has gone deep sea diving on afternoons like this one. He still hasn't been drinking after playing morning basketball at the courts, so he dives.

"I think he won't dive today because Scoob has been getting seasick on the boat," Andie whispers, as if not saying it too loud doesn't make her hope real.

Scoob barely gets out of the truck even with Pete helping. Scoob growls and gnaws on Pete's commandeered flip-flops.

"I think he wants an activity where Scoob

can just lay in the sun," Andie says softly.

Chewing on the flip-flops and spitting out the torn leather, Scoob sprawls in the sand, near one of the rusted pillars of the bridge – "yeah, it rusts in Avalon, too," Pete says, "even though the water tower says it's cooler by a mile."

Through a tear in the corner of my eye, I see a sturdy man walking purposely toward us, away from an official looking four-door car he swerved and parked near the rocks. In a blink, I realize it's my "buddy" even from 100 yards away.

I hold my breath. I haven't spoken to Rage since... was it the night at the bar?

Rage asks in a shaky voice, "What you catching, bro?"

"Nothing bro," Pete says throwing out a cast. "Just started, tho." He lowers the rod and shakes Rage's hand.

"You aren't even using bait," Rage says.

Pete gives him a fake half hug around the cop's Hawaiian shirt unbuttoned midway, looking behind him as if checking for handcuffs.

"What you doing down south here, crossing the bridge into Avalon? You usually don't leave the northern state of Strathmere," Pete pokes him.

"You know me, just checking out the vegetation," Rage says, trying to impress Pete, "I hear the American Beach grass, Sea Rocket, Bayberry, Black Cherry, Virgin Cherry below the bridge are in full bloom on this side, too."

"I only smoked grass here as a kid," Pete says, knowing Rage is mocking him.

"Well, speaking of breaking the law, crimes

against humanity, we didn't solve who beat up the cop, no new leads, or any leads," Rage says. "His family wants to take him off life support."

Pete throws out the baitless line, a long cast, as uncaring as if Rage told him there was rust on the bridge and salt water in the ocean.

"I'm going through my own pain," Pete says, "I don't think Scoob will make it through the summer... and the college kids still can't beat us."

"What would you do... if you were the family of the beat-up cop?" Rage asks, "I mean, what, man, would you do..."

"You know, I'm torn," Pete says. "Torn up like those flip-flops in Scoob's mouth."

"He deserved the beating. Right?" Rage baits Pete, hoping for him to snap like Jack Nicholson on trial in A Few Good Men.

My fishing line gets tangled with Pete's line. One of us has a fish on the line even without bait. Pete just cuts both lines.

Rage leaves without even looking at me.

Pete throws out a few more casts before saying, "I *sook* at this worse than basketball."

He picks up Scoob and hands me the rod. "Let's go up and see The Basketball Alumni Legends League... The-Ball League, whatever the fook that is," he says mockingly. "They play a showcase game tonight at Hagan Arena up at Saint Joseph's. We can grub, buy some fish to eat at Cavanaughs in Philly afterwards."

"Who the fook is playin'?" I ask.

"You guys might want to play in this new league after college instead of going overseas. I

know people who can get you both on a team...
together... you make a good team," Pete says.
"Like I said, the league is for college players a year
or two out who aren't good enough to play in the
NBA, but still want to play."

"They should come the fook down here and
play," I say while tapping Pete's heart with my
backhand. "They won't beat you old... you guys."

"They won't let me play in the league,"
Andie says, "Anyway, I'm going to Turkey... to
play in the women's league."

This hurts.

I lately figured we would be together - Andie
and me. We hooked up the weekend in Boston. So,
I know firsthand, if that is the right word to use,
about her plumbing. She knows I know. We don't
talk about her nature vs. nurture. We don't care
about what we can't control. We just care about
each other. Well, I care about her.

"You have to stay and take care of Scoob,"
I say. "Pete can't bring him on dives anymore."

"You won't miss me," Andie says, poking
me in the ribs with her callused hands.

Pete throws the fishing gear in the back of
the truck. He gently puts Scoob in the front seat.

"There are some good players in the league,"
Pete says, clearly not wanting to hear anymore
about Andie going to Turkey. "Hey, the grand
Dunph might be there."

"Who the fook they play?" I ask, trying to
sound into this league to a guy without sneakers
anymore. "They probably play indoors..."

"A team from Washington, I think a bunch

of old Georgetown and Maryland players," Pete says pointing from the top of the bridge at his Chucks floating out into the ocean.

He sticks his arm out the window and shakes Boo's hand. Pete stops on the down slope of the bridge as two teenage girls dressed like vamps walk by us. The one with the short, red-dyed hair waves at Scoob sleeping in the front seat as Pete opens the door, saying "Let me out. I want to go with my Chucks."

The two girls, younger than Andie and me, have four Chinese ideograms tattooed on their left shoulders. The tats look expensive. They are multi-colored. The girl with the dyed red hair has red and yellow letters. The girl with the long, straight black hair has green and yellow letters. They both wear a spaghetti-strap black top, making them look like every other early teenage girl drifting around Sea Isle, floating down from the Philly suburbs. Except for the tats.

"Girls, you don't know the difference between Shanghai and Shangri-La," Pete says, squinting at his Chucks drifting out to the empty horizon, "and you got those fookin tattoos."

"So, what? It's art," says the one girl with the straight black hair and perfect teeth. "Your feet are ugly."

Pete spits on his feet and rubs them. "Better? They are polished now," he says, putting one leg over the rail.

"Go ahead, Pops, jump," the red-dyed hair girl says while giving him the finger.

"Need help getting your other leg over the

rail," the black-haired girl says. "The world will be better with one less pair of ugly feet."

He stutters up Landis Avenue, stopping and going. Pete sticks one foot out the window. We park in front of Busch's For Sale sign.

"Art... Tattoos aren't art," Pete says. "Art is subtle, not in your face. Like Da Vinci's paintings... his work isn't for sale."

I can tell he wants to give us a lesson, but more to distract his mind off Andie. When Pete talks, it is always for one of three reasons: To entertain, to educate, or to erase. He would like this analysis of himself. I really think his stories remove him from his world, like the Saigon Airlift, to steal a metaphor he would use, to safer and happy and higher grounds.

"Specialists from the Center for Research and Restoration of the Museums of France found that Da Vinci used up to 30 layers of paint on his works to meet his standards of subtlety," Pete says, picking sand from Scoob's hair. "Added up, all the layers are less than 40 micrometers, or about half the thickness of Scoob's hair.

"The technique, called 'sfumato,' allowed Da Vinci to give outlines and contours a hazy quality and create an illusion of depth and shadow," Pete says, shutting off and then starting the engine up again.

At least he resumes being Pete, saying, "Da Vinci's use of this technique is exemplified in the Mona Lisa... not by lovely girls who fook up their beautiful God-given perfect bodies with Chinese tattoos they don't understand."

Andie appears to show an interest in art, which I know she was exposed to while growing up with Pete. "I thought," she remarks "Da Vinci's technique isn't well understood. Scientific study on it has been limited because tests require samples from the paintings."

"Sfumato is known by those who know," Pete says. "Sfumato is subtle. It's not like whites and black... race isn't as subtle."

"Or yellow, like the Chinese tattoo chicks," I say, trying to alter the conversation, but knowing his teaching won't change course.

Pete keeps preaching past his Hut and stops across the street where brown Uggs hang from a clothesline behind a duplex. He slips them on his feel even though the furry boots only fit halfway.

Driving again, his foot slips off the gas pedal. His stop-n-go driving snaps my neck. He turns around at the Dead Dog Saloon. Silence again while driving past the Sea Isle courts on JFK where a bunch of Division-3 looking kids play 'Knock Out' with their lovely moms watching, surely dreaming that their kids will play D-1 someday... and not turn out to be like Pete... and Andie... and me.

"Nope, race isn't as subtle as sfumato," Pete pulls from the front of his head. "Racism is like pornography, you might not be able to define it, but you know it when you see it, especially in America where JFK promised us a new world.

"He promised us Camelot, like King Arthur and the Knights of the Round Table, where justice ruled and all men were equal... and when men like

Sir Gawain honored their word.

"But, race is in our face. It's all around the world, like there's an unpopular Italian Black Minister and at a recent soccer match over there, a banana was thrown at a black player…

"Was it thrown at the player… or symbolically at the leader of the government because times are changing in Italy too?" Pete asks, not expecting an answer because I know he thinks the answer is both.

"Or over here, was it a coincidence when President Obama spoke the other day about racism in America, saying he was afraid as a black teenager growing up in this country and suggesting not much has changed?" he asks, but again not expecting an answer. "Or was he poking all the 50-year-old Bounce-passers who are already angry at him in America because the economy sooks?"

He takes off the boot on his right foot and puts the Ugg under Scoob's head.

"It's interesting how the track in Delaware is named Dover, and all white people go, since the cliffs of Dover in England are famed because they are all white faced," Pete churns from his recesses.

"A fookin coincidence," I say. "Maybe like the banana in Italy. But not like Obama talking about Martin, he was digging at mainstream America, that was no coincidence."

"Nothing's by chance, or Rochambeau as the French say," Pete spits out. "The White Cliffs of Dover were noble England's last defense from Hitler's hateful Nazi Germany."

"Is he, Rochambeau, a European player?" I

ask. Suddenly, Andie seems alarmed.

"No Rochambeau, not a soccer player bro, it means nothing happens by chance," Andie says. "Life isn't a game of rock, scissors, paper. God doesn't play dice as, Einstein said... the ball goes in the basket or it doesn't... some girls are born with twin brothers and other girls are born with balls...

"Let's go drinking... do what we do best."

Pete adjusts the boot under Scoob. Andie readjusts the Ugg.

"I don't feel like drinking tonight. You guys go out," Pete says swerving in front of the Hut. "But get home early, we are going to check out NASCAR, where going around in circles in life is all right, normal. The big race is tomorrow.

"Be back before the crawl of the night and bring back the Zen. I need the Zen."

We both say, "later gator" simultaneously, but Andie and I don't go out drinking, doing what we do best. We hold hands back to our Hut...

The morning ferry bounces away, hazing the contours of Cape May. I had never crossed the Delaware Bay. Looking back to the sand dunes of Cape May as if they are the Cliffs of Dover, all white and protecting the people from the evils of the world, I suddenly long to live there.

This NASCAR is like another world. There are miles of rows of side-by-side campers, flying flags on the RV's of favorite drivers, guys and girls of all ages holding beer cans in foam cup holders. Country music rips everywhere, blaring, "chew tobacco, chew tobacco, chew tobacco, spit."

A white dude, well they are all white down

here, tells us we need to pick a favorite driver and buy a t-shirt so we don't look so out of place.

We are the most normal ones here.

"How a-bout if we bring o-ut our Poulan weed whackers," Andie drawls, making the guy laugh as he hands us three cans of Budweiser. Pete gives the Jeff Gordon hat man his can back.

Each RV packs a roof satellite dish. There are a "*shatload* of portable septic trucks," as Andie says holding her peeling nose.

Merchants sell NASCAR inflatable seats and Hatfield meats. There is a pudgy guy pushing power window siding, whatever that is, there are some good old North Carolina folk handing out smokes and chew from Skoal and Marlboro. There is a table from Delaware State University, which I know from recruiting it is a D-2 black school, with white people handing out pamphlets deep in the back of a corner of the parking lot. A dude wearing an Obama t-shirt, with the president's head shaped like a banana, is standing between the Delaware State table and a guy wearing a Ricky Bobby t-shirt singing "The Hotel California."

It is fookin amazing how fast these cars go. Even more fookin amazing than everyone walking around with a beer in hand inside the track and how Big Brother allows anyone to bring in coolers filled with beer. I don't think they are afraid of a terrorist sneaking in anything here.

In the heat and with all the beers, my head spins like the cars zooming around the track. I am laughing out loud. As loud as I ever laughed, but no one can hear me with the car noise. I scream, "Even

414

the fookin whitey crowd all own seat cushions with their fookin favorite racer's face."

Really, they are all like preschool kids with their favorite cartoon characters on their lunch boxes. And they all wear their headphones, which I am told plugs them into the pit crew here at the Monster Mile. And the headphones even have the number of their favorite car on the earflaps.

The fans can't be more into it... except people begin to leave with 20 laps to go in the race. I can't even tell who is winning and they are leaving. I really like the fans here. Everyone's friendly and nice. I don't want them to go.

Pete hasn't sniffed a sip.

Nothing really appears what it seems to be. My life is going in a circle like the cars. I am learning without listening here, once again, like starting over, like racism in our country... just going around and around, in the same direction... like Loopy, the Jitney driver, like my networking.

Chapter 24

The rising late summer sun already delivers another hot Saturday morning at the courts, like so many days of past. Except, oddly, a lone bagpipe player wearing a plaid kilt wails down at the bay, promoting a new dawn.

The music floats with the high clouds, an eerie sad Irish ballad. While playing basketball with Pete and Andie and the Bounce-passers, I've heard a lot without really listening. But of all the sounds I've heard down here, this is the saddest.

Fighting not to get misty, I try to think of the game and the players. Usually there are a few newbies, guys down for the weekend, but they usually show up later, not knowing the Lids' Law.

A familiar face weaves like the music through the waiting players.

John Rage, looking trampled by life like Pete, like he was out drinking at the diner, walks purposefully toward the bleachers. He steps over Scoob without petting him... like the dog's nothing but a wet towel on the floor of Braca's.

"Pete... I need to talk to you," Rage says, not looking at me even though I am tightening my sneakers right in front of Pete.

"Whatever you need to tell me, you know you can say in front of everyone," Pete says somewhat confrontationally.

"The cop's dead," Rage bursts more with anger than with sorrow. "His family decided to pull the plug at midnight... I found out at 6 this morning."

"I can understand them giving up hope," Pete says stoically, "but why now ... why today?"

I think the insurance company gave the family a deadline before September, or at least that's what my dad said would probably happen.

"It's... Aug 28th the 50th anniversary of Martin Luther King's "I had a dream" speech," Pete answers his question to Rage. "His poor family must know. His family wanted him to be free... free at last to dream."

The shirtless Pete picks up Scoob, saying, "I don't feel like playing today."

Andie ties her hair up in a knot.

"What was his name, the cop?" Pete asks, turning back toward Rage. "What was Moonie Mann's *real* first name?"

"You know," he answers sadly, "I don't even know. *Everyone* called him Moonie."

We speed toward the Townsends Inlet Bridge. Without high-fiving the collector, Pete slows down at the top, peers into the ocean and says, spitting into his hands and rubbing, "What's done is done ... when done this could be a fine residence for an Irishman's ashes... if only the grand Bobby Sands knew of this portal to peace."

We cross the rusty bridge and turn left into the empty parking lot. "I want to take a walk with Scoob... alone," Pete demands.

The troubled soul mates walk a few feet away. They sit on the dune for an hour or more.

Andie and I wander around the Townsends Inlet Waterfront Park next to the bridge. We sit on a bench inscribed "Mary E DeFrancesco - Heaven on Earth" but not feeling like we are in heaven.

The American beach grass dances without care here in the wind where the ocean meets the bay, rmalleable like, bending without breaking.

The orange-ish concrete chips away on the bridge's foundation, where I kick sand on Andie.

Painted on one pillar, half in the water and the sand, is this faded orange basketball with a blue king's crown on top of the ball.

Carrying Scoob, Pete's trudges through the soft Sea Isle sand toward the flat water under the bridge where the ocean meets the bay. He kneels.

He slouches back toward us and rubs the graffiti from the top of the orange basketball, now bright as a full moon after he flakes away the sand.

We putter down Landis slower than a jog, past Busch's where I want to ring the red bell to stir Pete out of his darkness, and past the Coast Guard court where no one is playing, past the world of pretty moms pushing strollers and moving their lives toward the flat wave-less ocean.

We drive past the new Sea Isle courts going up JFK, over the bridge and onto Route 9, past the Seaville United Methodist Church with a still pond and a white Gazebo already decorated for a wedding, then straight past the Seaville Motel, where Routes 9 and 50 meet.

Pete leaves the truck running as he carries Scoob into the Marmora Animal Care, a one-story building with no cars in the parking lot.

The vet, a lady with short straight black hair and a tight figure, pats Pete's shoulder as he cuddles Scoob. Andie shuts off the truck.

We hear him talking through the closed door. We edge closer to the door when we hear a sob ... Pete sob.

"My daughter, Andie, always wanted a dog," Pete tells the vet, "but I never wanted one with work... and not having a mother around... and basketball on weekends... and drinking."

We crack the door. Pete's trembling hands rest on Scoob's head. He says, between sobs, how "Andie was five years old and I was worried she would never fit in... and never have friends... and need protection from the hating, unaccepting, closed-minded un-ephphatha world."

He slides his right hand over Scoobs eyes and says, "You remember how one day we went to a dog rescue shelter in Vineland 12 years ago this month and how Andie ran right up to you?"

Opening the door, Andie kneels next to Scoob and says, "You remember puppy, I turned to my dad with my hands folded looked up to the sky and said, 'thank you God for giving us Scoobie Doo... God answered my prayers last night.'"

Scoob sucks a last labored breath, and we hear one last sob from Pete... I can't look at him.

On the ride back into Sea Isle, on the causeway with the tall telephone poles supporting bending wires on both sides, Pete tells us as he held Scoob's head when the vet slowly injected the needle, "Scoob looked up as if to say dying was OK."

"I want you to be OK... Andie," Pete continues. "I want you to be always taken care of... for life...

"But I know the end in life isn't always OK… when I used to walk to grade school in Drexel Hill with Matty, we would meet at the corner… his block was flat while my was down-hill… then at the end of the school day we would walk back to the corner… he had a flat block to walk home and I had to walk up hill for a block… he would say every day that the last block for me is the toughest…

"I think the last… the end days in life will also be the hardest."

I reach over Andie in the middle seat and pat Pete's shoulder. "We'll get another dog," I say.

Pete only says, "I wish, like my mom, I lived a good, unsinning life."

"Unsinning?"

"I'm going diving," Pete tells us as we cross the concrete bridge back into Sea Isle, back onto JFK Boulevard, back past the courts with a kid too young to hit the rim, shooting air balls like me down on the Avalon courts.

We ask to go diving with him. He barks, "Too dangerous, you gots your whole life to live."

"Andie, I think it would be grand if you played basketball in Turkey," he adds seamlessly, rubbing her on the head.

"As for you Byrdie," he says while reaching over her to pat me on the head, "Over the highways and byways the pilgrim goes aflame with the name of my small black rose."

I knew this was extracted from the 17th century elegiac poem Roisin Dubh, the small black rose, and that this line was written anonymously. I know this because the Wiki page where I searched for clues about Pete is booked-marked on my phone...

Now Pete tells me... I think he is telling me something more... he is giving me more than a clue.

"He called me his small black rose," I say to Andie, reaching down as if to pick up Scoob.

"Indeed," she says painfully, mourning life without her dog, her childhood Gift from God.

There is really nothing for us to do without Pete. While he is diving, Andie slouches in Pete's chair. I slide in an old VHS tape. The Packers and the Chiefs are playing on the grainy TV screen. It must be the first Super Bowl. I fast forward to halftime. The Arizona band plays The Sound of Music and then morphs into the shape of a bell with a crack and plays Liberty Bell, which is the theme song of Monty Python's Flying Circus. That is something I learned from my dad watching TV when I was a kid. The Grambling band marches on the field and the two bands play the song This is My Country. There is the Waiting for Robert E. Lee song... then the shootout at the O.K. Coral...

I watch the second half. The Chiefs are driving when Kansas City quarterback Len Dawson throws the ball near the end zone. The Packers' No. 24 intercepts the pass. The announcer says, "Willie Wood brings the wood."

The camera closes in on No. 24 in the green jersey and zooms up to the bars on his facemask.

Willie Wood is black.

I stare at the TV screen, not remembering much except that the Packers went on and scored after the Willie Wood interception... then Vince

Lombardi was carried off the field.

Shaking Andie to wake her up, I ask, "Did you know Willie Wood was black?"

"He still is," Andie says. "Pete says he lives in a nursing home, in D.C. I think, these days."

We drink through the rest of the morning staring at the fuzzy TV, not changing the channel or removing the tape. Then we head over to the Springfield, hoping Pete will show up.

Strangely, Happy Hour is lively. The lovely mommies are drinking their fruity drinks. Pete isn't here to mock them for being so perfect and they can't hate him for being Pete... and then one of them liking him when really drunk.

Pete went on the dive over six hours ago.

At the Carousel, a 12-year-old boy tilts on an over-sized skateboard, riding on the promenade while watching his mom dance on the sand around the outdoor bar. A 12-year-old girl bends over the railing to kiss her mother, who is dressed in tight jeans and a midriff shirt like her daughter with popcorn in her braces.

The Springfield bouncers hold the door open for us like royalty. Dei sits alone with her legs crossed at the bar, but without her furry boots.

"Where the fook have you been?" she asks nicely, flipping her brown flip-flops with her sockless feet.

"Waiting for Pete," I say.

"I'm sure he's following his Destiny," she says. "You do know, Destiny, that's my full name? My half Indian parents were half hippies."

"I didn't."

"I can keep a secret," Andie says. "I did look up what your name means."

"Dei?" I ask.

"Yeah, in Injun, Dei means upward," she says, raising her beautiful brown eyes.

"Well, my last name is Ashe," she says. "I'm Dei Ashe … get it? D-ash."

"Pete called you… calls you Josey," I say.

"That's because of the Josey Wales scar I had down my right cheek," she says. "Why do you think I always sat to the right of Pete? I didn't want him to look at my scar.

"I got it lasered away yesterday… or the day before … or the day before."

The Mexican brothers' happy hour band has stopped. The jukebox plays. A couple-dozen of women line dance around the steel pole between the two bars. Younger girls shake and strut behind the bar near the stage.

Sirens.

As we spill outside, Andie looks like all her life she knew this wailing sound was coming.

With the echo of the siren behind him, Rage runs up the promenade, knocking over the kid on the skateboard. He bumps past a few moms, spilling their umbrella drinks.

"Pete's boat is empty," he huffs. "After this much time he would be out of oxygen."

I listen without hearing.

We drift back inside, as if Pete will be pissing on the jukebox. Andie hugs the steel pole on the dance floor. Rage pulls her away as she says, "The Springfield will never die" and I say, "Check

424

your history, the popular bars die first."

A Coast Guard boat speeds us out to see where Pete's empty boat drifts on the drab blue-gray water. His diving gear is gone... we search until after its dark...

For a few days after, maybe a week or two, the boat was kept docked at Pier 88, only a block away from the Coast Guard Station boat slips. There was yellow tape around the pilings. One night, Andie ducked under the tape and dove head first onto the middle of the 18-foot Boston Whaler.

She spread face down on the deck, looking under the captain's seat. She read my mind.

I faked trying to help her up as I reached under the captain's seat for the balled-up paper. Wrapped with white athletic tape and stuck to the paper ball was a thick white envelope. I peeled the ball off and handed it to Andie. We read the bold blue letters in the center of the envelope: Prudential "The Rock" Life Insurance Company.

She wrapped the envelope around her ankle inside of her sock, scrapping open a scab... dripping blood.

Sitting in the captain's chair, I flattened out the paper ball.

From under a light on the pier, Rage saw me reading the crumpled paper. I told him how I wrote my farewell to Pete while sitting on the captain's chair. I said I wanted to throw my words into the ocean, but couldn't...

Rage kept asking me what I wrote while I was reading the balled-up paper again and again at the Springfield after closing that night. He said I was sounding fooked in the head like Pete.

The summer crowds are long gone. The Mexican bros don't play anymore. Only the drunken winterers, the ones who rent out their homes in the summer, are here. It is September and still no signs of Pete... or what happened.

"Did Pete dive back down to decompress?" I ask Andie for the millionth time. "Did he come up too quick?... Did he run out of air?... Did he mix the wrong air?... He wanted to live? Right?"

"He had to come up too soon, but he would never do that," Andie says, convincing herself Pete didn't ascend knowingly too quick. "He's too smart... he wanted to see me get... taken care of."

I don't know. I don't think he executed himself like Crowhurst, but I don't know and won't say. I am killing myself for not talking to him about redemption...

Dei pulls up a stool between us.

I look again now at Pete's note I keep inside my iPhone case. Sitting between Dei and Andie, at the empty Springfield, I read every syllable on the balled-up paper:

"The Halfway Healers will always be a mystery to the unworthy masses, the Mad Monks to the searching souls, the Merry Mendicants to the adoring admirers, true romantics to the Romanovs, healers to the hangman, and curers to the cursed... the tides change daily, water disappearing somewhere, but the world won't change ever... calling me unawakened awareness... before running to the tomb like John and Peter to see the risen Jesus... or like the Halfway Healers hallway believing."

Chapter 25

The October drizzle splats rudely, mixing with my tears that want to be alone. We are back on holy ground for the first time since... no, we are not on the courts. We aren't waiting for winners.

The ocean blue St. Joseph's Church towers over the old white church where Pete's prayers didn't work.

The new church connects to the little one with the 13 steps of bad luck, the same number of steps to the gallows and the same number of loops in a noose, the same number of steps to Pete's Hut.

The wooden cross is gone from the side yard. That's where Pete went when he snuck out of mass to rest and to be renewed on so many hung-over Sunday mornings. How could a cross be gone? A large white sign has replaced it. Oddly enough it announces the arrival of the new church, which is already here, where we leave first in line.

An Irish flag, ragged on the edges, flies from some house, whose owner's name will never be remembered like Pete's. The tri-color shares the crisp morning air with a lone bagpiper wearing a plaid kilt and a green sash and wailing the haunting Harry's Game. The song, I learned by Clannad, is the same eerie ballad played that dreaded morning at the Avalon courts.

The half-filled church empties out down the main steps ... Andie and I start the funeral procession ... I wipe my eyes with the green sash draped over my shoulders.

Although no body was found, Fr. Devlin said

the Mass of the Resurrection.

After this Saturday service about a dozen of us begin our stroll through the streets of Sea Isle like Bloom did in Dublin. Not unlike what the 100,000 did for Bobby Sands, we do for Pete. Like I will do in Ireland too someday, for him.

We march hoisting Pete's soul through the streets of Sea Isle again, but this time with only half of the once bounce passing Lids. We carry his spirit in triumph around *his* town… like he did for his mom in Lake Tahoe, to show life it didn't win, to remind the mommies they can't mock Pete in church and like him at bars anymore, to taunt their husbands, who hated him on the courts and even more in bars, that their children will tell *their* kids someday of Peter the Great, a man, who if he had stood 6-4, would've been in the NBA.

But today no one lines the streets.

We parade up Landis without Uncle Matty, slowly and sadly at times, defiantly and dignified at others, while being stabbed with feelings of love and loss on each suffocating Sea Isle block.

I squeeze Andie's hand, squishing her melting M&Ms. No one stands on the streets to see us, approve of us… I know Pete can, does. No one else would see a half-black guy holding a white half-girl's hand even if they were there.

They would be blind to the feelings of love and not wanting love inside of me for Andie just like they couldn't see balls inside of her. They couldn't see that I am half white too, just like them. It is just that the other half isn't white like them. They couldn't feel the torturous burn of the melting

M&Ms either reaching my heart.

We trudge past Raffa's deli-grocery on the corner of 43rd and past the white beat-up house flying a new Irish flag... and a Scranton U. flag...

With our heads slumped, we walk past Lou's Dogs and the "best buns west of Madrid, baby," sign. I smear chocolate on my cheek as I wipe away a tear, trying to be strong like Pete would want. We walk up to the Sea Isle courts...

We pass the VFW, the firehouse, the police department, and the ambulance corps. No flags are flying at half-mast today like they flew for Whitney Houston...

I see Pete's stories in every window.

We walk back to the middle of town, straight down Landis Avenue, past Sea Isle Ice and Atilla's Gym, which could never mold a man as tough as Pete... once was...

We pass the Yacht Club of Sea Isle with its waiting list, past 69th-70th street, the one block triangle house with the New York Times and Philly Daily News honor boxes on the corner. The newspapers say nothing about Pete today...

We walk bravely past the row of old houses on the bay at Sound Street, which were battered by the super storm. They don't seem nearly as battered as my resolve without Pete.

We walk past the Townsends Inlet Civic Center, where no meetings are held to name the basketball courts on JFK after Pete Duffy... past the Coast Guard Base, where the basketball court is empty... where the guards have stopped searching for Pete, who might still be treading water, or on an island like Crowhurst, or swimming around the world… past Busch's where McMann Himself sings no more… where condominiums will rise next summer across the street from the new "in" place, Hank Sauce.

Who is Hank?

I trudge up to the chained front door of Busch's, banging the red bell with my knuckles …

We plod across the rusty Townsends Inlet Bridge, above the American Beach grass, over the bench inscribed this is "Heaven on Earth" and above the orange basketball graffiti, bright now as a full moon, on the concrete base of the steel pillar with the blue king's crown…

Andie lifts her sunken spirits and taps under my chin, saying "at least the Townsends Inlet Bridge will never die."

"Check your history," I say, "the steel bridges die first."

We all knuckle punch the toll collector, a young kid with blonde hair and no goatee or tears in his eyes… who Andie whispers "is Boo's son."

We drag our feet above the No Fishing sign on the bridge… past a fisherman catching a striped bass like this is just another day.

Life marches on as we parade to the courts, the bagpiper leading us plays on… Harry's Game again. I hum the Gaelic words out loud while in my mind sing the translated words I taught myself like Pete would've sung to me, "in war, no one wins, there are no winners, just losers."

Looking at the empty new courts, this sacred place where I met Pete, I say to Andie "There are no fookin winners." I squeeze her hand as if I'm carving a spearhead from a sacred stone.

"You can't be Pete," she scolds me with a whisper. "You can never be Pete."

"I'm still going to try and be as good as I can, knowing I'll end up bad," I tell her. "I could pray to be good, to do the right things in life, but God knows they would be just words in my head knowing how I really want to be just like Pete."

"I gots... gots to go," she chokes.

With her hair hanging over her eyes, Andie knuckle punches me and walks toward the mystical bagpiper. The three of us marched Pete's Path, stopping at each station of his crosses. They disappear toward Townsends Inlet Bridge. I'm alone again, except for my tears, like *that* first morning here at the courts, but without my earrings and dreads.

Chapter 26

In Braca's, where I first drank a beer with Pete, and learned to listen without hearing, I melt into a bar chair with a straight back. The rigid seat doesn't swivel like the old bar stools did, but no one is here to turn to and tell stories about Pete.

Lynchie is back bartending, however. It has been just over three months now since Pete... so I am drinking.

Andie has been gone for over a month, too. Not even a high-five for a good-bye. Good and gone like Pete.

I heard from Uncle Matty that she went to live with her mother in Turkey. She never took her cell phone. She abandoned Twitter.

I keep her phone charged. Every four minutes, before the phone goes to sleep, I tap the glass cover to see her screen saver picture of the Townsends Inlet Bridge.

"Lynchie, can you plug in the phone for me?" I plea. "Just in case she calls... "

I keep a bag of mixed M&M's for her and I put them on a napkin.

I'm in the middle of all the changes here - a new church, new courts in Avalon, and in Sea Isle, the new Braca's. But with Lynchie back and with every swig of the numbing cold beer, my head seems less resistant to accepting them.

Except, of course, Lynchie and all the beer in Sea Isle can't bring Pete back to the courts, or to the bar, or back to life.

There's a documentary playing on the TV

435

above the bar. It's about the 50th anniversary this month of the JFK shooting. Black and white photos on the flat screen show a laughing JFK playing touch football on the beach with his smiling brothers.

I am sitting in this bar on JFK Boulevard thinking not much has changed in 2013, in a half century except for the bar stools that don't turn.

Grand guys like JFK and Pete are gone, leaving the messes of this world to the rest of us. The Irishmen didn't even get to live long enough for their first bout with skin cancer.

"The only change in race over the last 50 years is now black guys use the N-word and white folk don't," I say to an acutely attentive Lynchie as he wipes the bar in front of me with his white towel. "Last month, Stephen A. Smith sounded like he used the N-word again on ESPN.

"Wasn't JFK supposed to fix America? Wasn't he supposed to bring on Camelot?"

I heard what Camelot was supposed to be from Pete and my dad's generation. But to me, without Pete, Camelot is no more.

"Wasn't MLK supposed to fix America, too?" Lynchie says, sliding me a bottled beer. There is no tap beer served here any longer.

Then Lynchie leans over. He holds the white towel carefully in front of his mouth, and he says to me quietly, "The cop who died had pulled Andie over for speeding early one morning. It was the same morning of the night he got beaten.

"She was on her way to a basketball game in Avalon and Andie told him she was speeding because she was having her period."

"The cop told her he had heard she could 'only bleed from her elbows when scraping them diving for loose balls' from her 'girl specialist' doctor from Camden. He said that the doc was in town vacationing, how he got pissed drunk one night, and how he told him she had internal testes. Then when the cop asked Andie how could she possibly have a period, she freaked."

"The cop was just doing his job," I reasoned to Lynchie. "He was trying to get to the truth, to ticket her or not. He had probably heard every excuse in the book."

Lynchie nods, "Cops are human, too."

"Did you ever tell John Rage?" I ask.

"No, I couldn't... wouldn't tell anyone about Andie," Lynchie says, wringing out the towel of a mixture of beer and water from the bar.

"That night, the cop was drinking and he started poking at Pete about Andie," Lynchie says back into the towel. "The cop never liked him because Pete always beat him at the courts. Though the cop had played Division 1 ball somewhere, he could never beat Pete in a pickup game. He hated that so much he stopped playing.   "The cop said some stuff he shouldn't ... not loud, but loud enough for me to hear," Lynchie says. Then, again leaning in closer to me he says, "I overheard enough to know about Andie."

"Pete was protecting Andie," I reasoned.

One night, when the two of us were alone at Braca's, Pete preached to me how during tough times with people, life was more like an ocean crossing and not like a river crossing.

He said on an ocean crossing, there is no place to put a person down. He said you don't want to throw someone overboard in high seas because of how they treated you. And sometimes the river is so rough and the rapids so roaring that you can't wade to the shore to put someone down who has hurt you.

He said that is when you have-to ride out the storm, or the rapids. He said all you can do is hope they don't pull you overboard with them. You have to hope they see your goodness, if you are truly good… and goodness will change them.

But he said if they are pulling you overboard on the high seas or rough rapids, or pulling a loved one overboard, then you have to push them before they take you or your loved one down with them. Not everyone wants to be saved.

He said you would never do this during rough times in calm seas, which he said you see some people do. He said it was better to fall overboard yourself during calm waters than push or pull a friend. And once overboard in the calm seas, the person might change knowing they were wrong or had hurt you. Or the evil exacta - both.

If not, you just swim back to shore. The swim will make you stronger, thirsty for mo' beer.

Lynchie taps me with the bar towel, snapping me out of my Pete's syllabus thoughts.

"Pete would've never thrown the cop overboard simply because he was black," I say into the towel. "He would've pushed him, though, I think, if he was pulling Andie overboard."

Lynchie pours my bottled beer into a pint glass. He wipes the dry bar top in front of me.

"Pete judged each situation by how rough the waters were, not by race, religion or repercussions," I say to Lynchie. "Let Rage think what he wants, let the others in town think Pete was just schizophrenic, bi-polar or just a mad man... let them think he killed himself."

A drop of sweat splashes into my pint. Lynchie wipes my forehead with the towel. I use the bottom of the towel to wipe my eyes, quickly.

"Remember when Lebron won his first NBA title and said he had to look at himself?" Lynchie asks. "Really, Pete just has to look at himself and judge... we don't have to judge him."

"Yeah, he liked Lebron," I say, trying to cheer up with another paradoxical Pete memory. "He wanted to be like Lebron on the court. He would've been if he was 6-8 and not 6-foot... he was that good... and worked that hard...

"I want to be like Pete even if it means spending time in Purgatory."

"Or Limbo. I want to tell you something else," Lynchie leans close and says. "Earlier in the night, Rage's ex-wife ate dinner with some of the other mommies. It was just after the usual dinner crowd when she came over to the bar here and started talking with the cop. He backed away, but she kept flirting... and she was doll-up tempting.

"Rage came in, sat by the fireplace in the corner and watched them talk for two and a half hours. When Rage made a fire the people eating complained, but he didn't put it out ... the cop walked her home and came back … that's when he ran into Pete… back here at the bar."

I unplug Andie's phone and put it next to the M&M's in the inside breast pocket of my North Face jacket. I leave the bar, knowing the next morning will be the last Saturday at the Avalon courts. Every player who is down for Thanksgiving will show up.

Maybe Andie will show up.

I leave Lynchie and Braca's, vowing never to go back, only going forward in life now. Unless… if Andie comes back.

Onward. Or beyond.

I arrive at the courts a few minutes after 7 o'clock. So much for going forward in life. Pete's Magnetic Reversion theory is twisting me, pulling me back and pushing me away at the same time.

I had decided not to play basketball for Ursinus while Pete is still missing… the funeral, the Mass of the Resurrection, was just for the Lids to talk about bounce passing, and the others from the courts, to be together with Pete one more time.

I wait for Andie to call winners…

I'm not too late getting here. The games don't start right at 7 anymore without Pete.

I think how Andie would've already taped both of her ankles in the truck, on the way over. How she still would've managed to wave to the kid toll collector on the Townsends Inlet Bridge while taping-up, holding our new dog and handing me a "dolla fif-tee" for the toll.

On the bench next to the courts, I quickly tape both my ankles, too. I don't have earrings to tape anymore. I am wearing my Los Angeles Clippers powder blue No. 32 jersey of my favorite player Blake Griffin.

Our dog, Scoobie Two, which I rescued as a puppy last week from the Vineland dog shelter, doesn't like being tied to the bleachers. But I can't let Scoobie Squared run around free. He brings too much energy, like Pete on the basketball court, and digs up old bones everywhere he goes. He brings me the sign-up clipboard with the broken chain from under the bleachers.

After a few four-on-four games - none of the Lids are here - no one waits for winners and no one talks about life anymore, the dog and I head back to the yellow rock of a house. The one Pete rented and the one I rent there now.

I walk down to the beach pretending to hold Andie's hand. I throw sand into the water with Scoobie Deuce. He must learn Magnetic Reversion.

But as I throw the sand into the ocean, it blows back in me face, which comforts me, really.

I think, the flying sand would be blowing back into her stoic face, too. She would run to the dry white powder, scoop up two hands full, run back into the foamy water almost up to her healed knees and throw the sand into the ocean. Again, the sand would blow back.

She would do this a few more times before running past me with specks of stand on her smiling face, saying, "Hustle up Hook, we got to go on... got to go down river in life like Pete."

I don't want to let go of Pete - like how I just hated it when Pete's stories ended at the courts and bars, at NASCAR races or on planes… or when I stopped hearing them, like falling asleep at the bar at Busch's during the middle of one of his tales and waking up with my fever dream.

I don't have the dream anymore…

Yeah, I know I gots my whole life ahead of me, but instead I think how I could be hanging out with this white, well whitish, basketball babe who stopped saying gots or fook…

If only I could go visit Pete and hear Andie bark "gots fookin winners" just one more time.

I wipe some sand on my Clippers' jersey and I sprint toward the promenade with our new dog. Scoob stops to sniff around the grassy dunes. Andie would grab him. She would jump the four-foot wall onto the promenade. She would run like a Monster-drink fueled Ethiopian marathoner in the Olympics with her bare and smooth feet.

With sand, all over us…

I walk up to the Sea Isle courts, right here on JFK Boulevard, where a bunch of middle-school age white kids are playing on the 50th anniversary of JFK's assassination.

The kids' moms probably don't even know JFK was supposed to change the world.

A tough-looking 12-year-old or so boy, wearing a Kobe Bryant No. 24 Lakers' gold jersey over his black hooded sweatshirt, dribbles a ball up from the bay and barks, "Winners."

Maybe he is still wearing his Halloween costume since the kid's face is so red it looks sunburned. His teeth are already clenched so hard there are white lines shooting out the side of his lips.

He inhales like he will spit, but doesn't.

He studies each older player like he will play against them for real one day in the NBA.

Sadly, little does this revved-up kid know this next game will be more real here, right now, than his dream of ever playing in the NBA.

Which is OK. He can be part of playing basketball down the shore, where each dribble forward he takes now pushes him back to a time when every dribble mattered, when winning mattered… where the better he gets, he will only be trying to get as good as Pete and the guys in Drexel Hill, who Pete watched play as a kid.

Basketball can never be better than it was back then… in Pete's day, in his neighborhood.

Tragically, this little redheaded kid has to live his whole life without knowing that in life there are no winners.

Should I tell him "there are no winners, boyo, just players and watchers?"

A lady walks up from the bayside. I hear her tell the Disney World-dreaming, 12-year-old boy to "be careful playing against the older boys."

She strokes the dog. I tell her his name. She says just "How cute little Scoob Two is" and saying how she "used to watch the cartoon when it first came out 50 years ago."

"Sometimes we call him Scooby Deuce," I say, wiping sand from the court off his back.

"Are you from around here?" she asks. It sounds like she has a real New England accent. She is watching her kid do dribbling drills courtside as he waits for winners.

"Sort of. Are you?" I ask for some reason, knowing she wasn't as soon as she said 'are.'

"Sort of," she says, "well, not me, but my son... he has ties here... a lineage, I guess."

I think how Andie would jump on my back now, I'd be carrying her, and how she would hop off my back as if she knew the lady was going to keep talking... knowing the story could be long.

Instead our new dog is on my shoulders.

"The boy's dad is from down here. He never met him," she says. "I only met him once ... one night, actually."

She smiles – or is it a grimace? She starts to walk away as if the memory stabs her spine.

"Where did you meet him? What did he look like? What was his name?" I ask rapid fire.

She turns around, shrugs her shoulder and says, "I actually never knew his name ... I always thought he was too interesting to even have a name... like a western cowboy in the old movies."

"Well where did you meet this mystery man?" I press, inching towards her.

"Ah, you would've never heard of the place... the Roisin Dubh, a swell bar in Boston, the weekend after the NBA draft," she says as I start to drift in a little closer to her. It is a Gaelic name that translates into the Black Rose.

"I will always remember the bar because this cowboy was like a black rose. He was dark on one side, but like a blooming rose on the other.

"Like he would talk about how race in America is still tense, pointing to all of us whites packed in the bar in Boston," she continues. "And then he would spill into a real outrageous story…

"Like, I will never forget, his old black gym shorts story."

She looks at the courts to see her son playing in a game against the older kids.

"Here sit on the park bench," I say, "right on the name of someone who didn't wear black gym shorts that sponsored the free seat for us."

Eagerly, the lady sits on the bench without looking at the swings. She starts telling the story as she zips up her New England Patriots jacket.

"The guy said he stayed at the Tucson Marriott over the winter for work, he gave lectures on leadership or something at the University of Arizona there and he would swim in the pool for a workout each day. He said everyday he would wrap himself in a pool towel and leave his old black shorts hanging over a chair to dry. He said after showering in his room, he would go back wrapped in a towel and get the shorts. He didn't want to get the rugs and elevator wet, he said.

"Anyway, one day he forgot to get the old black shorts. He went back that night and they were gone. They were his favorite black shorts.

The next morning, at breakfast, he said he saw a guy around his age and height wearing his old black shorts, so he sat down at the table next to him and his young wife 'gifted with a perky pair.'

"He said the waiter came over and asked how he was this morning. He said he was fine and relieved. He told the waiter he was bitten while hiking in the Sonoran Desert the day before, bitten near his privates when a scorpion got under his old

445

black gym shorts.

"He told the waiter his 'little guy' swelled up not naturally, or unnaturally is the word I think he used, when the scorpion sprayed him. He said he was OK after going to the emergency room and getting the anti-venom, which he said was the last dose the hospital had in stock since it was scorpion-biting season in the desert...

"He said the man wearing his old black shorts quickly shot up to his feet, saying he 'wanted seconds' to his perky wife half his age.

"He then waited a second, 'a perfect pause,' before telling the waiter how he was lucky since the scorpion's spray, if not treated in 24 hours, causes impotency and infertility.

"He said the absconder of his favorite black shorts dropped his plate of pancakes.

We laugh powerfully enough for Pete to hear. Peter the Great lives, I think... I tell myself.

The basketball game ends. Her kid shoots free throws, pounding his dribble on rebounds.

She said how pleasant it was talking with me before saying she hopes to run into this hell's angel cowboy with the black shorts story down here, even though she never knew his name or anything really more about him than the black shorts story, but does remember him saying he plays ball down in Sea Isle into the Thanksgiving Weekend... so he could meet his son.

"My name is Eva."

She yells over to her son, "Come on, we got a long day searching around Seanile here, let's go, Andrew."

The redheaded boy stuffs the ball under his arm and struts over to us. I look at him … and I see Andie. The lady looks at her son and stares.

"You sure you didn't know him?" the lady asks me. "Know anyone who would know him?"

I think of Andie and how if she was here and the lady said her boy looked like her, how Andie would probably say, "Nope, I'm black."

Night sneaks up early in late November. As I watch the sun set in front of us over the bay while still sitting on the bench, I see my bird friend, the Atlantic Puffin, flying overhead, the black bird flaps away right in the middle of the pack of white sea gulls, or bay gulls, heading out toward the ocean… south for the winter.

As I follow Puff's predetermined flight, over Braca's Café, and over the concrete green-painted promenade, I hear the waves pounding onto the bright-white beach, turning the sand hard and dark, the water and land coming together with each surge… and then pulling on each other… constantly mimicking life, knowing what brings us together always soon pulls us apart… mocking us if we choose to lose.

Chapter 27

The rain stops as I make a right turn off Route 9. The faint breeze from the storm blows this morning's Wawa bag out the window.

I drive toward Avalon on this stormy August Sunday morning. I haven't been back to the courts since late last summer... and that October day with Andie and the bagpiper... and then in November, but the games were just four-on-four... so yeah, I haven't been back to *the courts* since Pete was here a year ago...

The clouds open in front of me like a curtain to where our story together began ...

I stop at the courts because they are on my way. I am driving up from Cape May to Sea Isle. I'm heading for the house I just rented after getting a job on a fishing boat. That's after over a year of not working. Now I am doing judo instead of basketball... but that story is for another day... I have moved onward, at least halfway.

No one is shooting. Although the sun is breaking out and it is already 8 in the morning, not one old guy or young kid is even dribbling around the puddles on the new shiny courts. The signup clipboard is wedged under the bleachers.

The tennis courts are filled with players returning lobs over the nets to each other.

My head is still bouncing back and forth from talking to the fishing boat owner down Cape May. He started arguing with me for wearing my Blake Griffin jersey. The guy went off like he just read a newspaper editorial about Donald Sterling.

About how last April, with his team in the playoffs, he showed his colors by bashing his young oriental girlfriend for sitting at Clippers games with black guys like Magic Johnson.

My boss wanted to argue about how could I support the Clippers by wearing a jersey of a team owned by a racist. I just listened, though. I don't want to even discuss any more about race

I don't have the strength like Pete did...

My swing is empty, but I need some shade.

I sit under the Puke Tree.

I think how Andie would have pulled her baseball hat over her eyes in the truck, hugging Scoob Two, now nine-months old already, while I sat under the old tree. How she probably cut her long red hair months ago and how she would have looked so good sprawling out under the hat.

How she would've been laying across the front seat, sticking her feet out the window. The scars and scabs on her ankles all healed.

My hurt is shaded under the tree. I try not to think. I watch the swings. One is moving, but no one is pushing. No one is pulling.

My swing just swings as if nothing anyone does or can ever do will stop this motion.

I might have dozed off for a minute or so.

A blonde-haired kid climbs onto the swing. A lovely blond lady pushes him from behind.

"Hey," Catrina says, "you OK?"

Looking over, I say, "Yeah" and stare at her familiar face. She is still hot, the mom I met at the swings here last summer, the one I had barely shaken hands with in church, the one who argued one side about Martin and Zimmerman, saying she was only being politically correct.

Her face, though, looks different. Softer.

She grasps my hand tightly saying, or rather whispering, "Tough one last night, huh?"

I nod even though I haven't pounded beers, since Andie hijacked my dreams.

"It is no fun to drink without Pete," I say, knowing there is no way I could begin to tell her.

The chain on the swing squeaks, but only on the return to her.

"My boyfriend played here, we were to get married this year, in 2014… we have a three-year old, but he wanted to wait… I said I'd never get married again… but he didn't give me a chance… he split… my life is spinning out of control…

"Hell, he was younger than me anyway. Don't think he was ready to settle down at 41… I came over from church, picked up the baby from my mom… no one plays down here anymore for me to get him jealous when another guy hits on me… it always happened down here."

I blurt, "But ma'am …" as she speed-talks.

"Not that the old guys would always hit on me, actually most days they would argue when not playing … but there is no one to argue with about the 18-year-old African-American kid Michael Brown who was killed in Missouri by the white cop Darren Wilson last week," she says, sounding like an anchor woman reading the teleprompter.

"Do you want me to argue with you or agree with you?"

"No, I'm just saying. I live in Moorestown,

right outside of Camden, and a poor black kid is shot every other day there by another black man and no one cares but since a pale skin shot a darky, everyone cares … I think."

I look around for the broom Pete used to sweep the courts. I would rather sweep the puddles away than listen to her tired… troubled reasoning.

"The cop's guilty," she says, not giving it a rest. "The kid was just walking down the middle of the street…"

"Well, Brown did fight with the cop through the window of the car, at least from what I read," I engage with her out of reflex.

"Yeah, but the kid ran away, and he had his hands up when he was shot six times," she argues.

"Well some accounts said he was moving toward the cop," I say unable to accept only one side of the story.

"Well, damn, I can't imagine my innocent baby here getting shot as a teenager because of the color of his skin… because he is white," she says.

"Well some say he robbed a convenience store minutes before, that he stole cigars and pushed a store employee," I add, trying to assure her cops just aren't shooting teens for no reason.

"I guess you would defend the guy who beat-up the cop in Sea Isle two years ago?" she says. "You know the cop who died."

"I'm just saying life isn't always so black and white, that there are gray areas. I'm just saying there are two sides to a story… like a swing going back and forth.

"I'm just saying these Ferguson riots are

tearing the country apart," the lady adds. "I don't want my kid growing up in a country like this where blacks and whites are shooting each other."

The wind picks up as a young kid dribbles up to the courts. He is maybe 12 with his whole stinkin' life still ahead of him. He dribbles at the end where the breeze blows from the ocean to his right. He air-balls his first shot from the 3-point line, missing a few feet left.

The kid shoots an air ball from the foul line a foot or so left.

He shoots an air ball inside the lane maybe a foot to the left.

The kid will never know how to shoot in the wind down here. He will never know how to bring the wood.

The cell phone in my breast pocket rings. I drop it as soon as I hit the button to talk. From a puddle, I can hear "gots fookin winners."

I drop to my knees and yell into the phone, "Andie!" The Townsends Inlet Bridge photo blinks... the screen goes black.

Desperately I try to dry the phone. I wipe away the rainwater and my tears. I tuck the phone into my breast pocket. I turn and run to the truck.

Andie radiates from behind the wheel, holding a cell phone. Her hair is cut. She smiles. The missing tooth is, not missing anymore.

I dive through the open window, spilling the bag of M&M's in my pocket all over her.

All I remember next is Andie chases down another air ball by the 12-year-old kid.

"You got to shoot into the wind," I say. "You

got to use the resistance to get to your goal."

I go over to show him how to shoot the ball into the wind down here. He wipes his forehead with the top of his Larry Bird jersey.

"You have to use the wind, not to fight the wind," Andie says, rubbing against my shoulder.

"Aim to the side the wind is blowing," I say, leaning against her.

"Let the wind push the ball to the basket," Andie says, leaning back against me.

I bounce the ball to the 3-point line at the top of the key. I keep dribbling. I haven't shot a basketball with purpose since Pete ...

The ball bangs off the backboard hard to the right, comes down and hits the kid on the head.

"I'm Ok," the kid insists.

"Shooting into the wind takes practice down here," I say, hugging Andie with one arm.

"Shooting into the wind takes a special touch," Andie says, wrapping her arms around me.

"You can change your shot ... don't be afraid to change," I say. "You know Jesus says 'be not afraid' exactly 365 times in the Bible."

"Once for each day," Andie says.

"But I like to shoot alone," the kid says.

"You know, I knew this great man who visited Walden Pond a few years back to be where a man named Thoreau wrote in seclusion for two years. Well, 150 years later even Pete... our own Peter the Great... couldn't get a parking space at the National Historic Landmark, there were so many visitors there was a cop directing traffic and it was just a regular mid-week day," I tell the kid. "Even a lonely lake changes… life changes… you can change… our f-f-f … world can change."

We float over to the truck where Andie changed my life a few minutes ago. I don't even turn to steal one more glance at Cartrina's lovely ass and swirling mind.

I do look back to see the leaves blowing on the tree I was just sitting under. What? No…

The Puke Tree falls.

The trunk snapped a few feet from the ground. My tree crashed where I was sitting.

I stare at the fallen tree. Immediately, I realize that Pete has been with me, telling me it was not my time to go, telling me to keep marching on, to help kids with their jump shots, to somehow help people… help our country, help the world speed forward with race relations… or at least to be more accepting of our differences.

Ephphatha.

Beyond the felled Puke Tree, the empty swing still swings.

Chapter 28

The Sea Isle Wawa is unusually crowded for an offseason day. I'm waiting four deep in line to buy M&M's, both peanut and chocolate, for Andie, I peek down at the disheveled newspaper rack. On top of the messy pile, the USA Today still screams of "The Race Riots of 2015" in Baltimore, just like the news did last week.

I buy the paper since it is the first week of April and I want to check out how Derek Jeter is hitting. I throw the USA Today across the front seat of the truck, figuring there is all day to see if the Yanks sport a winning record or not. The paper unfolds on top of Pete's old little league scorebook.

We watch our dog, Scoobie Two, run on the beach. He likes sniffing around the dunes near the promenade. He is always bringing back driftwood, as if a gift for loving him. We sit on the sad steps below the pavilion.

After a few minutes of sniffing in the high dune grass and with a little bit of digging, our curious dog brings us part of a gray wooden oar.

On the end of the oar, the paddle end, there is a dark reddish stain.

Andie and I take the oar to the cops.

After a couple of weeks, Harry calls my cell. I pick it up without touching the leftover circle marked on the device after the consensual intercept of Pete.

Harry tells us that the DNA tests came back... the stain is a match for the blood of the poor Sea Isle cop, the one who died in a coma.

He says the broken half-oar matches a splinter of the half-oar at Bonz's Beach. He adds that according to his police source Cali-holi will be arrested tomorrow when the paperwork is done.

The next day we kneel quietly on a nearby dune where we hear Cal-holi confess that he whacked the cop. He wears a blue baseball cap rather than his Cowboy lid. He offers an explanation more than a confession, saying that the cop "hassled" him for months to leave the dunes, how he couldn't live at Bonz's Beach anymore, how it was the law.

Cali-holi removes the blue Sea Isle City police cap that was given to him years ago. It was a gift given to him for all his generous contributions. Rage cuffs him as he says, "I didn't mean to kill the cop, but only to give him "a real crime to worry about instead of hassling me."

Tucking his Hawaiian shirt in his cargo pants, Rage tells Cali-holi, "The cop was just carrying out my orders and those from above me."

We stand. Andie and I hug Scoob Two.

"I killed your wizard, too." Cali-holi yells to us as he is escorted down the dune, past Bonz's mailbox.

Harry calls back that night. He says Cali-holi admitted to sabotaging Pete's oxygen mix just to show how smart he was… like how he was a brilliant businessman right out of college … like how he changed the gas to a helitrox mixture of 26 percent oxygen, 57 percent nitrogen and 17 percent helium, which allows the diver a max depth of 44 meters or 144 feet and forces the diver to make decompression stops on the way up or else... like how Pete thought his trimix of 10 percent oxygen, 20 percent nitrogen and 70 percent helium would allow him to dive over 100-meters... like how it would allow him to come up without decompressing... and like how he is not a beach bum because he beat the cop and it took so long for him to be caught... and how he wanted the credit for the perfect crime by painting Pete as the suspect since he knew people would think Pete killed himself out of guilt for killing the cop... but how he also wanted to whack him because he felt Pete skated through life on B.S. and blarney... while he had the brains... how he wrote the jibberish final message found under the captain's seat and how he laughed how Pete's followers must have thought it was brilliant Pete at work again and followed the jibberish... and how he wanted to be caught, which is why he put Pete's updated paper of the mixed oxygen for his diving tank that he took from under the boat in the Bonz's Beach mailbox over a year ago... but no one cared about him and ever checked the mailbox...

With the sun poking over the horizon, we leave the house to check the mailbox. I forgot where the truck was parked since we haven't had any money for gas lately. Turning the corner, we see the truck's passenger side window open. The rain from the morning dampened the already yellow newspaper.

"At least Pete's scorebook and old newspaper clippings were covered by the USA

Today," I say, sliding the pile between us. "See, newspapers are good for something these days."

Andie pounds the brakes at the blinking red light on Landis and JFK when a recycling truck doesn't slow down when crossing the intersection.

"I was going to cruise through to try and save gas," she says as the newspaper and scorebook scatter on the floorboard of the truck.

The truck stalls under the flashing traffic light.

We are out of gas.

I paw at the paper and scorebook.

With one arm out the window, I read in the scorebook how Pete struck out his first two at bats playing for Mr. Rizzo and the Yankees. I read aloud how he was replaced in the fourth inning and his two subs both struck out once each against the Cardinals.

"You see the scorebook does tell time," Andie says as she pumps the gas pedal.

With one foot out the door, she turns the key one last time, but the engine doesn't kick over on just fumes. We slouch over to the swing set near the basketball courts. I read the paper aloud:

Streets of Baltimore are on fire... mob throws rocks at police... National guard called in... stores looted... Mayor calls for calm... in honor of Martin Luther King... who was shot and killed... a few days earlier... on April 4, 1968."

I stash the old paper back in the scorebook and flip over the USA Today from a few weeks ago.

Andie grabs the paper and reads:

Streets of Baltimore are on fire... mob

throws rocks at police... National guard called in... stores looted... Mayor calls for calm... in honor of Freddie Gray, who was arrested and died... a few days earlier... on April 19, 2015.

Chapter 29

We plop to watch Super Bowl 50 at The Rock. Andie stretches in his chair and puts her feet on the table right next to the paper on which Pete wrote his trimix ratio of 10/20/70 - 10 percent oxygen, 20 percent nitrogen and 70 percent helium. The paper we lifted from the mailbox.

On the other side of the paper he wrote: *the tides change daily, water disappearing somewhere, but the world won't change ever... be the change before running to the tomb like John and Peter to see the risen Jesus... or like the Halfway Healers, halfway believing."*

"Wake me up for the halftime show," she says with Scoob snoozing on her scab-free knees.

"Only if the Arizona and Grambling bands are playing," I say, shaking the video at her.

The Brit band Coldplay performs at halftime with Beyonce and her troupe of dancers wearing black leather outfits. Coldplay finishes up by playing Fix You while a video montage of the past 49 years of halftime shows flashes on a big screen behind the stage.

"Wake up," I yell to Andie when a short clip of the Arizona marching band flashes on the screen along with Michael Jackson, who is posed holding his package. "Her snore startles Scoober."

I flip on Andie's iPhone, kiss her Townsends Inlet Bridge photo, and log on to Twitter. Already tweets are blowing up how Beyonce was wearing a black outfit to signify the Black Panthers of the 1960s. And how her newly released video was anti-cop and how it shows people with their hands up in the "don't shoot" pose like when the people of Ferguson, Missouri protested...half the tweets salute Destiny's Child.

I Google "Super Bowl… Willie Wood."

A New York Times "Digital First in 2016" story from a few days ago pops up first. I shake Andie. I show her the photo of an old black guy wearing a Packers' No. 24 jersey slumped in a wheelchair, alone in a hospital-like room.

"Yup, Willie's still black," she says.

I read the article:

Willie Wood suffers from dementia. He doesn't remember the interception of Len Dawson. He doesn't remember the first Super Bowl.

Fook, old Willie Wood doesn't remember anything… not about the Black Panthers … not Vince Lombardi's 'winning isn't everything, it is the only thing'… not the Civil Rights Movement or Camelot in the 60s…

He doesn't remember the last 50 years… Willie doesn't, I think, even remember Pete ever bringing the wood.

Chapter 30

We haven't watched any TV since the Super Bowl, but tonight Villanova plays in the NCAA tournament championship against North Carolina.

Pete would've watched on this warm April evening with only Loopy the Jitney driver not in front of the TV. Pete would not even drink tonight.

I put down my beer and backhand toss his faded blue Villanova baseball hat to Andie.

"Put it on for show."

"Thanks bro."

"Give it back, though."

"Will do. Looks like the hat has one more miracle... one mo'."

"Indeed. Here we go... Nova."

The game is tied with four seconds left. Jay Wright calls a time out. He draws a play on the whiteboard. Andie grabs the 10/20/70 paper off the table and draws the play Pete showed Coach Wright at Twisties under the gas mixture numbers.

We crouch in front of the TV. Andie's hand and mine sweat together as we squeeze tightly when the ref hands the ball off at the baseline to Kris Jenkins... who inbounds for Villanova to Ryan Arch-something... who rubs his defender off a pick and dribbles across half court... wheels at the 3-point line... dishes to the trailer Jenkins... bang... at the buzzer... just like Pete drew up.

Villanova just won the national title... in Houston... with 0:00 on the clock.

Afterwards, Jay Wright thanked Mike Daly for his support. The gracious coach said how the

Wildcats had won for him.

Daly had died just a month earlier of a heart attack. In the moments before dying, he sent Wright a text, just like he did every day. This one was of his granddaughter singing the Villanova fight song. Wright read the text moments after his death. The game doesn't end when the clock strikes 0:00. Pete was right, of course.

Pete had taught us how, in 1971, when Mike Daly didn't play a minute, the Wildcats lost to UCLA in The Houston Astrodome, a facility which now stands unused next to the new stadium in which Nova just made madness, mo' magic.

I scroll through Twitter. I see a tweet saying the "Villanova magic of 44 is alive in 2016."

The tweets read in rapid messages:

Villanova had played in 44 NCAA tourney games going into this year since winning it all in '85... Nova had just beat Oklahoma this year by 44 points in the semifinals... the jersey numbers of the five starters added up to 44... the Wildcats "clawed" back to tie the game against North Carolina at 44... the Tar Heels' No. 44, Jackson, miss two critical free throws with 2:44 left... Ryan Arch-something played in his school-record 144th game... the victory, today, is April 4 or 4/4...

And St. Thomas of Villanova was appointed an archbishop in 1544... and how Villanova will go to the White House and meet Obama – our 44th president... the magic of 44...

The successive tweets end without saying anything about Pete... how The Pistol wore 44... how St. Joseph's Church in Sea Isle is on 44th

Street…

The July 4th weekend passes without us picking up a basketball. We take a long walk on the beach as the nation celebrates its birthday, honors its freedom, proudly pats its own back once again.

Earlier this week, though, on back-to-back days, police fatally shot black guys in Louisiana and then Minnesota.

America's Independence Day hangover ended with fatal fireworks.

"Let's play winners." Andie says, poking Scoob, rolling out of bed Saturday morning. "Time for our comeback tour, like *the* fook-in Who."

"Indeed," I say, unrolling a folded pair of socks from the top drawer and putting them on, one black sock and one white… but I don't care.

In the closet, I find my old Air Jordan sneakers… now with paint on them.

At Wawa, Andie buys her M&Ms and mixes them in one plastic pretzel bag. We cross over JFK Boulevard and putter up Landis Avenue past the new church and the new restaurant where Busch's once stood, past everything new.

In front of the bridge we are stuck behind a jitney bus dropping off last night's drunks. Andie's iPhone beeps. I read aloud a news alert from USA Today: *Cops shot in Dallas… a sniper fires on 12 police officers… five die at Parkland Memorial Hospital…*

"Parkland, that is where JFK died," I moan as Andie swerves around the jitney making another loop.

The black-and-white striped traffic

gate at the rusting drawbridge is broken in half and stuck pointing straight up, as if inviting us to cross over the stormy sea to the other side, as if steering us to heaven without racing to the tomb first to believe, as if telling us not to wait for someone here on earth to walk on water to lead the way across, as if pleading with us to be open… ephphatha… as if showing us to have faith in the cross.

Made in the USA
Middletown, DE
24 May 2017